HEAVEN'S SCENT

book one in the Heaven's Scent series

TANIA COOPER & RICKY COOPER

Other books co-written by these authors:

Between Worlds
(Book two in the Heaven's Scent series)
Love, Life and Naughty Bits

Books written by Tania Cooper:

Too Broken to Love
Too Easy to Love
Happy Little Horrors anthology
Cold – coming in 2016

Books written by Ricky Cooper:

Designated Infected
Designated Quarantined
Alienated anthology

Here I stand, helpless and left for dead.
Close your eyes, so many days go by.
Easy to find what's wrong,
harder to find what's right.
I believe in you. I can show you,
I can see right through all your empty lies.

Dance with the Devil - Breaking Benjamin

The Light Ones

ARIANWEN

They told me it's wrong.

'I can smell you, you feathered harlot. Escape me you will not, you stupid little creature!'

That I shouldn't tread so close to the heat.

'You think you can sneak into our world again and again and steal our master's possessions?'

That the abilities I possess could never protect me completely.

'You have walked our lands for the last time, you filthy whore! Now you will finally learn what it's like to serve a true master. He is going to be thrilled with such a valuable catch when we clip your revolting wings and lay your bloodied body at his feet.'

Protect me from the land where evil resides.

'Try as you might, the smell of your feathers gives you away every time you try and hide, try and sneak in and out of the village, taking what does not belong to your pathetic Lord!'

I continue to run with quiet haste through this forgotten forest, careful not to take a wrong step, my confidence slightly wavering as the Devil's Hunters nip at my heels. I need to trust my abilities and gifts to see me to safety as they have done for my entire existence. My cloak snags on the large finger of a branch, a slight tear appearing as I tug it roughly. My hood has fallen back, causing my long golden locks to fly wildly behind me, collecting tiny pieces of the dead greenery with it.

'Nothing will save you this time, you disgusting thief. I am that close to you, I can taste you on my tongue!'

When they're close, I feel a scorching heat that starts at the top of my skull, sending an echoing shiver through me as it slowly moves down to the back of my neck, making my light, delicate hairs stand to attention, and a soul-piercing ache race through my entire body as my mouth fills with a foul, sour taste that squats on my tongue. I know when this clinging taint fills me it's a warning that they are almost within reach of me. And this time … my senses tell me that they are about to make contact.

'Maybe our master will be so pleased with such a valuable prize, he will give you to us when he is finished with you! Then you will finally learn the true capabilities of us Hunters!'

I can hear the ruffle of his clothing right behind me, the heavy scent of ash and sulphur burning my nostrils like acid, a prickling feeling crawling over my skin as if their filthy claws are scratching me, shredding me, trying to claim me. I can scent four of them, closing in from all sides of me.

'You are ours for the taking, we will snuff your light, you will be damned to our darkness for eternity for your thieving ways.'

But … I can also sense *it!* Him, her, it, my eternal saviour, my guardian, a force I have yet to lay eyes upon, but its presence I have felt since I can remember, always lurking in the background of my life, always watching over me as I cross the border of my home, through the land of the forgotten forest and into the Devil's waiting room of death; the village of the condemned.

'We have you surrounded. Say your prayers little birdie, not that they'll be much use. Your Lord can't save you this time. WHAT! Her feathered scent has gone! Where is she? Who can see her? Move, you useless bastards, find the winged bitch, I will not lose her again!'

Danger was closer than I thought this time if my guardian needed to throw them off my scent. I endeavour not to let them get close enough to scent me at all. It very rarely happens, but my latest reclaim took more out of me than usual, so it took a while longer for my senses to return to full strength, and, by then, they were too close to easily evade.

'She cannot escape our grasps again! We can't go back to Lucifer empty handed! Find her!'

I can hear them turn to my left as they yell and scuttle through the rotting greenery away from me, chasing a dead lead, leaving me to once again return safely to my own world.

After my close encounter, I hastily make the dangerous trek back, towards the towering solid stone dragons that act as the gatekeepers, protecting our rapturous garden. I know my protective force, my guardian, is still nearby. I can feel its penetrating stare through the back of my cloak. But, as I turn my head sharply, hoping today my dreams of sighting my saviour will come true ... I am met with nothing but the dark trees and shrubs that line my path and blinds me to the foulness that lingers just beyond our borders. Disappointment washes over me, yet again, as I make my way back to my own immortal world.

Yes ... they continue to tell me it's wrong.

They tell me I can't possibly sense all the danger.

No matter how many times I try, try to explain to them that I can feel it, that I can sense it, that I can taste and smell it, it makes no difference. Try as I might, none of my kin will listen.

No one understands the true extent of my gifts, the true power that flows through me, an innate ability to sense danger before it falls upon me, the reason I can tread so close to the Devil's lair. Yes, they were close today, but were still unable to capture me; and yet some of my close kin still do not believe in what I do, and the risks I take. All they preach is how wrong all that I do is, that the souls destined for Hell have all had their fates written and that no matter what I do or how I try to help, I will not be able to save them. They are the damned, and unworthy of being saved.

My own kind, the pure white souls, the vengeance and salvation of those of mortal chains; we are Angels of God.

We were created to protect all mankind; to watch over, to guide, to save, and yet, most of my kin believe that not all of those souls we are charged with protecting can be saved. They believe that once their actions condemn them to the edges of Hell, there is no way to save their accursed soul; that there is no way to bring them back from the edges of evil and into our ethereal light.

But not I!

Something deep within my angelic soul, part of my pure innocent heart, part of the glorious vibrant essence that flows through my veins, tells me that all can be saved if I can reach them before they pass the point of no return, before they fall over the edge of eternal darkness.

When I walk the borders, those ragged, wasted, heat scarred lands between divinity and damnation, I hear whispers, whispers from the mouths of the condemned; but as hard as I try I can never fully hear the words they speak.

Yet as my feet draw me along this dead border between my world and theirs, I know it's the same three words every time. The whispered sounds they make, the ones that tease at my ear as I pass, are identical to all those that have come and gone before.

From the deep soulful baritone, to the high piercing tenor, I know the words they speak are the same. The words they have, those three, simple, whispered collections of letters are a name ... for me. I just wish I could hear what it is.

Are their words kind or malicious, my mind wonders? Do they want to feel my presence, the hope I bring, or would they prefer I left them alone to the fate they have been dealt?

I can only follow my heart, the intuition I was granted and do what I feel is right, what I know is right, what my heart and mind tell me I must dedicate myself to, and that is to save the souls that were wrongly sent to kneel before the fallen one himself.

Because I have a gift. I am a chosen one. I am a *Reclaimer*.

There are others of us, a small select group of chosen angels who have this title bestowed upon them. Despite their kinship, their friendship, our united camaraderie, I am beginning to believe the words that my kin have spoken about me, that I have the abilities above and beyond what my fellow Reclaimers possess. We can all sense when a condemned soul still has enough pure good inside of them that they still claim a right to walk before God, instead of the Devil.

When they call in need we seek them out in the village of the condemned. A vile place, where all souls are doomed to dwell until we, using our God given abilities to help, guide them to the light they so deserve. But this group of chosen ones, the only people these poor forgotten souls can count on to save them from eternal damnation, are not of the belief that all who call us can be saved.

But I, deep within every fibre in my body, feel that they can. I sense it deep within my immortal soul. I can hear their last shallow breaths gaining strength when I am near, I can taste their hidden good in the air that surrounds them. Their hearts beat to a sweeter tune, their very form giving off a vibrant energy, when they know they have a chance to release the good within.

I have an unexplainable connection to them. These destitute mortal beings, who are all but forgotten, are the reason I have been granted my gift. I am meant to be the only one who brings them back to the light. I am the only one who dares walk so close to the edges of Hell without care to my own safety, because these forgotten children deserve their chance at eternal peace.

My kind, the celestial beings, live in the most glorious, entrancing place ever created. Eden, the true Garden of my Lord and Creator. Its beauty, its richness, its vibrant essence *cannot* be matched, be it in the mortal or immortal realm. Nothing is as pure or as virtuous as the place I call home. The white light that surrounds my place of solace is the most enriching power that has ever existed, and it is a place of undiminished peace when a being needs it the most.

That does not stop me from venturing into the cesspit that is the waiting room of death, the edge of Hell, to Reclaim the souls that the dark one is wrongly taking for himself. I have endured a lifetime of insistent warnings and lessons on the power of the Devil, the master of my kin who was cast from the sight of our Father, Lord of Hell and progenitor to the dark ones that follow in his footsteps. History has shown his ability to make a person see what he wants them to see, manipulating the truth until you question everything that your mind and heart ever believed.

He has power over not only your mind, but your physical being, making sane minded people act in extreme, unimaginable ways. He seeks out your biggest weakness and uses it to give him the power to destroy you. He takes joy in the sadistic pain he willingly creates with his malicious sorcerer's magic. Torturing those souls suffering at the edge of Hell. Playing with them as if they are mere toys to be broken and cast aside, like the petulant spawn of a mortal. Using their screams of terror like a decadent song to bring joy and rapture to his enthralled minions and to give his twisted armies entertainment. He is the vilest creature that has ever walked these worlds.

But these warnings have been passed down from generation to generation, most of them from first hand accounts of the Devil's most hideous crimes, but it is still *not* enough to ever deter me from what I know I was created to do.

I have never come face-to-face with the vile creature of darkness, or one of his lurid demons, but I can feel them when they're near. When I venture too deep within the village of the damned, I know they can sense me, I know they feel my passage through the lands Lucifer has claimed sovereignty over as I can feel their unrest at my presence. The energy around me starts to heat up at their heinous excitement of having an angel in their midst.

They have, in some twisted game of cat and mouse, sent their Hunters, demons of the darkest order, to stalk us, to end our chances of saving those who seek our light. They are the most heinous of beings, ones who take malicious pleasure in trying to bait and ensnare one of us, wanting to strip us of our enlightened essence, to twist it and use it for the most beguiling of evil acts, to take our once divine force and twist it to only Heaven knows what. I know in my heart of hearts that it is something so far removed from my task that I am tainted just by the thought of it.

I must be wise and vigilant with every delicate step I take. A momentary loss in concentration could result in my discovery here amongst the decaying souls. I take every precaution I can, to move with no more than a whisper, my steps light as I'm huddled in the encompassing swathe of my protective cloak. It helps to contain my silver, vibrant glow, masking the power I hide within.

Its dark grey colour shrouds me as I move from shadow to shadow, the dark fabric blending like the waves of night within this sombre village that I walk. Bedded within the soft cotton lining is the true strength of its magic, a collection of pure enchantment.

Since I was a child, I've been walking the far edges of the Garden, which is touched by the fingers of the dark tainted forest. Every now and then, I would discover a type of small precious blue or red crystal, shining amongst the mixture of brown and green leaves on the ground. The first time I picked one up and placed it in my palm, I knew I was holding a great power, a force I knew I wouldn't understand until I needed to the most.

I believe for as long as I can remember, it's been the hidden energy within these crystals that allows my cloak to give me extra coverage, to be unseen by the dark army that is known for hunting my kind like a sport, but that's not the only protection I am blessed with. I have with me my guardian, a *rapturous force* that I always feel, and its mystical energy surrounding me when I enter this dying land. A force that seems to wrap itself around me when darkness gets too close, making me feel safe, protected, invisible to the malevolent and prying eyes that seek to clip my wings.

When I am drifting between the makeshift dwellings closest to the vile cliff that drops to Hell is when the force is at its strongest. It seems to know when the danger I am encased in is at its highest peak. I know the instant it is close; I experience an overwhelming sense of peace and safety, a sense that washes throughout my body like the drifting of the mortal world's tides.

My heart beats like the wings of a bird, undetected by anyone but myself, I feel a prickling sensation race over my entire white delicate skin, making me shiver slightly. I can hear a slight intake of breath and a whisper as I force myself to breathe. The scent of warm ashes mingles with a sweet smell, something akin to the apples that flourish in the gardens of Eden. I can actually taste the sweet fruit floating amongst the air. All my senses come alive.

Except one.

My sight.

I've never laid eyes on this mysterious entity. Each time I turn, there is nothing within my gaze but the dreary world of these suffering beings. Yet I know it has always been near, for almost a lifetime. I feel it lingering on the edges of the forest, behind the trees, following me all the way into the village, waiting for me to complete my deliverance of the sallow souls, so it can see me safely back to my own land.

I know it's not a Heavenly spirit or a guiding light. I can feel that it is of human form, but as much as I try, I have never been able to catch a glimpse of just what embodies my guardian and saviour. Maybe, just maybe, I want it to be of that form so badly, that every singing fibre of my being has left me blinded to what it really is.

I have a desperation to find its true source that is so fierce I know one day I will be brave enough to venture far within the darkness, just for a chance to find the truth. Even if that means risking my own self-worth, I just have to know *who* or *what* my eternal guardian truly is.

2

Seventh Circle

ALBION

The air around me burns, shimmering like gossamer as I stare up at the vaulted walkway that spans the water slicked stone barrier staying my exit from this cesspit, a cesspit that has been my home for as long as I can remember.

I raise my face to the heat licked air as a small hand clutches my elbow, sallow, paper thin skin grates over my sweat stained form; the rasping tug of the collar at my throat makes me shiver as talon like fingers sink into the flesh of my elbow.

The putrid stench of their breath fills my nostrils, overpowering the vapid pall that lingers in the air around me. Its shimmering yellow haze makes me squint as I turn my head slightly, willing away the stale odour of rotted flesh and curdled eggs.

'Time has come, Albion, for you to take your father's place. The winged servants of the false messiah need to see the face of their lords and masters; one of their own is waiting at the pass.'

Taloned claws tug at my neck as I feel the runes in my collar glow, their heat seeping into my scorched flesh as the lock at my throat clicks. The burnished bronze latch snaps open as cracked and brittle flesh pries the symbol of my indenture from around my throat.

'Now, Albion, your master awaits. This is not a position given lightly. You will be sent to a place where none of our kind is meant to tread.'

My feet weigh me down as I stride towards the cloaked and scowling figure, his glowing yellow eyes, colder than the deepest circles of this despotic pit, bore into me as I walk forth.

I feel the faintest quiver of fear in the pit of my stomach as I stop in front of him. Nothing, nothing could have prepared me for the cold anger laced stare that bears down upon me. The sheer wall of malice and hatred that stands there makes me quail like a pup scrabbling for the safety of its mother's shadow as the weight that falls upon my form forces me to my knees, even as my pride and honour compels me to stay my course.

A malicious smirk twists his face as he stares down at me, the stench of a millennium of hatred and death rolls from his slowly unfurling wings as I watch from the corner of my eye. Moloch slips away into the shadows, his withered form retreating from where his master had trod. I push my shoulders back, feeling the runes carved into my flesh ache and burn as I let my wings unfurl, the parting flesh of my back sending a sheet of ice cold anguish through me as I show my true form.

'You called, Sire?'

His lips curl, the glowing fangs that line his mouth glittering in the burnished glow that fills the air. Dancing shadows play across his face and vanish at the sight of their ethereal light. Even in his fall from the gates of that spoilt child they called a god, some vestige of my Lord's angelic past remains untainted by the passage of millennia that our kind has spent in this dank and stagnant tomb.

'Ah, my newest Hunter. Your father served me well, Albion. His passage through the borders of our world were met with trembling fear and the feather laced scurrying of my woe begotten siblings.'

I watch as his fingers flex, the calloused and leathery skin stretching over the undulating bones of his knuckles as he reaches out, placing his hand on my shoulder, my whole form tensing for the briefest of moments as I look up into the cold yellow eyes that bear down upon me.

'So tell me, are you ready to follow in your father's footsteps, Albion, to cleanse our borders and return to us the souls we hold claim to, from the feather laden curs that threaten our very dominion and the sanctity of the souls sent to our ...'

He pauses. My gaze resolute, I watch his mind turn inwards as a snide, almost sardonic, twist curls over his lips while he pats my shoulder.

'... tender care. My brothers and sisters think they can flaunt our boundaries with abandon, scurry through our lands and homes like the locusts my father cast down upon the Egyptians, snatching up the souls within like spoilt children at a friend's birthday. Their greed knows no bounds, Albion, and I ask you, are you ready to defend our lands from it? To kill for the safety of all who stand at your back?'

I bow my head, emotions that I had long held at bay curling through my heart and soul as I feel his hand lift from my slowly trembling form. I knew from birth that my task was pre-set. I was thrown headlong into this steaming world of horror and desolation with one task lain in my path, to be a Hunter.

A Hunter, a killer of angels. The long held beliefs of those arrogant winged heathens fall limp at my feet as my task and title sink into my mind and soul. This single solitary task, nay my very existence, hinged on my being one of the few with the ability to snuff their effervescent light from this Hell spun world that surrounds me.

I raise my head as Lucifer, my Lord, my Liege, my King, steps back, his wings falling away from his frame. Their taut, scaled leather encapsulate him as I push myself to my feet, words tripping from my lips before I feel any recognition of what I am saying.

'By my life, or my death, I will serve you, my King. I will scour these lands clean of the filth that dares subjugate our people. Like my father before me and his before him, I will raise my hand against all that the false Idol has sent to our shores and will not rest until I have felled every last one of them.'

I watch as he turns away from me, a beckoning finger cast over his shoulder. I follow on, the soft fluttering of his featherless wings flirting with the air as my ears strain against the howling, guttural calls of the callous minions that chatter and squawk in his wake.

'Your station carries great weight, young one. Very few of your fellow warriors are given, or even granted, the abilities you were birthed with; your father was my best Hunter, my most adept killer, and none that have come since have ever surpassed him in skill or lethality.'

A smile teases my mind as I approach the bottom of the spiralling flight of stairs which wind their way up the walls towards the vaulted walkways that circle above. The echoing clank of mailed feet and the guttural grunts of the feral beasts that patrol them night and day swirl around me as I make my way up the never ending cavalcade of steel and wood.

'You will depart from my presence, Albion. I have little desire to face the glaring light that bathes the surface. My brothers have long sought a chance to put to rest their wayward sibling, namely me; and I do not seek to give them a chance to do so.'

He stares at me, his cold yellow gaze questioning as I finally come level with the lord of my creation. His sneering lips quirk once more, a more playful stance turning them from a vision of malicious hate to something more like pride.

'Go child, your path awaits, walk it with pride, my Hunter. Oh, and Albion, don't hide what you truly are.'

I bow low, my wings curling around my shoulders as I hook the razor tipped talons together, drawing them tight around me as I step into the mouth of the tunnel that leads deep into the arms of my own destiny.

A sense of trepidation and pride flows through my veins as I stride down the darkened hallway. Guttering torches and heat scorched sconces line the way. I reach the thick iron studded door, my hand settling against its warm and pitted surface as I push it open.

'Barbatos, are you here?'

My voice rings around me like a bell as I listen to the near silent crackle of the coals in the furnace. Its thick oak bellows hang silent at its side as I watch one of Barbatos' slumbering serfs, the diminutive creature curled on the handle like a puppy. The sound of claws on stone draw my ear as I step further into the heat licked room, the air shimmering as I cast my gaze about me.

'Barbatos, I am here for what is mine.'

The loping wheat coloured form slips past me, the crackling coals slowly fading as the room fills with the vile, visceral tones of rending flesh and shifting bones. I watch Barbatos twist and morph into his true form. I turn my gaze from him, bile rising into my gullet as thick swathes of dead flesh hit the floor with a pattering splat.

'Still can't watch that, hey boy. So, what did the Angel send you here for?'

I feel my stomach boil as I listen to Barbatos' words, my hands balling tightly upon themselves. His eyes fall upon me as he lifts a cloth bound bundle onto the bench that dominates the room, swatting aside a squealing serf as he begins to peel apart the package.

'Calm yourself, boy. That Angel hasn't been here nearly as long as I have. My existence pre-dates the Jews' march from Egypt. I pre-date the creation of man itself, so before you go and unleash your ire upon me, child, just remember to whom it is you are speaking.'

I force myself to relax as I draw my ire and rage inwards. The boiling cauldron of emotion in my stomach pushes up from my core as I watch the thick, oiled sheet of hessian fall aside; glistening mail cord leather meets my gaze. Barbatos waves his hand at it all as I lean forward.

'This is what you came for, boy. Use it wisely.'

The sunlight burns my eyes as I crouch, hunched against the howling winds that sweep across the scorched earth that surrounds the gateway to my home, my dominion. My eyes ache, my ears twitch as I wait, staring into the city below; the jumbled collection of ramshackle huts and buildings tease my mind as I watch the skittering passage of the myriad of forms that weave their way through the alleys and streets.

Their shimmering essence surrounds them all as I stare down upon them from the shadows, from the edges of my own oblivion, their scent coating the air as I watch the poorly veiled forms of my prey flit through the world around us all. One question fills me as I sit, my armoured and shrouded form bathed in shadows. The slow chattering grate of the blue and red crystals in my palm sooth my tarnished nerves.

I am a Hunter, I was born a Hunter, I am pledged to Lucifer's service as was my father before me. But, why am I so torn? I watch my prey and the cattle they have come to save swirl and dance before me like dust on the wind and yet, even as I draw my sights on one of those self indulgent, arrogant winged heathens, I cannot pull the trigger. Something deep within me, this rolling ball for which I have no name, this inescapable sense of self betrayal stills my hand while I watch them, their life hanging on a hair as my finger aches for that one final squeeze. A feral growl fills me as I draw my aim away, my body shifting before I even consciously realise I am moving.

My mother's words fill my ears as I stalk forwards, moving with the shifting grass. The winds sigh over the slowly rolling waters that seep from the edges of the grey forests before me, that inescapable border between my world and theirs.

'All is not clear in our world, Albion. You are not of just one world. You, my little one, are so much more. Watch over the one who captures your heart and they will, in turn, watch over you.'

And here I sit, as I have for so many years, for that one moment where I can see *her*, the one those chattering and fearful wretches cry out to, their little 'Angel of Mercy,' and my Little Wing. My mother's words ring true. I *have* watched over her, even if she doesn't know it, just as she has over me.

The chattering of stones to my left fill my ears as I drag the scent of this one wayward waif through my sense. My eyes drift closed as she slowly dances past me; the fresh clean scent of pure air and apple blossoms draws at my mind as I move, falling into her wake as she moves further from me. Her movements are fearful and full of flight as she slips through the cracks towards the border, my brethren fast at her heels. The beads in my hands click as I fall to the left. The snarling face that greets mine falters.

'Albion, brother, what ...'

His words fall silent as I watch my blade shear through his skull, a glittering arc of crystallised blood pattering to the floor around me. I draw my blade slowly free as I watch his corpse glow and slowly crumble, the wind drawing it in as it turns to ash before my eyes. The scent of charred flesh and ashen bone fill my nose as I turn, watching her whispering form vanish into the tree line, her head turning in my direction as my unheard whispered words fill the air.

'Fly, Little Wing, fly.'

The dirt at my feet lingers as I kneel in the grass choked pathway, my fingers plucking the glowing crystal orbs from where they lay. The small pouch on my hip jangles slightly as I pull at the draw string, the blue and red gems within casting out an almost ethereal light. I let the still warm orbs slip from my fingers as I watch her slip completely from sight, the ball within me settling. I turn and move away from the edge of the forest as the low rumble of the stone monoliths that bar my passage fills the air and, once more, my Little Wing is beyond my reach.

As I watch the last fading whispers of her ethereal essence drift apart, their golden strands splitting on the wind, I turn, my eyes shimmering as I let my vision twist. The dancing light of the heathens fill the air as I watch another of those feathered invaders drift from the mouth of an alleyway; with nary a sound, I move. My leather clad feet pull me through the grass as it sways around me, the blade in my grip shivering as it senses the blood that it lusts after. Barbatos' words ring in my ears as I near closer to my prey, my lips pulling back from my teeth as I reach forwards.

'Remember boy, her hunger will cry out to you, scream inside your skull like the cawing of a harpy, but never give into it. To give in to that lust for blood is a death sentence, Albion. Too many Hunters have, and I don't want to see Abara-weiser's heir become the next target of Lucifer's blood hounds.'

Lucifer's blood hounds, the Dolophonos; my core chills at the thought of them. These angels fear my kin, but the Dolophonos make me and my brothers cry like children alone in the dark, screaming for their mother's embrace.

The silent assassins of Hell, rampant wraiths of smoke and malice, soaking in the anguish and pain of everything and everyone around them. Malachai, the shifting red eyed master of the order, shadowing my mind as he stalks through the layers of our nightmares.

My hand reaches out, my studded knuckles reflecting dully in the glaring light of day as I slowly spin my blade in my grip, the razor edged dagger turning across my bare palm as I lunge forth. Cupping satin flesh, I drag my quarry's head back and sink the screaming blade up through the angel's windpipe. The cold rush of air over my cheek makes me smile as I watch the cobalt coloured glow of its essence pour forth, spilling down as I pull the dying angel back into the alleyway.

Drawing my dagger from its neck, I drive it deep into my prey's chest. I feel it sink past the being's ribs, through supple, dough like flesh as I relinquish my grip and let the angel slip to the floor, my blade still lodged in its chest. I stand over the gasping heathen and stare down into her slowly fading ocean blue eyes.

'Ah, a woman. A pity such frail beauty was doomed to cross my path here. Sleep now, little lady, and know that Albion, son of Abara-weiser, sent you to your rest. You should feel honoured to be my second conquest of this new day.'

I can't help but feel my heart fall as I watch her light fade with the twist of my blade, its cold edge slicing through her stomach. I drive forwards and up, my arm lifting her from the floor, the blade sinking through her heart. Her final, almost mewling gasp meets my ears as her body begins to fade, the shimmering specks of light and golden glowing dust rising from around her as she drifts apart.

A deep well of self-loathing and pity rolls through me as I kneel in the dying energies of the woman I have just silenced for eternity. Plucking her cloak from where it lies before me, I wipe her blood from my now cooing blade before slipping it into the sheath at my waist. I am a Hunter. I should rejoice at the death of my prey, exult at their death as the energy from their slain form flows through me, soaking my core in a buoyant drift of manna. Yet, as I kneel here amongst the scattered remnants of the angel I just silenced, I feel nothing but regret and hate. Not at her for being an angel, but at myself for having silenced her inner light and beauty. My mind draws forth images of *her*. I stare at the blood stained cloak at my feet, the slowly cooling pools of cobalt blue send coiling wisps of glowing light into the air as I think of all I would do to keep *her* safe from harm and all I have done to keep the hands of my brethren from her throat.

With an echoing sigh of pain and regret I force myself to my feet and move down the alley, my feet and body guiding themselves as I choke down the welling emotion that threatens to drown me.

3

Misunderstood

ARIANWEN

I've never had to fight.

I've never had to truly prove my strength. I've always relied upon my gifts and abilities to move unseen from my bright incandescent white world, through the dreary greys of the forgotten forest, to the dark blackened village of the condemned and even towards the glow of fiery red at the edges of Hell.

I have come as close as one can to being face-to-face with one of the Dark One's Hunters, and yet I have always managed to evade their grasp, even when I have been close enough to them, to one of these despicable and shameless creatures, to be able to taste their vile stench in every breath I took. I was close enough to see its disgusting hateful eyes glowing with scorching heat that seared all the way through to my deepest darkest crevices.

That pitiful excuse of a being belonged hidden in the morbid tunnels of Hell, that destitute world of vile and rampant sin where it will be destined for an eternity of pain and hatred; and yet its sole purpose was to rise to the surface in search of a celestial prize to take back to the one he kneels before. That one that takes joy in casting a dark, pitiless blanket over every shred of virtuosity that it can find.

If it wasn't for my ability to stop my own breathing, still my heartbeat, and cool my body instantly until I was as close to death as an angel could be when I sensed danger was upon me, I would have been the next prize for Lucifer's collection. Instead the Hunter only stilled his footing for a brief moment before turning in the opposite direction.

'Arianwen, did you hear what I said?'

My mother's voice resounds in my ear as I make my way through the door of our home, still lost inside my own thoughts. I close my mind off to her bitter yowling's as I try in vain to make a hasty retreat, not wanting to get into another debate with my mother who seems to think it would be easy for me to cease the calling I have had bestowed upon me, as if it would be easy to cut off something that is so much a part of my being as much as a limb is to my physical body.

'Arianwen, you know you can't continue this childish dalliance. You can't keep venturing into that cesspit of darkness; prancing so close to the edge of Hell, all hours of the day and night; it is not the behaviour of a future bride of Gabriel. You must start showing everyone that you are worthy of taking up a position beside one of our greatest Warriors.'

The words that exude from her mouth are making my ears bleed. How does she know me so little to not understand that I was given the gift of re-claiming because it is my birth right, it was what I was created to do? I know that I am one of the best amongst my kin, and without me, many helpless souls would wrongly fall before the dark lord.

'Mother, please stop this illusion that I'll one day become Gabriel's wife. I don't want that position, I've never wanted it. I've told you many times before that it's not what I'm meant to be. There are far more suitable candidates than I. Why are you pushing so hard for something that you know would make me miserable?' My mother's loud gasp I'm sure can be heard throughout the entire garden.

'How dare you mock such a respected position? You are beyond fortunate to have even courted with the idea of teasing his eye.

How could you so willingly flout such a prestigious honour? You need to give up your childish ambition of changing the path of souls that are already lost to their impending fate and finally accept that this *is* the path you're bound to tread. Not all souls can be saved, I know that.'

Sometimes I feel such a hatred radiating from my mother's every pore each time she has broached this subject; it's something I will always struggle to comprehend. I know every mother's maternal instinct is to want the best for her child, but how could she possibly not see that the path she has me walking towards is not the path that I am destined to take. And how can she truly not understand since she was a Reclaimer herself for a short time.

I can no longer take part in this torturous repetition; time and time again I have been hounded and I can take no more. It seems to be the only source of dialogue between us of late, and I feel like no matter how many times I show my ire at her words, she can't see past her own fickle musings. I turn to walk back out the doorway as I feel my mother's hand snare the edge of my cloak before I can retreat.

'Please, Arianwen, I need you to see that I'm only saying this for your own good. Do you truly understand the magnitude of the danger your calling has put you in? Reclaimers do not normally walk as close to Hell as you do.'

'Mother, you know I do, but you must understand that what I do is who I am. It's threaded through my entire body. It flows through my veins like the blood that keeps me alive; without it I would cease to exist. I am the only one who can walk that far and I am not going to cease that.'

I turn before she has a chance to mouth her response. I need to clear my raging thoughts, to erase the words she has spoken yet again. I'm not sure there is a single person in this light land that completely understands the person I truly am. The person I am destined to be.

✦ ✦ ✦

As I walk along the winding paths through this exquisite masterpiece of divine nature, I can't help but be eternally thankful for the life I have been created for. This divine garden is life at its purest. I am truly blessed to be able to experience such splendour each day of my life. I feel such astonishment each time I take in all the glorious colours that flow through even the smallest of the delicate flowers that carpet the soil on which I tread, to the branches of the canopy of tall flowing trees that dance above me, showing only glimpses of the azure blue sky, to the sound of the crystal clear water in the stream that winds itself through this heavenly garden, giving life to everything it reaches.

'Arianwen, your steps still hold much fight in them. What heavenly creature are you trying to stomp upon?'

I jump in fright, too lost in my own thoughts to even notice the great Anatiamoros is right in front of me, smirking at my angry scowl. I instantly bow down on one knee out of deference before my liege lord and the oldest most respected Reclaimer in this heavenly world.

'Stand, sweet child, and tell me why there is such anger surrounding your aura?'

I rise and slowly lift my eyes to meet his, trying to control the sudden assault of emotion that has flooded my senses and let my words tumble out with haste.

'I fear I may never be able to show my loved ones my true self. No matter what clever words I try, their minds are set in solid stone, when the *truth* is on a rolling pebble.'

I take a deep breath, not wanting to give in to my emotions and appear weak in front of my greatest mentor and a man I see as the grandfather I no longer have.

'Arianwen, in all my years I have seen it near impossible to change the minds of those whose life is defined by the deepest seated need to protect their offspring.

'If one sees even an ounce of harm enveloping their child, it can turn mild mannered mice into the fiercest of lions, ready to fight and protect with their entire being.

'You are as strong as your mother is and as her mother before her, so don't assume that the words she speaks are not coming from her own personal experience and the experience of those who came before her. Her words are out of love, not anger or stubbornness.'

From the one person I thought would completely understand my plight, comes the realization that maybe no one will ever understand who I truly am at my core. I smile just to acknowledge his words, but find it impossible to respond.

'Is there something else child? You seem to have more than just anger surrounding your aura. There seems to be a changing light approaching one of your many celestial layers, but I can't seem to put a name to it. Just please do me one small favour, be extra wary, child, when you are moving from our world to theirs. Evil can show itself in even the most unexpected form.

'I can sense a change upon you that may be anything but light. There seems to be a shift in our worlds that is making our great one feel unease, which is why I feel that Gabriel has seen fit to call a council of all the legions leaders to discuss what course of action, if any, may need to be taken. But you didn't hear that from me.'

He winks and grins at his comment.

'Go and find your peace, Arianwen, and know that only *your* heart will hold the secrets of the path you must follow.'

I bow my head before moving past him, my feet leading me towards the place that holds my heart the most. As I walk away, my mind drifts. I breathe in all the glorious perfumes of nature surrounding me, I close my eyes, hoping it will wash away the turmoil I feel bubbling inside. The sweet smell of the gardenia flowers always seem to rise and joy my heart, and the scent of the lavender bushes that my legs sometimes brush upon seems to always provide me with clarity. But it's the giant floating lily pads slowly dancing across the lake that are always whispering my name upon the winds.

As I reach the water's edge, I slowly rise to the tips of my toes, stretching my neck, tilting my chin up until my eyes meet the blue sky above. I release my wings, my body stretching as I push out, their pale feathered lengths, basking in their freedom, lifting me, letting every single downy feather slowly unfurl as I begin to leave the solid ground below me. I slowly float forward until I reach the centre pad, the beat of my wings soft as I drift quietly, slipping through the air as I fan the waters below me, dropping an inch at a time until I finally land, barely causing a ripple on the surface of the water. I slowly lower my body down to a kneeling position, contentment filling me in the one place that always gives me complete solace.

With hands on my knees, I lean forwards, my eyes falling on my reflection in the clear, glass smooth water, my three auburn feathers to the left of my cheek, clearly standing out amongst the pure white surrounding them, a constant reminder that I am, and always will be, different from the rest of my kin and that the wing they adorn was once considered a morbid disfigurement. The slight teasing and ridicule I had suffered for it being smaller than its twin when I was a young child would always sit in the back of my mind. It grew in time, as did my awareness to what I was created to do.

As much as I need to clear my mind, Anatiamoros' words invade my thoughts; the fact that my mother may be speaking from personal experience is nothing new to me. I can see it in her eyes that she holds many secrets, secrets that she hides from me, secrets that she willingly draws back from the edges of her visage and keeps in the depths of her soul, far from the glaring light of day.

I suspect that her younger years were not as smooth as she portrays them to be. But surely by sharing those secrets with me, we may find a common ground to speak upon. But whenever I try to delve deeper into her soul, she shuts down and tells me not to live in an unattainable fantasy.

How can she say that? This life is all I have ever known; my father and mother were both chosen ones in their youth, as were their mothers and fathers before them. Her anger rises further when I have mentioned that. Deep within, I feel someone from our heritage was once human, a privilege I have dreamt about since my earliest memories. My mother has always dismissed them as colourful childhood fantasies without a word of truth to them and I shouldn't continue with such fanciful thoughts at my age, which seen through human eyes would be twenty two.

But I know they are true. And I feel that the truth will be presented to me in time, when that information will have a direct impact on the path I will follow. Anatiamoros' singular comment, 'Only *your* heart will hold the secrets of the path you must follow' is what's playing with my thoughts the most. I know what I feel in my heart is true, that I am to save the desperate forgotten souls that no other Reclaimers have ever had the ability to reach, that I am to deliver them to God so they can receive the eternal peace for which they are entitled.

But ... I also feel that another path will be put forth to me in my lifetime. I can't explain it and yet I can feel that there is more to my life than I first thought. I have forever felt like a part of me was missing, like a part of my soul was gone, pulled from me and cast to the winds that roar through my world. When I was younger I thought these feelings stemmed from the one smaller wing I was created with, that the ridicule I was subjected to brought forth all the worry and doubt that hounds me; but, through it all, as I have aged and my wings matured, I know that it's more than a child-hood stunted growth, more than the lingering vapours of childish insecurities. It's deeper, more meaningful, like a part of my soul is missing a piece.

I try not to think about it often, because it hurts to feel like I am not whole, to feel like I am lacking in some way. Sometimes when I have dwelt on these feelings, it has taken my strength and I can't do that to the human beings that would have to face eternal Hell forever without me.

I suddenly hear it!

Another calling! Someone in pain. Someone in utter distress. Someone who is experiencing unthinkable fear. Even if I tried, I couldn't ignore the need in me to end these poor humans' suffering with a peaceful journey to their final resting place. Heaven.

I slowly take flight from my place of rest and gently land on the bank of the river, before making haste on foot through the garden, towards the stone dragons that are the exit from this place of bountiful life and into the start of the world that the forgotten ones reside in. We are detected more easily in flight so on foot I go.

As I begin to pass these large stone gatekeepers, a rumble rolls through their granite forms, vibrating the ground that I walk on.

'I know, I know. I can sense a shift in our worlds too. Something *is* about to happen. But I will be safe, my friends, and I will return soon like I always do,' I tell these caring and once mythical creatures who watch over all from our lands.

Their low growls are still slightly rolling the earth as I make my way through the forgotten forest, with its old decaying stumps and leafless dry branches stretching out like claws, wanting to catch a piece of you as one passes. The once soft green moss under my feet has now turned a lurid lifeless black, barely crunching as I start to make my silent decent into the village of the condemned.

I can feel the rising tension in the air, its electric atmosphere encircling my throat in a vain attempt at strangling me. But I must not give in to its malicious distracting force. I have a job to do that is more important than what is trying to shift the balance of these immortal worlds. To me, the soul in need is my first priority, and my second is not being discovered amongst these suffering beings by one of the dark one's atrocious hounds.

As I whisper through this village, flitting between the ramshackle dwellings made of broken long forgotten buildings and the remnants of all of God's long lost creations, stepping on the ground that's a mixture of poisoned mud and a lifetime of human waste, trying hard to completely shut down my sense of smell so I can bare this inglorious scent, I can feel the unease growing rapidly within all of my senses; every sinew in my body is winding tightly, waiting for something to make itself known.

As I approach the door and reach for the handle of the dwelling I have been called to, I notice I can still hear the rumbles of the gatekeepers far off into the distance, which only heightens my awareness that evil is close at hand.

I let my eyes wander quickly around this city of Hell, making sure not a creature nearby has scented my aura, before I pull the handle I'm gripping tightly down and open the door with practiced silence.

I enter with a soft glide, instantly seeing the being in need. A young woman, whose one wrong decision has seen her banished to these edges of Hell, lying in an old, moth eaten and ragged pile. The jumble of rags and straw that she has cobbled together is little more than a heap of trash, not what any sane being would call a bed. I move to her side, grabbing her hand, bringing it to my lips as I reach out my other to gently place it against her cheek, her skin cold and slick with fever's kiss.

'You have nothing to fear, sweet one. You are a child of God, and I am here to guide you back to his waiting arms. The good you still have deep within your soul will see you back to where you belong. Close your eyes now, child. Feel the warmth I have for you and follow the light until you are home.'

I give this poor soul every piece of celestial virtue I have to offer, sealing her within it as I send her on her way, my will to see her safely home swaddling her like a child's first blanket. Watching as her eyes slowly glide shut, her entire being becoming an orb of luminous light, rising high from the bed. Her human shell starts to dissolve into a mass of glittering aura, like sunshine dancing through a window pane, turning into her true soul of pure rapturous light, before slowly dancing, twirling and disappearing into thin air, now on her way to the peaceful land.

I take a moment to truly appreciate the astonishing force that is the human soul. Its journey from God's hands, to its human form, to its lifetime on earth, then to return to its Creator to receive eternal peace for its services to mankind, is nothing short of a miracle. A miracle I long to be blessed with during my lifetime.

But before I have time to get lost in my thoughts, I feel the ground beneath my feet start to quake. The heavy rolling rumble brings me back to the realization that I need to return to the safety of my realm before this mysterious energy shows the force it holds within.

I grip the door handle ... pause ... listen ... and start to pull down slowly, trying to avoid the tell tale click of this ancient mechanism. When no noise presents itself, I grip harder and pull ever so softly towards my waist, letting my senses become aware of what surrounds this dwelling, before leaning slightly through the door frame to let my sight take charge for a moment.

The damned all seem to be unaware of the shift in energy as they go about their daily existence, threading through this waiting room of death. I step out with extreme caution, letting only one foot at a time step on to the wretched soil beneath them. I turn to the right, slowly easing past the corner, my head turning with a rising sense of unease as I make my way towards the back of the decrepit building, gradually rising with each step as I make my way up towards the forgotten forest with no more than a whisper.

I *feel* more than hear the presence of something descend from a rooftop and land with a slight rustle of fabric a mere step behind me. I instantly gasp before I realize my need for silence in this woeful village. Fear starts to thread its way with haste throughout my core, making my heartbeat fasten without my control as the horror of what may be behind me starts to realise itself within my thoughts.

The sudden recognition of my own thoughts, pushing forwards the fact that I know exactly what creature is behind me, the force of it almost knocking me senseless with disappointment soaring through me at not sensing this earlier. I recognize the foul stench of Hell whispering around my head as the trickling heat of danger winds its way around my entire being. I know to survive this close encounter I have to have all my wits about me. I need to draw on all my gifts and abilities to have the strength to face this terror, to face the deception that Hell's minions can weave in my mind, to push aside their veils and curtains and find my way into the light that I claim as my home. I know this vile demon behind me has the upper hand with my disadvantage being my back is turned, so I know it would be pointless to try and outrun it. I need to turn and face the Satanic Hunter and outwit my way from this diabolical situation.

I slowly begin to turn, watchful for a weapon or talon claw. A single twitch from this behemoth, the merest movement of its intent to reach out and connect with my light flesh, and I would be undone; but as I let my eyes fall upon the chest of its dark, leather clad form in front of me, I notice there is no movement from my enemy at all; it's as if it has suddenly turned to stone, only the steady thrum of its breathing and beating tones of its heart fill the now silent air.

But I am wiser than to fall for evil's trickery and not for a second will I let my defences fall. I let my eyes gradually rise, moving over the tight old black leather that adorns its muscled body, surprised by what my vision is showing me. My eyes are drawn over lines of muscle and sculpted flesh, all of which is pleasing to my eyes; this demon, this servant of Hell has a very defined and humanlike visage which looks firm and full of incomparable strength.

I am surprised that this is the form that evil is showing me; it is far from vile or hideous, as the images that all of my kin are led to believe, and what I have always thought a demon close up would look like; and yet all my beliefs are cast asunder as I bear witness to this silent Adonis that is so close to my eyes. I cautiously raise my head, preparing myself to look evil in the eye for the first time.

I need to remain strong, I need to show no fear. I need to remind this Hunter that I will not become his prey today. As my eyes continue their ascent over his massively broad shoulders that are holding onto two copious arms that look like they could crush the earth, to his thickened neck of soft, cream coloured flesh, slick with sweat, where I can see the only movement in his sensual presence in the form of two large veins pulsating with excitement at rapid speed, to his wide chiselled jaw that extends to two gloriously high cheekbones that seem to beg for my fingers to grace them, that is framing two plump glistening deep red lips making promises beyond my limited knowledge, mesmerizing me as I struggle to hold my wits together.

I'm unable to comprehend this vision of confusion, my mind struggling to compare this humanlike male species with that of a woeful demon. As my eyes are taking in this extraordinary sight before me, I feel something boiling inside, something growing and gaining speed like lava inside of a volcano about to erupt, a heat that is soaring through my veins.

His nostrils flare as I almost reach his glass balls of hatred. I take a large breath in as I prepare to face one of the sons of Hell itself. I steel myself for what I'm about to see as I let my eyes reach their final destination.

An almost deafening roar reaches my ears as all my senses are left in awe. I gasp as I have an instant recognition of the beautiful aqua blue globes that are staring back at me with as much unbridled adoration in them as I am surely showing in mine. I know I have *never* seen into these eyes before, yet as we both continue our appraisals, I know exactly who I am staring at, as this creature in front of me has been a part of my life from my earliest possible memories, a silent shadow to my own life and footsteps.

My body is frozen as my mind tumbles. I know I am in shock, this sudden and all too unbidden revelation leaving me helpless in front of this towering beast of muscle and brimstone! This demon, this Hunter who is standing tall over my small frame is my saviour ... my guardian! My mind refuses to acknowledge what my heart and soul know to be the truth, that the comforting aura that has followed my every move from the moment I leave the gates of Eden to the second that I return, is him!

It's always been him!

4

Devil's Stare

ALBION

I sit watching the sun dip, the soft cooing hum of my sated and slumbering blade tickling the back of my mind as I rest the heavy lump of rune etched, hand forged metal against my palm and thigh. The thick barrel of my father's pistol rests in the crook of my thumb as I let my eyes travel over the scroll work and inlays. I roll my hand over the shimmering chamber, the thick slug like bullets filling them like nails in wood as I listen to the heavy oil choked click of the mechanism as I rotate it round by iron coated round.

My great grandfather had carried this, and his father before him; throughout my family line this weapon was passed from wielder to wielder, father to son, father to daughter, wherever the powers fell; those that carried this, carried it with pride, just as my own father had before me. As I stare at the ebony handled weapon, my mind is awash with thoughts so dark and depraved that the tinkling lights of sorrow and self-hate are crushed beneath their tumultuous form the itch starts.

That teasing ache in the back of my skull fills me as I lift my gaze; my senses scream as the familiar scent flirts with me. I push forwards, rolling up onto my haunches. My eyes snatch a glittering glimpse of golden light and I know once more my prey is abroad ...

and yet, through it all, I feel nary a tremor of excitement. It is more a settled resignation at the thought of claiming another unwitting life, a life that has just happened to cross my path and one that would have continued to flourish had it not scurried through my ever watchful gaze.

Biting the inside of my cheek, I trace my fingers over the runes on the barrel, feeling them glow hot beneath my hand as my blade once more begins to sing for blood.

'I know, you'll be sated soon enough, and I will be damned once more.'

I hear and feel the shivering hiss that my blade bleeds through me, my scalp itching as I let my fingers slip over the hilt, a soft cooing tumbling through my soul as the animalistic core of my insatiable weapon senses the tender touch.

Stepping forwards, I feel the ground leave me as I drop from the rock outcropping that I've made my home. My cowl snaps and my body tenses as I plummet towards the floor. Even as I sink into the waiting arms of the rock strewn crevasse below me, my eyes never leave my prey, their shimmering wake drawing me to them as they skitter like rats through a sewer.

My gait is easy and steps light as I make my way towards that effervescent glow, the golden trail of purity making my stomach clench; the blade at my hip shivers in the afterglow of the slowly evaporating mist. Sinking to one knee, I cock my head to the side as I listen to the clamorous bustle of the market not one hundred meters from where I now rest. The pattering of fevered feet reach my ears as I rise, my form already moving as I leap, my pace nimble as I haul myself up on to the flat roof of the squat building one of these sallow hairless apes called a home. The corrugated sheeting beneath me rattles slightly as I surge forwards, the stench of excrement and fear mixing into a heady, bile inducing miasma that threatens to steal the air from my lungs.

They scurry from door to door, hovel to hovel, as the lowest rungs of this foetid pit live like swine in a mire of eternal sorrow, while others barter and caw over poorly made trinkets that aren't worth the polished pebbles they're made of.

The wind shifts around me as I scan the dilapidated world, my eyes shifting as the world melts into a shimmering haze of grey. The blue glowing shapes of these hairless apes moving like spectres as the shimmering golden silhouette of my prey stands, its form bursting like a super nova as I make my way forwards.

✦ ✦ ✦

Stars burst through my vision as I crash to the floor, my mind screaming as the flesh at the base of my back separates; the heady scent of my own blood and the vaporous corruption of my prey turned hunter flows over me.

'Abara-weiser's heir, really, I was honestly expecting something far more impressive.' His sneering face bores into my own as I roll forwards, the torn flesh of my back already stitching itself to-gether as I come to my feet. My mind tumbles as I curl my hand around the hilt of my blade; its fervent shivering sends a rolling vibration through me as I slowly step to my left; my strutting opponent smiles as we circle one another. His gait easy, overly confident as I wait for his opening move.

'Estrastiel, I thought it was you. My brothers never were a match for you. How many of them have you sent to oblivion now?'

A smirk stretches his sallow features as he weighs the blade in his grip, his eyes shifting from me to the gilded pommel resting against the edge of his hand. 'Not enough it seems.'

A low growl settles in my throat as I feel that intensive familiar tickle, the tingle that settles in at the base of my skull, the vibrating shiver that lets me know she is slowly getting closer.

Estrastiel's attention wavers as he senses her arrival. The sudden blooming of intensive calm that rolls through the air fills the world around us both as his head turns towards my Little Wing's arrival. I grin, his eyes slipping closed as his body goes limp. She draws ever closer; springing forwards I drop low, my blade slicing upwards, its cawing hum filling my mind as I feel his flesh part, its tip slipping through Estrastiel's lungs and deep into his spine.

His body seizes, feet scrabbling against the metal beneath us as his blood flows over my hand; my lips graze his ear as I pull him close to me, his eyes spinning as his body tries in vain to understand what is draining the life from it. I pour all of my rage forth as I lift his twitching form from the floor, my hand sinking into his ravaged flesh as a rolling ball of hate and malice fills me.

'Never take your eyes off your enemy, Estrastiel, you never know when that first strike will fall. Alas, this seems to be a lesson you've learned a little too late.'

I scythe my dagger to the left, his eyes falling blank as I let his body drop from my grip, my blade's warm cooing sending a sated shiver along my spine as I wipe his blood from my hands; my eyes shifting as I feel my Little Wing draw near.

Her golden laced glow fills my vision as she passes me, mere feet below, her radiance blossoming over everything as she struggles to contain her inner light. The yowling animals from all corners of Hell rise, their twisted auras filling the air as I slowly follow her glittering wake, hoping against all that life has taught me, that they somehow pass her by.

I watch as she pulls the cloak tighter around her slim body, the rippling mottled swathe of cloth hugging every curve and angle of her lust coaxing form. My wandering gaze falls to the swell of her tight posterior as she slips through the shadows of this rust and filth bitten land, begging hands and pleading eyes snatching at her as she wades through the destitute and the downcast.

I try in vain to tear my eyes away from her; the swelling in my body and soul makes me bitter with myself as I desperately search for a way to push from my mind the want and lust that my Little Wing is now drawing from me. I knew they were there, these unbidden feelings, ever since her first tentative blooming as my innocent Little Wing went from a shy violet to a tender rose.

The wavering shadows and shifting material does little to hide her innate sexuality. As I slip from the edge of the roof, my fingers curl through the gaps in the rafters. I hang there, like a spider stalking its dinner, silent and unmoving as my sweet temptress finally vanishes from my view. The overwhelming wall of love and calm shifts and undulates as her cloaked and cowed form vanishes through the door below me.

With a soft muffled grunt of exertion I drop, my feet kissing the ground as I roll to my feet, the oily tendrils of my brothers' searching auras brushing my own as I push outwards my anger and will, sending a boiling wave of malice and hatred out like a wall of water, heaving aside their pitiful attempts at stealth and subterfuge.

I listen to the wind, feel the warmth of her grace kiss my death seared skin as the contented sighs of the hairless apes around me float on the air; the gentle whispering of that one singular name filling my ears as I slowly rise to my feet, wiping the sweat from my eyes and brow as I breathe her heady scent in.

Running with as much silence as I can muster, I leap. My hands curl over the edge of a roof as I haul myself upwards, the clinging taste of her purity coating my tongue as I stop, my eyes shifting once more as I stare down into the room below, its contents masked by the slabs of pitted stone and wood beneath my feet.

Creeping forwards, my body tucked and hunched low, I reach out, my fingers curling through the iron ring set into the worm eaten wooden hatch in front of me. My eyes drift closed as I silently plead for it not to squeal in rust coated agony as I draw it up from its centuries' old resting place.

I watch as the room swims into focus, the glittering glow of her new claim filling the room as the soul leaves its tired and world fevered husk; she turns, her glowing blonde tresses bouncing against her nearly armourless form. I shake my head at the ill prepared woman below me; how could she move through such a desolate and deadly world as mine without some form of protection around her?

I close my eyes, a silent prayer to myself bouncing within my skull as I vow to make right the wrongs that have befallen my sweet angel. Easing the panel back into place, I move towards the edge of the roof as my Little Wing tentatively makes her way from the doorway below my feet.

I grit my teeth, my need to see her safe at war with my own selfish desire to see her face to face, even if it is for but the briefest of moments. My fingers bite into the crumbling stonework as I stare at her diminutive form mere feet below me. Should I finally show myself to her? Should I really shatter this dream she may have crafted about who it is that shadows her every waking moment in this woeful place? Can I, son to a Demon Knight and murderer of her kin, truly show her that the one person in this entire pit of death and depravity that doesn't want her soul on a plate is also one that has caused her the most pain?

I cannot say what makes me move, but before I even have the conscious thought of finally showing myself to the angel who has gripped my every waking moment, I am plummeting like a comet to the earth. I am falling and, as my feet hit the floor and the dust falls around me, the realisation swims into focus. The realisation that no matter what my decision would have been, this, right here, right now, was the only right one.

I watch her stop. Her hands softly twitch as she begins to turn, my breath stilling in my throat as I reach up and pull my mask aside, the cold air spilling across my cheeks and chin as I drag the hardened leather down letting it bunch around my fingers. My eyes widen, the heavy guard slipping from my grip as I watch her turn to face me. I feel the soothing, vaporous caress of her nature as my body uncoils, the tension and anger melting from me as I stare down into the bottomless iced violet pools before me. The intensity of her gaze undoes me as I feel my core boil, energy racing through me igniting everything I have fought so hard to contain as our eyes lock. The world around me and this glowing vision of faith and compassion falling into an all consuming silence that envelopes us both completely.

Nothing could have prepared me for the vision that stands

before me. In all the years I had spent on the fringes of her life, in the shadows of her world, keeping her safe, keeping my Little Wing safe from the darkness that stalks her. Not once did I dare ever show her what and who I am. But now here I stand, helpless, open and bare as I gaze down into the eyes that hold confusion and understanding in one single look. I lift my hand and slowly cup her chin, the shivering passage of grace and energy that flows through me, as my calloused and battle worn flesh meets the smooth silken alabaster of her flawless form, makes me want to fall to my knees as she continues to stare up at me.

I open my mouth to speak, my words dying in my throat as her hand rises, encircling my own as she turns her face, bringing my palm to her cheek, her eyes sliding closed as she sighs softly.

If devils could cry, if we possessed the ability to feel anything beyond anger and hatred, I know that my soul would scream out like a child lost in the dark as I stare down at the angel before me. The unspoken words that drift between our eyes linger, teasing the air as I feel her move against me, the soft tender curl of her fingertips against my palm, the brush of her hair against the bruised and battered flesh of my knuckles, the gentle warmth of her breath as it slides along my arm, sending a rippling shiver deep into the depthless black that stands at my core.

As she lifts her head, I slowly drop my hand, my skin tingling and palm throbbing at the loss of the silken flesh that had been in my grasp, its warmth and cleansing taint seeping through me as she steps away, that merest of motions sending a wave of pitiless sorrow through my soul.

The look of utter incomprehension explodes through her eyes as she stares at me, her chin quivering as her eyes brim with sorrow. I yearn to sweep her close to me, to hold her in my arms and whisper that I am the only one in this world that she need not fear ... and yet, I know all too well that if I were to move, her mind would shatter, sending her fleeing from me like night does from the dawning of the sun, her feet carrying her back beyond the monoliths that stand vigil over the gates of Eden, and so far beyond my reach that I would have no hope of ever seeing my sweet Little Wing again until the day of my own reckoning.

I watch her eyes widen as we both sense their approach, that growing hollow numbness that fills the world with a carnal fear, their malevolence filling the void around us like water seeping into a cavern. It is like a soothing balm to my rattled nerves, but, despite its all-encompassing familiarity, it still feels as foreign to me as the hairless apes I am destined to wander amongst.

My eyes fall to hers as I watch her shiver, her whole form quaking as the blanket of fear and loathing settles around us smothering the world completely.

I lift my hand, needing to feel her once more, to feel her flesh beneath mine, to have my fingers curl over the back of her willow slim neck, but I pause, knowing that if I do the spell between us will shatter completely. I slip my iron caster from where it sits on my hip, her eyes brimming as she tenses with absolute terror as she watches my arm move.

'Run Little Wing!'

The words trip from my lips as I drop my hand from where it lingers, the scent of her still clinging to me as I push her aura away, ready to turn. Her mouth opens in a wordless cry of refusal as my eyes settle on hers once more.

Her steps falter as she moves away, as the blanketing evil that had so besieged our unveiling appears. I listen to her steps slow, feeling her eyes upon me as I pour my rage forth, my form shifting as I turn, my eyes burning a sulphurous yellow, a last bellowed command tripping from me as she stares into my soul. I want to scream at her to run, forcing her away from here, but all that pours from my lips is a guttural roar. My gaze lands on the black pulsating spectre of evil and hatred that stands in the doorway to my left, coils of black vapour folding out of it as I advance.

The chequered grip of my weapon sits tight against my palm as I make my play. My arm rising, I bring the iron caster to my eye, the nickel plated sights aligning as I squeeze the trigger. A thick pall of vapour seeps from my nose and mouth as I feel my ears and eyes shiver with the concussive kick of the caster.

I surge forwards, my rage and fear pooling into one insurmountable river as I taste my own blood. My blade screams in my mind as I grasp its ridged handle, drawing it from the sheath with such ferocity that it sparks against the gilded guide that surrounds its mouth.

The metallic scent of blood and sweat fills my nostrils as I stare at the grinning face of the demon before me, his scaled and reptile slim form bending with all the coiled grace of a cobra as I carve at the air around him.

My head snaps backwards as I feel his heel connect with my jaw, my vision bursting into a shimmering wall of light. I stumble, my caster rising as I fire half blinded and stunned at the impact. A vicious, taunting laugh goads me forwards as I once more squeeze the trigger of my weapon, the percussive flash casting shadows around us.

'I had hoped my eyes were deceiving me, brother. That the piece of angelic cunt that you let scurry free was just one more toy for Abara-weiser's heir; seems that you have fallen further than the rumours lead many of us to believe. Consorting with the heathens is beyond forgiveness, Albion; but then again, I never did like forgiveness all that much.'

The blanket of hatred and fear that surrounds me falls away, my rune scarred form standing bare as I stare deep into Abezethibou's eyes, his half naked form dancing around me as I parry and deflect blow after blow, feet and fist descending upon me as I twist free, my voice rising as I find a moment's reprieve from the deluge of blows that descend upon me.

'How can you stand against me? How can you do their bidding? After all they put you through, chasing the Israelites and following those foolish Egyptians into the red sea. Beelzebub doesn't care about you, he doesn't care about any of us. His testaments to Solomon of your rising to power were as empty as his promises to my father.

'Who pulled you from that prison? Who dragged your centuries' drowned body from the depths of that torturous cell? Me, not them! I beg you, lay down your arms, brother. If you stand against me, then you will fall, of that I promise you.'

My words ring in my ears as I watch his stance shift, anger and pain surging through his eyes as he flies at me. His leg sweeps upwards as I duck, my blade crying out in ecstasy as I sink it deep into the flesh of his knee. Vein, sinew, muscle and tendon part like silk as I pull my exultant weapon free. Abezethibou's leg sinks to the floor as blood pours free.

I spin my blade over my palm, driving the pommel hard against his temple as I ensnare his neck in the crook of my arm.

'Please, brother, I beg you, don't make me do this!'

Abezethibou's lips curl into a vicious smirk as blood seeps across the dirt encrusted floor.

'I pray you fall, Albion, you and your heathen whore. I pray you fall.'

My eyes slip closed. Resignation fills me as I send my blade sinking downwards, his flesh parting as I drive it deep into his heart. Wrenching my blade from his chest, I let Abezethibou's limp form fall from my grip. I turn, my vision shifting as Arianwen's shimmering light fades into the dark around me.

The soft thrumming of the living guardians fills the air as I sigh, a weight falling from my chest. I step out of the room and into the fast approaching nightmare that blankets this blighted land around me; my heart rests easy as I know she is safe once more.

5

Impossible

ARIANWEN

I am being fooled!

It is the only possible explanation. The Devil knows no bounds, I've had that lesson drummed into me for my *entire existence*. He would use any force of evil to capture even an ounce of our all-encompassing essence.

So why is my soul telling me that all I feel is real? That no matter how much I try and deny it, I know that I just witnessed the truth standing a mere inch from my physical body, joining with mine in the briefest of moments. How can it be that all I have come to rely upon to keep me safe, to watch over me every time I walk so close to evil ... is evil itself?

As he stood over me, my body and soul completely over-shadowed by this mountain of flesh before me, his presence completely smothered my entire delicate form, yet ... I was without fear. How can that be? He is a fiend. He is evil. He is a demon! Yet, in some strange way ... he is also ... mine.

How can my pure thoughts be thinking such things? I am an Angel of God, a being of pure and holy light. I should not be thinking this way. It has to be the Devil's trickery at play. Am I not as immune as I thought I would be to his malicious illusions? But as I let those words settle into my thoughts, in the deepest part of my being, I know they are not true.

He is a part of me, he always has been. I just can't see how it's possible! Demons and Angels have been eternally at war, arch enemies of the deepest order since creation as we both vie for supremacy in these immortal worlds. How could this Satanic Hunter of my very own kin make me feel like I am complete for the first time in my existence? How can I, an Angel of God, have feelings towards this hideous creature at all?

I had no control over my physical body when we were face-to-face and I lifted my hand to gently grasp the back of his large weathered one holding tightly onto my chin. That direction of my limb came from somewhere very deep within my soul. But as I made a connection with his heated calloused skin and turned my face slightly to bring my cheek into his open palm, I felt like I had finally found my missing piece and the soft sigh that floated past my lips was a sigh of relief. Relief that my internal visions of my guardian being of humanlike form were correct. That now, as I sat in my saviour's grasp, I could finally be at peace, my soul could rest in the gentle clutch of strength that surrounded me

But realisation that I had just touched a demon's evil flesh twisted itself around my relief, strangling it with such a mighty force that I had to take a step back, as my body started to quiver, not only from the shock of this reality but also from the loss of his touch. Unwanted emotions started to brim my eyes as my feelings were threatening to overtake my normally very careful thoughts.

Grief unexpectedly flew through my senses, our eyes still spellbound with each other, as I realised this may be the end to my unexpected saviour's guardianship over me. Now that I know the true source of my eternal keeper, how could I ever feel safe again? How could he continue to follow me as closely as he has done for my entire existence?

We both sensed at the exact same time the all too familiar presence of another demon as my larger than life guardian growled, 'Run, Little Wing' in a deep and sinfully sensual baritone which instantly vibrated over me, its rolling warmth raising goose bumps through my body as I trembled in its wake, giving a warning as fierce as the stare that exuded from his aqua blue eyes. Then, as my feet haltered, he released a deep, fear laced and rage filled growl.

That's when I turned and ran with haste, not glancing back, too fearful that my emotional mind had betrayed me and that the most extraordinarily intense moment of my life would turn out to be nothing more than my imagination. I ran with fear, with anger, with confusion at his words 'Little Wing' and with emotions I had stirring inside that were as alien to me as being a human would be. I moved with a speed I had never thought I possessed, unsure now if I would ever be safe in these immortal worlds again.

As I reach the edges of this dying forest and start to see the reaching fingers of Eden's life force beneath my feet, I realize that the ground is still quaking beneath me from the growls of the eternal stone dragons, protectors of my world from the evil that now seeps into the pores of my skin.

I raise my head, looking towards the entrance as I slow and make the final steps to my place of rest and peace, and yet I can't. I cannot bring myself to take that one last step. I feel like there is now an invisible wall preventing me from entering. I have been touched by one of the Devil's creatures! Am I forever tainted now? Have I betrayed my own kin by allowing his touch, by internally craving it as soon as our eyes meet, by whimpering in loss when his touch was absent? I can feel an underlying force that tells me my existence will never be the same again.

Emotions make me weak at the knees as they give way and I fall, hands stretched out to support me, landing on the sacred soil that marks the entrance to God's home and the rumbling earth stills. Silence suddenly engulfs me; the only sound to grace my ears is my own ragged, heavy breathing and the thudding of my franticly beating heart pounding against my rib cage. My entire body is tense and wound up, my blood curdling with speed. I feel like I could explode from the build-up of pressure pumping through me.

I feel something foreign, a liquid slipping from my eye, flowing through my long lashes and slowly rolling down my delicate face, taking a path it has never ventured before. This can't be happening! This is impossible! Our eyes may water with emotion, but never before this moment have I heard of a *tear* escaping down an angel's cheek. Tears are a human weakness, and yet as I feel the warm liquid continue its path down my pale skin, I know this single tear is a sign that my path has now taken a starkly different turn.

'Don't baulk, child. This is still thy home. Thy quaint form shall forever be welcome here. There will ne'er be a need for fear amongst thine own kin. Dry thine eyes, stand fast as a new path shall soon be revealed to thyself.'

The soft old world language spills from one of the granite creatures standing tall and proud on either side of me. The heavy grating of stone against stone meets my ear as its head turns to look down upon me, its carved eyes holding more wisdom than I could ever hope to possess.

'How … how can I move forward after my entire existence was just torn to shreds revealing a piece of my being I may never be able fathom? How can I possibly continue my life's calling now that I feel less invincible knowing the true source of my guardianship? For many human lifetimes I was able to move unseen, unheard, through the twisted veins that feed into the pit of Hell. But now … what worth am I to the souls that call my name if I have lost the ability to trust my gifts to deliver them safely to the gates of God? What will become of me if I lose my calling?'

Panic starts to rise throughout my aura as my thoughts become entwined with too many visions to make any sense at all. I am confused beyond reasonable thought. What is happening to me?

'Child, calm thy thoughts. A panicked mind will not solve thy calamity. Only peace will bring thine answer to thyself. Thou art stronger than thou think. Rise now, child, feel the comfort of thy home. Thou will always be safe hither.'

I rise to my feet and look forward towards the only home I have ever known, its peace somehow slightly tainted by my recent encounter. I reach a hand up to wipe at my single tear, collecting it on my slender finger and bringing it to the front of my face. I watch as the transparent liquid slightly glistens in the sunshine that flows down over my form. I bring my finger to my mouth, curious to experience all of this wonder as my tongue darts out to collect this miracle of mine, its salty essence surprising me as a calm starts to settle over my scattered thoughts as I swallow its celestial brilliance.

I *am* stronger than this moment.

I am wise enough to confront evil in whatever form it presents itself to me. If this *is* one of the Devil's many deceptions, I will not fall prey to his vicious games. I will walk with caution but not with fear, I will take my next steps with the experience I have learnt and the experience bred deep within me. I will move forward with an opened mind but I will guard my heart like a fortress. I will not again be distracted by these new foreign emotions. Whether they be true or trickery, I am determined to find out the truth.

I step forward, breaking through the silent barrier my mind has placed in front of me, taking tentative steps forward feeling a peace that can only come from my home. All the fear and confusion easing slightly with each step I take.

I need time to truly process what has just happened. I'm still not convinced it was real. How can it be? How can a demon be the force that has been watching over me for my entire existence? How could he have gotten so close to me without detection? How could such a vicious creature be the source of my safety and comfort? And why did I feel such a rush of affection with his words, 'Run, Little Wing?'

I gasp, now realising he was referring to my once stunted childhood affliction. He remembers my little wing? No! No, no, no, no! This must be Lucifer playing with my memories, invading them, finding my weakness, twisting it into new false words to make me feel, to force me to care, to make me doubt everything that I have ever been taught. But why is my soul screaming for me to open my heart and feel, feel what I just experienced at the touch of my guardian's large weathered fingers, the lifelong connection we have always had finally making sense as our eyes met directly for the first time.

Lost in my confused thoughts, I don't realise I'm no longer alone until someone grips my forearm, instantly stopping my steps as I let a small squeal escape my lips.

'Arianwen, thank the heavens you are safe. Estrastiel's grace has gone, I can no longer feel it or see it in my mind's sight. I don't understand, he was too wise to fall for a Hunter's trap. But as soon as I felt his grace disperse there was a shift in our worlds. Two powerful almighty forces in these immortal worlds came together as one volcanic energy, then silence. Nothing but silence. Like every conceivable world just paused as one, waiting for an event to happen that was out of all of our control. Estrastiel may have stumbled upon something he shouldn't have which has now cost him his life. Something is not right here, something is coming child, we must make haste. Gabriel has called for all Generals and Archs to convene. Tell me child, what did you see out there? What could you feel? Gabriel will want you to recount your experience in the village.'

Anatiamoros is practically dragging me as he is speaking, his harried form guiding me towards the crystal like castles at the foot of God's gates. Panic starts to rise up from within me, my throat feeling thick and tight as we get closer to the great hall where all of our leaders are gathered at the will of our Arch Angel. Grief over Estrastiel hits me hard as I realise I know what type of wretched creature has taken his life. The same type of creature who I just let place his fingertips upon my silken skin.

Before I can even think of a way out of this diabolical situation, the ancient carved wooden doors open upon our arrival, their heaviness making their hinges groan under their immense weight. I have to think fast, I have to remain calm, I can't let them see my internal struggle, my guilt, my deception, my admittance of having courted with the enemy, my want, my affection for one of the dark ones, my weakness that I know will start to show in the tiniest of changes to my body language.

As soon as my first foot is in the door, the raised voices start to hush and even though I keep my eyes down out of respect for the

Archs and Generals, the leaders of our kin. I know every set of eyes in this room is slowly turning to watch my advance. They are all boring a hole in the side of my head, reaching, searching, trying to discover what I know.

Do they know where I have been? Do they know that evil has touched my celestial aura? Can they see the demon's fingerprints embedded on the surface of my delicate skin that feel like they are screaming out loud like a flashing neon sign from one of earth's buildings? I know they can't see them, but to me, they feel like they have been eternally imprinted into the pores of my flesh.

When we come to a stop, I begin to slowly raise my eyes. They know, they know something is different about me. I can see it in their curious stares. A few of them raise their noses slightly, as if they have caught the smell of the lingering scent of my recent encounter. Gabriel's brother and commander, Michael, stares at me with anger before taking a menacing step in my direction.

'She has just returned from the village; its vile smell still lingers in her pores, which is one of the many hardships a Reclaimer must endure. Nothing to be alarmed about, Michael,' Anatiamoros says as he puts a hand up to stop his advancement upon me.

Silence falls upon the room as Gabriel's stare finally captures my eyes, his frown lines evident in the look he is giving me.

This great wide hall suddenly feels claustrophobic, like a small closet as the walls begin to close in around me. Absolute silence descends upon us as Gabriel seems to be trying to read my mind.

'We are so thankful that you made it home safely, Arianwen. It would have been a great loss to us *all* if you had not returned. Please recount for us what you experienced in the village.'

There are no safe words that can flow from my mouth. I feel like whatever slips from my lips will reveal too much. I can sense all in this room are already suspicious of my being here so I'm finding it near impossible to hold my composure, as it is, without trying to think of words that can save me from this moment. I know I must speak, speak words that are not all truthful.

'I was performing my duty. My charges were crying out to me, a soul needed guidance. My focus was on them and our survival. The end of days could have come, my lord, and I would have spared it nary a glance.' I say in the calmest voice I can muster, even as my stomach begins to tie itself in knots as I shrink under his ice laced gaze.

'Come now, my dear, you mean to tell us that such a great Reclaimer as you could have missed something that tumultuous? Two of the greatest forces that have ever appeared suddenly join to one all mighty eruption and then silence, and you can say you sensed nothing? You're telling us that someone who has been so *highly* vaunted as being the most spiritually aware of us all could be so blinded by *one soul's cry* as to miss an event that has shaken our realm to its very core?' Gabriel retorts, as sarcasm drips from his words. If I let his arrogance seep into my aura I know I may slip up.

'I felt the earth rumbling, which I assumed was the dragon keepers' growls that sometimes accompany me when they are being too over protective. But as for some overwhelming force, it was unfelt by me, my lord.'

Gabriel's frown deepens as my words sink in. I know he is not happy with my answer. As I hold my breath waiting for his reply, Anatiamoros speaks first.

'My lord, it takes our entire being to reach a soul and guide it safely into the arms of our King. This momentarily leaves us with not much else to sense with. For Arianwen, this may have been when these mysterious forces were at play.'

I am thankful for Anatiamoros' defence as it seems to break the spell that the others were under as conversation starts to slowly arise again. Gabriel gives me a stare that I cannot decipher, so I bow my head to break this connection, hoping he will not feel the need to address me again.

I then sit in silence as the hall around me descends into a babble of heated discussion as to the origin of the possible forces that could have caused such a shift in our worlds, still feeling their glances upon me as I will this uncomfortable meeting to an end. Could it be Lucifer trying to lure us to begin a war? Or maybe creatures from another immortal world seeking a response that will warrant a battle? Or could it be some of our own that have fallen to the dark realm, wanting to take vengeance for being cast out of Heaven? Many ideas are thrown into heated debates while I sit here, controlling my body's responses to words such as Demon, fallen Angels, dark forces, explosive connections, spies, all the while very much aware of Gabriel's constant stares.

I know that it is me and my eternal guardian they are all trying to discover, but I am yet to understand this powerful shift in worlds that our connection created myself. I need time, time away from here, away from doubting stares and words dripping with hatred to fully comprehend the meaning of the two of us finally coming eye to eye and the power this meeting seems to have created. Could it be true that our single touch has created some type of almighty force that has been felt by all that grace these lands? Or will it all turn out to be another one of the dark lord's games, created to cause a war for his own entertainment?

I see a set of large booted feet standing in front of me, almost touching my own, as I look up into the menacing stare of Michael.

'You are no longer needed. You can leave.'

I slowly rise, not breaking his stare, his body language showing signs of anger towards me as I slowly take a few steps back until I reach the large doorway from which I entered, where I turn and cautiously walk away. I hear the meeting drawing to an end, my name on the lips of several as I pass them in my caution laced haste.

I feel like running, I feel like screaming, I feel like letting the new experience of tears run like a river down my cheeks. I am frightened and confused by the events of the last few hours. There is so much tumbling around my head, so many things to think about, so many things to consider. What do I do now? Where do I go? Who can I talk to without putting them in danger? To have been created in a world of constant love and support, I feel incredibly alone at this very moment. I feel like I have betrayed my kin, yet when I was standing face to face with a demon ... I had never felt more complete as I did in that single moment.

I quicken my pace as I make my way through the vast winding

paths of the most beautiful garden ever created, as I feel anything but beauty inside of my twisting thoughts. What is happening to me? I have always had an answer for everything, but now... now I feel like all of my wisdom has deserted me in my most desperate time of need.

I scream as I collide straight into a solid male chest, the thick muscular frame making me stumble as I try in vain to stop the shrill scream that tumbles from me. As I regain my footing, I raise my eyes quickly to look into the questioning stare of Gabriel as I take a step back.

'Don't tell me the always strong and extremely composed *Arianwen* is feeling fear seep into her eternal soul?'

I can't believe he has sought my presence here, alone, in the garden as soon as his important gathering came to an end. I have only ever seen Gabriel in the company of others as it is customary for anyone this great Arch has shown an interest in to always have a chaperone present out of respect for her pure innocence. But the look he is giving me now is far from innocent.

He takes a slow step forward as I take one back, his eyes questioning my reaction to him.

'Is there information you withheld from that meeting, Arianwen?'

I slowly shake my head no, too cautious to use my voice.

'Hmm, I'm extremely good at reading your body language, I have been paying attention to it for quite some time now my dear, and it's telling me that you know more than you are willing to share. Out with it, my sweet angel. Tell me what you know.'

As nervous as he is making me feel, I will not crumble under his questioning. I must stay strong.

'I shared all I know at the meeting tonight. I did not witness or feel anything that was out of the ordinary in that wretched village of the damned. I am not holding anything back, my lord,' I say in a voice so calm it surprises even myself.

He takes another step forward and I force myself to stand my ground, which seems to bring a smirk to his face. He slowly reaches out to push a strand of hair from my face and tucks it behind my ear which he slowly caresses. I can't help the slight jump at his touch as it surprises me he has made contact at all.

I look left then right in hope of finding someone who can break this uncomfortable encounter.

'Surely we are both old enough to not have a need of a chaperone watching over our every move, *Arianwen*. You could be mine soon anyway, to do with as I please without the watchful eyes of a single person. How I would relish owning you completely, my sweet angel.'

His voice drips with lust as he drags my name out, twisting it into a childish keening whine as his hand travels from my ear to my cheek, his head moving ever closer to mine. I turn sharply from his touch, uncomfortable that he is so close to me. He grunts in anger as I take a step back.

'Tread carefully, Arianwen. Danger can present itself in many forms and it will bid you well to know that I can find out any secrets you may be keeping. It will be better for you in the end if you come forth with them of your own accord.'

His eyes widen as anger fills his voice, then with all the flourish of a scorned peacock he turns and retreats back in the direction of the great hall.

This is all too much! Why is this happening to me? All I have ever done is serve my Lord by using the gift I was created with, helping the human souls in need. Time outside of that was spent quietly, working around the garden, helping to cook feasts for special occasions and spending time with my family. My time outside of the village of the damned has been peaceful and uneventful. So why, now, is all this unwanted attention coming my way?

I have never seen Gabriel touch a young lady's face before, let alone show any other emotion but complete composure. So to see the sea of emotions he just showed me is unsettling. But I do know if he had any idea of the secret I am keeping I wouldn't have been allowed to leave the great hall. If he had any idea that one of his fellow celestial angels had stood still and willingly allowed a vile demon Hunter to make contact with her pure white skin ... I could be banished from my heavenly home.

Vile demon? *Vile demon*? The vision that is swimming in my memory ... is anything but vile. I recall my eyes' travels from his sculptured chest, over his larger than life broad shoulders, all the way up to those entrancing aqua blue eyes that harboured many secrets, secrets he has spent an eternity trying to hide, secrets he unknowingly allowed me to see for all but the briefest of moments, secrets I have no intention of finding out. Because I know now, that any curiosity I may have about my eternal guardian will bring danger, not only to myself but to my entire kin.

Whatever almighty force we created by our first meeting should never be allowed to happen again. For if our joint power can create such a significant shift in both our immortal worlds, to bring on the talk of unnecessary war, then I won't be a part of it. I will have to learn to live with the unanswered questions I feel the need to seek. For I will *not* take a chance of becoming a possible pawn in one of Lucifer's woeful games.

I have reached my home, the place of peace and happiness. A place I so need to seek solace in at this very moment. When I open the door my mother whips around, ready to growl my name, but when she sees the expression on my face her frown disappears, only leaving an expression of utmost concern. She opens her arms out wide as I stumble forward desperate for her safe embrace.

6

Retribution and Hate

ALBION

I stand staring into the dead eyes of my former friend as his blood slowly slips from my blade, sweat and anger seeping from my every pore as the world drifts back into some semblance of coherent focus.

'I told you time and again, brother, you never were good enough to best me.'

Rage boils up through my heart as I grip his corpse by its limp throat, lifting it from the floor, my eyes burning with anguish as I scream into its slack and lifeless features.

'Why, you stupid coward. Why do this to me, why make me take away something that can never be given back?'

A small squeaking gasp snatches at my ears as I let my hand slip open. Turning my head, I catch sight of one the sallow hairless apes that burrow and scratch out a meagre existence in this dead burrow of lifelessness.

'So, I am not a demon, brother, is that what you said? I'll show you just how well these wings suit me.' A malicious sneer twists my features as I push myself to my feet.

'Come here, girl, I have something to give you.'

I almost laugh as she tries to run, my anger and lust filling my mind as I snatch her backwards into my grip by her hair. Part of me rails at what I am doing as I tear at her clothing, the tattered remnants of another life hanging from her dirt smeared body like an empty sack as I rip it from her. The pale flush of her skin stark against my own as I grind her face into the wall, dust flying free with her every breath as I feel my length harden in my trousers.

'It's at times like this that I love the fact you're already dead. You hairless apes are always so willing to receive but never to give anything in return; now I can just take what I want. The dead need never care.'

Her squirming thrills me even as I feel my throat constrict, a small part of me dying as I reflect on what it is I am about to do. Am I truly going to do this, even if she is nothing more than a lost and wandering soul of a long deceased woman, am I truly going to defile her to prove my worthiness to a people I know I do not belong to?

My cares are tossed aside as I feel my length slip free of my trousers, the pulsing heat of my girth pressing deep into the cleft of her backside as I feel her squeal and tense beneath me. 'No ... please ... don't ... I won't say anything, I promise ... let me go and I promise I won't say anything to anyone.'

She pushes away from the wall, her back curving against my time honed flesh. I push my hardened girth between the quivering flesh of her backside as I lean over her, my body engulfing her completely. 'There is no pleading. You're a shadow of a long dead creature, and every demon knows the dead can never speak.'

I feel my length catch at her puckered ring, her whole form tensing as I slip on downwards, my goal slowly slipping along my engorged flesh; the heat of her body soaks into me, the life that courses through her soul showering me in a saddened blanket of self-loathing as she all but screams in terror as I drag my pulsating erection free of her quivering cleft. 'Shall we see just what your body can offer me?'

I stare at the body pinned beneath me as my whole being slips into this beast that calls itself Albion. My hips drive forwards as my swollen head meets her fear slicked cusp, my rigid length spearing deep into her quivering depths as she wails in pain and fear, her eyes glued wide as she thrashes against my grip and my ever invading girth as I force my full core into her.

Tears roll across her skin, carving paths through the dust and grime that clings to her as I piston into her. Words trip from my lips as I pull her head back, my eyes staring into hers as her mind struggles to comprehend just what is being forced upon her. My internal struggle threatens to break me apart.

'Seems you have a lot of give to you. And here I thought I had found the one simpering piece of hairless trash that hadn't been pried open by the filth here.'

I stare into her, my reflection dancing in her tear filled gaze as I continue to plough myself ever deeper into her. I tear my eyes from hers, disgusted with the sight that shines back at me from within them. Even as I bend forwards, my tongue snaking over her sweat stained skin, I can't help but feel an empty elation at the form that is slowly being crushed beneath me.

With a vicious jerk I drag myself from her, throwing her to the floor with a pain laced bark as she strikes the compacted dirt at my feet. Curling into a ball, she stares at me as I walk towards her, the ragged dregs of her clothing pulled tight around her as she cowers into the corner, her eyes never leaving me as I grab the back of her head, my other hand encircling my shaft as I press my head to her lips.

She turns her head as I watch her last efforts at defiance, my hand leaving my shaft as I send a searing slap across her face, making her gasp and whimper, my hips driving me past her lips as she starts to cry once more.

The florid impression of my hand glows on her skin, her blood mingling with her tears as it slips in a diluted paste of anguish from the corner of her mouth. I watch her throat swell, my girth sliding down her gullet as she struggles to breathe around my all invading shaft.

With a grunt of exertion I push her head down onto me, listening to the fitful choking emanating from the waif at my feet. I stare down at her as I feel my seed rise, spilling from me in thick ropes as her fists beat at my thighs and hips, heavy grunts leaving me as I feel her tongue desperately trying to push me from her mouth as she struggles to breath. I wrench myself free as the need to vomit fills me, the growing wall of revulsion and self-hatred drowning all I had felt mere moments before as I stare down at the coughing and battered girl at my feet, my seed dripping from her mouth as she quivers, retching into the dust.

I close my eyes as I turn, the sorrow in my heart at war with the exultation my demon blood feels at the act I have just performed in its name. Forcing my flaccid girth back into the confines of my trousers, I flee the scene of my blood's crime.

Tearing blindly through the alleys and back streets that have long been my surrogate home, doorways, windows, the bodies of these misplaced souls flash past me as I run. My anger and self-loathing guide me as I scream inside my mind; my world tumbles as I slip sideways into an open doorway, screams filling my ears as I feel something splinter under my falling body.

Pushing myself to my knees, I gaze around me, the stunned and frightened eyes of young ones meeting my own as I feel heat burn over my skin, the smell of wood and coal mingling with the metallic taste of hot metal as I begin to take in what lies around me.

'I was wondering when you would come crashing in again, boy. Last time was when your father came seeking you. What had you done again? I think you had been caught stealing apples from the overhanging branches outside Eden, hadn't you?'

I look up at the figure standing before me, his small frame swathed in a hooded and sleeveless leather coat, the front pitted by blackened scorch marks, the scent of burnt hide wafting across the air, its subtle odour mingling in amongst the overpowering amalgamation of food and fear; thick soled boots crushing pottery and food alike hold him aloft. Scarred and grubby hands enter my eye line as his voice once more permeates my mind.

'If I remember correctly, your father came in, all fire and brimstone, literally in his case, and dragged you out leaving smouldering footprints in his wake; what I would bet my life upon you not knowing is ... he returned three days later, with a small chest full of opal and gold and paid for the damages to my home and to my forge wrought from your little spat with that upstart, and rather overzealous, angel. It was Estrastiel, if I remember correctly, although I don't think that will be the case this time, am I right, Albion?'

I shift my weight, bringing my legs under me as I start to rise, his hand curling around my own like a vice as he hauls me upright. My shins ache, my leather and mail trousers are stained with my own blood, splinters of wood and pottery greeting my gaze as I stare at the shattered earthenware and smashed wood that had been his dinner table.

'No, Garth, you're right. There will be no opal or gold, there will be no remuneration; I am not my father.'

Garth stares at me, sardonic laughter in his eyes as he motions behind him and moves away from me.

'Come with me, it's abundantly clear that you, my boy, are in no way your father, but that doesn't mean you can't clear your debt in another manner.'

The light dims as we cross through the rest of Garth's home, the slit windows in the thick earth skimmed walls drowning the light, casting paper thin sheets of golden dust filled illumination across our path. Images flash through my mind, of me being led by my father's hand into the heat washed centre of Garth's workshop.

I can still remember my first sight of the glowing forge and billowing smoke that curled through the chimney of the hearth and the taste of heated metal that clung to the air like wet cotton on cold skin.

The memories that assail me render me mute as I follow on in the stout blacksmith's wake.

✦ ✦ ✦

Sweat rolls from me as my muscles scream for rest, images of the girl's terrified eyes boring into me as I send the heavy cold forged hammer down upon the heated sheet of steel. The edges fold and roll as I send blow after blow down upon it. Visions of my Little Wing fill my head, washing the tortured memories of that desecrated waif from my mind's eye; I stare at the sheet of red hot steel before me as its new form begins to take hold, subtle curves emerging from the still glowing metal as I once more send the hammer crashing against its surface.

Plunging the searing, heat soaked plate of steel into the bath of ice water, I watch as the surface boils and writhes, steam bathing my skin, its white miasma coating the air as an ear withering hiss fills my ears. Lifting the heat dulled plate from the water, I stare at its mutely reflective surface, my features distorted and twisted in the water sliding over its still warm surface.

'Not bad, boy.' I turn and glare at Garth, his mildly condescending smirk making my ire rise as I set my budding creation on the bench to my right.

The bench's thick chipped and stained surface, a symphony of order as I pick up the twenty ounce hammer and line up the metal punch, the resounding clunk makes my teeth itch as I send the heavy pointed shaft of tempered metal through my slowly evolving work, small holes littering its edges in a regimented line.

I stare down at the shaped and hammered metal that rests on the table's surface, the scribe cutter in my hand dancing over its face as I trace and etch a deep rolling pattern of weaving curves and swooping angles. The coiled form of two birds' heads appearing before my eyes, their layered forms rising from the edges of the metal, their beaks settling around the cupped swelling of the plate's upper edge.

'Not bad boy, not bad at all, although I doubt this is for you.'

I grunt, the noise rising from my throat as I stare at Garth from the corner of my eye. 'Mind your tongue Blacksmith, remember who and what I am. You may have been my father's ally and personal smith, but I am not him and as yet, despite my honour binding me, do not hold you as such.'

Garth simply smiles and pats my shoulder, his grip firm as it tightens slightly on my leather sheathed form. 'Nor would I expect you to, young master Weiser, nor would I expect you to; but may I suggest something? Leather padding would be a sound addition as well as bracing on the sides and across the top of the chest.'

The leather sits cool and smooth in my palm as I stare at it, Garth's words fresh in my mind as I begin to set the cotton wadding into the pockets I have made. Pressing it into the steel plate in front of me, my fingers begin to tremble slightly as my mind slips into a fantasy. Pictures of her glowing violet eyes, long golden trusses and supple body locked with mine, my hands dancing over her skin as she pushes against my fluttering touch. I feel the first stirrings of my own entrapped lust and violently push the thoughts aside before anything else steps into my already dallying thoughts.

I cast my gaze over my work, a small measure of peace and pride blooming within me as I lift the Bradawl from its resting place and carefully push it through the leather using the holes as a guide. A sudden bark from outside the shop makes me start, my concentration slipping as the Bradawl pierces the boiled hide and sends itself into the flesh of my palm. I grunt in pain as I pluck the tool from its resting place in my hand, the hot scarlet taint of my blood painting its tip as I watch the hole begin to knit itself closed.

Slipping the rivet through the centre of the padding, I set the thick bracing plate against it and slowly hammer it shut, the rhythmic progression lulling me into a shallow stupor as I move methodically through them all, each hammer blow sending another image dancing through my head, the curve of her neck, the way her smile made her eyes dance with light ... and then all at once it is shattered by the image of the girl I had so destroyed, the light I had so defiled in my own need to sate my inadequacy at my dead kin's words.

7

Hideous

ARIANWEN

Visions swirl behind my closed lids, taunting, teasing, dragging me through a very dark place. The red steam that claws its way out from the centre of Hell, tortured painful faces frozen on a helpless scream, heavy cloaked immortal creatures with eyes darker than a moonless night sky, white silken flesh tearing from bone with streaks of blood smearing its pure surface, firm carved sweat slicked muscles adorning an arm that is reaching towards me pleading for me to place my hand in its grip, dark shadows behind trees with red glowing eyes slowly caving in around me as I try to run from their capture.

I toss and turn as evil dances around my dreams, not giving up, not giving in, in its relentless torture of my thoughts. Enough! I scream internally, these newfound tears watering my eyes as I fling my legs over to the side of my soft feathered bed, naked feet hitting the cool surface of stone as I stand and reach my hands up to my eyes, trying to rub away the residue of the Devil's illusions.

Even in the safety of my home I can't escape the reality of my situation. I feel like I can barely breathe, my throat tight with emotions and fear. I need to find my calm to be able to have a chance at any coherent thoughts.

My light steps are near silence as I make my way towards the front door, grabbing my ever comforting cloak, swinging it up and over my shoulders as it shrouds my body in safety, reaching up and back to pull the soft silk hood over my head, I then reach for the door, opening it quietly as I take my first step out into the bright shining moon. My restlessness starts to recede instantly as I stand in stillness looking up into its magical aura.

Earth's natural satellite sits proudly above the atmosphere, its luminous surface holding more power than any earthling could possibly ever begin to understand. Four and a half billion years of secrets and wisdom in its ability to move more than just ocean tides. Its celestial beams bringing solace and calm to many who know its true powers. As its soft rays dance in the reflection of my eyes, I take a deep breath basking in the transcendent glow it veils over my form.

I move slowly through the moonlit garden, not knowing where to begin in my understanding of all that has happened to me. I am torn between a desperate, almost primal need to see and question my lifelong guardian, needing answers to so much my life has yet to reveal to me. Yet I also have an innate need to do what's right for my kin and protect everything that surrounds us Angels of God.

If I pursue the answers I so desperately seek, I could be risking all of this beauty that surrounds my celestial home and everything good and pure that inhabits it. If I take a chance and believe that what I experienced standing in my eternal saviour's presence is not the Devil's trickery, and it turns out that I am indeed being played by their evil intentions, then I may lose everything that I hold dear to my heart.

I finally reach my favourite place, peace settling over me like a wave as I lift up onto my light toes, spread my glorious wings out wide, feathers uncurling like a new flower in the morning sun and fly over to my favourite giant lily pad and land in the middle of the crystal clear lake, away from everything but my own internal battle. I close my eyes, enjoying this silence as I try and centre my warring thoughts and let time disappear for now. I finally feel the first rays of the new dawn washing over me as the beautiful sunrise warms my body and brings to life this heavenly garden I call home.

How could I do anything to risk this beauty, full of life and peace? How could I bring unrest or the possibility of war to the tranquillity and solace that resides here?

I can't!

I won't!

No amount of need or curiosity is worth risking the life of the ones I love and cherish. If I am meant to know the answers to my questions, they will come to me in time. Until then ... I have to forget my guardian even came into my life no matter how much an insatiable craving has started to grow within my soul. I will squash it down, conceal it, not give it power to taint my thoughts. I will not let it rule my head. And I will protect my heart from all the emotions screaming to get inside.

I am so lost in my thoughts it takes me awhile to realise that Anatiamoros is sitting on the lily pad next to me, silently watching the anguish twist tightly around my body. I look up into very concerned old gentle eyes and unwanted tears fill mine.

'Arianwen. Talk to me, child. I know you have a mind full of troubles and I feel it's more than just the concerns that the leaders are having at the moment.'

Could I tell him? Would he understand? Would he believe me?

These are questions I will never know the answer to because I will never risk putting him in such a dangerous position. So I just offer him a shake of my head, answering no to his question. He frowns for a few silent moments but doesn't question my lack of an answer.

'Our leaders are very concerned, and so they should be. A force with such extreme power as what was shown yesterday has never been felt in all of our histories. We all need to tread carefully until its source can be found or *it* shows its intentions to our world. Until then, we need to refrain from going into the village until we are sure our safety won't be compromised. I know it may hurt to ignore the calling of the ones in need, but we must, just for a little while to ensure the safety of our entire immortal world. This all could be Lucifer at play. Let's not fall for his games.'

He gives me a sad smile before he rises to his feet and flies away, leaving only but a slight ripple in the water below his resting place. Yes … he is right. It could all turn out to be Lucifer and a way for him to create entertainment for himself and his vile minions. Even if it's not, what could possibly come of my interest in my saviour? Questions may be answered, but then what? Nothing! Nothing can come of his reveal to me except trouble. Trouble and danger. But why does my heart start to ache as soon as those words slipped from my mind?

I look down at my reflection, knowing that the faint finger-prints embedded in my chin can only be seen by my mind, yet my heart knows they are there, and as I raise my hand and run a single fingertip over the spot that his rough fingers gripped me, gripped me with a gentleness I can't understand, I know there isn't a force in either of our immortal worlds that could ever erase the imprint from my soul.

I gasp as I hear another tortured soul scream in terror, pleading for my help, crying from the twisting darkness before suddenly falling silent. What is happening? There has never been silence after a calling before! The soul only receives a silent peace when we have arrived at their side and safely delivered them to God's waiting hands. But that tortured scream is still racing around all of my senses, begging me to go to it, pleading with me to take away its pain, its suffering. How could Anatiamoros possibly expect me to ignore something that is a part of my entire essence?

I am torn! I know the danger, I know the risk, but a soul cannot control its timing of need. I try to ignore, I try to block it out, pain shooting under the entire surface of my delicate skin. I wince as the pain intensifies, wanting to scream, wanting this horrible unnatural feeling to leave me at once. The physical and mental pain is almost unbearable. I can't ignore. It's not *in me* to ignore! I have to go. I was created to help all those in need and that's what I'm going to do.

I tread with extreme caution as I enter the dreary dying forgotten forest that was once as vibrant as Eden, before the war of immortals' most powerful worlds destroyed its life force. I take gentle steps, my feet soft, catlike so as not to rustle even one dry leaf, not wanting to bring even an ounce of attention my way, wanting to slip in without a single creature noticing my presence. We are unable to use our gift of flight in this world between worlds. As soon as my feet leave the solid ground beneath it the atmosphere changes, which can be heard like a siren calling out to all of the dark prince's entire army of evil, signalling directly to my whereabouts.

I near the first dwellings of this decrepit village, carefully using all of my senses and gifts to feel for any dark creatures caving in. I am still very aware that this could be a trap created by the Devil, but I know in my heart it could also be a true calling of a soul in desperate need, and that ... I cannot ignore.

I come to the dwelling the calling came from before it fell silent. All my senses are extremely heightened as I see large footprints at its entry, walking to and away from here. I am as vigilant as I can be as I grip the edge of the already opened doorway before slowly turning my body into the darkness of the large room.

The smell hits me first before my eyes even have a chance to adjust to the filtered light coming from an old grimy windowpane at the far end. That's the smell of evil and terror twisted together in hideous pain. I turn fast, trying to see every corner of this dungeon of vileness, the smell so strong I can't be certain of my safety here. My eyes adjust, and when they do I know there is only a single figure in this room.

It takes me a slight moment to register what my eyes are showing me. A sight I have never seen before now, despite coming into this waiting room of death thousands of times over my existence as a Reclaimer.

I move slowly forward, the figure coming into focus as I get closer; the atrocious violence I see before me has my stomach retching, making me want to run screaming from here, never to return to witness these vile acts of the Devil and evil that bows at his feet. I can smell that what's left of the human shell of this soul is female; her sweet innocence still lingering on the edges of this beaten and bloodied form lying in the dirt at my feet. Shredded cloth adorns her body like clothing, barely covering her seeping opened flesh, showing glimpses of bone that has splintered, floating among fluids that shouldn't be seeing the light of day.

Her body is twisted, limbs that were crying out in pain, reaching to protect itself from the force that was strewn upon it, now broken and hanging loose inside the flesh that encases it. Deep festering scratch marks glow a sickening red outlining the curve of her hips, the flesh so fragile, now shattered so completely it could fall from her petite frame with a touch of a light breeze. All fingernails but two have been ripped from their place with a desperate attempt to claw away from this heinous act of evil's pleasure.

She is no longer breathing but I can still sense a slight flutter in her chest as her heart tries to wait for the moment it can walk in peace. I struggle ... for the first time, in proceeding with the job I was born to do. The painful vision in front of me has shattered my heart and speared my soul. This once living creature had already passed from her mortal world, so why did one of the dark forces have to torture this beautiful human again, when waiting in purgatory is enough of a torture in itself?

As my eyes begin to blur with tears, I know that there is a strong possibility that my own guardian and saviour could easily commit acts as vile as the remnants of the one before me. Why? Why did my lifelong protective force have to turn out to belong to Hell, belong to a world that relishes the most hideous of acts?

I take a deep breath to calm myself, needing to concentrate on the soul in need that is now in my arms, lying in a torturous heap. I brush the damp strands of hair that are stuck over her eyes as I whisper.

'Sorry, beautiful, for the pain you have endured, for not reaching you in time to save you from this last act of violence against your still pure soul. You are going to be rewarded for enduring such grief. Your soul will be given an eternity of peace and solace in a place that is more beautiful than any mortal dream your mind could have ever imagined. Rest now child. You will arrive safely in the hands of your maker soon.'

I can't help but lean in to offer a small soft kiss to this once vibrant creature's forehead, as I use my gifts to ensure her safe travel to a bright celestial world far from this dark and malevolent place.

As her body rises, turning into the true form of a glistening soul, I rise and once more scan its disgusting final resting place as I make my way to the door, pained that such a village even exists where souls need to wait at the edges of Hell to receive their eternal destination orders. Suddenly weak from the visions I was just a part of, I fall to my knees just outside the dwelling I came from, uncaring as to who sees me, unfazed as to the danger I am in, here, on my knees. How can such an immortal world co-exist beside Eden, the most rapturous entrancing place ever created?

As I lift my hands from this lewd soil, I feel sick. Sick at the thought of the creatures that have walked on this ground before me and the hideous acts they partake in on a daily basis. I want nothing to do with them. Any of them, even my guardian, because what I just witnessed lying in a shattered heap is the work of the evil creatures that reside in and around this cesspit. I will never find life's answer anywhere near this sin. I need to get away from here. I can't handle where my thoughts are taking me.

I make my way back through the forest to the only place that can possibly cleanse my soul after the darkness that was just spilled into it. Anger now taking over as I stomp on the moss strewn floor beneath my feet, wanting to scream and fight and make all of the darkness go away.

Just as I'm about to reach where the forest recedes, allowing Eden's life force to take over ... I feel him. Watching me.

I turn with disgust and anger radiating from my aura, remembering the poor broken soul I just had draped in my arms. I hate him. I hate that it has been he who has been watching over me my entire existence. Times when I felt safe and protected, it was evil hiding in the shadows. I cannot stand to look at him any longer so I turn to leave.

As soon as I take one step, he is there, standing in my path, towering over me, completely encasing me in his presence, glaring at me with a look of confusion on his face. I turn from his glare, suddenly confused by my body's reaction to him being this close. I am beyond angry, yet I feel my internal forces settling for the first time since our last encounter. How can that be?

He grabs my chin with a foreign softness that throws my thoughts into disarray, turning my face gently until our eyes reach again, tilting his head slightly to the side with a frown, silently asking me where this anger has come from. That's when I see it! I see something so unexpected in his eyes I feel like my entire being is free falling.

I can see deep within his dark tainted soul, the good that so desperately wants to taste freedom. It's franticly trying to reach me, calling to me for help, pleading with me to rescue it from the lifelong shackles it has been lying beneath. Anger starts to flare to life in his features as he realises what I have discovered, something he has kept well concealed from all other beings until this very second.

Could this be true? Could this be why he has been near me for all of eternity? Has this spark of good been drawn to the light I have inside? This doesn't make sense! How can good an evil co-exist within one being? It can't, it's impossible! I'm thinking this must be an elaborate illusion by this demon before me, but my soul is telling me that the good he has locked tightly inside ... is real!

This is too much. I have no idea what to do standing here in his mighty presence. I need space. I take a step back and turn out of his grip as I take a step away from him.

'Wait!' he shouts, his sinful voice making me stop instantly. I refuse to turn, shake my head no and take a few more steps away.

'Wait!' he growls in a terrifying tone. But I won't give in. I only turn my head halfway around as I mouth the word 'no' again.

In a nano second he is next to me and grabs me by the back of the neck, turning my head, forcing my gaze to meet his.

'You dare defy me, Little Wing?'

I want to melt in his arms at his endearment, I want to submit to his dominant voice, but I know I can't. I have to stand my ground if I'm to survive what this man does to my body. I have to hold onto my anger to fight this war of words.

'You have never had power or authority over me for me *to* defy you. You don't own me!' I say as strong as my nervous voice will allow.

'Are you sure about that ... *Arianwen*?'

I gasp. 'You know my name.' I whisper, the words barely coming out of my mouth as my heart and soul comes alive at the sound of my name flowing over his beautiful lips. My heart rate quickens as my breath fastens. All my nerves come alive as the surprise registers within my brain. *He knows my name.*

He looks surprised to have said my name as well, as his eyes blink at a rapid speed. I can't! I can't fall for this, I can't believe this is true, that these feelings he evokes so easily within me could possibly be real. How could a demon create such joyful pleasure within my heart? I brace myself as I anchor my being to the solid ground beneath my feet as I growl, 'Let go of me, *Demon*!'

He raises his eyebrows at me, only to then tighten his grip on my neck, silently challenging me to fight the hold he has on me, searching my eyes for my retaliation.

'You can't hold me here, *Demon*. Let me go before my kin come looking for me.'

He just keeps staring at me, not talking, not letting go, just searching, searching my eyes for something, but for what? I don't understand what he wants me to say. But he is making my anger rise again, giving me the strength to resist his power over me.

'I will give you only one more warning, you *vile Demon*, let ... me ... go!'

His eyes crinkle in rage at my taunting words as he tightens his grip yet again on the back of my neck, pulling me closer to his face as he bends down towards me, our noses almost touching as I hear his breath panting in a silent rage.

'I'm not only a Demon, I am the son of the Lord and Knight

Abara-weiser. I am a man. I … am … ALBION!'

He screams in my face, letting his built up anger go free. That name! That name feels like it is a part of me. It always has been. I have always known the name of my true guardian, it has been forever etched into my soul which has hidden it from me for eternity, until now, but how can that be? His name is a part of me.

'*Albion,*' I whisper, testing those words across my tongue and letting them float over my lips. He looks alarmed, almost shocked as my words hit him in the chest like a stray bullet. His mouth slowly drops open as he looks like that stray bullet just hit him straight in his heart. Suddenly his grip on my neck is gone as this larger than life man drops heavily to his knees before me.

8

Following the Light

ALBION

I stare at the fruits of my labours, the dull unpolished metal sitting stark against the black leather that filled its concave form. The etched sides glow with warmth in the orange hue gloom of Garth's workshop. My eyes trace over its swirling lines and engravings, the intricate details wrought by my own hands and yet, as I stare at the slowly emerging piece of armour before me, I can't help but feel a sense of awe at just what I have created.

I have spent so long honing my skills for one purpose, the art of death, the ever expanding vault of knowledge locked within my mind leading my body to one inevitable purpose, to kill, to take the life of another in the service of my master and lord and yet this, this work of art, this amalgamation of steel and leather has left me reeling; reeling at the fact that my own hands drew these things together and created the unfinished work that now lies atop Garth's bench.

I know in my heart who it is for, who it is destined for, destined for the one person in this entire universe I would gladly kill and die for. A wry smirk tugs at my lips. If I am truly honest with myself, if she wished it, I would hunt God himself, tracking him to the ends of time if it meant seeing her smile one last time.

Turning from the doorway I set my eyes to the road ahead, the twisted lanes of the warren about me leading me, driving me forwards through this den of iniquity. The cat calls and beckoning fingers trying in vain to entice me into their little black pits of vice and sin. I snort in disgust as I stride past them, vapid calls besmirching my endowment following in my wake as I feel the all too familiar tug at my senses.

The winding world around me fills me with a loathing that I have rarely known. How can these hairless apes allow themselves to be trodden down this far, to be ground underfoot like insects, crushed into the dust beneath my feet; and yet, as I cast my eye abroad, I can see that they're all striving to better themselves despite it. I cannot fathom the effort it takes to pull yourself up from such a fall, their squalid existence a pale shadow of what they had in life and yet they all seem, for the most part, content.

Her call grows with every step, her familiar light washing through me the further I stride from the bilious centre of this carrion hoard. My mind burns with the sights and senses around me as I'm drawn further and further from the quiet heat licked contemplation of Garth's workshop.

Little Wing's glowing aura fills the sky with an amber bloom that only she can create. My heart races in my chest as I near the edges of the village and its condemned people. The silent tugging call of her soul curls through my own, making my knees weak as I reach the precipice, the shadowed edges of the fall to the forest below giving me pause. Dare I take this last step, to plummet into the lands that have spelt certain death to all my brothers and sisters too foolhardy to enter, to enter a land where even the forest itself loathes our very essence?

Steeling myself, I step, the temptation to unfurl my wings drowning me as open air greets me; as I tip forwards, the rippling canopy of green below rushes towards my falling form. I stare wide eyed as the undulating sea of leaves and lumber, the standing towers of sentient wood, rise to my plummeting body.

My mind screams as my wings push at my skin; nothing will draw me faster to my goal, only the ever approaching pain makes me second guess my choices. Reaching out, my fingers kiss the bows of the trees around me, hands snatching at branches and leaves as I drive myself into the waiting grip of the forest.

Limbs and twigs crack and snap as I slide down its length, leather tearing and skin splitting as I grow ever closer to the floor below me. Pain spears through my side as I lose my grip, plummeting to the ground.

With a bone rattling thump, I hit the needle and leaf strewn floor beneath me, my split skin sending rippling lines of pain through my mind as it begins to slowly sew itself back together. Gritting my teeth, I tentatively cast my eyes to my right, the thick pine branch curling its way from my side, my own crimson life's fluid snaking its way along the knotted and gnarled stave.

With a barely checked yowl of pain I pull the shattered branch from my side, my knees buckling as blood and torn flesh falls free, pattering to the floor beside my quaking form. My breathing cuts like glass as I hear the wet crackle of my own flesh beginning to knit together, the cold flood of air over the open wound making me want to vomit as I begin to slowly push myself upright.

Stepping forwards I wince, the newly repaired flesh of my side still tender as my body shifts, tugging at the virgin strands of skin and sinew, and still through it all her call pulls me forwards, urging me on as I stride through this twilight world of light and shadow.

Drewen groan and shift, twisting their skyward limbs to block my path, branches swatting at me, tearing at my leather armoured shoulders as they try in desperation to drive me from their world; I have always loathed this place, these withered husks of bark and timbre fit for little more than kindling or bed posts, and yet, I can see what would have once been a great and wondrous forest full of light and laughter. Have my kind so polluted this world that even the all-encompassing forces of Eden fall short of restoring what has been lost?

I let my mind fall empty as I am once more pulled forwards by the flowing golden light of my Little Wing. I cannot fathom how so much power can be locked within such a diminutive form and yet, as she bleeds her raw energy into the forests around us both, I cannot help but marvel at it. The sheer weight of her might lost to her, but all too obvious to all of those who would seek to undo it.

As I make my way past the twisted fingers of these omnipotent trees, I cannot come to terms with the question that has so vexed my mind. What chance did I ever truly have, what chance was there in this tangled web we have woven between us that I would ever be able to pull myself free from her bewitching light? I step through the line of brush before me, her pull stronger than ever as my desperation grows, my need to feel her beneath my fingers, the gnawing hunger that so drives my wanton desire for her presence. To have her eager all-encompassing glow overwhelm my darkness entirely as I pull her lithe and willowy form to my own, her supple softness moulding against me, as I claw at the answers dancing out of my reach in a desperate bid to know what it is within her that has driven my heart and soul to distraction.

My eyes itch and ache as I see her glittering aura flow through the trees that stand like sentinels in my path. My loathing for these hunks of hell spurned timbre deepens as I push through the boughs and branches, their needle sharp spines slicing at my cheeks and brow. I finally stumble clear, my heart hammering in my chest as I cast my gaze upon the woman that has so captured me.

In that moment, as she stares up through the woven canopy of green that stands at the final reaches of her land and my eyes travel over her light bathed curves, the man that I am fades to nothing, my entire form falling away as I stand naked and afraid in her presence. Her reaching touch draws from me the shy and frightened child I had thought long since lost in the depthless black that fills my core.

I watch as her mind slowly draws her back to the world around us, her body twisting, turning with the grace and flow of water over stone, her violet eyes locking with mine as a small smile flirts with her lips for the smallest moment as I take a small tentative step towards her, her gaze tracking my every movement.

I watch the smile fall from her lips, her gaze tumbling into blackness and hatred as her aura turns to the darkest of depths of midnight. Her eyes blaze with contempt as I slowly make my way forwards towards my Little Wing. The sheer ferocity of her ire makes me falter, my resolve waning as I finally come to stand before her once more. She turns to go, disgust plain on her marble white features, the smooth curve of her cheeks rising, twisting into am almost feral sneer as she begins to turn from me. My arms hang like lead at my sides, my mind awash with a storm of fear and confusion as I try in desperation to reach for her. With my last ounce of will I lay caution to the wind and throw myself into the depths of my demonic heritage, my body dissolving into the wind as I appear before my startled angel towering before her like the dragons that vie to keep me from her world.

'Please, wait.'

Her anger overwhelms me, pulsing into my soul, flooding through me like the tides. I lift my hand, feeling her soft skin beneath my fingers as I cup her jaw; my heart hammers in my chest as I feel her flesh connect with my own, her warmth and life flowing through me, seeping through my body, filling my very soul. I stare deep into the violet eyes that fill my dreams and my waking thoughts, pleading with her to stay, to stay with me, here in this one moment, to show me where all this sudden hatred and anger has arisen from.

Her words spurn me, filled with venom and spite, each one sending a barb through my heart, burrowing deep into my core as she pulls from my grip. I call to her, my voice near pleading as she steps from me. She casts a glance towards me, my anger rising as her eyes meet my own; I close my eyes, drawing from within my own hurt and rage at this little upstart.

I bellow at her, my voice shattering the self-imposed veneer around my headstrong angel as she stops dead in her tracks, I pull her to me, her body moulding to mine as I stare down into the violet pools that threaten to drown me completely.

My muttered goading question sets her ablaze, fire dancing within her as she pushes against my chest. I let her slip from my grip, a small smile ghosting across my features as I watch her rail against my will, her body saying more than her weak willed protests ever could.

She hammers at my chest, fire coursing through her as she screams at me to release her, my grip slipping clear of her slender arms as she stands, chest heaving and eyes glowing with anger and malice.

She calls me demon as if the word is a spite laced insult upon my very being. She curses me with my own label as if it denotes who I am to my core. I am the son of a Demon Knight and a Courtesan to Lucifer himself, I am Demon spawned of the purest reaches of Hell, and yet as I stare into the eyes of the Angel that holds me so unknowingly in her palm, my title, my genesis, skewers me like the sharpest of blades, piercing me through to my core and on down into the depths of my very soul, shattering my entire being.

From anyone else, be they kith or kin to this alabaster beauty that stands before me, the words would ring as hollow as the beat of their heathen wings, but from her, from the one woman in all of the three realms that can undo me with a glance, it is all too much to bear.

I ensnare her once more in my grip, drawing her as close to me as I can, my face mere inches from her own, the soft caress of her breath on my lips making my heart hammer in my chest. My voice streams forth as I scream at her, the proclamation of myself filling the silence that had so entrapped us both, my words echoing through the glade of half-life as I lay my name clear to all who would hear it, my anger and fear lying plain to see in one tumultuous exhalation.

She stares at me, eyes wide, glowing and iridescent like a violet moon. I cast my gaze upon hers as I stand mute, my words still resounding through the world around us both. Her questioning eyes fill my own as I lay all bare before her, begging her to see beyond the darkness, beyond the tainted evil that has drowned me for an eternity, to the source of who I truly am, to the part of me so lost beneath the black that even I had begun to question if it was little more than a figment of my own malicious mind.

Her hand rises, slipping across my jaw as she pushes herself to the tips of her toes, the tip of her nose brushing my own as she undoes me with a single whispering breath, my name slipping past the rose pink lips that are echoing my own.

My knees buckle as I crash to the floor, my vision dancing as, all at once, the darkness within me falls away, seeping from me like water from a shattered glass, leaving nothing behind but all that I had sought to bring to the light. How can this Angel, this woman, bring from me all that I have struggled for millennia to find with a single word?

I stare with unseeing eyes as she kneels before me, her hands lifting my own to her cheek. The touch of her skin upon my own courses through my veins like fire as she traces my fingers over her jaw; the soft silk caress of her hair against my calloused knuckles ripples through my heart as I slip my hand from hers, pulling her to me in a single instant as my lips find hers. I draw her to me, her body entwining with my own as I throw wide the doors of my soul and finally let her light shine upon me, casting me anew.

All at once urgency and wanton need take control, her lips coveting mine as I press her to me, my fingers sit entwined in her hair as my grip once more settles over the back of her neck. Nothing can contain the ache that burns through me, igniting my loins in a tempest of passion and need as I press myself into her. The layers between us are stifling as I let my hand roam, slipping across the swell of her buttocks, my fingers sinking into her supple flesh as I draw my tongue over her lips.

The taste of her, on my tongue, on my lips makes me shudder, my heart hammering in my chest as I once more graze her tongue with my own. The scent of her arousal fills my senses as our bodies sink to the leaf and needle strewn floor. I can feel her grinding against me as her moist centre presses deeply into my loins, my throbbing length aching to respond. I can all but taste her wetness seeping through the gusset of her cotton panties, drenching her dress and soaking my leather and padded cotton trousers as she presses ever harder against me, her heat drowning my mind and driving me to distraction as she nips at my bottom lip.

Who knew such a sultry, sexual vixen lay beneath the demure visage of my captivating angel. I close my eyes, uttering a silent prayer to whoever listens that I am the first and will ever be the only one to draw this side of her to the fore.

Awakening

ARIANWEN

Wet heated flesh glides over my delicate lips, sliding, sucking, biting at the corners of my mouth, causing a delicious hurt like sensation. His tongue, soothing where his teeth just caused pleasurable pain as it travels along the seam of my now swollen lips, pushing through, demanding its presence be acknowledged as it dances with my own, petting, rubbing, causing a wet friction that travels all over my entire form as he devours me completely, taking control of all my senses. His tight grip on my hair at the back of my neck is unforgiving as it anchors me entirely to his hard trembling body.

His large solid form is moulded and fused to my every curve and crevice, fitting me perfectly, like he was created *just for me*. The heat between us is hotter than the edges of Hell as it races over my body, lighting every piece of my flesh on fire until it feels like a raging inferno engulfing my skin.

His other hand travels from the middle of my tingling spine between my wings, slowly down over my white floating dress, feeling me, memorising every dip and rise as he reaches the top of my buttocks, spreading his fingers wide, pushing further down and slowly but firmly adding pressure, controlling me, moving me to where he needs me most, until I feel my wet centre start to part beneath my panties and wrap either side of his leather clad heated manhood where I can feel both of our thumping pulses begin to entwine as one.

Every vein in my body is pumping with blood rapidly as my heart struggles to cope with this sudden influx of sensation that is completely foreign to my entire existence. We are both releasing pheromones that are rising and swirling together. The scent of his masculine excitement is seeping from his every pore, floating, dancing around my head. After a lifetime of lessons and research on human beings, I know more about them than they know about themselves, and I know with utmost certainty that what my body is experiencing now is *arousal.* And what an entrancing experience it is.

Every inch of my body is reacting in its own unique way. I have a prickling sensation all over my skull, as if a thousand pins are trying to penetrate my almost exploding brain. Small droplets of sweat are forming on my forehead, slowly gliding down my face. My breathing is barely there as I gasp at his tongue's constant intrusion as my own tongue starts to tingle with fire.

The pressure of his chest against mine is making my nipples sting and ache for more attention which I can feel all the way down to the apex of my thighs. My heart is beating franticly against his chest like tiny fists pelting his leather armour around his heart. The once slow and almost dormant butterflies that reside in my stomach have now taken flight and are creating a sensual burn that's swirling and tingling just beneath the surface of my skin.

The ribbon of arousal is rippling through my entire body, slithering down low until it reaches the apex of my thighs to my hot centre, where my body's juices are overflowing, dripping down my legs, soaking through all of my clothing, drenching his own that's pressed against mine, letting off a scent that is intoxicating, making it blatantly obvious what my body is asking for. I want to feel a deeper connection with him. I want him to claim me. I want to feel him move inside of me.

I gasp loudly at my unexpected thoughts as I try to pull out of his grip, but that only makes him tighten it more, feeling as though he may separate my hair from my skull, which only fuels my body's excitement. He rises us both with ease to our feet as his lips start to move faster over mine in an almost panicked manner. I am lost! Lost to these new sensations taking over my heart and soul making me want, making me need, making my body beg for more as I release my own tongue, slipping it out to trace his rich red plump lips, tasting his excitement and arousal and the saltiness of his skin.

His throbbing length that is snugly placed between my panty covered folds is pulsating at a rapid speed as it continues to harden and grow against me with every passing second, taking on a life of its own. Its passionate movements rub my bud of nerves, exciting my body further, taking me to a high cliff, holding me on the edge, on the edge of something I'm yet to understand. His lips continue a sensual dance with mine, unrelenting, not stopping, still licking and biting.

I feel like my body has come alive for the first time in my entire existence. My heart is swelling with the depths of emotions I am feeling for this man. Even though I am anchored tightly to him, our bodies are slightly swaying, rocking together, seeking, demanding more of a connection, wanting to break through the barriers that our clothing has created.

He growls low in his chest, beautiful vibrations flowing throughout his entire entrancing body which transfers to mine, making it sing to the rhythm he is creating. My heart is feeling things I never thought my immortal being would ever be capable of.

The emotions I'm feeling for him are overwhelming, all-consuming, and utterly and completely intoxicating in every way, making me feel light in my head, unable to think clearly as my body's response to this demon's actions are out of my control.

This demon ... demon ... he is still a demon! I pull my mouth from his with every piece of strength I have left as I start to push against his chest. Panic fills my eyes as I realise who exactly it is that has caught me up into his almighty web. We stare into each other's eyes, still both panting, struggling to breathe with each rise of our chests. I have to go, I have to leave, this is wrong, this is dangerous, this can't be, I shouldn't be feeling the things I am.

The simple truth is ... I am an Angel ... he is a Demon ... our worlds cannot come together like this. It is forbidden, it is wrong, it can never be!

He seems to have this realisation at the same time as his grip slowly loosens on my neck and he glides his other hand away from my body. Still holding lightly onto my neck, he pleads with his eyes for this moment not to end, for this emotion not to disappear, for our heart rates not to slow. But I was wrong to let this happen, to *want* it to happen. For both our safety I have to leave now. I twist my neck out of his final soft grip and turn to run to the safety and comfort of my homelands.

'Arianwen!'

I freeze at his commanding tone. I turn slowly, meeting his intense pleading gaze. 'If you have to go, I understand, go slowly and carefully, but never ... will you ... run from me again!'

I am frozen to the spot with his loud, yet heartfelt command for me not to run from him. This simple sentence has a profound effect on my heart as I look into his beautiful blue eyes. Eyes that are now claiming me as his. I slowly take a step backwards, not breaking our gaze as I try and decipher what it is that his eyes are asking from me.

Is it to stay, to promise to return, to acknowledge his claim over me? The emotions I see swirling in his intense stare are too many to name. It is like with this single glance, he is laying his soul at my feet, filled with all of its lifelong secrets and begging me to handle it with care.

I continue walking back slowly, step by step, finding it hard to break away from his entrancing eyes, feeling my own fill with moisture as my emotions begin to take over and the realisation that I am completely lost to this being in front of me finally takes an unrelenting hold of my soul.

I finally turn and walk away, slowly, one step at a time, feeling his watchful glare, doing what he has done for eternity, watching until I return to the safety of my world. It is him. It has always been him. I know in my frantic soul that he has always been a part of me and somehow I know he always will.

I stagger slightly as the aftereffects of our encounter continue to ravish my form. My legs feel weak, barely able to support my body. There is still friction between my thighs with every step I take, feeling sensitive beyond the realm of possibilities. My body's natural juices are flowing from my still pulsating centre, travelling down my entire thighs. My breasts feel enlarged as if they're about to spill from the top of my corseted dress. My lips are tingling and swollen to twice their size as if they were stung by a bee; my tongue is numb, floating lazily inside my mouth. I can still smell his scent clinging to every inch of my body, making it hum from my head all the way down to my toes.

I am walking in a trance, my aura beaming in the sensual afterglow of his touch, trembling with emotions and feelings now soaring through my veins like blood, feeding my heart, nurturing my soul, awakening every nerve in my entire body; the sound in my ears is deafening. I feel a change deep within, one I knew was always going to arrive, yet I had no idea that it would show itself in this form, the form of a demon, a demon who has been guarding over me forever, a demon who has enlightened my heart and shown it the possibility of a range of human emotions, a demon I know who holds many dark secrets in his soul, the darkest one being that he is hiding the good inside he was created with. My soul knows this to be true. I can feel it, I can smell it, I can sense it, I can see it deep within his eyes and I know this is why our worlds have been forever destined to collide. And I know that it is my destiny to help him discover why he was born with the blood of a good man.

Lost completely inside my own thoughts, I don't even realise I have walked past the dragon gatekeepers, into the garden and have arrived at the entrance of the humble cottage I call home until the door bursts open as my youngest sister Caronwen almost falls out of it.

'The great ones have called a meeting for all of us kin to attend. I wonder what could be so important,' she rushes to spit out. Then frowns as she looks me over.

'Are you feeling unwell, sister? You look a little ill; your cheeks are burning red. Is everything okay?' she now asks with great concern. I can only imagine what my appearance is showing my sister. I need to move from her now before she sees too deeply.

'I'm fine, little one, just rushing around to get all of my chores done before the meeting. Who knows how long it may go for? What time are we expected there again? I forgot.'

She just shakes her head as she answers, 'In one hour. Don't be late, or Mum will be mad.' She grins at me.

I go inside and into my room, grabbing only the essentials I need and then make a hasty retreat out and towards the hot thermal bathing springs, needing to hide what my body has been through only moments ago. I move quickly and quietly, not needing anyone to stop me for conversation at this very moment.

As I reach the edge of the warm water, thankful that the place is deserted, I place my personal items behind me and begin to strip away the layers of my tainted clothing, my body sensitive as each item slides over my skin. Standing there, as naked as the day I was created, I slowly walk into the pure sacred liquid that I know is going to wash away his scent and masculine essence from my body.

I walk until the soothing water is up to my shoulders and begin to wash away a life changing moment. My body still pulsates from the memory of his large hands gripping me tightly as I brush my hands over my delicate skin, hoping to hide from my kin the touch of a demon.

My flesh is still tingling with the effects of being brought to life as each glide of my fingers over my flesh reminds me of his every touch, gentle, hard, wanting, needing, claiming. Yes ... he has claimed me as his, and even though I know in my head that it is wrong, that it cannot work, my heart and soul have claimed him as mine.

As I wash away my dark encounter, my body is remembering

what he made me feel, how he made me feel, and starts to respond to the lightest of touches. I close my eyes and instantly see his hungry stare. I can smell his scent, feel the heat of his body as my entire being yearns for more as I glide my hands over my form imagining that he is still here with me, that he is holding me, that he is kissing me, that he is devouring me.

My fingertips over my now swollen nipples cause a sharp tightening in my stomach, creating a delicious ache to bloom and spread throughout my being. My hands smoothly glide down low over my stomach, trying to relieve the enticing ache as my fingertips continue to slowly travel further down until I reach the now alive soft and moist centred bud that holds all of the sensual tension that is still built up in my body, begging for a release.

As my fingers slip through my folds with the intention of washing away my body's sin, I quietly moan and can't help but imagine that it is his calloused touch wanting more of me, demanding I give in to his want, to his desperate need, to this coming together of two destined souls. My breathing is now coming in pants as I wait in anticipation to my body's reaction to the pressure I'm now placing on my throbbing centre.

I gasp as I hear a branch snap on the shore, opening my eyes, looking around franticly as realisation sets in as to what my hand was just about to do. I can't see or hear any other movements, but I have a feeling that someone is near, that someone is watching, that someone knows what my thoughts were just singing. I rush out of the water quickly, crouching down with modesty as I reach for my towel and cover my body. An uneasy feeling settles in the pit of my stomach as I carefully dress myself under the cover of my towel. Does somebody know where I have been? Do they know what I was washing away? Do they intend on punishing me for keeping company with the enemy?

The air around me is thick as I sense eyes upon me but I'm yet to see them. I can feel a dark aura nearby and know that my safety may be compromised even though I'm in my own world. Fear starts to trickle down my spine and prickles my scalp as I try not to show my internal worry. I dress swiftly but without panic as I gather the rest of my belongings from the ground and move slowly away from the shore, keeping my body language calm.

I hear another snap of a branch, this time to the left of me but I control my reaction, not showing that I heard its sharp sound. I deliberately let a small smile show on my face at a bird in a tree in front of me, trying to concentrate on anything other than my fear. I hear the slight rustle of fabric as I look ahead, noting that I still have quite a few steps to go until I am in a clearing and out from the coverage of the trees that surround the springs.

I hear the crunch of a footstep on the leaves that have carpeted the ground and know that whoever is following me is coming closer. A slight breeze moves past me, bringing a scent with it. A scent of the flowers that reside here in the garden mixed with something spicy that slightly burns my nose, something I haven't smelt before but something I can feel that has a darkness to it.

I'm about to reach the clearing when a sudden large force of air pushes from behind me as the carpet of leaves on the ground cries out loudly close behind my back, I brace myself for some sort of contact as I leap the last step and stagger into the clearing and look forward in the distance to see a group of three young boys laughing aloud as they all walk in the direction of the outside amphitheatre. I turn sharply, ready to defend myself, when my eyes are met with nothing but lush trees and small bushes.

My eyes dart left and right as I try in vain to see who it was that was following me and had come ever so close. Fear wants to take over as I realise what I sensed was danger, here, in the safety of Eden. How could that be?

I take a few deep breaths, trying to calm my fractured nerves and carefully scan my entire surroundings. In the distance I can see people starting to move towards the meeting place, all chatting and walking with ease, not a care in the world, and that is how our world should be. But I know that danger was near, near enough to reach out and catch me in its grip, but I just don't see how it is possible unless ... unless it was someone from within these walls that surround my home. My heart starts to beat faster as I struggle to comprehend any of my kin wishing harm or ill will against another unless they suspect I have caused danger to us all. Someone may have seen ... seen my encounter with the demon who now owns my heart.

I have to shake this feeling because no one but a Reclaimer ventures into the forgotten forest. I have to pull myself together with every piece of strength I have to once again walk amongst my kin, not showing that one of their pure angels is now indeed tainted.

After taking another very careful look around, not seeing anything or anyone hiding in the lush foliage, I turn to head home and join the rest of my family at the meeting for all kin.

10

A Jealous Silence

ALBION

I watch her move away from me, move away from us, could I call it us? Yes, what had transpired defied explanation and left me feeling a sense of completion for the first time in my life, but, through it all, I was left with a sense of loss, a loss at the moniker of what we now had, and a loss at my angel's all too sudden departure from my embrace.

I feel the tendrils of envy and jealousy coil themselves up my spine. Despite the unspoken bond between us both, I know in my heart that she will always be at their beck and call, and that, for all my self-control and will, is not something I can abide; if silence can feel jealousy then at this very moment, it's reared its head and bellowed to the sky announcing its birth.

I sit for a moment listening to the creak of the trees around me, their ire and need to see me gone from their realm, waning as I drink in the silence. The echoing limitless wall of nothingness that is punctuated by nothing more than the shallow groaning of these ancient elms and oaks and the twittering of the birds around me.

Rising to my feet, the sod and fallen leaves beneath me cling to my legs and backside. Their cold, slightly wet countenance leaching through my leather armour and into my skin. Dragging my hands across my dew slick form, I stand tall, my hardened member straining against the clasp of my trousers, its length almost painful as I move towards the path and my sulphur stained home.

'She could have at least popped the cork on this bottle, leaving me like this is just cruel,' I grin to myself.

My climb is filled with thoughts of lust and heated sensuality as I scramble and claw my way from this unforgiving land of sentient timber. The mud and dust cling to my skin as I pick my way up the steep near vertical pathway that leads into the carnal house that I call my home. The blast of heat hits me in the face like a smith's hammer, chasing my breath from my lungs like Cerberus casting his ire on all that pass through his gate.

I feel their eyes upon me, the questioning glances of the behemoths that patrol the edges of the fall, their hulking forms filling the air with the stench of rotting meat and stale sweat as they pass me by, the planks beneath my feet groaning in protest under their armoured bulk. Images of my angel fill my mind even as I descend into this sulphur swathed pit that has drowned my every waking moment in fear and anger, my sense of trepidation grows as I move ever onwards; I feel sweat roll down my spine, chilling my very core, the sense of my being watched rising with every step I take until it is almost too much to bare.

What has she awoken in me, these warring feelings that vex my very soul, I cannot pull from my mind the truth behind them and yet, through it all, I know that she has woken a part of me I so longed to bring to life myself. Why then after my millennial existence has it taken the chaste and fervently frightened kiss of my angelic enemy to wake them inside of me? Have I really become that separated from who I truly am, have I distanced myself from my own truth so much that it has taken that one act of tentative kindness, and dare I say love, to draw out what I so wished to claim myself?

My mind tumbles through a maelstrom of chaotic noise as I finally reach the entrance to the under croft and the land of my woe begotten kin. The scent of charred meat and sex fills my nose as I push the doors aside, the raucous laughter and thrumming music that assails my ears makes me want to flee to the quiet sanctity of my own oasis, but, I know I have to slip on the mask I call my face and persevere. With a heavy cry of joy I feel an arm ensnare my shoulders, the slack and drunken face of my kinsman filling my vision as he slurs my name, the foetid stink of his breath making me retch as I carve a smile into my lips and I roll from his grip, a joyless laugh tripping from me as I clap my hand on to his sweat laced shoulder.

'Well met, brother, but, I need to wash the heathen stink from me, line one up for me and I will return. Tell Agares that there are a couple of runaways in the village that need to be dealt with, I spotted them on my way back in but was too damned tired to pursue them, besides, it's that crocodile riding bastard's job anyway.'

I watch as Alp nods, the patchwork multi-coloured hat on his head wobbling as he staggers away from me towards the bar. A smile tugs at my lips as I watch him shift his form into a willowy woman and slide up alongside one of my more unwary kin.

Muttering to myself I move towards my cell at the top of the spiral tower, its ragged and pitted form rising out of the far corner of the under croft like a broken finger, its tip sinking into the thick smoke smeared stone over our heads. My mind hums, buzzing like a swarm of enraged bees as it sits in my skull, saturated with the fractured thoughts of Arianwen and all that she has drawn to life within me.

The blooming seeds of my own sanctity taking root in the pitiless black that boils within my core. Can I truly poses a shred of light within me, can this fractured form that I call my own body and soul contain anything other than the depthless cruelty and depravity that boils around me? Even now, as I cast my eyes to the milling bodies and writhing lumps of limbed flesh that surround me, I see nothing but lust filled carnal want and lascivious need. Can I really have it within me to be more than these beasts that rut and grunt in the throes of primal copulation and drunken debauchery?

Do I really wish to remain a living cell in this body of overt avarice and gluttony? Shaking my head, I force my weary frame up the spiralling staircase heading towards the dark, cool, blissful silence of my chamber. Arianwen's scent drifts through the warm, sweat soaked air around me, filling my mind with a cool sweet calm that I have only ever felt when I am near my source of redemption.

The noise of the bar below me fades to a dull rhythmic thump, the minute tremble that worms through the soles of my feet a soft but constant reminder of just where I am. With a sighing grunt I let the sweat and blood stained jerkin that so clung to my form fall to the floor, the tear in the back an all to stark reminder of just how close I came to losing my life in that warren of vice and virtue that sits on the precipice of my kin's kingdom.

I stare at the scarred and rune etched flesh that is my body, my image warped and misshapen in the battered mirror pinned to my cell's wall. I can still feel her slender fingers on me. The memory of their soft touch igniting trails of fire down my chest and stomach as she ground against me, makes me stir, an agonising ache boiling through me as I draw my eyes away from the polished sheet of beaten metal and move towards the damp riddled shower.

The water pours down upon me, searing my dirt and grime smeared skin as I lean against the wall, I feel the skin around my shoulders tighten as the water slips over the puckered and ridged scars that hide my wings, those taloned and scaled shackles of my forbear, an all too stark reminder of who and what I am.

The searing heat rolls down my spine as I drag my head upwards, breaking through the scalding stream. I reach up, dragging my fingers through my matted and gore stained hair, their ebony strands clinging to my face and neck as I pull the carrion filth from them.

A soft gasp echoes past my ear as I turn towards the door, her shadowed form standing silhouetted in my doorway; I stare at her, my heart hammering against my chest as she stares at me, I feel the scars on my shoulders begin to itch and split as she begins to walk towards me.

'I always knew you were an impressive specimen, Albion, but I had no idea that you were so ...'

She pauses as her eyes travel up and down my body, appraising me as if I were a slab of meat hanging in a butcher's window.

'... well equipped. I must say whatever piece of meat you have been skewering is very lucky, I dare say you'd split any one of those hairless apes from quimm to chin if you speared them too quickly; that can't be very satisfying for the son of such a well travelled Knight as Abara.'

Her lips curl into a condescending smirk as she steps closer to me, moving slowly to my left as she trails her fingers across my chest and over my shoulder. I feel her fingers graze along my lower back, my lank and sodden hair sending glistening rivers of water along my skin, the chilled air of my cell raising my skin in a stippled map, raised lumps blossoming across me like the skin of a plucked chicken.

'What do you want, Lilith? I have told you, we are not coming together, you are not going to be my betrothed, you are nothing to me; so tell me what you want or remove yourself from my sight.'

Her eyes dance with barely concealed anger laced laughter. I push Lilith away from me, an indignant squeal rising from this demoness that stands so besotted with me. With a snort of anger and derision, she folds her arms across her chest and glares at me, her eyes tracking my every movement as I pull a clean set of trousers up my still damp legs.

'The King has called a meeting. He needs all the legion heads there and seeing as you command the sixth, I was ordered to bring you to him.'

I cast a glance at her as I lift a clean shirt from my dresser, the coarse woven cotton shirt draping itself over my form like a bed sheet. Moving to the door, I stare at her, my eyes saying more than any of my barbed and venom laced words ever could. With a snort of anger she moves past me and out onto the balconied walkway that borders my cell.

I call after her vanishing form, 'Tell the King I will be there. As for you, disappear before I make you disappear.'

'We have to prepare. There is something coming, a shift. I defy you to say you have not felt it!' The doors swing open in front of me, the gathering throng of Generals and Knights turn to watch me move to the fore and take my seat, the carved onyx chair fitting me like a glove as my head rests against my family's crest. I turn my gaze to Abaddon, his eyes boring into Lucifer's as our King sits atop the dais, the three tiered platform lending him a commanding view of all whom he has created.

'Yes, I have felt it. I have felt the forces shift. I have felt them move and yet, not one of you, not one of my commanders, not one of the men and women who guide my legions can give me a reason or cause for what is casting this tumultuous ripple through the very fabric of our realm!'

I watch with more than a measure of caution as Lucifer pushes himself to his feet, his black and claret swathed form rising, anger radiating from him like the pulsing of the sun. 'So, tell me, Abaddon, as one of those same men, what exactly are we supposed to prepare against when not one of you have the faintest of glimmers as to what the source of this ...'

I shift in my seat, my hand falling to the blade in the small of my back as I turn, ensuring I have a fast exit from this entombing chair. I know exactly what they have felt, I know exactly of what they speak, I would have to be as blind as the ferryman to not know its true nature.

'... power is. How can it exist between our land and theirs and neither of us chance upon it before. Pray tell, Abaddon, in all your wit and wisdom, how can you explain that?'

I cough into my fist as I spot a slither of an opening, a chance to direct their attention away from their slavish hunt for the 'source' and onto a more open and obvious threat. Drawing my King's attention away from the stunned and shaken General he is now mere feet from, I speak.

'Sire, if I may. I have been abroad these past five weeks and have sensed this thing's arrival, and yet seen nothing. I have gone from the edges of Eden and those damned Dragon gates to our very doorstep and back again, and as yet have to see anything amiss; whatever it is, it hides itself well, but I fear that is not our most pressing issue. I can assure you, we are not the only ones to have felt this. Not three days ago I took down two Reclaimers and one of Michael's damned scouts. They are searching for this thing already and if we don't do something about them, it may tip the balance in their favour, and that is not something we can allow. They are already ahead of us in terms of military strength. We cannot afford to lose any more ground to them. Look how far they have pushed us back from the village.'

I pause, letting my words hang as a soft murmur creeps through all of those gathered in the chamber. I study my commander as he drinks in my words and their none too subtle guidance.

'You raise a valid point, Albion, come take the floor. You, above all of my commanders, have seen the heathens' movements first hand. Enlighten us all.'

I push myself to my feet, digging my fingers into the arms of the chair beneath me to hide the trembling that suddenly rolls through me as I move to the centre of the room. The eyes of my peers bore down upon me as I stand before them. Never, in all my years, have I felt more unimportant and more significant in a single moment, as the battle scarred and tried and tested men and women before all, waiting for me to speak. Me, a Hunter living in his father's shadow, now holding the attention of every demon lord and knight in the seven circles.

Finally, finding my voice, I lay out all that has befallen me, twisting the truth to suit my own needs as I watch them sip at the stream of lies and half-truths I pour forth.

✦ ✦ ✦

The gathered members of Hell's elite slowly dissipate, the energy pulsing in the air, lending a nervous tension to everything around me as I catch Lucifer's gaze lingering on me. With a nod, he beckons me to follow him as he moves towards his private residence, an almost indecipherable look of pain and resignation on his features as he moves towards the double doors flanked by two of the hulking behemoths spawned from the depths of these seven circles.

'Do you know why I was cast from grace, Albion? Do you know the genesis of our people; do you know the true origin of these seven Hells and how I came to be the "Demon" you see before you?'

I take a seat opposite my King, a look of resigned pain and failure etched into his ancient features, the youth of his angelic routes tarnished by the passage of millennia and his incarceration in these despotic realms.

'No, my King. I have heard rumour and conjecture, but I know better than to pay credence to the twittering of my kin.'

Lucifer chuckles as he pours a measure of a fire licked golden liquid into one of the cut crystal tumblers on the small table in front of him.

'I am far from the oldest here, Albion, and some of those twittering as you put it, come from some of those men and women who even outstrip Michael in their life span. Barbatos is one of them. He is far older and wiser than you or I could ever hope to be and yet, he shows fealty to me ...'

I open my mouth to speak, to apprise my King of just what people like Barbatos have said of him, but I find my words dying on my lips like fruit on a withered vine as he raises a hand, turning to me and offering one of those amber filled tumblers before taking a seat opposite of me.

'I know what they say, Albion. I know how free spoken Barbatos is and it is something I accept. I may be ruler here, I may be in possession of more power than any other being here, but with that power comes a need to be mindful of just who it is that you rule. Do you understand what I mean, young Weiser?'

I buy myself some room to think, my mind tumbling as I sip cautiously at the glass in my hand, the warm earthen taste filling my mouth as it casts a trail of fire from my tongue to my stomach. I let the silence linger for a while longer as Lucifer studies me, his eyes probing my every expression and movement as I try to coalesce an answer. Setting the glass in my hand on my knee, I slowly begin to reply.

'My father taught me that no matter what, a man's power comes from what he does in defence of others and not in the betterment of himself. That is something that I have strived to live true to. With every life I have taken, every action I have perform-ed, I have always lived with the thought that, through my own actions, another of my kin lives free for another day; I am sure, my King, that is what you set out to do through your actions in remembering those who answer your call, who act in your name carrying out the orders you give, striving towards the betterment of our people by any means necessary.'

He smiles lightly at my reply as the hearth crackles, the oak logs filling the air with a dusky warmth that seeps into your very soul. I sit, waiting for any sign of a reply from him as the silence swells, rolling over all in a thick miasma that seems to choke the air.

'Well put, and your father was a good man, an even better soldier and an excellent General, but, you haven't answered my original question, Albion. Do you know what caused my fall?'

I sit silent once more. There was many a rumour and tale surrounding Lucifer's fall from grace, but, as far as anyone was concerned, that was all they were: rumours and tales, not a fact or truth amongst them. I sip at the glass in my hand, the amber liquid within glowing in the fires light.

'Love, Albion. I was cast out because of love and my own foolish pride. I wanted man to see God as I did, to follow him as I did, before I became Satan to those simpering homo erectus. I was as you know me: Lucifer, bringer of light. I had God's ear, I was his chosen leader; I commanded every legion of Heaven, they all looked to me for guidance and I gave it willingly. Why? Because I loved them. Then with a glance, I was cast out because my ideals and wishes for my father were not of his own design. The bastard son and my own brother threw me from grace, casting me into a new role as the prince of their own alternate ego. Love was my downfall, Albion. Do not let it be yours.'

Lucifer's words ring through my mind like a bell, resonating down to my very soul. Thoughts of Arianwen slip through my mind as I slowly weave my way through the bustling throng of chattering idiocy. The world passes me by in a blur of noise and confusion; bodies morphing together into a shapeless mass of sweat and lust filled moaning. Alp slips through the crush to my side as I near the foot of the stairs once more, his hand finding my shoulder as I pause, letting him gain my attention for the briefest of moments.

'She wants you, you know that, don't you? She will never let her desire for you wane until she has had you.' I tense for a moment, my mind whirling with panicked curiosity at his words, Ari's face filling my vision as Alp smiles knowingly at me.

'Lilith has had her eyes set firmly on you from the moment you took your father's position as commander of the sixth legion. She never loses what she has her eye on, Albion, you of all people should know that.'

With a soft pat on Alp's shoulder, I turn him back to the gyrating crush that heaves around us, before I move up the ever spiralling staircase towards the darkened hole in the wall that is my cell. 'I do know that, Alp, I do know that. Still doesn't change a damned thing.'

Day drips into night, as night bleeds into day, my mind running rampant with the fractured, feverish dreams spawned of my fears and doubts. Nothing can save me from the calamitous storm that rages within my own mind. Can I truly weather the assault? Can I keep my façade intact, when everything around me is vying to drag it from my form, threatening to reveal to all my kin what I so desperately want to hide?

Can I truly lie to myself, deny all that I know to be true; is the truth that I feel within myself really drawing me one step closer to my ultimate end, will all she is willing to give the key to my downfall? I was once told, 'To thine own self be true,' but how can I, when I know within my heart that I must lie to survive, that I must lie to all those around me to simply keep my truth from spelling destruction of the woman who owns my heart?

I leave the sweltering heat and pounding music of the under croft behind me, moving through the bustling corridors and walkways of the circle that is my family's dynasty. I search desperately for an answer as I brush past the lumbering mountains of dim witted flesh, a disgruntled grunt leaving them as I vanish into the pale white glare of the sun.

The air washes over me, blasting the heat from my skin as my sweat licked form shivers lightly in the new dawn sun. My feet lead me forwards as my mind continues to race. I know in my mind and heart that I cannot put her in that danger. I know I cannot risk seeing the death of someone who owns me, mind, body, heart and soul and despite it all, despite the fact it will cripple me to my very soul, that, to save the woman I love, I have to let her go; I feel my heart lurch as the decision takes hold, a sense of dread and finality filling me as I reach the fall, that bitter and fractured precipice crumbling beneath my feet as I stare at the woodlands below.

Dangerous Kin

ARIANWEN

As I walk along the centuries old cobblestone paths, a few steps behind the rest of my family, letting the smells of this divine garden soothe my rattled senses, all I hear is whispers from my fellow angels as to what this meeting could be about. Conspiracy theories of all shapes and sizes are thrown around as we all walk as one, waiting to hear what our great ones have to say.

As a Reclaimer and my parents being former Reclaimers we are seated at the bottom with the rest of our gifted kin in the first few rows of this ancient amphitheatre. Straight in the direct eye sight of Gabriel, who is standing silent, as still as stone amongst the other quietly chatting leaders of our world.

His eyes bore into my skull, not blinking. I feel as if he is willing all of my secrets to the surface to then be laid at his feet. People are walking around him and in front of him, but he is not letting his stare escape my eyes. I feel raw and naked with his intense stare as I imagine him knowing what I have recently encountered. I can't help the heat rising to my cheeks as I swallow past the strangling lump in my throat. If he knew, surely I wouldn't still be sitting here.

A slow smile starts to appear on his face as I know he is sensing my discomfort of his blatant gaze, as other people around now stop and look towards what has captured this great one's attention. I don't need anyone else looking closely at me, I just need to get this meeting over with so I can go and hide in the privacy and comfort of my home.

As Michael begins the meeting by welcoming and thanking everyone for attending today and introducing the leaders who are all on the stone stage beside him, Gabriel has yet to turn from my eyes. Is this because I am to be the topic of conversation? Have they all figured out that it was the meeting of Albion and I that seems to have created this almighty shift in our immortal worlds? Did one of their spies come upon us today without either one of us sensing them? Am I going to be strung up for trial in front of, not only my entire kin, but my family as well? My poor younger sisters, having to witness such a shameful act.

I struggle to keep my composure, Gabriel noticing the hammering rate of my heart as his sly smile now turns to a frown right before Michael calls for him to speak. I can't hear his first words as my blood starts to roar behind my ears and my heart beats franticly with the possibilities of what may happen to me. What pulls me out of my self-inflicted panic is my youngest sister's hand that grabs and grips my own tightly, as Gabriel's words finally reach my brain. *Possible war, the Devil's trickery, don't wander alone, don't stray too close to the borders, we still don't know what it is we are dealing with, but its power grows stronger by the day, we must stay alert at all times, more spies will be sent out, you are all well protected, no need for panic.*

I can breathe for the first time since sitting down, now realising it is not I who is the cause of this meeting, but my sister's still tight grip on my hand makes me realise the frightened innocence that is radiating from her every pore. She is still so young and has yet to learn the full lessons of the Devil's evil acts. And I, her big sister who she looks up to, could be the cause of her learning way too soon that good and evil do, in fact, cause wars that can affect us all for many lifetimes to come. I would never do anything to put her in danger, or any of my family for that matter, but I know that what I allowed to happen today could be the biggest danger we all face yet.

As I look around at all the innocent faces of my family and kin, I feel sick to my stomach at what my selfish acts could possibly cause. I would never risk our beautiful peaceful life and the importance we hold in the human world by seeking answers, emotions and pleasure for myself. Whatever reason fate made the path of a Demon and Angel cross in such a way, I can have no part of it anymore. I will not be the cause of pain and heartache to my people.

The meeting continues with the same musings, asking that we all help each other and be a little more cautious in our daily lives, but to also have faith in our God to guide us to a safe existence. We all get up as the meeting ends and make our way towards the stairs that lead up to the top of the theatre to return to our homes. My sister's small hand is still in my own, holding on tightly, looking for guidance.

'Arianwen. A word please.'

I don't have to turn to know who has asked for my presence, but I am thankful he has done so in front of other people this time, instead of seeking my company in solitude.

I turn and bow with respect then rise, drop my sister's hand and take tentative steps towards Gabriel, noting the wide smile on my mother's face as he tilts his head slightly to the side with a gentle grin and offers his elbow for me to take. As I slip my hand softly in the nook of his arm, he gently places his over mine as he leads us towards the back of the theatre. I'm unable to stop the shiver racing throughout my body, which doesn't go unnoticed and if I'm not mistaken, rises a slight chuckle from him.

After a few steps, we arrive at the back of the stage and stand in front of the collection of small pine trees as his grip on my hand increases in pressure slightly as an indication to look up at him. When our eyes meet he just stares straight at me, still with a slight grin, not saying a word, looking, searching, all the while I'm trying to control my body language, trying not to show how uncomfortable he makes me feel. I'm sure any other rightful aged angel would love to be in my position, standing here looking into the eyes of one of our greatest leaders, desperate for his attention, dreaming of being chosen as his bride, standing beside such a handsome, strong man, but not I. He does have lovely masculine features, strong lines and is very sculptured in body, but I have never had an attraction to him in the least. The only feeling I have ever had towards him is that I suspect he is not as calm and pleasant as he appears to most. I have a feeling that he is harbouring a dark side, a side I never wish to meet.

He continues his silent appraisal of me as my face begins to flush, his grin increasing as he enjoys the signs of my discomfort. I fight to maintain my composure and panic as it feels like he is trying to uncover all of my recent secrets and encounters. Finally after what feels like forever, he leans in closer to my face and I can't help my body's reaction as it goes rigid at his closeness in the near vision of others that are still within the amphitheatre.

'Arianwen, my dear, you are going to have to learn to control your *childish* reactions to me. I can't have my possible future bride flinching with nervous embarrassment every time I touch her, now can I? And believe me, my sweet angel, when you are officially mine, I *will* be touching you ... often. But I have a feeling you may just like that, *Arianwen,* am I right? Somehow I feel you're not as innocent as you seem, my delicate angel. For one that is *so* in touch with the spiritual realm, I'm sure you're just as *in touch* with your own inner needs? Hmm, or does that only come out in you when your body is surrounded by warm water?'

I gasp at the knowledge that it was Gabriel who was watching me, watching me wash away the sins of my body and the one who made me feel danger in my own once safe world. I go to pull out of his grip but he only tightens it.

'Don't be afraid of my knowledge, *Arianwen*. It was quite an arousing show you displayed, like nothing I have experienced before from an angel as pure as you are. It just makes me want our wedding sooner rather than later, because now I know on our first night as husband and wife, you are going to pleasure me more than any other being has done before. And if it wasn't for my pledge to our Lord to uphold all sacred vows, I would take you *now* to the privacy of my own chambers and have my way with you, official ceremony be damned.'

'Please let me go,' I whisper, as I drop my eyes from his and try and pull my hand from his grip, but he will not let go.

'I think we need more meetings like this, my sweet angel, so you can feel more comfortable around the man that could become your master. And I have a feeling that I need to keep an eye on my wayward angel as I am yet to be convinced that you are not hiding something.'

Two of the leaders come closer to us, trying to catch Gabriel's attention, so he makes a show of softly grabbing my cheek with one hand. He slowly leans in to give it a delicate kiss before pulling away with a soft smile on his face as he turns to walk with the other men.

My body starts to tremble as I feel like I could collapse onto the hard stone beneath my feet. The danger I felt at the springs was real, it laced the air around me, raised bumps all over my skin. I scent the darkness in the air and now I know it was Gabriel! The danger came from not only one of my own kin, but also one of our most powerful leaders! I have always felt there was a darkness behind his eyes, but is it dark enough to cause harm to one of his own? What would he have done to me if he *had* caught me in his grip? I tremble further as a sick churning begins in my stomach. Did he know what I was washing away? Oh dear lord, how long has he been following me?

I jump and gulp in a large breath as my mother places a soft hand on my shoulder. 'Oh, Arianwen, that was such a sweet moment to watch. Everyone can clearly see how much you mean to that man. Half the theatre was still full as he placed a kiss upon your cheek. I hope you now know how important you are to him, my dear.'

I can't release a single word around the tight closing of my throat. I have fear and uncertainty swirling around my head. I know I can no longer put my kin in danger by seeking the attention of my demon, but is the only alternative the attention of a Dark Angel? What will happen if he does get me on my own?

I can't help the tremors that are overtaking my form as my mother frowns at my reaction. 'Arianwen?' She questions with concern in her voice as I raise my watery eyes up to meet hers. My eyes are silently begging her for answers, for guidance, for reassurance that I will indeed remain safe in my eternal home, that she will have understanding for all of my actions past and present and that, above it all I will always have the love of my mother.

'My darling daughter, so wise beyond her years, I know in my heart you will choose carefully the right path to take. Your pure soul will help to guide your choices, child. Have trust in it.'

My youngest sister Caronwen once again comes up beside me and grabs my hand as she smiles up to me so sweetly. I swallow down my emotions and draw on the strength I was created with to offer her a smile back.

Then my other sister, Brianne, the middle child of our family, grabs my other hand as she whispers up to me, 'That was the sweetest most romantic thing I have ever seen. He actually kissed your cheek. I have never seen him kiss a cheek before. You must be very special, Ari.' She beams at me.

These two beautiful sweet young souls beside me are the biggest reason why I must control my feelings and emotions for my demon guardian, why I must push all that my heart and soul wants deep down to the darkest parts of my being, why I mustn't seek answers where danger lies and let them come to me if that is my fate. I must protect my family and my kin from darkness, even if darkness resides amongst our very own world. I will not risk this beautiful world I was created in for my own selfish reasons. I must focus on *why* I was created at all, and that was to be a Reclaimer and guide the lost souls of God's children to their rightful resting place. That is all I will allow my mind to concentrate on. And I will find a way to reveal to my mother why I am not destined to be the bride of a Dark Angel. I will have faith in God's plan for me.

As we all return home and settle down for the night, I can't help but feel unease at Gabriel's words and actions. I check my two little sisters' rooms twice, as well as all doors and windows to make sure they are locked, something we have never had to do before. As everyone else finds peace in their slumber, I am yet to lay my head down to rest. My mind racing as to what Gabriel may have planned for me, and how much he really is going to be watching me. I am yet to witness him venture past the protective walls of Eden, but that doesn't mean he hasn't done so in secret. He sends out his army of angels, but that doesn't mean he never ventures out under the shadows of his own protective cloak. He is one of the most powerful angels ever to have been created so he has gifts more powerful than I could ever imagine. I'm sure it's an easy task to go wherever he wants undetected, including following me to the edges of Hell.

I look outside my bedroom window and up to the glowing moon high above my heavenly world and wonder what part it has played in the recent upheaval of my once centred, controlled and peaceful existence. Its power beyond the realm of all our worlds. I watch as its radiating glow descends down upon the divine garden outside my window, casting silvery shadows over the night fallen quietness, shadows that my tired weary eyes are still searching franticly for any sign of danger lurking. I will move Heaven and earth to ensure my family's safety even if it means I have to protect them from one of our own.

I feel my eyes starting to take on a lead like state, as I struggle to keep vigil of the abstruse night sky. My head is lulling heavily on my shoulders as I slip slowly down, away from the window as my head finally hits my pillow. But peace I cannot find. My dreams are awash with darkness and evil and shadows moving, reaching to grab me, to take me to places unknown, to places that smell of lurid deception and reap sounds of painful screams. I have visions of Gabriel watching me at the hot thermal springs, flying and landing right behind, grabbing my hair as he stifles my screams with a solid hand over my mouth. Grabbing, taking, forcing me to yield to his want, to his power. Black clouds float above then descend with an almighty speed as I see a flash of Albion's face, before he lunges for Gabriel, taking him under the depths of the water. Next, I see black soft moving air creeping low to the ground and start to seep its way through the garden, reaching for innocent angels, trying to suffocate all living things, screams of children filling my ears, the horrified looks on my sisters' faces as I try in vain to reach them, only to be held rigid, fixed in place, my world around me crumbling like wet pastry, slowly disappearing before my eyes.

A scream escapes my throat as I sit up straight, clinging to the wet bed sheet that surrounds me, wiping the sweat that is stinging my eyes, gulping large breaths as I try to replace the air that was torn from me by the horrors in my dreams. My mind still manic with all I have experienced in only a matter of days. I have no understanding as to why, now, have I been chosen to face such difficult trials and tribulations when all I have ever done is serve my Lord completely. But regardless of the reason, I know what it is I need to do, and that is to ensure the safety of my family and kin and this glorious immortal world we are privileged to call home.

I am still unsure of how to deal with Gabriel's musings and declarations, but I am certain of one thing, and that is I need to see my demon guardian one more time, to make him understand that what we have started cannot continue, that I need him to promise to stay away from me and my world.

Surely he knows that the powerful feelings we created as we came together can only lead to trouble, heartbreak and possibly the destruction of all we hold dear in our immortal worlds. The sharp pain in my chest tells me that it will already hurt walking away from him now. I can only imagine the depth of the pain if we allowed this to continue any further.

There is no use trying to return to slumber when my heart and my mind are at war with each other. I need to get this over and done with if I am to concentrate on my true calling and then find a way to evade any more of Gabriel's dangerous advances.

I pull my cloak tight around my form and slip the hood over my head as I reach one hand out to open the door. Before I step out into the pre-dawn light, I turn to once more check that my family home is safe and to pray that no harm will ever come to those that I love dearly. I close the door behind me quietly and then search with my eyes for any sign of movement from the edges of the shadows nearby. I then close my eyes and use all of my senses to search for anything that may indicate that danger is near.

I listen for a rustle of leaves, the hint of moving fabric, I smell the scent of blossom floating on the light breeze, something so familiar I am sure it is only the glorious smells of the garden it brings with it. I reach my hands out to my sides, releasing my wings only slightly as I use my feathers to feel for any vibrations around my aura that may indicate someone else is close by. When I feel a comfortable silence engulf me, I move slowly with care, taking each step with caution, feeling a sense of dread that I have to be this careful in my own safe world.

I move through the garden and towards the low purr of the dragon gatekeepers of our world, who seem to be waiting for me. When I stand directly under them, between their twin granite forms, their purring stops. 'Tread with care child, thy world around thee is changing, bringing danger closer to thy home. Listen to thy soul and believe in thy faith.' I hold dear to me the care these ancient beings have for my welfare.

I choose my response carefully. 'But what if my head, heart and soul are all telling me different things, great ones?' I ask with a pleading tone to my voice.

'Find the common theme they are trying to betoken thou. They are *all* a part of the, and are *all* of equal importance. Thou will feel deep within when thou hast discovered their message, child.'

I smile, walk over to place a hand on one of their cold stone curves and then walk to the other and place my hand there before slowing walking into the forest and the beginning of darkness.

I only have to take a few steps before I feel my entire body start to come alive as it senses his, and I know he has also felt my presence. My heart starts to beat faster, making my blood flow with beautiful speed through my veins, causing a vibrating hum that seeps through my entire being, giving it an ache I have never felt before.

My delicate ears can hear in the distance his large heart beating against his rib cage, trying to sing a song with my own. A heated electricity rises from my toes soaring through me all the way to my scalp and exploding through to the sky above like fireworks dancing in vibrant colours. His scent now invades my mind as every step brings us closer to this copious power that only grows more with every meeting we have, a power that I know could be capable of destroying our worlds.

This thought makes me stop in my tracks after only one step into a small clearing. I must not let these feelings overtake me, I must keep control, I must ignore the shattering anguish that is splintering my soul. I have to do what's right. I have to end this before it gores any further! He continues his pace but then slows when he sees I have stopped completely, his slight grin now fading to concern when he takes in my expression and coming to a stop himself.

I take a moment to admire this handsome strong solid being who stands mere feet from me, as my eyes well with tears at just how much this demon has taken a hold of my heart in such a short amount of time. He stares as if he can see straight into my soul, a soul that's about to say goodbye. I brace myself and try to draw on the strength I have within to break apart and walk away from the biggest impact of my entire existence and the one and only person who has ever made me feel truly *alive*.

I take a deep breath, fighting hard not to give in to the trembling cry of my heart at the words I'm about to speak. 'I came to say goodbye.' His mouth opens slightly but he remains as still as stone as I continue, pushing through the pain in my chest. 'This ... this force we have created by coming together could destroy both our worlds and I will *not* risk that. Please ... please promise me that you will keep your distance from me and my home.' Those last words catch in my throat as the emotion starts to strangle me.

'Arianwen.'

One ... softly ... spoken ... word.

That's all it takes, for my head, heart and soul to come together as one, in understanding and love. Yes, that's the one word that they all agree on. This ... is ... love. Love. An emotion so potent that not even all the mighty powers in Heaven and Hell combined could harness and control or even destroy its ties. Its ties that bind two hearts together as one. That one softly spoken declaration of my name from the mouth of my demon holds more conviction in it than all the sermons I have heard for an eternity. The gatekeepers were right, I would know the moment I had the answer and this is that moment. What we have created coming together is not a power that will destroy our worlds, but a power that may one day save them.

I take the last remaining steps until I'm directly in front of his towering muscular form, looking into his large desperate blue eyes as my soul rejoices at being allowed to accept the piece of itself it always knew was missing. I reach a hand up to cup his weathered defined cheek, needing to feel our connection. He rests it upon my delicate skin and closes his eyes with a loud sigh that tugs at my heart with emotions that are so new to me.

'*Arianwen, please,* don't ask me to do this, don't ask me to say goodbye, because you and I know I cannot. As much as we should or need to, I know I cannot do as you ask, my sweet angel.'

He slowly raises his head so his eyes reach mine once more, as he desperately searches for the answer he needs, the answer he wants. I let him see deep into my soul at the emotions that are swirling around as I let my lips form a small smile, his eyes becoming hopeful as he waits for my words.

'Albion, I am *scared* at what may lie ahead for us, but I too now know that I could never say goodbye to the only one to have ever captured my heart.'

He sucks in a loud breath. His top lip trembles slightly as he speaks. 'Are you mine, Arianwen? I *need* to hear you say it, I *need* to hear you to tell me that you are truly mine.'

I can't manage to release a single word past the lump in my throat so I just nod slowly as a single tear seeps from my eye and slowly slides down my cheek. He grins ever so slowly as he reaches a finger up to my cheek to catch my falling tear with such an unexpected gentleness from this dark and rugged demon. He then places his finger in his mouth, tasting the salty essence of my body as his smile spreads over his entire beautiful face.

He then reaches for me with both his powerful hands, bringing me so close that our noses touch as he whispers, 'You are mine, you are everything to me, Arianwen.'

I can't help the joyous smile that spreads over my entire face as I finally feel like I have found my destiny. But the happy feelings that are spreading fast throughout my body are instantly turned to ice as we both jump and turn with fear at the sound of applause coming from behind Albion.

'Well, I must say, that was such a *touching* moment, brother! You must have truly lost your touch. Such a shame for such a great Hunter. I dare to say that if you have to resort to such theatrics your skills most assuredly are waning, especially if you have to use them to snare yourself a new toy. But I can understand the effort, even if they are waning. The theatrics pay for themselves when snaring this piece of winged crumpet.'

Fear starts to invade my body as my senses realise exactly what type of creature is reaching out his claw like fingers, brushing them across my feathers as if he is trying to draw my essence from me with his reptilian touch.

'She is such a fine toy indeed. This alluring piece of angelic tail is the best prize I have seen in a long, long time. You are going to be crowned a king, Albion, when you bring her back to share with the rest of our brotherhood, or is she going straight to our dark lord?'

12

Of Dreams and Virtue

ALBION

The fall, this barren patch of scorched and scarred earth, the definitive barrier between my land and theirs, an area purged of all life and left as desolate as the face of the moon. Michael has been said to have made his stand against Lucifer on this spot, their clash scarring the earth here to the very core of our world, cleansing it for eternity.

This is it, my final chance to turn back, to face my choices and take the arrows that are cast at me and my Little Wing, but can I truly do that, can I honestly put my own feelings before her safety. Can I be that selfish?

With a shuddering, almost melancholy draw of breath, I cast my arms wide, tipping myself from the edge. My wings spread from me. A searing lance of agony slices its way through me as the scaled leathery extensions of my being snap open, pulling me from my swan dive and sending me soaring through the crisp morning air.

My senses scream as I pass over the blanket of mottled greenery, the glowing life force of the forest's myriad of residents glittering like the night's stars, their scurrying owners squealing in terror as my shadow passes over them, sending them all diving into burrow and nest as I begin my descent into the emerald void below me. The wind teases my ears as I circle downwards, my ever shortening descent taking me further and further through the bows and trunks of this haven of wildlife I so loathe.

My feet kiss the loamy needle strewn floor as I feel my wings retract; the sickening sensation of my own bones realigning, making me shudder with disgust as I slowly close my eyes. My senses shifting, moving through the ether around me as the world comes alive, its face born anew as I slowly take in all that is surrounding me, the faint chattering click of carrion beetles as they devour the carcass of a squirrel.

The soft snorting of deer and boar fills my ears, the grunting of these dirt chewing sacks of meat and offal mingling with the world around me as I move towards the winding pathway, its rough uneven surface littered with twisted and buckled stone work, a glimmering spectre of a world long since past. The etched fascias staring up at me from the floor beneath my feet as I pick my way towards the clearing.

I can feel her presence drift towards me, her aura teasing, searching, reaching, seeking me out. It bathes my soul in a warmth that only she can give me, her soul grasping at mine, wanting to connect with me on the deepest level only an immortal can experience. I reach back, my aura blending with hers as I trace it through the twisting avenues and pathways that surround me to their source, to the woman that I adore and hold in my heart. Yet as I trace my way forward, soaking in the teasing, glowing pathway that Arianwen has lain at my feet, I can feel this malevolence overshadowing it all, drowning my mind in a deathly shadow that fills me with dread. Its cloak like form surrounds her aura, threatening to smother her, encase her in a mire so deep that I am not sure I could ever hope to pull her free of its cloying grasp. As I step closer to her and this malevolent blanket, my chest freezes. I know now that I have to end any contact with my wondrous angel, if for no other reason than to see her safe. I have to see this through for her sake, I have to see this to the end even if it means breaking my own heart in the process.

✦ ✦ ✦

The trees part, the light dappled clearing opening out before me as I step free of the darkened confines of the canopied pathways I had trodden only moments before. My eyes alight on the winged beauty with whom I am so completely enthralled. Can I truly do this, can I really deny the love I feel for her, can I in all honesty end this completely? If I am to be true to myself, then I know I cannot, but despite my all-consuming need to have her in my life and heart for as long as I shall live, it is all too clear to me that we must part, for the sake of not only ourselves but ultimately both our worlds; but now as she stands before me, her eyes locked with my own, I know that I can never leave her side, I can never leave this winged goddess I so adore and covet even if it means condemning us both for eternity.

Her words drill into my heart. Is she truly asking that of me, asking of me the one thing I know I cannot do? I open my mouth, begging her with my eyes, her name tripping from my tongue. My soul bleeds as her eyes sink into me, her hand skating over my skin sending ripples of agonising pleasure through me as I see the finality that echoes in her eyes. Leaning into her touch, I close my eyes, a deep sigh rolling from me as I force back the welling of raw emotion that is threatening to drown me.

'*Arianwen, please,* don't ask me to do this, don't ask me to say goodbye, because you and I know I cannot. As much as we should or need to, I know I cannot do as you ask, my sweet angel.'

She smiles at me as my eyes reach hers once more, her eyes glowing with light, deep violet pools that lead me straight to her core, her soul laid bare before me as her sumptuous rose pink lips draw me in, her words flowing through my mind as she presses herself to me. Her voice makes my heart race despite her declaration's of fear, her words trickling down through my heart as her voice trembles, words of devotion falling free as she buries her head into my chest.

'Are you mine, Arianwen? I *need* to hear you say it, I *need* to hear you tell me that you are truly mine.'

I watch in awed fascination as a single crystalline pearl slips from my angel's violet eyes, crawling across her flawless alabaster skin. Lifting my hand, I rest my fingers against her cheek, the glittering orb of her tear rolling over my fingertip as I lift it to my lips, tracing the cool diamond essence of my violet eyed queen across my tongue. The salt tang makes my body quake as I feel her roll down my throat, her angelic aura blooming through me as I sigh deep within myself.

'You are mine, you are everything to me, Arianwen.'

I watch a joy filled smile bloom across her features, my heart hammering in my chest, a sense of completion filling me as I begin to lean in, her lips calling me forth as I pull her tighter to me, her soft supple breasts pressing into my chest as I slowly glide my hands over her lithe body. Her warmth flows over me as I close my eyes, breathing in her scent as she pushes herself up towards me, her moist warm breath billowing across my neck and chin just as a wave of chilled malice fills the air.

'Well, I must say, that was such a *touching* moment, brother! You must have truly lost your touch. Such a shame for such a great Hunter. I dare to say that if you have to resort to such theatrics your skills most assuredly are waning, especially if you have to use them to snare yourself a new toy. But I can understand the effort, even if they are waning. The theatrics pay for themselves when snaring this piece of winged crumpet ...'

I watch as he moves around behind Arianwen, his lecherous gaze making my blood boil as he reaches out; his skeletal fingers flickering across the light downy feathers that edge her wings.

'She is such a fine toy indeed. This alluring piece of angelic tail is the best prize I have seen in a long, long time. You are going to be crowned a king, Albion, when you bring her back to share with the rest of our brotherhood ...'

He pauses once more, meeting my gaze as I feel my ire begin to break through the dam around my heart. 'Or, is she going straight to our dark lord?'

I stare at my kinsman, the crest seared into his leathery flesh bearing the house of Udai, his snakelike eyes boring into my own as I hold his gaze, anger coursing through me.

'She is going nowhere, "brother," this one is mine and mine alone.'

A sneering grin rolls across this peon's face as he shifts his stance, his prepubescent wings unfurling from him as he growls deep within his throat. I watch in an almost amused urgency as his hand falls to the short sword at his hip.

'Prepare yourself, brother, a prize such as that winged harlot belongs to our lord, not one of his foot guards.'

I snarl as I feel Arianwen move, her winged silhouette dancing between us as the upstart moves to attack, his fist connecting with my angel as she is cast from my gaze. My rage boils free, overflowing and engulfing my mind, an ache rolling through my skull as I feel my skin split, my horns breaking through my scalp as I charge forth with a guttural roar.

I drive my fist forwards, my hand reaching for this boy soldier's throat. My fingers close round his neck, the thick, rope like fibres rolling underneath my grip as I draw him towards me. The sound of a blade sliding over the mouth of a sheath greets my ears as I pull him towards me.

Pain lances through my side as I lift this whelp from the floor, the metallic scent of my own blood filling the air as I close my free hand around his wrist, the blade clattering to the floor moments later.

'You shouldn't have drawn on me, boy, but that is nothing compared to the pain you are about to receive, not only for the wound you have lain to me but in penance for laying finger to my woman.'

His voice comes in a choked and gargled gasp as my grip tightens, his eyes burning with hatred as I watch his free arm curling upwards. His mouth foams as he forces the appendage between us, a flare of grey tinged light fills my eyes as I am catapulted backwards, landing with a bone rattling thump.

A wry chuckle slips from me as I wipe blood soaked dust from my jaw and cheek. The whelp stands there, chest heaving and eyes glowing red and bloodshot.

'A soul caster. Udai must be getting desperate to be pulling you from the toy box, boy. Do you have any idea how many of your kind, the abominations spun into being by Udai, that I have cut down in my rise to the head of the sixth legion? Do you, boy?'

The insignia branding in the boy's chest starts to fluoresce, a shimmering blue light flowing forth as I crouch low. I ease my blade from its sheath, the wolfen core screaming for blood as I begin to circle to the right, easing my glutinous weapon into a more solid hold. The boy feints with his left hand, sweeping his leg right at my knees. Dancing away, I smash my fist down, the pommel of my weapon driving hard into the joint of his ankle, a snarl of guttural pain leaping from his lips as I push forwards, seizing my advantage.

He staggers backwards as a blinding burst of incandescent light fills my eyes, stunning my mind in a flash of white hot agony as the whelp vanishes before me. The pattering sound of feet is my only warning before his razor edged weapon cleaves the air in twain where my head had been mere moments before. My blade scythes upwards as I feel the air ripple around my head, the metallic clang of steel on steel taunting my ears as I twist my grip, feeling the edge bite into this boy's wrist, tendons parting and blood coursing over my arm and shoulder as I roll free.

His screams fill the air, carrion crows rising like souls of the lost, their shadows dancing over us both as they flee the sound of his anguish. The whelp's twitching hand hits the floor with a wet thunk as his cold wrought blade tumbles free. I turn my eyes to him, his eyes bulging as he stares at the ruby red fluid pumping from the stump that once held his hand.

'I told you, boy, you're not the first caster I have torn asunder, nor will you be the last; how sadistic and self-loathing can you be to want to shear off pieces of your own soul to throw pretty lights at your enemy? Are you truly that idiotic, child? But it matters not what you are or what you aren't, do you wish a fast end to this, or are you going to continue this wanton act of futility?'

His eyes burn into me as I watch the branded emblem ignite, undulating walls of light flowing across him as his eyes shimmer, bursting as his body begins to split and fracture. 'I'll show you futility, Hunter. I may be taking my own life, but you will be torn down with me. Here is the true power me and my brother casters hold. See the heat of a truly free soul!'

I throw myself aside, my body landing atop my angel as this wretched cur finally casts himself from existence, his corporeal form shattering in a searing ball of heat and energy, his soul vaporising all it touches as it billows out from him in a rolling wave. My skin crackles slightly as I push myself upright, my body screaming at me as the final dregs of my enemy's burnt soul fades to nothing.

I stare down at my arms, my armour crumbling as I move, twisted and heat scorched flesh peeling and sloughing away as I rise. The scent of my own roasted flesh sits, squatting like a fat rat on my tongue as I stumble to the side of my soul mate.

The scent of her hair fills my senses as I stare down at her, a wry smile finding its way to my lips as I shift my weight to my knees, brushing my sweet angel's hair away from the side of her face. I shake her shoulder gently, her name trickling from my lips as I watch her soft features searching for a sign of acknowledgement.

'Arianwen ... my love ... answer me. Please, my sweet, answer me.'

Panic rolls through me as I turn her onto her back, my eyes searching her soft and motionless features for anything. Franticly I let my hands wander as my mind slips into a time honed zone, my fingers searching, teasing, sensing every undulation, every movement, every facet of her form as she lies there as silent as a frozen grave; the scarlet rent in her smooth seamless skin standing stark against her pale visage.

Lifting her limp and unconscious form from the floor, I feel her feather light frame roll into my grip, ruby red droplets falling in a glittering string from her cheek as her wings tickle my skin. The scent of charred and burnt leather filling my nostrils as I lever myself upright and walk cautiously back into the darkened warren of trees and shadows.

✦ ✦ ✦

The door clacks shut behind me, the gloom filled hovel doing little to alleviate my fear and worry as I move through what remains of this shack's furniture. The torn and gutted remains of an easy chair fills one corner, the squirming pink offspring of a family of mice filling the air with a discordant melody as they squeak for their mother.

I push past the twisted hulk of the roof, the slanted shafts of light punctuating the air, dust swirling and dancing in their golden radiance as I duck low, moving under the fungus choked beam and twisted sheet metal that blocks my path. All the while, she hangs limp in my grasp, her downy snow white wings tickling my blistered skin, her glowing radiance soothing my seared flesh as I move through this squalid façade.

I stare at the wall in front of me, the rock face baring the scars of a thousand passing generations. I feel my way with my eyes, my gaze travelling along its ridged and chipped fascia guiding me, as I turn my head searching for the slither of what shouldn't be. The dancing edge of rock latching onto my gaze as I move forwards, a twisting serpentine tunnel emerging before my eyes as I step through the gap, disappearing into the very heart of the cliff before me.

My chambers open out like the halls of a cathedral as I move towards my bed, the raised shelf of granite rising from the floor like a plinth. The thick fur that covers my one luxury standing stark against the dark rock that surrounds me and my unconscious love.

My footsteps echo, casting a rapacious cadence as I stop gazing down at my angel as I slowly, with reverent care and tenderness, lay her on my bed. The thick mattress moulding around her slender form as she sinks into the padded top. I smile as I perch lightly next to her, brushing the stray strands of hair from her face, the wound in her scalp already stitching itself together as I watch the wavering golden luminescence slip from the slowly closing tear.

Watching that glowing laceration slowly erase itself from being, I feel my heart lurch. I turn away, my stomach churning with the knowledge that my inability to protect my soul mate, the one woman I truly love, is the reason she now lies wounded and unconscious on my bed. I lift the pelt slowly, drawing it up across her legs, settling the thick bear skin over her as I turn away. My self-loathing boils up from my core as I move towards the shadowed workbench in the far corner of the connecting chamber.

I watch as my breath fogs and swirls, hanging in the air before me as I move away from my bed, walking through the low ceilinged passage, into the my work chamber. I snort at my own fanciful thoughts as I reflect on just what my angel is lying upon.

A mattress, the cotton swaddled collection of feathers and springs cushioning her form, something so commonplace for one of Arianwen's lineage. It is not something a demon would ever find themselves owning, and yet, here I am, in my hidden home; this swathed secret hidden by the ancient rocks and long lost home of a family long since forgotten to the annals of time.

I run my fingers across the runes etched into the monumental walls around me, bearing the sight of Angel and Demon alike, reflecting on that one source of vanity I have ever succumbed to.

Kneeling before my hearth, I pluck the split lumber from the pile, laying it atop the kindling and char cloth. Laying my finger at the base of the rag tag pile, I whisper, the soft mumbled incantation spreading through me as I drag my nail along the split and feathered kindling, watching it glow and smoke before, with a flick of my wrist and sudden snatch of my distended nail, it bursts into flame. The heat and rolling *whoosh* of pummelled air assaults me as I push myself upright.

Heat slowly begins to chase the chill from the air around me, the hearth's dancing glow casting spectral shadows, their dancing wavering forms an all too accurate imitation of that seething den of debauchery and my cloying cell that I so long to forever leave behind. Sitting at the bench, I draw back the oiled cloth. The shimmering of polished metal and boiled and waxed leather greet my eyes as I lift my tools from the block and set to work.

My mind dances as I push the final rivet through the thick cloth backed hide, my anger searing through me as the tools slip from my grip, my hands curling into fists as I pound them into the top of the bench, my knuckles tearing, my blood coursing through the torn and ragged flaps of skin soaking into the wooden surface beneath me; I grit my teeth, franticly staving off the need to scream.

How could I have been so careless? How can I protect the woman I love when the first instance of our truly coming together is punctuated by this? My eyes travel through the dancing gloom to the softly breathing form that lies swaddled in my bed, my heart hammering in my chest as blood seeps between my fingers. I feel my nails slowly extend, piercing my palms.

She was hurt because of me. She was in danger because of me, because of my lustful need for her, I will always be a source of danger to her; this scuffle with another of my twisted kin proves this better than my own words ever could. She stepped between me and my assailant because of what we have between us, even when she knew she was woefully outmatched. She now lies unconscious on my bed because of me.

If I hadn't ended that whelp's life, the outcome could have and would have been vastly different, and I don't know if I can face that again.

As One

ARIANWEN

The feel of something soft under my fingertips awakens me with haste as my eyes shoot open looking for danger. My last memory of standing between Albion and one of his kin vividly comes to life as my heart starts to race and my breathing comes in quick gasps. I sit up straight and push backwards with my legs, my back connecting with hard stone. I stretch my arms out in front of me, ready to defend myself as my mind slowly begins to catch up and realises I'm no longer in the forgotten forest. My eyes search the darkness, seeing nothing but stone walls through the flickering of light which seems to be coming from a small fire in a connecting room.

My head starts to pound. I brush a finger over my forehead and feel raised flesh that my gifts have already started to heal, but my memory cannot supply me with how it came to be there. I should have fear, I should be wary. I have no idea where I am, but ... I know I am safe because I can feel *him* nearby and know that he would never allow harm to grip me. I look down and notice that the softness beneath my fingertips is fur, white fur, I think, and it is covering something soft. I look towards the edges of the pelt, my eyes straining in the dull light and recognise a mattress, something similar to what my family and I have in Eden.

I can sense that my guardian has slept on this same bedding, but I'm finding it hard to comprehend such a rough vicious demon caring for such soft luxuries. I can smell his scent everywhere as I run my fingers through the fur beneath me and start to believe he has brought me to where he resides, to where he calls home. Does a demon even use the word home? My comfortable feeling starts to dissolves as I realise I have no idea how my guardian or his kin lives or even behaves away from the hunting I have witnessed them perform.

I have always felt as if I had enough life experience and teachings to know all there is about the evil ones, but as I sit here in a darkened cave like room, on soft bedding, in the residence of a demon, I begin to believe I am not very knowledgeable at all, that I still have a lot to learn, a lot to experience, yet I'm unsure if my angelic essence is truly strong enough to withstand the struggles and danger which now seem like a definitive part of my future.

I know I have to move, I know I have to return to the safety of my own world, but I am suddenly nervous to see the demon that I now know with complete and utter certainty has claimed my heart as his. There are so many unknowns between us, so many unanswered questions, I don't know where to start. The last time I saw him, I was standing between him and one of his brothers and I have no memory as to how that ended or how much time has passed. Is he hurt or injured? Has his fellow kin gone to get reinforcements? Is that why we are hiding amongst stone walls? If so, how will I return safely to my own home?

I will not find these answers hiding in my guardian's bed. I have to face him sooner or later so I shuffle to the edge, my wings tucked away tightly under the skin of my sides and place my bare feet quietly on the cold rock below me. A chill rises up my spine as soon as they land. I look around but cannot sight my head piece, white boots or my cloak anywhere so I rise on my naked feet and slowly step towards the flickering glow which is calling from the other room as a shiver racks my body. I brace a hand on the curve of the rock and take a deep breath to brace myself for the sight of the man who has claimed me.

I slowly take a step, moving with an experienced whisper, unsure as to what my eyes will find when my body turns this corner. I slowly lean into the edge as I bring another step around. The light of a large open fireplace is what hits my eyes first, but they are quickly overtaken by the presence of his larger than life form sitting astride a stool, bent over with his head in his hands, seeming to be lost in his own thoughts. He has not detected my aura yet so I take the time to admire all that he is.

His broad back, white cotton stretched tight across it showing every line of his muscles. His dark silken hair hanging down, caressing his neck, brushing his shoulders. His large rippled arms, elbows resting on his leather clad knees, hands reaching up, wrapped on either side of his head, his fingers buried in his hair. His shoulders up high around his neck in a tense position, heat, fear, uncertainty radiating from his every pore, and something else, dare I call it ... sadness?

His fingers slide out from his hair. He sits up straight; he has felt my presence yet he doesn't turn as he speaks. 'I'm sorry you were injured, it shouldn't have happened, it will *never* happen again, I promise you that,' he says in a low growl.

I know it is not aimed at me, but at himself for what I can only guess is the small bump on my head which my body has all but healed. I'm unsure as to how to respond, but he blaming himself is making my heart ache. I take the few steps to stand directly behind him and place my small soft hand on his large shoulder and whisper, 'It's okay.'

'No it's not!' he roars as he stands, knocking over the stool he was sitting on, and turns to face me. I can't help my reaction as I jump and take a step back from his looming angry form. He takes a step towards me as I take another back, his forehead wrinkling with concern at my flinching as he takes a large deep breath.

'I'm sorry, Arianwen,' he says in an almost whisper, pleading with his eyes for me to accept this apology. I go to open my mouth to speak but my words are lost looking at the depth of emotions so strongly showing across this demon's face. The man who makes me feel like my heart has only just discovered how to beat for the first time.

He comes closer and I welcome his advance this time; his eyes bore into mine as he lets me see through his façade and all the way through to his fragile soul. He slowly reaches a hand up towards the lump on my forehead, gauging my reaction before finally and very softly makes contact, slowly gliding one of his fingers over the raised flesh in a tender caress. He moves his finger down to my skin, his touch electrifying, before bringing up his other hand to cup both of my cheeks, cradling my face within his strong protective grip, looking at me with such a sweet innocence that completely disarms me.

He leans in calmly and places a feather light kiss on my small wound, making me melt in his hold, then pulls back to once more catch my gaze. *'Arianwen,'* he breaths out in an almost prayer like plea as he leans his forehead against mine. A plea for me to see the real him, to take a risk on this dangerous liaison, to take a risk and open my whole heart up to him. A Demon, an eternal enemy of my kin! Oh God! How can I risk putting my world and my loved ones in the danger this connection will bring?

Before my panic has a chance to rise he leans down and lays his lips gently upon mine, holding me firmly to him as his lips move over mine, his taste and touch sending me into delirium as he takes a large breath in, consuming my essence, letting it dance over his lips and slipping down into his all-consuming depths. My heart is pounding in my chest, trying to break out and grip him hard, never to let go. He brushes his lips back and forth slowly over mine. I moan into his mouth ... and that's all it takes for the gentleness to cease.

His fingers move to entwine in my hair. Gripping my scalp firmly, he pushes me backwards until I slam against the rock wall with the force of his body pushing into me. I yelp at the pain when my body hits the solid surface.

'Arianwen,' he pleads with me, begging me to submit as his hands move from my hair slowly to my shoulders and make their way leisurely down my arms, pushing them behind my back until

he grips my wrists, bringing them together to be held tightly in one hand, as his other hand reaches up to cradle the back of my head so my body is no longer against the unforgiving rock surface behind me. His body still pressing into my every curve as his lips start to devour me.

He is consuming me, taking what he wants, what he needs and giving me all the emotions he has to offer. His tongue pushing into my mouth, demanding that my own joins this sensual dance he has created. The friction that arises shoots through my entire body until it reaches the apex of my thighs, setting on fire the bud of my arousal as it swells and throbs with need, begging for more as his body moulds perfectly into mine. My body's juices now flooding my panties as it goes into overdrive with heat and need.

His lips grow urgent as he pulls back slightly to bring his tongue out, tracing my lips in an agonisingly slow pace, lapping at my very essence as I pant into his mouth, *'Albion.'*

His name tipping from my lips sends him into a frenzy. The hand that was holding my wrists lets go and spreads over my entire buttocks, pushing me further into his throbbing leather covered length, causing my bud to burn further. He is pushing, trying to get closer, trying to crawl inside my own skin. He moves his hand down further until he reaches between my legs and brushes my centre lightly.

I gasp loudly at the contact and throw my head back in pleasure as my body feels like it could explode into a million small pieces with the next touch.

He growls deep inside his chest as the hand between my thighs lifts up hard in one movement, my legs rising and wrapping around his solid waist in an utterly natural response. He grunts as he pushes to me, back against the wall, still carefully cradling my head in his large hand, his lips continuing to dance over mine in an all-consuming pleasure.

We are both panting, almost gasping for air, our heartbeats racing in time with the other as he grinds against my centre where I can feel his throbbing length grow.

'I need to feel you my sweet angel, I need to feel your soft moist

skin beneath my fingertips. But if it's no, then tell me now as I can barely restrain myself,' he says into my mouth, pulling back slightly to look into my eyes, looking for a sign of uncertainty.

I want this, I want all he has to offer, my mind, body and soul feels like it is alive for the first time and I don't want these feelings to stop! I want to grab them, embrace them and return them to him. I give him my answer by leaning in and using my tongue to trace his lips in a bold move I never imagined myself being able to do.

He bends his knees slightly to give support to my body as he moves his hand from under me and around between both our bodies, between the wet heat we have already created as my hands reach up to grip his shoulders. He gathers my white dress up into his fingers and pulls it up higher and out of the way as his hand touches my stomach, splaying his fingers out wide and pressing in firmly, making my ache grow as he slides it down until he reaches the top of my panties and continues to push down slowly until he reaches the wetness that has seeped through them.

'I can't wait any longer,' he growls loudly as he moves his hand to the groove of my thigh and pushes my panties to the side with his thumb as he lets two fingers slide softly over my wet centre.

He sucks a large breath in as he growls again, bringing his fingers back up and this time pressing firmer as they glide down and *into* my wet folds.

'Albion!' I scream out, unable to contain the pressure that is building up inside my form, bubbling over as I lean forward and claim his lips in a heated kiss.

He takes control and bites my lip, sucking it firmly into his mouth before releasing it and soothing the swollen flesh with the petting of his lips. He brings his fingers slowly back up again before pushing down through my slick folds and continues further until I feel his fingers at my entrance.

I tense, tense at my desperate want, at the unknown, at the fear of what my body is about to experience, at the fear I may never be the same after this encounter, that I may never be able to return to my quiet reserved life again without the thoughts of my demon racing constantly through my mind. He doesn't give me a second longer to think about it as he pushes one finger into my centre, my quiet moan dying in the shadow of his load roar.

'My sweet, sweet angel!' His scream of passion echoes off the walls of this granite room, igniting every nerve of my existence.

He doesn't hold back as he adds another finger and groans as he slides them both in and out, creating a delicious friction that is driving me crazy.

'Albion, please!' I plead, plead for a relief to the agonising ache that has taken over my whole body, an ache that is burning in my stomach, an ache that is building with every slide of his fingers in my wet centre. I feel a building that threatens to overcome me, but I want it, I want to feel everything he is giving me, I want this experience with him, only him.

I feel like I'm going to lose my mind as every part of my existence hangs on the edge of oblivion as he continues to devour my mouth with a fast frantic kiss that is seeping into every pore of my body while he continues moving his fingers, quickening his pace as he pants harder into my mouth as I whimper into his.

I'm there … on the edge … waiting to fall …

'No!' I yell as he pulls his fingers free from me as I painfully hang on the edge.

'Oh, my sweet angel, you deserve more than to be taken up against a wall,' he says in a gravelled tone as he embraces me harder to his body, wrapping one arm around my waist while the other supports my buttocks, lifting me to him as he carries me to the room I woke in.

He stops at the foot of the bed, holding me tight, staring into my eyes with the deepest emotions I have ever seen on another being before. 'Mine,' he whispers. I nod at his heartfelt declaration as his lips gently glide over mine. He places both knees on the bed, still holding me tight as he shuffles up the bed before slowly lowering me down until me back connects with the softness of the fur.

He then proceeds to kiss down my entire body. Slowly across my jaw, moving down to my neck, to my collarbone, where he bites before soothing it with his tongue which then draws a line down to my still covered cleavage. He begins using his large fingers to unbutton my white cotton dress, not breaking his sensual lips from mine, but after only two, he grunts in frustration and rips it open instead, from the top all the way to the bottom hem. Buttons fly and land with subtle clicks on the rock ground bedside the bed as he wastes no time in reaching behind my back and ripping the straps of my brassiere, flinging it behind him as he removes his lips from mine and bends down to connect them to one of my nipples.

I scream out at the pleasurable pain as the sensual burn travels all the way to my wet centre, my body arching up underneath him, making us fuse together even more as he pushes me back down deep into the soft mattress. His hard shaft almost breaks though my delicate cotton panties, burning, wanting, needing to feel him bare at the centre of my arousal. He laps at my nipple before moving to the other, giving it a bite which makes me scream into this darkened room.

He continues his travels, biting, licking, kissing down my entire form until he reaches the apex of my thighs and places a hard kiss on the top of my panties that makes me moan and wither beneath him.

'I need to taste you, Arianwen. I need your sweet juices flowing over my tongue and down my throat,' he says without giving me any time to let those sinful words truly set in as he rips my panties from my body, throwing them to the side and then brushes his tongue from my entrance, through my folds and pushes it against my swollen bud ... and that's all it takes!

I scream with all the air I have left as a raging inferno explodes around my centre and races through my entire body. 'Please, please Albion!' I scream and scream as the sensation sets off fireworks all over my sensitive skin, from the inside to the outside of my trembling flesh as he continues to lap up all the juices that are flowing like a stream from my bubbling centre.

'Oh, my sweet angel tastes better than anything in all the immortal worlds combined,' he rushes out as he pushes his tongue all the way into my dripping core.

I scream at such a delicious intrusion. The feeling of his thick, hot, coarse tongue moving, rubbing against my entrance and into the sides of my internal walls is taking my breath away. I gasp as my body struggles to come down from the massive high it just experienced as I feel it building again.

No! I can't! I will not survive another fall from such a great height, I am still seeing stars behind my eyes as my head floats in a dazed state, swimming in a sea of euphoria.

'I need more, I need one more, my Little Wing,' he roars as he replaces his tongue with two fingers, pushing in and out franticly as he uses his tongue to lap through my folds and over my bud that is swelling with each pass.

I thrust my hands in his hair, wrapping my fingers around the silken strands and pull hard as I try and anchor my body to this world. His arousing growl vibrating against my throbbing bud adds to the erotic sensations he is creating with his tongue. I never knew pleasure could be like this, this extreme, this frantic, this explosive, this consuming! I had imagined it to be slow, sweet, gentle and civilized but this ... is anything but civil. This is wild, fast and utterly raw!

His tongue presses hard on my centre as he curls his fingers to the front of my internal walls, creating a new sensation that pushes me over that edge of pleasure once more. 'Albion!' I scream as I struggle to catch my breath, desperately trying to gasp in some air, feeling faint as I fall fast once more and land with an earth shattering crash beneath his large looming body.

'I need you, I need to feel you, Arianwen. Tell me, tell me I will be the first and only. Tell me you are truly mine,' he desperately pleads with me. I can barely register his words as I feel him move over me, removing his leather trousers before settling his weight against me once again.

I have been feeling his hard shaft moving against me, but this, feeling his heated, sweat licked naked flesh throbbing against my swollen bud is extraordinary! He uses his knees to spread my thighs wide as he stares into my glassy eyes, searching once more for any hesitation as to what's about to transpire. One side of his mouth starts to lift in a seductive smirk as he leans over my body and positions himself at the entrance of my core, the tip of his heated manhood teasing my entrance as my body tenses in anticipation. He pushes in slightly, my body clamping up at this foreign intrusion, uncertain as to how to react.

'*Let go, Arianwen,*' he whispers in my ear and then claims my mouth in a soft slow kiss, trying to calm my body, and I am lost. Lost to him and how alive he has made me feel. And I do exactly what he commands me to do.

I let go ...

He pushes all the way in with one hard thrust, making me scream out in pain and pleasure as I feel a tear, breaking me away from who I was, to become who I'm meant to be and that is his, to own completely. The intense pain at his manhood's rampant intrusion is slowly bleeding into pure pleasure as my body rises to meet his, asking, begging for more. He grabs my arms and pushes them above my head, holding my wrists in a tight grip, not moving, frozen in time, savouring this feeling as we finally become one. The feel of him pressed firmly against all my internal walls is almost too much to bear as I yet again struggle to breathe in amongst this carnal lust.

His intense stare shows me that he is only holding on by the finest of threads as he begins to draw himself from within me, dragging his heaving throbbing flesh along my over sensitive walls as he almost slips free from my unforgiving grip, to then drive himself deep within my writhing core again as I can't help the scream that escapes my lips. 'Albion!'

He attacks my mouth in an almost insatiable frenzy as he reaches one hand down and under my knee, bringing it up high to my chest, driving in deeper, embedding himself in my clutching core, giving me more pleasure in a single movement than I've had in a an entire lifetime.

'You are mine, and I am incapable of letting you go. You are my addiction, Arianwen, and I want more,' he proclaims as he thrusts in repeatedly, not slowing, not stopping, taking everything my body is offering him. My juices are flowing like a river all over his solid shaft. I feel that now familiar build starting again, giving me an insatiable yearning that travels all over my inflamed flesh.

He lets go of my wrists and brings that hand down to my breasts, kneading, pinching my nipple, twisting it to the point of pain before his lips disappear from my mouth and latch onto the nipple between his fingertips. He sucks hard, his excited growl vibrating the sensitive skin surrounding it as he then uses his teeth to cause a more euphoric pain at the same time as he sends his hand down, shooting between my legs, pinching the centred bud of my arousal ... sending me over the edge of oblivion.

I scream his name over and over again, begging, pleading for this to never end, pleading for him to catch me as I fall from a greater height than my own wings have ever reached. My body trembles and pulsates as if all my nerves are screaming at once. Every piece of my entire body has come to life in a way I never thought possible.

His movements over me are now as chaotic as a tumultuous storm as he pants and growls, finally losing all control, and what an exquisite sight it is to see. He thrusts twice more before his final thrust results in an cataclysmic explosion, his essence pouring inside of me like a raging heated river, joining with mine, dancing as one, two missing pieces finding themselves after an eternity apart.

'Arianwen!'

Water forms in my eyes then rolls down my cheeks at the depth of emotions I can see swirling inside his beautiful blue eyes which are now trained on mine as he continues to move slowly inside of me, calmly pushing and dragging, finally releasing our mighty grips, both of us eventually coming back down from the clouds of lust to the lands of our immortal worlds. He settles his weight gently between my legs, still inside of me as he softly kisses my tears away while whispering my name over and over again.

He cradles my head in one of his large strong hands while he uses the fingers of his other to slowly trail over all of my sensitive skin, raising bumps as he moves from my neck, down my collarbone, softly between my now swollen breasts, over my stomach and slowly back up again, all the while laying feather light kisses all over my face. The fact that he can turn from a ravenous lust filled beast only moments ago, to this soft sweet man needing this gentle touch, just melts my heart even further.

I bring a hand from behind his neck and slowly run it down his cheek, wanting to return his loving caress, wanting him to know the depth of my own emotions. He leans into my touch and releases a long sigh, as our wordless actions speak volumes amongst this stone cavern that we lie in. If poets and writers from the many lifetimes of the mortal world have written about such extraordinary heights of love, what words could possibly describe what we, two immortals, just experienced? I doubt there have been any words powerful enough to describe it in all of the worlds combined.

14

Lust and Caution

ALBION

I cradle my angel in my arms, her sweat licked form curling against me as she trails a glistening path of tender kisses along my neck and chest, her lips fluttering over me like the wings of a butterfly. I tense sharply as I feel her teeth close on my nipple, a mischievous giggle emanating from my winged lover.

The shimmering mirth in her eyes makes my heart dance as I lay my lips to hers, her essence soaking through me as I roll her atop me, my angel's thighs sliding along my sides as I feel her soaked wetness press into my abdomen, the warmth leaving a glistening trail along my carved flesh.

'You own me, Arianwen, always have. From the very first moment I laid eyes upon your gold laced form, you have captivated my very soul. I am yours mind, body, heart and soul, and I would murder God himself if it were to see you for but a second longer.'

I slip my fingers along her smooth cream tinged skin, her warmth flowing through me as I trace the curves of her hips, a soft sigh rolling from her lips as I slowly, teasingly walk my fingers along her ribs. A gentle smile blossoms over her flushed features as she begins to grind her silken folds against my stomach, her pink flushed form shivering as I drag my nails along the sides of her breasts.

A shuddering gasp of excitement and pleasure meets my ears as I graze my lengthening nails over her nipples, the sensitive buds of rose pink flesh hardening once more under my slow, teasing ministrations. I watch in gleeful fascination as her eyes shadow, her core quivering against my skin as I feel her heated cream slip down my stomach, trailing down over my smooth shorn pubis, coating my shivering agates in her juices, the pink tinge making my heart weep as I roll upwards, my lips folding around her hardened buds as I draw my teeth over the softly wrinkled flesh.

Pulling my lips from her wet nub, I purse my lips, blowing gently over the overtly sensitive bulb, her back arching against me as she squeals, her folds rippling against my skin as I draw back, my thickened member slipping through her soft wet centre, bolts of exquisite abandon rolling through me as I push myself from the feathered slab beneath us, lifting my heavenly maiden with me.

She clings to me, her hips driving her sodden core along my length as I move away from the warm and lust filled sanctity of our bed. She never stops, her movements becoming frantic as she pants into my neck, the moist warmth of her breath rolling down my chin as her wetness carves a trail down my stomach and along my urgently throbbing length, my need to release burning through me as I near my one true source of selfish vanity.

The water pours down over our naked forms, my hands drifting over her body, the sheer sensual flood making my heart hammer in my chest as she leans her back against me, her pert, toned backside pressing into me as she lifts her hands up, reaching over her head as the slim digits encircle my neck. A hum of utter contentment lifts from her as she submits to my every caress, her eyes fluttering closed as I clutch the thick pad of natural sponge in my hand and send its water soaked mass slipping over her engorged nipples and on down over the flat edifice of her stomach.

The swell of her mons greets my wandering hand as the sponge slips from my grip, my fingers and palm sliding over her water slicked form, slowly vanishing into the wanton depths that call to me from between my angel's thighs.

The feel of her warmth clutching my searching fingers makes me swell further than I have ever been before, the rapturous pain throbbing through my loins as I curl my fingers, the mix of our conjoined essence flowing over my probing digits as I slowly, delicately draw them from her. The supple shiver that rolls through her as I finally draw free of her tender clutching folds makes my heart sing. I lift my hand to the level of my eye, the glistening fusion of our most intimate connection coating my palm as the water pushes it from my grip, the pale tinge of red that slips down my wrist, dripping to the floor below filling my mind as I feel my lover move in my grip.

'Ari ...'

My words are a mere whisper as I feel my little angel melt in my arms, my lips scant millimetres from her ear, strands of her glistening hair clinging to my chin and cheek, as my fingers once more travel over her sides, the rippled line of skin that dances under my fingers drawing me up towards her shoulders as I flick my tongue over her ear lobe.

'My light, my love, I ...'

She turns in my arms her firm breasts pressing into my chest as her lips find mine, a soft smile dancing from her lips to her eyes as she catches my lip between her teeth, her soft bite tugging at my skin before, with a soft pop, it slips free of her nibbling grip, her words stilling my voice.

'I know, Albion, I know, there is no one in these worlds that I would ever give my heart to, I have never felt more safe or protected than I do with you.'

I stare into her eyes as she intertwines her fingers with my hair as I lose all semblance of logical thought.

'I will always protect you, come whatever may, Angel or Demon, friend or foe, nothing will pass, nothing will break our bond or my promise.' She lays her head on my chest listening to the beating rhythm of my heart, as my words continue to fill the space between us. 'But, above all this, Arianwen, my angel, my light ...' I cup her chin once more drawing her gaze to my eyes.

'I love you.'

I watch her glistening violet orbs, they scream at me, telling me, 'Yes, I love you too,' but the words never come. The simple string of dedicated affection never making its way free of her plump rose tinged lips, as I lock her gaze firmly with mine. Indecision and doubt warring within her, fighting against the affirmation of our union and love that I know she feels, deep within the core of her very soul.

The look of utter indecision spears me, carving its way through my heart and down into my soul. I feel the shuddering wave of pain and anguish break over the rocks that are forming around my heart, keeping the pain from my shores. I throw myself into the arms of my own need and desire, drawing my angel to me, my lips once more finding hers as I sink into her embrace.

Her arms snake around my neck as I pull her water soaked form to me. I feel her wings unfurl, water cascading over her crystal white feathers, their downy forms folding around us as my burgeoning length slips along her quivering, passion soaked velvet, her sex blossoming around me as she draws me in, her taught, firm legs folding around my waist, the simplicity of her movements in pure synchronicity to my own. The natural almost instinctive action drawing us closer together than I ever thought we could be as a winsome, lust filled gasp fills my mouth, her tongue dancing over mine, my angel's warmth engulfing the hardened length of my spear as I sink deeper into her sheathing silk.

I feel the soft kiss of her feathers along my skin, my fear, anger, sorrow melting away, soothing the raging indecision and pain that has so plagued my living memory. Never before have I felt such completion, such utter peace, as I have when I am in my angelic lover's embrace.

Her weight settles into me as I push us both forwards, the cold stone sending a shiver through us both as I feel it press deep into my arm. Ari's clutching warmth tightens around me as the shocking cold rolls down her spine, my hips driving me ever deeper into her slick depths as she gasps and pants into my neck, her bruised lips cupping my collarbone as I feel her teeth sink into my leathery skin.

A deep ecstasy filled growl rolls up from the depths of my stomach as I slide my hands over her hips, her firm buttocks filling my hands as I dig my fingers into her pliant flesh, forcing her down onto me as I sink ever further into her wet warmth. The need for release rising from me once more as I feel the remnants of our lust and love filled joining flow from her, spilling out from my angel's core, soaking me in our conjoined purity.

A guttural growl peels from me, boiling up from my chest as I feel my agates tighten, sending searing jets of my pearl white seed deep into my angel, her silken folds clutching around me as she casts her head back into the steaming stream of water that cascades around us both, a soft keening groan slipping from her lips as she joins me once more in rapturous bliss as her body releases all to me.

I trail my fingers over her skin as we lie swathed in the thick bear pelt, the flickering glow of the fire casting dancing spectral forms across the caverns wall. I breathe in deeply, her scent mingling with the cherry filled smoke of the burning logs. My lips graze her shoulder as I let my hand dance over her stomach, the soft undulating muscles rippling against my fingers as I feel her shiver against me. I let my wings slip free, curling around my angel as she burrows deeper into my grip; my mind swirls as I feel this cold wave wash over us both, a drawing sense of foreboding filling us as I feel my angel tense.

'Ari, tell me what is it that plagues you so much, this pall of malevolence has shadowed your every step for a dozen cycles and as much as I endeavour to, I cannot find its source. Please, my love, tell me what is it; I cannot bear the thought of something threatening you that is so beyond my reach, the knowledge that I could do something to rid it from your life and was unable to do so, for the want of its name would tear my soul apart.'

She turns her eyes, finding mine. A soft smile teases her lips as I brush stray strands of corn golden hair from her brow, the silk strands gliding along my calloused skin as I stare down into the iridescent violet pools that have so captured my soul.

My lips find hers in a soft longing kiss as the warmth of the fire washes over us both. Drawing away from the tender moment, the taste of her on my lips and tongue, I once more beseech her to tell me what is shadowing her every moment. A chaste look of fear laced bemusement flickers across her face as she looks away from me, the tension that settles into her saying more than words ever could.

'Is this shade of a creature really so great that you are afraid to speak its very name, Arianwen?'

I cup her chin drawing her gaze to mine once more, my fingers pressing softly into her jaw. Her gentle caress passes across the taught chapped skin of my knuckles as she turns her cheek into my palm, her eyes slipping closed slowly as she sighs, her voice soft and low as she finally begins to speak.

'Albion, I don't know what you're sensing around me, but please, there is nothing shadowing me, there is nothing darkening my steps. The only force I feel when I am out there laying claim to the lost and the weary is your comforting energy, the one thing I gladly accept from all of this. Please, my sweet, believe me, there is nothing out there, man nor beast.'

Shifting my position, the dull ache that fills my backside drains away as I pull Arianwen into my lap, my arms folding around her as my wings fold back, heat flooding over us both as the crisp chill of the night's air begins to leech slowly into us both, the soft breeze that flows from the narrow entrance.

Pushing the pelt from around us, I plant a soft kiss on my angel's neck before gently lifting her from my lap and pad quietly towards the door, dragging the concertina timber and leather door across the entry way.

I feel her eyes upon me, moving over my naked form as I turn back towards her, her eyes roving over my body as I smirk, her words ringing in my head casting a dark river of doubt through my mind as I cock my head to the side slightly, watching her eyes move in tandem with every step I take, a slight chuckle echoing from me as I finally reach our fur lined nest.

'Ari, I know what I felt and what dogs you even now is like nothing I have ever felt before. It's deep and filled with anger so pure that it makes the malevolence of my kin seem like love's first kiss. Now please, my darling, don't cast me for a fool, tell me the truth.'

I watch her eyes darken as she turns away from me, her arms folding across herself as the pelt slips from her shoulders and bunches around her hips, a soft whimpering sigh lifting from her lips as she turns her back on me.

'Please, Albion, don't force this from me. I am not sure what it is myself. I know it is something dark, something close, but please, do not make me put a name to something I am unsure is even real; I have left it lingering in the shadows of my own world, the small dark spots of Eden that hide all of God's little secrets and I fear that this, whatever it is, is one such dark secret. So I beg you, please leave it be, if or when the time is right I will tell you, but for now can't we just enjoy what little time we have together.'

I nod, watching the pleading look in her eyes swell, the echoing thank you that ghosts behind it all casting aside the pain and fear she had felt mere moments before. With a soft sigh, Arianwen once more leans into my embrace as we settle into the cocooning warmth of the animal fur as the hearth fire continues to crack and snap.

'What are we, Albion, what can we really call us, this situation we are so wrapped up in? I struggle to find a name for any of this.'

I slowly run my fingers through her hair, the solitary blonde strands that slip down the side of her face curling between my fingers as I struggle to find the words she wants to hear.

'Arianwen, I honestly don't know. I do know I love you. I have from the very first moment my eyes caught your aura trailing through the branches of that ancient apple tree. I would sit for hours and watch my little angel play, your laughter filling my dreams even then, as I trailed in my father's footsteps; but as for what we are, well, we are what we are, an Angel and a Demon, although I detest that word. I am a living being, not some vengeful spirit humans can call forth with candles and chalk circles. We are also two complete polar opposites, you, my Little Wing, are a Reclaimer ...'

I feel her shift in my arms as my fingers trail through her golden tresses, a soft smirk lining her features as she latches hold of my hand, pulling it towards her as she plants a soft playful kiss in the centre of my palm.

'And by rights I should have shot you the moment I saw you. I am a Hunter, Arianwen. I am the enemy your kin so fervently rails against. We shouldn't be here, be like this, and yet I cannot imagine being anywhere else. I have never felt so contented and at home in my entire existence. Nothing will ever be enough to explain just what it is between you and I, explain what it is that brings about such a solace and boundless energy that echoes out from us every time we are near one another, and I for one, my little angel, hope I never find out.'

I pull my arms tighter around her, the soft warmth of her skin against mine sending sparking shivers through to my very core as I once more settle into a comfortable position. The scent of her hair fills my nostrils as I breathe deeply, pondering the state we are slowly slipping deeper into. Can we really be the cause of the calamitous force that has so shaken the cores of our individual worlds, can our joining have really brought about the start of a war six millennia in the making?

If that is the truth then by rights, can we, as a pair, as a unified couple, allow this to happen for the sake of our own union? I know in my heart and soul if I had to make a choice of my kin over Arianwen, the slumbering angel in my arms, then it would be her each and every time, even if the choice cost me my own life, but this ... this could mean anarchy, war, and a loss of life so great that I doubt our two worlds would ever truly recover.

I glance down at her soft features as the golden light of the fire plays over them. Can I truly be that selfish, can I condemn two worlds to possible total annihilation all for the woman I love?

Yes, yes I can.

Loss

ARIANWEN

I feel it.

It still lingers with every step I take.

Every brush of the top of my inner thighs against my still swollen centre shoots lingering pleasure through my entire body. I feel alive, I feel electric, I feel completely sated for the first time in my life. The afterglow of my and Albion's sensual dance is making me feel more powerful than I have ever felt before. I feel like I could conquer all the worlds in a single day.

I can still feel the echoes of his touch, the memory of him roaming over my entire body scorched into my mind, touching flesh that had never been touched by another being before. His nails scrapping over my nipples making me want to scream in ecstasy, his hands, fingers, and tongue tracing all over my form, licking, biting, sucking, memorising every dip and curve. His astounded awe at the sight of the pink tinge on his fingers from the taking of my virginity. The look of absolute calm and pleasure deep within his eyes that were showing me all the way into his dark tainted soul.

I became a different person in his embrace, braver, sensual, confident, wanting, needing. Without thinking of it I was returning his sensual acts. I was boldly touching, biting, unfurling my wings and swathing him in them as my legs naturally moved to wrap around his waist. His constant need to slowly touch and pet me, like I was a soothing balm for his torn soul, was so unexpected.

He told me I owned him, I, an Angel, own a Demon? But as I question this, I know without a doubt that he owns me. He completely and utterly owns me. How could he not? After openly and easily confessing his love for me, how could I not let him own my entire being? I wanted to say it back, I almost did, but fear caught the words and lodged them in my throat. I know I feel it, but if I say it back, I open myself up to the possibility of being shattered so beyond recognition that I may never be able to put all the pieces back together again. I do love him, but I feel that if I let those words out I will never be the same again, in more ways than one.

Lying in front of his fire after we shared our bodies over and over again was pure bliss. I had never felt more adored by another being than I had in that single moment. And for him to pick up on the darkness surrounding my aura, which I believe is a hidden side to Gabriel, is slightly worrying. If Albion was to sense that darkness while I am in Gabriel's company, what would he do? Knowing how strongly he feels for me, his reaction could be extreme and put us both in danger within both our worlds. Would he be so careless as to try and enter Eden? Oh dear, I hope not.

I can see the fierce emotions he holds for me, and the many lessons I have learnt over the years about humans is that their strong emotions are what get them in trouble the most, so I can only imagine what type of trouble an immortal's powerful emotions could cause. Destruction, war, death!

It's hard to think about the danger we have placed ourselves in by allowing our emotions to rule our head, after what we both shared in each other's embrace, which was sacred, beautiful and complete bliss. How can I let my mind wander to the darker side of our union, the worry, fear and risks?

Is this what starts many wars? Someone choosing love over their loyal duty to their kin? Because I know now, after Albion's heartfelt declaration of his love for me, he would struggle to choose his demon brothers over the woman whose heart he holds in his hand and I know it would be the biggest heartbreak of my life to choose my family and kin over the man who is the other half of my soul. How could one possibly let go of a piece of themselves?

I know that if we continue the path we have now started, it will end badly. There will be no winners in either of our worlds. And what if we can't pick up the pieces after all is said and done? What will happen to us? If either of our leaders were to ever find out about us, we would both surely face the penalty of death. Then what would all this have been for?

I know that there has to be a reason that Albion and I have crossed paths at this point in our lives, that we both feel like we have found a missing piece of our souls, that the force we have when we are together is greater than either of us, greater than either of our worlds combined. But what is the purpose of it all? What are we supposed to use this power for? These unanswered questions are what has made my pleasurable feelings fade very fast as reality slowly starts to seep into my pores.

The reality that, no matter what the reason is for Albion and I finally meeting, I am still an Angel, he is still a Demon, and both our worlds are on opposite sides of good and evil. These are the things we can never change.

So I refuse to dwell on them just for this moment, living in the sensual memories of what we just shared for a touch longer, indulging in the knowledge that I am loved more fiercely than I ever thought possible as I raise my hand to place a finger on my still swollen lips while my other hand holds my cloak tightly, covering my torn dress.

I need to clear my head of such lustful thoughts and concentrate on my duties to my kin. I need to step back into my reality for a while. But that's easier said than done considering my entire body is still humming from his every touch, his every kiss, his every intense stare into my soul.

I shake my head, trying to lose the images that are invading my thoughts and concentrate on making my steps take me to where I need to go. I slip into my home quietly, thanking the heavens that nobody is home so I can slip into a new dress, shoving the tattered remains of Albion's passion under my bed before exiting quickly. I arrive at the enormous vegetable garden in Eden, the fresh smell hitting my senses and soothing my soul, overflowing with just about every delicious edible food there is.

I grab an old wicker basket and start to make my way down one of the many pathways between the squares of lush vegetation. One can come here to collect food for their own family's meals or to help collect for a large banquet or ceremony that has been organised. But now, it is perfect timing for me to gather examples of a collection of vegetables and take them to our learning centre for the little ones.

One of the many tasks I love in my beautiful world is to assist in educating the littlest ones in all aspects of our lives and that of the mortals on earth. Their innocent and inquisitive questions have me giggling constantly, giving me a smile that I can still feel in my cheeks well after the lesson has finished. They are so eager to learn, but what I enjoy most is their endless affection when the lessons are over and I am graced with thankful cuddles from little arms and kisses all over my cheeks from tiny lips. They are just so happy and adorable.

I can see them up ahead, all sitting in a circle, their full attention on whatever their teacher is currently talking about, when an uneasy feeling washes over me. A prickling feeling runs up my spine as I fasten my steps towards the children. I can feel a presence close behind me as I take the last step before I reach the children's circle.

I don't turn, I don't acknowledge whoever it is so close to my being, I just say a quiet hello to the children and join them on the ground, crossing my legs just like them, which some giggle at, and try to concentrate on what the lesson is about today.

I can feel eyes boring into the back of my head but I stay strong and refuse to give into the urge to turn my head slightly to try and catch a glimpse. I'm thankful when the teacher finishes her lesson and tidies up, ready to leave as I grab my basket of freshly picked produce ready to get lost in educating our tiniest of angels. The more I talk, the more my mind relaxes as I become completely engrossed in my teachings and the small smiling faces before me.

Just as I'm wrapping up today's lesson I feel a hand softly land on my lower back, my body instantly going rigid as all my senses tell me exactly who that hand belongs to.

'Arianwen,' Gabriel whispers near my ear before moving from behind me to stand in front of the children. 'Good morning, little ones.'

He addresses the children in a soft sweet tone I have never heard released from his lips before. The children all bow their heads politely as they already know this to be the way to address one of their leaders.

'Have you all enjoyed your lesson today?' he asks as lots of little heads nod with enthusiasm. 'Miss Arianwen is a lovely teacher, isn't she?' He receives more tiny nods.

'I think she is very special too,' he whispers and gets lots of soft giggles as I try to comprehend what game he could be possibly playing with these type of questions.

All the children's mothers have started to gather around, ready to take them home, as I hear the first of the whispers start to spread. Speculation as to the depth of attention Gabriel is openly showing me compared to the other girls who could possibly be in the running to become his bride.

I distract myself from such idle gossip and walk towards a friend who recently had her second child, whom she offers up freely to me for a cuddle. The small sweet bundle barely stirs as it is transferred to another set of hands, fitting perfectly in the cradle of my waiting arms. What a sweet little cherub she is: perfectly smooth alabaster skin with rosy red cheeks and soft, miniature plump lips that are moving slightly in a suckling motion, as if she is dreaming of her next feed. Such a gloriously happy creation a baby is, the best that God has to offer.

'What an adorable little cupid,' Gabriel coos as I jump slightly, raising my eyes to his face, not realising he was standing right in front of me. He runs a finger gently down the beauty's cheek in my arms, looking at her with a sweetness which inexplicably puts me on edge.

'I must say, Arianwen, a baby in your arms is a delightful sight. Maybe that is something we could work on during our first night as husband and wife.'

I gasp as he lifts his eyes to mine, looking at me with an unmasked hunger and need that raises bumps on my skin, and not in a good way. Not like ... *Albion.*

Oh, Albion.

My guardian, my saviour, my lover, the man who has the key to my heart. A man who could never ... never be able to give me the precious gift of a child. This thought causes an instant stabbing feeling in my heart and leaves my soul screaming in pain. I turn from Gabriel sharply and return the sleeping cherub to her mother before moving towards where the children are playing a game of chasey, their laughter rising and floating in the air, saturating all that surrounds them.

When Albion and I shared our bodies, there was no need for such human concerns such as protection. Legend has always dictated that it is an impossibility for an angel and a demon to create a child together, which is something I would have to give up if I was to consider a life with the man who is gripping my heart so tightly.

As the little ones' laughter rises louder, my heart grows heavier with the realisation that the gift of a child would never be presented to Albion and me if we are to continue the path our hearts are willing us to follow.

A feeling of lead settles in my stomach at a loss I am yet to even experience. I turn to find Gabriel still watching me as he continues his conversation with some of the mothers. He was right; if I was to accept what he is so blatantly offering, a baby could become a possibility sooner rather than later.

But as I study his possessive stare over me, I know deep down in my soul I would never be happy in a union with that man. I would never blossom, I would never have the freedom to continue my calling, and Reclaiming is something I will never surrender. If I was to marry Gabriel ... I would lose myself.

As I turn from his intense stare, my eyes lock into a glare, a glare coming from Michael. I have barely said two words to Michael in my entire existence, yet have always felt his dislike towards me without a clue as to why. He is our quiet leader, always watching, always in the background letting Gabriel be the voice of our rulers, yet he is the one who holds the most power amongst us angels. His capabilities are legendary throughout our immortal world, but by looking at him you would never know. He always seems to be playing second fiddle to Gabriel, but we all know that it is Michael who makes the final decisions about our kin before it is put to our true Lord.

I refuse to turn away from his probing eyes, silently standing my ground, not wanting to give him fuel to accuse me of hiding something, trying to appear stronger than I am in his presence, trying to hide all my secrets away tightly where he will never uncover them. A child trips in front of me, so I move forward quickly to pick the poor little thing up from the ground, but after brushing off her dirty hands she is off to a sprint again. When I return my eyes to where Michael was standing, he has disappeared. I sigh loudly, releasing the huge tension I wasn't even aware I was holding onto.

Some of the mothers come over to say goodbye, collecting all their children, ready to return to their homes when I see Gabriel also making his way to me. I tense before he reaches me and I can tell by his small frown that he noticed. He waits patiently for this group of goodbyes to be over before approaching me, one hand reaching out, his fingers running through a loose strand of my hair blowing in front of my face before moving his hand down to take one of mine, bringing it to his lips, kissing it gently as he squeezes it slightly.

'Until next time, *Arianwen*," he croons to me before letting go and moving away, giving a nod to the remaining mothers and their children.

I can't help the shiver that races over my body at his touch and suggestive tone as I turn to say a quick goodbye to the remaining mothers before my hasty retreat. Visions of Albion still fill my mind as I ponder over all I would have to give up just to remain in his arms.

No chance of motherhood is just the beginning. I would surely lose contact with my family and the rest of my kin if they were to find out, ensuring no chance of a wedding ceremony, which also means I would never be entitled to a halo, which is presented to the new bride and groom as a sign of their commitment and ability to now bear children and also enhances the individual abilities they are already gifted with.

But it's the biggest part of me I could never chance losing which has my soul twisting in pain. My calling, my gift, my reclaiming. This is what I was born to do, it is not something I could ever turn my back on. It is me! So why do I feel as if Albion is just as big a part of me as my calling? How could they both co-exist within me? I feel like I wouldn't survive if I lost either one of them. So how do I move forward from this moment when my entire being is so confused and conflicted?

I don't have a moment longer to contemplate these thoughts as I have come to an abrupt halt, with a very firm hand wrapped tightly around my arm. I gasp and use my free hand to cover the sound when I realise it is Michael's angry grip I am now in.

'You may have Gabriel under your spell, but I am not so easily fooled, Arianwen. I know you are not all that you seem to be, so know this, I will be waiting and watching you closely for the moment you slip up and show your true self.' He then squeezes my arm further before letting it drop from his grip and stomping away.

My true self. My true self! I have been nothing but a loyal and committed angel to my Lord. Always going above and beyond what has been expected from one single person. I have an innate and desperate need to please and help all that surround me, even going further than any Reclaimer has done so before by walking the red singed edges of Hell itself to save the souls crying out for me, who would have otherwise been left to kneel before Satan himself.

There have been whispers my entire life that I was created to be one of the most spiritually in tune angels to these humans, who dares to walk where no other angel has walked before to ensure the safe passage of the souls who have the right to return to their Father.

My only indiscretion has been to follow my heart and soul into the arms of the enemy to my kin, whom I know deep within every crevice of my being is also a piece of me, a part of my soul that I always felt was missing.

The way I'm drawn to Albion feels like it is completely out of my control, like this force we have when we're together needs the two of us to exist, that it just *has* to exist, that it is greater than the two of us, greater than both our immortal worlds combined. I never had a chance of resisting such an uncontrollable need.

But now I know, not only do I have to be mindful of Gabriel's attention to me, I now have to be mindful of Michael's shadowing of my every step. How could I possibly meet with Albion again with the constant threat of Michael following my trail? He must already suspect something has changed within my aura if he has suddenly decided I am hiding something worth finding out.

I need to clear my head, I need all these current players wandering around my mind to disappear for just a moment of peace. I decide to throw myself into all the chores I can cram into one day.

I return home and help my mother with all the cleaning of our house. Then I head to the main fountain in the middle of Eden, which is situated in the middle of a giant field of every exotic flower known to man, and quite a few that aren't, to help pick and bundle them up into bouquets that will be situated around the halls of all our official buildings. I spend the entire day and well into the night offering my help to anybody in need.

By the time I'm ready to head to my family's home, I am utterly exhausted. But it's what my mind needed today, some time to not think about my woes and troubles, some time to just remind me that the worlds are bigger than just I.

I am just about to reach my door, looking forward to a deep

sleep within the comfort and safety of my own bed, when I hear it. A calling, a soul in need, in need of the gifts I was created with and something I know I could never turn my back on.

I take a deep breath, trying to wash away some of the day's exhaustion, looking up to the moon as I exhale and brace myself for what is to come. I turn and only take a few steps when I sense someone watching me. Finding out who it is, is not my priority; my mind is already consumed with the job I have been tasked to do, so I keep on walking towards the gatekeepers and the world beyond.

Just as I'm about to stand beneath the larger than life stone creatures, my follower makes himself known. 'I hope you don't mind me shadowing you, my sweet angel?' Gabriel speaks softly. Shock at who it is has rendered me momentarily silent as I struggle to comprehend why he is here, as he takes my silence as an opportunity to continue speaking.

'I thought it might be a good idea to see exactly what my possible future wife does when leaving our world behind to enter enemy territory.'

What! How dare he think this is some sort of game where spectators are invited to watch. I stumble with anger as I try to respond.

'You ... you can't just stand by and watch. It is a delicate process which requires my full attention. It would be dangerous not only to the soul in need but also myself if you were there as a distraction.'

His lopsided grin makes my anger grow. 'Arianwen, I have been around a lot longer than you, my dear, and have walked within their world many times in my existence and yet ... I am still here. Believe me when I say, I too, have the ability to go undetected when it is needed.'

Panic starts to settle within me, the knowledge that no matter how clever my words are to try and change his mind, he will still follow me. But that's not why the panic has gripped me.

One word ... Albion!

He would have already sensed me standing here on the border, waiting for me to enter this forgotten world which lies between his and mine and while he waits, he will also sense Gabriel. I just have to have faith in Albion to know that showing himself to Gabriel will only spell disaster for not only him and me, but also the worlds we live in.

With a nervous step, I turn from Gabriel's still smirking face, trying to drown out his presence, trying to concentrate on the soul who desperately needs me and not on the rising panic at what Albion is going to see, as Gabriel trails me through this dead forest and into the waiting room of death.

I can sense him straight away, he is close, but my sight has yet to discover him and I don't want to alert my shadower to his whereabouts, so I concentrate on the task I must complete. Gabriel whispers something to me I'm unable to hear and have no desire to, so I turn and whisper back 'Quiet please,' which just increases the stupid grin on his face.

I turn back with more determination in my step and fasten my pace as my reclaiming skills start to take over my being, my senses becoming highly alerted to everything that is moving around me, every aura, every force. Everything with a breath is now part of my focus as I need to ensure the safety of the soul I will be delivering to my Lord and also my own.

As I approach the dwellings on the fringes of the village, I start to slow my pace, needing extreme care to step on the same ground that the Devil's minions constantly roam on.

The humans roaming around these decrepit buildings are oblivious to our presence and the fact that one of the most influential angels to have ever existed is right behind me, being as stealthy as he claimed he could be.

We reach the dwelling that encases the soul which has called to me on such a deep spiritual level that it cannot be sensed by another being, mortal or immortal. I hear their cry, not from within my ears, but deep within my soul itself. I feel their pain, their fear, their sins which have left them teetering at the edge of Hell. I feel their anguish, their hope, their lingering good inside which is what will grant them passage back to their true Father and Creator.

My eyes scan our surroundings, using my sight to search for anything out of the ordinary. I use my hearing to pick up on the slightest of sounds, of anything that may be closing in on our location. I open my mouth slightly, taking a slow breath in to taste any danger lingering in the air. Then I close my eyes briefly, letting all of my senses come together to create a sixth sense that allows my aura to detect any evil that may soon arrive to harm the soul in need, or even myself.

My hand reaches for the door, my palm pressing flat against the slowly decaying wood barely hanging on its hinges as I push ever so slightly, testing for the protesting creaks of this ancient timber. I push forward, making sure the noise doesn't rise above a whisper, as the door gives until we have enough room to slip through. Once inside I turn to close the door before I turn around and scan the rest of this dwelling for any hidden entity.

Once I'm satisfied with our safety, my eyes land on the dying soul who has called for me. It is a young man, barely out of his youth with what once would have been a slightly rounded boyish face. His body is reacting with panic as I slowly make my way to his side where he is withering in utter agony on the hard timber flooring. I make eye contact with him and instantly his body responds, relief washing over his pained features as his pleading eyes beg for me to take the pain away.

'You are safe now, child, I am here for you, I promise to take the pain away and give you a safe journey back to your Creator.'

He closes his eyes on my last words, a small smile gracing his child like lips, my hand finding his, giving him a comforting squeeze as I place my other hand on his forehead. As soon as my hand connects with his clammy skin, I have instant flashes of the life this young man has lived. From joyous childhood memories, to his first heartbreak over a girl, to the wind blowing in his hair whilst driving his first car, to the strike of grief at the loss of a parent, to following the wrong crowd trying to forget his sadness, to one rainy night, blinded by desperation and pulling a trigger he never intended to pull on an innocent bystander, to standing on a street corner as revenge drove his way, halting the young life that he had barely started.

My soul cries for the young man in my hands, so much to look forward to, yet one wrong decision rips his future from him. I press my hand harder to his forehead, drawing my essence from deep within my body and transferring it to him as his body lightens, ridding itself of past pains and sins that once leaded down his form. My touch becomes softer as his soul starts to leave the shell of his body, slowly rising from its earthly encasing to reveal its true source, a bright heavenly light not seen by any earthling's eyes, its glistening luminous force too glorious for the eyes of a mortal.

I let go of the body under my touch and watch it slowly drop and evaporate into nothing but dust. I cup my hands under the gleaming light of the soul, using the power I have contained within my entire form, giving it the final strength it needs to make its way back home and into the peaceful arms of its Lord. It rises and swirls, dancing with joy at its freedom from the shackles that life placed upon it.

As I watch the final strands glittering towards the small crack of light shown through the broken roof of this tired old house, I turn, readying my senses to once again search for any danger that may have been alerted to the act I just performed. As my eyes reach Gabriel's, I notice something I have never seen in them before. I can only best describe it as sheer amazement at what he just witnessed first hand. As I go to step past him he softly grabs my arm, staring intently into my eyes. He doesn't speak, he just stands and stares at me in silence. I feel like he finally sees the true gift I have, that he finally understands my true power and what my calling means to me.

As he's about to speak, I pull out of his gentle grasp and reach for the door, again moving it with no more than a whisper. Knowing the true danger I am surrounded by is always heightened after I do a reclaim, as it is hard to mask the force of a soul who has been granted peace. I take in my surroundings once more before I make my way out of this dwelling and head towards the forest and the safety of our own world.

But before I can take more than a few steps I freeze, sensing Albion almost within arm's reach. I close my eyes and silently beg him to please remain hidden, to please not increase the danger that already ensnares our union. I feel Gabriel's touch on my arm, forcing my eyes to snap open. I refuse to acknowledge his presence, refusing everything about him. Instead I quicken my pace, desperate to put distance between the man who holds my heart and the man who blatantly wants to hold claim over it.

I move quickly, my sole drive to see myself safely out of the village and through the forgotten forest, heading towards the gatekeepers with pure determination to put as much distance between Albion and Gabriel as I can. I note with slight trepidation a tree that has clearly been split in half and dread starts to fill my stomach as I feel exactly whose hand was responsible for it. I send a silent message hoping that he will restrain himself and stay hidden amongst the shadows of these dead trees.

Once we pass under the granite dragons I still refuse to slow down, desperate to free myself from my shadower as soon as I can. I cannot shake it, a deep foreboding boiling within me, making my stomach churn. I turn, feeling sick to my stomach that Albion had to witness him near me and fearful that the one who proclaims his love to me will have sensed the darkness that I feel within Gabriel.

I reach the steps of my home, unsure as to how to say goodbye, just hoping that Gabriel will make it short and polite so I can lock myself away safely within my family home. Again, he just stares with unmasked awe as he stands silently before taking a slow step closer.

'Arianwen.' He says my name with but a breath of air, making me feel uncomfortable.

'I am at a loss for words at what I just witnessed in that decaying village. I knew you had a great power within, but could never have imagined it was as potent and strong as I just laid witness to. You truly are remarkable my, sweet angel, and my eyes will never see you as anything else again.'

He leans in closer and places a kiss upon my cheek as I force myself not to stiffen at his touch, not wanting to draw any more attention to myself than is already there.

'Until next time, *Arianwen*,' he coos close to my ear before turning and heading towards his own home.

I shiver, watching his retreating back, at the thought of him and Albion being in such close proximity to each other and the disaster that could have been created.

My thoughts drift to the man that owns my heart and the life we have fallen into together that will guarantee we could never meet in the open or be as free as two young lovers discovering the joys of each other's affections. We will never have anything that could be described as normal. If we endure the hardships of our forbidden and dangerous love, then we are guaranteed nothing but pain and sorrow.

Will our love even survive living in two separate worlds?

16

Anger and Restraint

ALBION

I lie staring up at the ceiling, the scent of my angel's sweet nectar wafting around me as I watch the small fireflies and cave dwelling caterpillars make their way across the cave roof, their small glowing forms shimmering like the night's sky as they move across the black rock, the pressing sensation filling me as I ruminate on the mountainous deluge that hangs above me.

I swing my feet to the floor, striding towards the mannequin, its stained and torn form holding my armour. I cast my eyes over the wall behind it, my family's coat of arms staring down at me. I close my eyes, feeling my father's eyes upon me as I kneel, my voice echoing through my home.

'Father, I need your help. I need the guidance I so often scorned that you had always so freely given, please. I am at a crossroads and know not which way I should turn. Please, father, you have always shown me the true path to walk, but now I fear I have strayed so far from it that I can never find my way back. I am risking it all for the love of the enemy.

'I know in my heart, in my very soul that she is the one to complete me, but to seek her love, to keep it could mean the destruction of everything. Help me, father, I am weak and know not what to do.'

I stare at the crest, its rampant golden lions encircled by two sets of crossed sabres drawing my eyes to the centre. A lone line of cursive script stands stark against the white centre panel of the shield. *Vende omnia quae Mors*, all that which we sell is death.' The words burn into my mind as I hear a voice, not my father's rumbling baritone, but the soft soothing lilt of my mother's words, like honey in my ear as I drop my gaze to the floor.

'If death is all we sell, then how can I embrace life? How can I find the depths of love and longing I know I feel, if all I can give in return is death? Mother, please tell me, how can I only return her love by granting her bloodshed and pain? I know in my soul I am capable of more, but all that marks our path to each other is the burned and charred husks of the dead and betrayed, pitted bodies of my fallen brethren and those heathen angels that dared bar my path to her side. Mother, please, tell me now, how can this be all I can give in return?'

Silence greets my ears, the flickering shadows around me moving to the throbbing heat of the fire as I hear it hiss and crackle. The silence tells me all I need to know, even in their quietest of moments my parents grant me their wisdom. I know I am capable of more than dealing out death and destruction. In my soul, I know I am destined for more and it is time I found my true path. The one I have left behind is no longer the one I am bound to walk.

✦✦✦

Light streams around me as I push through the shattered remains of the squat building that shrouds the entrance to my home. The smell of wet grass on the air flirts with my senses as I rise from the mangled hulk of timber and blitzed masonry. The watery haze of the new day's sun bathe my features as I pull the boiled leather jaw guard up, the warmth of my own breath lathering chin and lips as I move. My fingers claw at the cliff side as I draw myself upwards towards my perch, the outcropping beckoning me forth as I heave my limber form up and over the edge, the softly rippling canvas sheet hiding me from view as I survey the world below me.

The spicy scent of the meat market draws my eye as I watch the bustling merchants setting their stalls for the day's trade as the minute horde of waifs and strays filters amongst them begging and snatching at scraps and cast offs as their canine companions bark and yap. Turning my gaze to the west, the lemon yellow orb fills my vision as a glinting makes me frown. A sudden itching fills my scalp as my eyes widen, my mind screaming at me to move. I throw myself to the right as the stone shatters where my head had been mere moments before.

Crawling, creeping, slithering like a snake across the plateau, I pull my long gun from where it sits, the oak case crashing against the stone beneath me as I lever it open. The scent of gun oil and dust clogs my nostrils as I roll onto my back, the oilcloth wrapped bundle sitting heavy against my chest as I lie shrouded by the raised edge of my perch.

The heavy viscous mineral oil coats my fingers as I pull the cloth from around my father's most coveted weapon, the gleaming ebony stock shining as I drag the cloth free and dump it unceremoniously back into the box, the polished brass breech catching my eye as I cradle the weapon in my arms, slowly rolling onto my stomach before crawling once more, with infinite care towards a small v-shaped gap in the rocks. Settling the telescopic sights against my eye, I search for any sign of my assailant, for the tell-tale glint of their weapon in the sunlight.

'Father, guide my aim, let my mark lie true and their end swift, and if the worst should come to pass, I beg forgiveness.'

My senses heighten as I feel the prickling kiss of Arianwen's presence on the very edges of my reach, her familiar aura brushing my own as I pull my weapon tighter to my shoulder. My urgency rises as I search for the heathen who so nearly claimed my life. I know that no Reclaimer would wield such a weapon, but one of Gabriel's Sleepers would, the creeping agents of that strutting peacock that so beleaguer and stalk my fellow Hunters. A flicker of movement draws my eye as I slowly track my aim to the left, the shadows drifting all too quickly as I slow my breathing, the sound of my own heartbeat filling my ears as I wait for that one moment, the point between the rhythmic thump of my life's music where everything stills and their life ends.

The weapon thumps against my shoulder as its echoing bark rolls across the mountain side. People below me yelp in surprise as they all flinch and scurry for cover. A shock of straw blonde hair tumbles from the side of a roof, the angel's slack grip letting its weapon clatter free to the floor as I continue to scan for their partner. Too many of my kin have come to lose their lives for this one simple mistake.

A feather strewn burst of movement fills my scope as the dead angel's partner takes flight, the thump of their wings reaching me like the distant rumble of thunder on the wind as I rise to one knee, my sights following their path through the skies.

'Flap, flap, little birdie, fly on home.'

I let my aim slip away as the angel fades from view, a small smirk playing over my features even as I mull over the ramifications of what has just come to pass. The fact is that I have just lain waste to another of my lover's kind, another soul purged from existence for all eternity, and yet as much as I know it will carve a path between me and my Little Wing, I feel no remorse for the life I have taken. I sit safe in the knowledge that if I hadn't, it would be my life fading into nothing and my darling angel would be left alone in this cold and heartless world that we both call home.

I stare around me, the shattered rock and flapping canvas telling me everything. I pull together my meagre collection of tools and food, wrapping it all in the billowing canvas sheet before tying it around my back. I kneel, pulling together the brittle dry remnants of my fire pit, piling on anything that contains a shred of my aura and scent before dragging my finger over it. All the soft mumbled words tripping from my lips as it smokes and then with a soft rush of heated air bursts into a glowing ball of guttering orange.

I feel my angel drawing nearer, the overwhelming scent of her aura cloaking my mind and soul in a blanket so thick that I have to fight to be free of its grip. Slipping forwards, I drop from the plateau, the air snapping around me as I land amidst a cloud of startled crows, their indignant cawing grating at my ears as I push forwards, searching for her once more, the glittering glow of her standing like a beacon to my eyes.

I move silent and slow, my form hunched as I feel the pressing weight of the weapons at my back. The smell of the smouldering remnants of my hunting hide drift on the wind as I dance like a cat up the sheer wall ahead of me. Fingers and toes find holds and cracks that would be invisible to a lesser Hunter, my body undulating and moving over the cracked and crazed mud bricks.

The summit vanishes behind me as I slide into a crouch, my body pressed tightly to the stone work as I see my angel begin to emerge from the haze of damp mist that hangs around the fall. Her glowing aura, so natural to my eyes seems broken, her form taut, bleeding tension as she moves like a drunken mannequin.

My brow furrows as a scent traps my mind, my anger rising as I watch a shadow shimmer in her wake, the spiced aroma all too familiar to my mind; my teeth grind, I feel the sharp bite of pain as one chips, the spiralling slither of white enamelled bone spearing into the roof of my mouth as I fight to leap from my perch and send my blade deep into that Angel's throat!

'Gabriel, you spineless cretin, how dare you stalk my woman. I will rip your wings from your spine and your life from your body before you lay a single finger on her.'

I watch Ari pause as she turns her attention my way, our eyes meeting for a fleeting moment; even though through the mist and silence I know she could never see me in a thousand lifetimes.

But as I stare through the swirling fog, I swear I see her lips drift into the smallest of smiles as our gazes linger in each other's direction, even as Gabriel's black laced aura closes in on hers, his fingers flicking through the stray strands of her hair as she moves into the streets and beyond my sight.

I sink to the rooftop beneath me, my ire and rage swirling through my chest as I sink my fingers deep into the mud coated stone, my talons carving through my flesh as I feel my true form begin to take hold, the skin of my scalp splitting as I roll tumbling from the roof line crashing into the powdery mist soaked lane below.

Clouds of sand coloured dust lift around me as the mist swallows me whole, its ice cold kiss sinking into my heat licked flesh as I stagger towards the scorched earth of the fall. I have to put distance between us before I lose control completely and bring harm to the woman I know is mine.

The pain that sears through my every sinew makes me want to scream even as I sink to my knees, the edge of the fall filling my vision and the squirming forest below calling out to me as I feel my scalp split, the ridged horns of my father's line curling free as I slump over, falling into the waiting arms of oblivion as I tumble, my wings snapping like wet silk as I sink into blackness, the pain and anger claiming me completely.

I push myself upright, the world around me shimmering, vibrating with the energy of a million pulsing lives. The thrum of the trees, the pulsing drum beat of hearts and souls all screaming into the ether, one voice of infinite power rising through my ears as I cast my eyes about me. Her scent fills my mind as I breathe in deeply, her footprints glowing golden as I make my way deeper into the seething heart of this shimmering mid world.

I raise my arm, my taloned fingers drifting over the bark of one of these self-righteous columns of firewood. I feel its echoing cry of pain as my talons dig ever deeper into its fibrous core, the glistening sap oozing free as it rolls over the lengths of hardened bone that had once been my fingers.

I curl my hand upwards, the tree's trembling scream burning through my mind as I move. With a roar of anger and hatred, I drive my arm upwards, cleaving the whimpering lumber in two. The echoing crack of splintering oak fills the air as I watch its light quiver and die around my arm, its glowing sap soaking through me. My chest heaves as I feel my horns slowly begin to recede, the pain of this helpless Drewen simmering softly as I draw myself back from the edges of madness.

My mind reels as I feel the overwhelming cry of a new reclamation, my fear spiking as my body responds in kind. With a sickening bubble of my own flesh, my talons and horns vanish, raw flesh sealing them away from sight as I run for the fall, my wings forcing themselves free as I climb into the chilled crystalline sky.

✦✦✦

I watch her move, the glow filling the shallow scraping of a home, the holed and wind shorn timber doing little to hide her from my sight. Her ethereal glow shines from every crack and split, filling the air with a warmth and loving radiance that only she could bring forth. I feel my anger melt from me even as his sneering form flickers through my vision.

I draw closer, my feet dancing over the compacted dirt and stones, my fingers finding their way to a shattered side panel. Slowly, I ease it away, feeling her warm light bathe my very core as I watch the charge in her hands begin to turn.

A shimmering orb rises free as I watch the boy draw his final breaths in this world, his form fading, dancing motes of orange and gold glittering like stars in the sky as it all swirls into the golden orb in my angel's hands. Her eyes shift, turning the purest violet as she lifts the glittering ball high over her head, pulses of blue dancing from her fingers cascading in waves over the boy's soul sinking into it, its brilliance blinding as I stare enrapt in what I am bearing witness to.

I move from the wall as they turn, silently slipping through the brazen light and away from the prying eyes of those I know can bring her harm with naught but a word. With the grace of a cat I make it back to the relative safety of the roof, the hardened mud still shimmering softly with the impression of my own aura, my eyes aching as I stare at the red and blue light that shivers like oil over water. I drop my hand, watching the shifting energies of my own soul move like smoke around my fingers. I hear her leave, my reverie broken as they make their way into the street below me.

Her quiet steps are mirrored by that preening cur. I feel the anger that eats at my soul begin to stir. How can I hold such jealousy against an angel I know my woman holds no interest in? My mind whirls as I desperately drag at the thought, a small itching chink of light searing through my mind as I feel Gabriel's aura reach out, that familiar taint sparking deep within me.

The feeling that, all too recently, had visited me in a far more intimate way. The realisation crashes over me like a collapsing wave, the deep chill the feeds into my bones, my heart seizing as I rise to my feet, my anger flaring, hatred clawing in my chest as the knowledge that the darkness that has so plagued my sweet Little Wing is now traipsing in her wake.

How can she allow something that she fears so violently and completely to shadow her wake? This vindictive, malevolent cluster of feathers and arrogance stalking her so closely that her very aura billows and ripples in protest, weaving away from him like smoke on the wind; I cannot fathom how my angel would let this come to be, and yet here he is, with his smirking lips and lust filled gaze, following her every move like a lovesick puppy.

The shadows close in, my footsteps muffled, their sound crushed by the sheer weight of the world's bated breath as I stalk ever closer to my heart's keeper and the bothersome gnat that she has so attracted. Chirruping insects quiet their arrhythmic cadence as I pass, the dead weight creeping ever closer to my crouched form as I stalk their footsteps.

Arianwen's soft blossom soaked fragrance filters through on the wind, undercut by an odour so soaked in its own arrogance that it almost chokes the air from my lungs. Drawing my mask up and tight across my chin, I push through the thickening under-growth, coming in line with my angel and her would be suitor.

I feel the familiar gnawing in the pit of my stomach as I draw closer, my blade keening in the back of my mind, crying for the blood of my prey. I force it down, smothering the itching tickle that is pricking at the base of my skull. Sitting there, calling to me, like an aching wound slowly being filled with the salts of the world.

I watch him lean in, his lips smearing themselves over her skin as my rage and jealousy break free of the confines of my chest, howling to the moon that now owns the sky. I almost rise to my feet, my talons bursting free of my skin as I feel my scalp rip in two, the sound of tearing silk filling my ears as my patron's horns soar forth, curling under my hood and down the back of my neck.

My body writhes as I feel my skin ripple, my clothing stretch-ing, groaning in protest at my shifting form, my true nature unfurling, flying free for all too bare witness to. I watch her, my eyes shifting back and forth from the cool blue that she so adores to the sulphurous yellow they truly are. If she saw me now, if she saw what I really am, beneath the veneer of man that is so pasted over my demon's brow, she would cut me down where I stand.

A deep growl rolls up from within, filling my throat as I sink my talons into the loamy soil beneath me, my mind whirling as I push myself to my feet. That kiss seared into my mind, the look in his eyes as his lips touched her skin, the shift of her shoulders as she turned her head, the spike and swirl in her aura as she felt him upon her. I cannot fathom it. Did she want it, did that contact come willingly? Everything in her body stance tells me no, but her aura and scent says something else altogether different.

I feel my wings rip themselves from my flesh, unfurling as I sink my talons into a trunk of a tree. Tearing it from the floor, I hurl it at the guardians, their heads turning my way as the thick oak log crashes into their gates.

'What right do you have to keep her from me, what right? She is mine and mine alone! You guard these gates like they are enough to bar my path and willingly watch as she is defiled by another. Her heart belongs to me!'

Their eyes stare down at me, impassive, all knowing, even as I stand before them, my true nature bare for all to see, I feel no malevolence from them, and yet they still bar her from my sight. The swirling wall of ethereal light that shimmers between the bars of these invisible golden gates hides all beyond them.

'You harm her and I will burn your kingdom down around you, do you hear me? You will live in a palace of ashes for eternity if she comes to harm at your hand.'

My voice echoes off the silent stone sentinels as I turn to the woods around me, my taloned fingers glowing as I drag them along the trunks of the trees. The Drewens' terrified screams make my lips curl into a feral grin as I watch them begin to smoulder and burn.

As my wings beat, fanning the flames, I cast my eyes back to the gatekeepers and the angels that lie beyond them, my whispered words making the dragons growl.

'Let this mark you as a warning of what will come lest my words be heeded.'

✦ ✦ ✦

I sit, the slow thumping of my heart burning through me as I watch the sun descend, bringing an end to the turbulence of the day. The taste of betrayal mixes with the sour note of the unknown. I feel the slow melting of my flesh and bone as my flesh suit once more takes hold, the sheer film of man that my angel has so fallen for slithering across me like water over glass.

I force myself upright, my visage a mask of two worlds, the slithering liquid skin still reclaiming its place as my face, the burnt red skin of my kin falling beneath the pale face of this world's downcast.

A chill washes over me as an emerging pack of shadowed figures melt from the world, their glowing eyes and hushed guttural whispers mingling with the air as I turn to face them. My head cocks to one side as I stare at them, my eyes dancing over each in turn as their black swathed forms shift into reality.

A quiet hush descends, blanketing the world in silence as their chattering words coalesce into one reverberating voice. 'The Master wishes to speak with you. Come now, he does not appreciate being left waiting.'

I stand mute as the light plays over these shades of former beings, their bodies wavering in the cool air that filters around us all. My eyes widen slightly as one of their faces is brought to light by the thready rays of the sun, the scarred and burnt flesh rippling with the passage of carrion beetles and the hatching puss soaked maggots that are slowly eating their way free of their living cocoons. I force myself to keep my eyes level and passive as their leader smirks. His teeth are blackened and rotted; thick mucus weeps from his gums as I incline my head, my eyes never leaving his as my steps break the frigid silence.

'Wise choice, Weiser, your father wasn't so sure of his actions when he was ... summoned.'

I feel my muscles tense; the desire to draw my blade and drive it deep between those magma red orbs is all consuming, and yet, somehow I stay my hand; my fingers tingle with need, the need to curl over my blade's grip, to feel the smooth leather bindings against the palm of my hand, but still my feet carry me forwards, away from Lucifer's blood hounds and closer to the unknown.

Heat rolls around me, the fresh, newborn soft flesh of my skin suit shrivelling at the sudden deluge. The burbling passage of liquid stone filling my ears as I slowly make my way down the spiralled ramp way, sinking into the pit from which I was born.

The heavy drip of sulphurous water mingles with the gargling hiss of rolling steam, the air thick with moisture as my rune carved skin begins to burn. I grit my teeth against the pain that suffuses me as my babe fresh form is ripped from me. My stomach churns as I feel my true form fly free, drawn from me like venom from a snake. The unbidden disrobing leaves me retching as I stumble down the final steps, my hands skating over the water slick stone as I fight to keep my feet beneath me.

The need to vomit swells from the depths of my stomach as I watch the once newly formed shell sink to the floor with a sodden splat. The hiss of scorching meat fills the air as the scent of roasted pork invades my nostrils. The screams of the lost and fated roll across the heated miasma that hangs in the inferno. Grasping hands reach from boiling pools of glowing magma, the tear soaked cries ringing for eternity from the walls around me. The wretched and downtrodden husks who are destined to claw and tear their own flesh from their heat boiled bodies as they try in vain to wrench themselves from the cauldron of pain and terror they now languish in.

A heated, bloated hand latches onto my ankle, rippled flesh rising from the boiling flood of liquid rock, sightless eyes set into a desiccated skull staring up towards me as its tongue lolls from its mouth, barely forming the plea for clemency that oozes forth. The words trickle around the bubbling remains of its own innards.

'Please ... please ... I beg you, release me from this torment. Don't leave me here.'

I kick its hand away, refusing to look into the pleading, tear laced eyes. I feel a small lurch in my chest as I hear the hissing, terror soaked scream vanish beneath the thick roiling flame licked pool at my feet.

The archway opens out ahead of me, the creaking groan of over tensed wood mingling with the rattle of metal as the methodical click of the rack is drowned out by the agonised screams of those trussed upon it. The echoing pop of distending joints soaks my mind, the gelatinous sucking of cartilage and sinew slipping under the pervading curtain of agony and fear.

My sense of trepidation is rising, the howls of the condemned still fresh in my ears; why has my lord and king chosen here of all places to hold council? It's a question that I just cannot fathom.

Even as I delve deeper into these halls of pain and abandon, one thought fills my mind, Gabriel. Gabriel and his putrid form lathering itself over my angel's skin. I rouse myself from my damnable reverie as I take my last steps.

His aura and sheer presence press down upon me. Even before I am fully in the room, my mind boggles. How can one being hold such unattainable power? It bears no credible source. How could that heathen progenitor bequeath such ferocious energies to a being little more than a child in the eyes of time? I stand here aghast at the weight of it all, the realisation of what could possibly lie ahead for me settling in like lead in my gut.

Could they know, could they have somehow traced her through me? No, it's not an answer that deserves contemplation. I spent so much on ensuring our paths were held invisible even to their most adept of hounds, and yet, how can I be sure? How can I know for certain that I am not stumbling blind into their arms, how can I be certain of anything? I could walk through this door only to find a blade in my chest moments later.

Would Lucifer be that conniving? Yes! Will he be now? Of that I cannot be sure. With all the wariness of a newborn babe I take the step. Be it to my own demise, of that fact I will all to quickly come to find an answer.

'Albion, come, join me.'

The carved bone tea set that anoints my gaze gives me pause; the rune carved skull that sits as the sugar bowl bears the stark white teeth of one of Lucifer's former kin. Surely he would not have kept such a lurid trophy?

'Ah, I see Acrestrian has caught your eye. He was one of my top lieutenants until he had delusions of grandeur and led a one man coup de tat; needless to say it did not bear fruit.'

I stand mute as he plucks two lumps of crystallised sugar from the severed top of Acrestrian's skull, the bleached bone flickering in the glow of the candles sat atop the others that ring the room around us both, their hollow black gazes glaring at me from every nook and crevice that abounds the soot blackened walls.

A soft chuckle draws me back to the situation at hand. Lucifer's sardonic gaze studies me as I try in vain to remain blank faced and stoic under the mounting pressure. The finger bone sugar tongs click and clink as one by one he lifts and drops the white glittering cubes into the steaming cup in front of him.

'Feeling a bit unsure of yourself, Albion? Surely the captain of my Hunters and the head of the sixth legion cannot feel off put by a few desecrated skulls of vanquished enemies; or does the sight of former kin and heathen alike make you feel queasy? I dare say the soul caster lying in a pile of ashes in the northern sector would hold a different tale if he could talk, although Udai has been overly hasty in deploying them into the field. Young pups one and all, you made sure of that fact when you set to the task of taking control of the sixth legion. Nicely done by the way. I haven't seen better work since you rescued Abezethibou from Solomon's prison, which brings me to my next problem. Abezethibou ...'

I feel my heart lurch in my chest, my blood running cold as I watch my King raise the steaming cup to his lips. The cold calculated smile that turns the corners of his mouth makes my spine shiver as I feel a cold sweat trickle down between my shoulder blades.

I try in vain not to shake, my shoulders quivering with the barely repressed need to flee. How can he possibly know I am connected in any way to either of them, and if by some twist of fate he does know, is he aware of the myriad of other gutter dwelling scum I have culled from our ranks in my need to see my angel kept from the grasp of harm's army?

No, I need to still my thoughts and my heart. The sound of its methodical beat is filling my ears, drowning out his words, and right now I need to hear exactly what is being said more than I need my heart to beat. Her life rests on what I am sure is about to be said, and I have to get it right.

'One of my best fighters, to be sure, and a top ranking lieutenant, has suddenly been struck off the legion's roll. So that is, what now ... at least a dozen of our command cadre, and who knows how many of the rank and file, simply snuffed out? Then as I move about my days as King of Hell, oh how I detest that title, I find that my head Hunter and General of my sixth legion is for all intent and purposes asleep at his post. That he is falling into such dereliction of duty that his own kin and fellow warriors are being ripped asunder under his very nose ...'

I watch every twitch, every minute tick as his ire mounts. The cup in his grip shatters as his voice rises with his anger. Shards of enamelled bone spear into his flesh, sending rivulets of glittering sapphire coloured blood to the floor as his eyes glow a deep sulphurous yellow. The skin around those now yellowed orbs splits, charring until the once creamed skin turns the colour of coal.

Never before have I seen behind the cultured veneer that he so paints over his brow. Never before have I seen the true face of the creature that was cast into the flame, but I did then. I saw beyond the veil, I was granted the misfortune of having the curtains peeled aside for the briefest of moments and staring into the face of evil.

For those few seconds, that scraping in the dusts of time, I was shown the true face of Hell and it terrified me.

I stay silent, Lucifer's shoulders slowly relaxing as he smooths out the folds of his house coat, silence enveloping the room. I drop my gaze to the floor, the miniature pools of sapphire steaming as they slowly begin to boil away to nothing. A deep languid sigh fills the spaces between the silence as I remain as still as the rock that surrounds us, not daring to breathe let alone utter a syllable in response.

'You're a good soldier, Albion, and an outstanding leader, which is why, rather than have you adorn the walls with the rest of the failures and traitors, I will grant you one chance, one chance to prove your worth to me once more. Find this malodorous inconvenience that is so plaguing us and eliminate it. I want you to erase it from existence, it and anything else that comes across your path. A group of the best Hunters you have to offer are waiting at the gateway. Take them and go. Go do what your father trained you to do ... and one final thing, do not fail me again, Albion. Your father never did. Do not dishonour his name by losing yours.'

I remain there, a small nod my only reply as I watch him wave his hand in the doorway's general direction. I take that as my cue to depart and turn, marching from the room with a measured pace, forcing myself not to do what my mind and body is screaming at me to carry out. To flee, to run now would be the last thing I ever did, that single act of cowardice would be followed with the swiftest end any being will have ever known.

I reach the outer fringes of the ninth circle, the stench of rotting flesh and flayed skin diminishing with each step before I finally allow myself to relax, hoping that I am far enough from his sight that I can finally relinquish the hold I have over my burgeoning fear. I lean against the tunnel's wall, my chest heaving as I feel my stomach lurch. The sound of my retching echoes through the silent walkway. The liquid splattering of my stomach's meagre contents fills my ears as I continue to heave, emptying my body of all but my own organs. Even now, I am unsure of their safety as I cuff away the stagnant string of bile and saliva that clings to my lips.

Pushing away from the wall, I turn, heading away from the site of my own disgrace and the steaming pool of fear and bile that now lies coagulating in the corner of the tunnel. I need to see her, to know she is safe, but how can I? I can't very well risk her discovery by one of my own simply to sate my own desire for comfort. As this thought permeates through me, I find myself staring into the faces of sixteen of the highest ranked Hunters under my command. I stare at each of them in turn, the battle scarred and patched armour that clings to them showing a lifetime of experience and pain. I nod, moving between them and towards the ramp way as they turn one by one and follow on in my wake.

17

Understanding

ARIANWEN

I step out into the new morning's light, enjoying the heated rays touching my skin, giving me a glow of newfound peace as I watch the sky shimmering in hues of orange and gold. After another sleepless night, I desperately needed this small moment here to bask in the simple pleasure of a sunrise. I breathe in deep, the scents of this magical garden seeping in deep, saturating all of my senses as I relish in this magnificent place I call home.

But as my mind starts to awaken and wander, the peace of this moment slowly starts to fade. I feel that tinge of stress forming at the base of my skull, threatening to overflow and reach into my brain, ripping this beautiful morning from me.

Having Gabriel shadow me last night, knowing that Albion was nearby, was painful and frightening. I don't want him to think that I had willingly invited Gabriel to follow me and I was fearful that he would show himself and confront Gabriel, which could have been the start of a war between our worlds. A shiver runs down my spine at my last thought. The threat of war is not something I want to dwell on. Not only would it mean an end to the relationship Albion and I have only just created, but it would also mean the end to some of my kin or possibly family members.

No! I refuse to think about that! I will move Heaven and Hell to prevent such a wretched event ever beginning. I know that what Albion and I have is beyond dangerous, but I now know that what has brought us together is more powerful than both our immortal worlds combined; it is greater than the two of us. We were destined to fall into each other's embrace, although the reason why still evades me. But I have faith that all will be revealed to us when we need to know it the most.

And after hearing his declaration of those three little words straight from his heart, the heart of a demon, I know that regardless of what fate reveals to us, he holds my heart and I never want him to let it go.

A lost feeling has now settled into my soul. Where do I go from here? What do I do now? I have no answers to these questions. It seems that no matter what I do, what direction I take, it will all lead to danger for more than just Albion and I. How can I move forward when being with the one I feel is my destiny will only spell destruction? Is that why fate has brought us together? Are we meant to be the start of a war? That can't be possible ... can it?

Why would fate gift us with such powerful emotions of love and lust, making our hearts both cry with magical joy, only to destroy it all with heartache and pain? My heart and soul refuses to believe that is our path. I believe that we have been brought together for good, not evil, and that the force which is created when we are together will one day have an important purpose amongst both of our immortal worlds. But until that reason is revealed to us, we need to act with caution in everything we do, together and apart.

The loud whistling melody of a group of birds above my head snaps me out of the gloom that was threatening to blanket me and reminds me to smile even when my lips feel like they can't. I take one more deep breathe in of this morning's fresh crisp air before taking my first tentative steps in the light of this new day.

I leisurely wander through all that this garden has to offer. The smell of jasmine floats around my head, mixed with the distinct smell of citrus from the nearby orchard. The bright colours of the newly waking flowers shining rainbow like shards of light throughout the morning mist which is slowly evaporating in the sunshine's rays. I head to the edge of the blue crystal like lake and crouch down, running my fingers through the purest water to have ever existed in all of the immortal worlds.

I look at my reflection and see something different, changes within me that no one else can see. Instead of a young girl's sweet innocent face shining back at me, I see a woman's face, one that shows wisdom, experience and ... dare I say it ... love? Is this the look of love? A glow to my entire being that has gone unseen by my eyes before. A glow that not only shows love but also happiness. Yes, despite the dangers surrounding our coming together, there is happiness there that I have finally found someone who I feel will truly see the real me.

But I am still fearful to say those words aloud, to say them to Albion, to say them to the demon I now know I love completely with all of my heart and soul. I love him. Oh my ... this is love. This feeling twisting deep within my heart, this feeling winding itself like a vine around my soul ... is love. A feeling I know will change my entire existence. I will never be the same again. I have been changed for all eternity from this day forth.

I ... am ... in ... love!

Then the fear hits me. In all my years, years of lessons about the humans, about how their strong emotions become their weaknesses, and the strongest emotion they have ... is love. Yes, love has been known to endure the greatest of pains and hardships and has helped many humans to survive feats they wouldn't have been able to surmount without it.

But it has also been known to cause many a sane person to act foolish in good and bad ways, to make decisions that have not been for their own good, to cause an ailment called obsession where one loses their own identity in the chase for another's love that is not freely being offered.

And it has been well versed in legends and myths to have caused many of the wars throughout all of our histories. And I cannot willingly allow the chance of a war to start because of my own selfish needs to fill a missing piece of my soul that I have been longing to discover for a lifetime.

But does that mean I will be destined to suffer through the possible alternative, a life standing beside Gabriel? I have pushed this issue to the back of my mind, but I know that if Gabriel was to choose me for his bride, there would be no way to refuse. Our oldest books show that no one has ever refused the hand of one of our leaders, it's their right to ask for whomever they wish, and to try and refuse would bring a great shame upon my family.

But why should I be subjected to a life of misery? Apart from my recent encounters with Albion, I have been nothing but a loyal and faithful follower to my Lord and all of my kin's sermons. Surely that should count for something? I growl deep in my throat, my head feeling like it could explode with all of this turmoil fighting for space within. I have never had this much to think about until now. Now I feel like I hold the burdens of all the worlds upon my small shoulders, without a way to rid myself of them.

'Arianwen, talk to me, child.' I jump at Anatiamoros' voice above my head. As I look up into his old, smiling grey eyes, I feel nothing but admiration and affection for this man. The longest serving Reclaimer who has lived many human lives over and over again, and someone who has always been my teacher and mentor in all aspects of my life. But the affections I hold most for this man, are the affections one would have for a grandfather.

My own grandparents moved from this world when I was but a baby, so I have no recollection of them. All that I know has been passed down from my parents and elders within our kin or within the pages of our history books. My mother's parents were also great Reclaimers who were involved in more than one war in their time. They passed by sacrificing themselves to save others during the last great battle of our world with Lucifer and his demons.

Which is why it took Anatiamoros many moons to talk my parents into letting him begin my training as a Reclaimer. It wasn't until they witnessed me save the soul of a deer within Eden's forests as a child that they finally could see how easy and natural it came to me even without the guidance and training normally required to achieve such a level of saviour. But that has not stopped their worry.

They too were Reclaimers, but not for long. As soon as they fell in love and married, they decided to devote their lives to each other within the walls of Eden and raise a family instead. Most Reclaimers only perform their duty for a short time as the concentration required to perform it can eventually wear you down. But the rare angels that were born with such a gift, like I, have the ability to do it for their entire existence, which is exactly how long I can see myself doing it.

And the kind, loving, aged man staring at me with concern on his old weathered face is the only one of my kin to truly understand how much reclaiming is a part of every fibre in my body.

'You know you can talk to me about anything, Arianwen. Unloading one's problems to another can lighten the load on one's soul. So give it a go,' he says with a slight grin. He always seems to be happy. Even in the most stressful of situations, he can still manage a smile to lighten the mood.

'I'm not sure what to say,' is all I can manage in a whisper.

'Let's sit.' He motions for me to follow as he walks over towards a bench sitting on the grassed area surrounding the lake. I rise and follow him, sitting down next to him, suddenly fearful he may already sense what is causing my woes.

'I can see something in your eyes, child, something that has changed. Please talk to me. I promise not to judge.'

His last words bring water to my eyes as I struggle with what words exactly to say to him. He notices my discomfort and takes pity on me, giving me the words instead.

'Love. I can see love in your eyes and I'm guessing it's not for Gabriel given the uncomfortable body language you show whenever he is near you.'

My jaw drops open at his more than correct statement; the shock must register on my face as his grin begins to widen. 'New love always has the same effect, a beautiful glow to the cheeks.'

He winks and makes me smile, but I am still cautious with my words. 'I do feel love, but it's ... not easy.'

He gives a little laugh at my words. 'If love was easy, my dear, it wouldn't be worth fighting for, now would it.' My only reply is a small smile.

I wish I could tell him everything, about an Angel who has fallen in love with the arch enemy, a Demon, and how I finally feel complete when I'm held in his embrace, how I feel truly alive in a way I have never experienced before. I wish I could tell him everything. But not only am I unsure of how far his support of me would stretch, I don't want to put him in any danger.

So I sit here torn, wanting someone to talk to and give me the much needed advice I need, but scared of the repercussions of that conversation.

'Why are you not shouting it from the roof tops or taking leisurely strolls around the garden hand in hand with the man that has so captured your heart?' he asked with his head tilted and a curious expression on his face.

'It's ... complicated,' is all I can say, even though complicated doesn't even come close to how twisted my situation is. His face grows serious as he considers his next words.

'Don't feel pressured into a life or a position you know would make you feel miserable and possibly prevent you from continuing your true calling. You have a right to absolute happiness just as much as the next angel, so don't think you have an obligation to make everyone else around you happy over what you truly want for yourself.'

I fight to contain my emotions at his beautiful words, but it does pain my heart a little that he is assuming that I'm in love with another angel and the reason we can't be presented as a couple is because of Gabriel's interest in me. I so badly want to tell him about Albion, about the man who holds my heart and soul, but I know I may never be able to say those words, even to him.

'I'm yet to see a way out of my situation with Gabriel. He has made his intentions clear, not only in public, but he has also approached me in private. I just don't know what to do.'

Anatiamoros' frown becomes deeper. 'He has approached you

in a private setting, without a chaperone around?' I nod at his response, and his face becomes very serious.

'Arianwen, I'm not sure how to say this without arousing fear in you, but I need to share with you a feeling I have, about Gabriel. I can sense, quite strongly, that Gabriel has another agenda for you, that maybe he is wanting you and your companionship for your power, not just as a wife to stand beside him. I am yet to pinpoint his exact intentions, but if my premonition becomes clearer I will speak with you instantly. Please, until then, be wary of his presence. I know he is one of our great leaders, but history has shown that not all angels have acted in a heavenly nature. Be alert, child, when he is near.'

I'm shocked that he can feel that the Gabriel that is shown in public is not the real Gabriel. I am relieved that it is not only me that can feel the darkness within Gabriel.

'What is the darkness that plagues Gabriel?'

I ask the question before I even have a chance to think it over. Do I really want to know the answer?

'There are many conflicting legends as to how Gabriel came into the position he is in today. And I think that is to throw anyone off the true path he took to get to where he is. Nobody knows the truth but God, and he wouldn't have given him such an important role alongside Michael if he didn't think he could do his job, which is to help protect the world we live in and the world in which the humans depend on us for. Many a great man has done things they wished they hadn't just to protect the ones they love. Not just men, but also great leaders.'

This I understand. 'I would do anything for the ones I love. I guess that means whether it's good or bad, I would do what it took to protect them.'

He nods his head at my words. 'Yes, love is very powerful and can be very intoxicating at times. Don't let your new love consume you to the point you forget your own path, Arianwen, but also don't let true love slip through your fingers because you're afraid to fall. Sometimes falling is the best part.'

I smile at his words which feel like they have shot an arrow through my heart. I would hate for fear to be the reason I was to lose Albion. What if I never got a chance to reveal to him my true feelings? That is a regret I do not wish to live with. But as Anatiamoros grows silent, it is regret that I see burning his eyes.

'Did you have a family once? I've never heard you talk of them. If it's too painful please ignore my question,' I say as he remains silent. I'm about to put him out of his misery and say 'it's okay' and leave, but then he answers in a very quiet voice.

'I knew my calling from my earliest memory. I always knew what path I would take and, once I became a Reclaimer, it was like I had blinkers on. I could barely see a life outside of what I did and the souls I saved. In quiet moments, I would think that one day I would love to fall in love and start a family, but as the years went by, that thought got further and further away from me, until one day, I realised my chance had withered away. I had aged too much to even consider a life outside of reclaiming. I hadn't realised, until I saw my reflection one day and an old white haired man was looking back at me, at how much time had actually passed.

'Do I have regret? No. It would have been nice to share my life with a wife and children of my own, but I don't regret a single day of following my true calling in this existence of mine. I have been blessed to be a part of everyone's life here in Eden. I've seen babes grow into cheeky children, children grow into curious teens, and teens grow to become great men and women such as yourself. I am so very proud of your achievements, Arianwen, and your commitment to your calling even when those close to you aren't as supportive as you wish.'

My eyes water as his kind words that tug at my heart. He is a true grandfather even if it is not through blood. He gives my hand a soft squeeze as he rises.

'Now enough talking to old men, off you go and be young and free with the one that holds your heart. But, Arianwen ... be careful at the dangers your heart may lead you into.'

He gives me a kiss on the top of my head before leaving me sitting here alone, wondering if he truly does know who exactly it is that holds my heart.

I need to see him, I need to tell him, I need to fall and take a chance on love, take a chance on fate helping to make this work. Love between an Angel and a Demon, could there be a way to make it work? I am not so naïve as to realise that what I am seeking is an impossibility. But my soul, relishing in finally finding its missing piece, is telling me that this is meant to be, that I just have to have faith. That I just a have to believe.

We will have to be very careful in all the worlds we tread in. Every step, every movement we make together will have to be carefully thought out. Until we can both figure a way to make this union safe, we will need to be on a higher alert than normal. If we keep it discreet, a secret, hiding away from prying eyes, we can continue to see where this love takes us. I can do this. *We* can do this. I just hope he still believes that I'm worth all the possible danger we will likely encounter meeting between worlds.

Finally a sparkle of hope blooms and starts to spread within my heart, winding around the love I have for Albion. A man I so desperately need to see at this moment, the man I crave to embrace me and hold me dear to his heart, a man who takes me to such heights, I forget my own name. Oh how that last thought has my stomach muscles clenching as the butterflies in my stomach start to take flight. I need to go to him now.

As I leave the stone gatekeepers behind and enter this for-gotten world in between, I can sense him instantly. His scent invades my senses, spreading like a poison through my veins, boiling my blood and making my heart beat rapidly as my breathing intensifies. I'm alive, in this moment. Even though he is not yet standing in front of me, he makes me feel alive.

My feelings grind to a halt as I sense other Hunters within this dying forest. I know it would be safer to turn around and wait beyond the walls of Eden, but the Hunters have never stopped me before. If I hear a soul calling for me, I find a way around any evil obstacles and always reach them in safety, so this should be no different.

I let my body adjust to the other beings nearby, noting that there are sixteen others surrounding Albion, a small army I am guessing, that seem to have completed their tasks and are now heading towards Hell. What they were doing in the forest in such large numbers I cannot comprehend, but now I have one purpose and one purpose only: to admit to Albion exactly the extent of my feelings for him.

The memory of him saying those three little words to me with such emotion and conviction just melts my heart. This man is so much more than a demon. He has good inside, good that out-weighs any evil that has been bred into him, good that is so desperately wanting to escape the confines of his once closed off soul. Good that is the reason for us crossing paths. Have I been brought to him to rid him of all his sins? Maybe, just maybe that is part of it.

I can feel the moment he senses my presence, the stress that was holding his shoulders up high around his ears slowly begins to release as he barks orders out for his fellow Hunters to return to their under croft. He stays grounded, ensuring each last one of them has obeyed his commands before he shifts slightly, facing my direction, lifting one corner of his mouth into a slight grin.

I watch as he turns slowly, moving stealthfully, taking each step carefully as if he is stalking his prey, the hunger he has in his eyes for me so blatantly obvious as he moves in closer. The intensity he is watching me with is heating my body before he has even laid a hand on me. How can one look have so much power over me?

I came here to tell him I love him but as he takes his final step in front of me, the words are lost in my throat as one of his hands grabs the hair on the back of my head, pulling me towards him roughly as he smashes his lips against mine.

18

Damned if You Do, Damned if You Don't

ALBION

The landscape shifts and rolls as I make my way through the dust caked streets of the village. The stone faced kinsmen around me move as silently as shadows as they drift through my eye line, each little more than a glimmer before vanishing once more into the darkened spaces of this world.

My eyes burn with the heated wall of energy around me, the bobbing shapes of these hairless apes and the glittering trails of my prey weaving through each other, intertwining in a patchwork of colour so vibrant, so over abundant with life, that it makes me ache with the sheer voracity of it all.

With short motions and ice laced glares, I send them off after their prey, the medley of duos moving in tandem, each pair never straying far from their partner. With the grace of dancers, they shift through door and window, drift from roof to roof as silently as the wind.

I kneel, watching their progress, my senses tuned as tight as a harp's strings, the air shivering as I follow it all. Strands of golden light and energy leading me away from the vanishing dogs of death and closer to my own private salvation.

The tickle of her rippling energy flirting with the edges of my consciousness, teasing my ego with each touch as I finally reach the fall.

My eyes shift, the cream tinged glow of her golden yellow aura fills my vision, the cloak around her shoulders masking her from sight to all but me.

A harsh burst of colour makes me wince as two of my Hunters unfurl their true forms and vanish into the canopy below. The dirt beneath my fingertips hums with ancient malice as I let it trickle through my fingers. The fall. I have always hated this place, their combined stench all too engrained into the very core of this scorched patch of malignant earth.

'What did Michael do, Lucifer, how did he win against you?' I muse.

Rising to my feet, I watch as one after another they descend, brothers, sister, husbands and lovers; each pair drifting down to the green blanket below.

✦ ✦ ✦

The Drewen tremble, their frightened quivering setting the world alight in a shimmering, shifting haze of light. I lie, silent as the grave as they begin their approach, this cluster of Sleepers ferreting through the brush in a pale attempt at stealth. These are supposed to be the elite stalkers and intelligence gatherers. I listen to the whispered grunt of condescending disapproval filter through the leaves to my left.

A low growl of anger boils up from my throat, silencing them as I push my coiled reach out to its limits, tasting the air for any semblance of a sign that she is amongst them. A small brush makes me grin as our searching ethereal hands meet, the soft kiss of her embrace filling me as I softly nod to those around me.

'Take them.'

The overwhelming ferocity that boils forth gives me pause. I watch as one Huntress ensnares the hair of one Sleeper agent, her girlish squeal echoing as her killer's fingers curl tightly through the silk blonde tresses. I see her eyes widen as her head is yanked backwards, leaving her throat exposed to the world as the Huntress' fingers sink into the soft pliant flesh. Undulating rivers of sapphire spill out around the invading digits. I watch in morbid fascination as the glistening cartilage of the girl's throat crackles and splits in her killer's grip, the wet snap drawing a grin from the feral woman as the agent's eyes begin to darken, death already sucking the life from her as her gossamer silk robes are dyed with her own life's essence.

The expression is always the same, disbelief and shock mingling with an arrogant refusal to acknowledge that an 'Angel of God' was bested by a demon. These pitiful children wouldn't know a true demon if they saw one. Even now, they are meeting their end at the hands of children and blood lusting teens. I turn my back on the melee, the sound of screams and clashing steel blurring as I walk deeper into the forest, my own blade snarling in my mind as I twist it around my hand.

Sixteen of my best they may be, but not one of them deserves the title, spoilt children of forgotten, washed up warriors, their armour little more than an ill-fitting suit passed down from one would be killer to the next. I feel a small pang of guilt as I crouch here watching this all unfold. That doe-eyed girl had never even seen a true sunrise and yet there she was, her throat in the hands of an overzealous child, ripped from her like the stuffing from a toy bear. Where's the honour in that? To die drowning in your own blood, choking as your lungs fill with what was once pumping through your veins. I cannot stay here anymore. I push myself to my feet.

These children are not my kin, they're not Hunters. They're malicious cretins that glory in slaughter. These fledgling sleepers were nothing more than mice before cats, so ill prepared for what lay beyond their borders. They deserved better, better training and a better send. The sounds of their screams follow me as I walk, pushing through the foliage around me until the sounds of that school yard scuffle is little more than a murmur in my ears.

I need to see her, to see my angel. The gnawing in my soul is carving away at me, driving my mind to despair as I reach out, slapping aside the panicked feelers of the Sleepers and exultant clapping grasp of those hedonistic children. My senses pricked for the smallest sign of her, the merest hint that she is here.

I find her, tucked away in the bowl of a large oak tree, her cloak pulled tightly around her as she hides, oblivious to the merciless slaughter of her kin. I softly tease the edges of her aura with my own, even as the distance between us stretches beyond count. I straighten my posture and turn back to the butcher's floor that these pups now frolic in. I know beyond a shadow of doubt that if she were to find this carnal dance, to find this butcher of Heaven's footmen, that there would be nary a chance to stop her before she dove forth and joined the fray.

My voice is harsh, uncaring and devoid of praise. I loath the very sight of these simpering children. I know this was Lucifer's idea of a punishment more than a test of my abilities. Burdening me with these useless sacks of skin and malice, his ear twisted by another fellow "Warrior" hoping to hobble me and make way for a more pliable sixth general.

'Go, take yourselves back to the under croft, none of you are to remain here. I will deal with stragglers myself. Bathe and repair yourselves, not that I expect you will have much to garner as wounds; these hatchlings were not even worthy prey.'

I watch a few sneer at the slaughtered pile of flesh at my feet, my ire pouring over them as I turn, my eyes shifting as I glare at them.

'Show some respect to those you have slain; they died with their honour intact. Pray that you can claim the same when your time comes. Disrespect the fallen again and I will butcher you where you stand. Now disappear, remove yourselves from my sight. I'm sick of looking at you.'

I turn, the harsh hacking cough of someone's final breaths filling my ears as my senses follow the departing flock of depravity I was so saddled with. Picking my way amongst the carrion floor, twitching hands and shattered bones littering the way, I find one blue eyed dove, her wings pinioned to the floor by the limbs of an oak. The twisted ends skewer through the soft flesh and deep into the earth, rooting her to the spot. The pain that dances in her eyes strikes deep within me. If this is what they're all too willing to do to her, what would they do to Arianwen?

I kneel, my hand stroking her brow as I feel Ari's energy move, her eyes watching my aura shift and undulate as I draw it in close to me. The fear in the girl's eyes says more than her blood drowned words ever could. My thumb moves over the punctured vein in her neck, the flow little more than a trickle as her once flushed skin begins to pale, the plaster grey sheen of death licking its way over her.

'This will hurt. I'm sorry. I thought they had more honour than this. Rest child, and I will make this quick.'

I press down hard, her eyes widening as I seize the chance and rip one of the stakes from the ground, her wing snapping back, the jolt rolling through her as her lips open in a silent scream. I slip my free hand around her neck as I move my hand to the other wing, my thumb once more pressing deep into the wound, sealing the flow and prolonging her life for a moment more.

I watch tears flow as her wings finally close, the tension in her body melting as I ease my pressing from her neck. With a tender motion I wipe away the glittering pearls and draw my blade from its sheath, settling the cold point beneath her breast, the fluttering of her heart shivering along its edge and into my soul. I close my eyes, willing away the anger that had so plagued me moments before.

'Sleep now, little dove, your pain is at an end.'

I drive my blade deep into her heart, her eyes snapping wide for the briefest of moments before she slumps to the ground, her body going slack. A soft smile plays across her features as the final dregs of light leave her. Golden pearls fill the air as she begins to dissolve, her ethereal soul being cradled by the winds of her maker as she is called home once more. I watch her form collapse, vanishing in a mist of dancing glitter and light, a silent vow screaming in my mind as I rise to my feet. The sixteen will come to know me well before the night is through. They will bring honour to their names and to the sixth. This slaughter today is a stain they will wipe clean with their sweat and blood, of that I will make sure.

✦ ✦ ✦

She stands there, her head cocked to the side as my heart hammers in my chest, the echoing thump searing through my brain as I reach for her. My lips latch on to hers, their smooth silken brush crashing through me as I encircle her waist pulling her against me, the press of her breast against my chest sending a chill along my spine.

If demons could cry, I would; the burning hitch in my throat smothers everything that drifts up, I turn my head, my lips gliding with a fierce passion over hers as I push us both into the thick trunk of an oaken Drewen. Her glowing golden tresses catching in the bark as I lift her from the floor.

My length strains against the threads of my crotch lacing, her warmth begging for my touch as I feel her heat blaze against my leather coated abdomen. She curls her legs around me as I feel her arms snake around my neck, her tongue coaxing mine as I grin, my smile drawing forth its mirror from the sweet angelic vixen in my embrace.

'Oh, how I missed you.'

My whispered words find their way free of the roiling smoke filled crush in my throat. Her hands slip from my neck, trailing over my shoulders and down my arms, plucking and tickling at everything they touch. I feel her searching grasp reach my waist, trailing over the rippling flesh of my lower stomach as she drags her nails over my belt line. The feel of her on my skin sends a pulsing line of blissful heat through my very soul as I draw her lip into my teeth, pulling at it as I tear her blouse apart. Her fingers tease my bindings, searching for a way to the rampant source of my lust.

I turn her tentative fingers away as I rip the lacing apart, my length springing free as Arianwen's soft grip ensnares my shaft, sliding along my ridged flesh as I drag her dress up and over her hips, her hand guiding me to her sodden cleft, her slickness sliding over my length's end as she slowly draws me along its wet lips.

I groan deep in my throat as she shifts. I lift her hips, driving myself down into her. Her warmth envelopes me completely as I feel her clutching core grasp me, drawing me deeper, closing around me as her fragrant essence flows free, soaking my agates in their viscous honey. Her lips slip from mine as I draw myself from her before driving my swelling length as deep as I can into my angel. I feel her chin against my neck, her breath warm and moist on my skin as I begin to drop into a steady lust driven rhythm.

Her panting breath drives me to distraction as she gasps at each thrust, the wet smack of our heated dance fills the air as she sinks her teeth into my skin, the snatch of white pain sends my fangs snapping free as I drive myself ever deeper into her welcoming silk. My guttural grunting echoes her gasping moans as I feel my blood well from her bite.

The wet warmth of her tongue on my skin makes my agates tighten as she glides it over the puckered puncture in my shoulder. The bitter bite of her slim slither of pink flesh darts over the raw holes, exciting me to new heights as I bury myself to the hilt in her dripping core.

My floodgates fall open, the torrent of need and raw desire that fills me wipes away everything, letting my animal lust rise to consume all I am. I grab her arms, pinning my gasping angel to the tree beneath us as I pull myself from her.

My hand finds her throat as I curl my right through her hair, turning her, lifting her from the floor. I plant my slim angel face first against the sentient tree, her hands finding purchase as she sinks her fingers into its rippled bark, pushing the side of her head against the coarse skin of the Drewen as she whimpers in my grip.

I slip my hand from her neck as I drag my nails along her smooth skin. Pin striped red weals mark my passage as I sink my fingers into her firm round cheek, teasing the flesh of her backside as I run my slick length against her flushed and pouting coven; with a heavy, sudden thrust, I send my rigid meat deep into her quivering core as she all but screams at the pressing flesh boring into her.

The sheer abandon that rolls through me is intoxication beyond belief. I feel my mind slip, falling into a chasm so deep that for the briefest of moments I am simply gone, riding on the waves of our mutual ecstasy.

The sound of our lust filled love shatters the air, her body arching against me as she screams. Her sweat racked body trembles as I delve deeper into her nectar soaked core, my shaft slipping through her silk walls as I feel myself tighten. My end rises as she writhes and gasps, pinned to me by my ridged shaft, our connection as pure in that moment as it has ever been.

Her head rolls backwards, a strangled, whimpering, orgasmic cry echoing from her lips as my seed pours free, filling her, spilling into her as she pushes back against me; her hips grinding into my stomach as she throws herself back against me, sending us both tumbling to the floor as I slowly slip free.

✦ ✦ ✦

A soft hum of contentment drifts up from the woman curled against my chest as my fingers trail lazily through her hair. The flecks of bark and the soft graze that skims over her cheek stand as testament to what had just gone on between us. I feel her fingers trail over my neck and shoulder, her fingers finding the small dips in my skin as my flesh continues to slowly knit itself back together.

I feel the coarse grain of the flecks of moss covered bark as they grate over my knuckles. The play of her hair through my fingers lulls me into a stupor as I comb my finger along the soft blonde strands of silk, watching the speckled rain of flaked timber glide free as she curls against me.

Nothing in that moment could have been more perfect. The utter and complete satiety, in both my heart and my soul, the swelling of love and hunger swirling into one glorious culmination of carnal and emotional exploration. The sheer ecstasy that unfurled, sweeping us both along in its turbulent wake, only to leave us gasping, drenched in our own satisfied desires, teetering on the edge of slumber in the dappled light of the trees that softly coo around us.

The pall of comfort is shattered in an instant as a crashing wave of carnivorous malice envelopes us both. I roll to my feet, bringing Arianwen up with me, spinning her behind me in an instant as I stretch my senses outwards, washing away the playful stupor that had so lulled me into a false security only moments before.

'Go, now. I know these Hunters, if they find you here, they will not hesitate to flay you alive. Run, pull your cloak about you and move as fast as you can, straight to the gates. I will draw them away; go!'

I watch her eyes harden as she opens her mouth to reply, her words stilling as she sees the ghost of anger and fear in my eyes, try as I might to keep it from her. With a soft nod she pulls her hood up and over her vibrant locks and disappears into the brush, the soft rustle of leaves filling the air as she vanishes from my sight.

Lost Words

ARIANWEN

The sound in my ears is deafening as my blood still pumps with rapid speed through my body, making me sway slightly as I step towards my home and away from the man who just made my heart soar and my body sing.

His frantic attack took me by surprise as his lips took mine in a vicious, yet sensual grasp. I could taste the adrenalin running through his system, mixed with fear, longing and love. I could barely catch my breath as he devoured me like a starving man, a man who was in desperate need of his woman, and my body responded instantly, turning me into a frantic mess of lips and hands.

I was so taken aback by his frantic actions that by the time he let his grip ease and ordered me to return to safety, I had forgotten what I went in search of him for. I never got to return to him the collection of those three emotion filled words. I desperately want to go back just to tell him I love him, but I can still sense his fellow Hunters around his aura so it's best I just continue on my way.

I'm almost at the gatekeepers when I hear a calling. Even though the other Hunters are still near, I have to go. I could never turn my back on a soul in need, I wouldn't be me if I did. I take care in walking the long way around, out to the far edges of this dying forest before cautiously turning back in and heading towards the village. I no longer feel the presence of Albion or the other Hunters, assuming they have entered the pits of Hell, but that doesn't mean I drop my guard. There are many an evil creature lurking amongst the walking dead.

I reach my destination and enter the broken down hut which offers little protection for me or the soul seeking safe passage back to their maker. I know I have to take extra care to remain unseen so I pull my cloak tighter around me and reach back to place the hood over my head, in hopes of smothering some of the luminous light I emit when performing a reclaim.

My senses are heightened beyond measure as I draw every last piece of power and strength from within my body to enable the soul to seek their way back home and through the shining white gates of Heaven, to be welcomed with love and happiness from the ones who have passed before.

As I exit this almost fallen down shelter, I hear a heart wrenching scream of absolute terror shattering the peace I just created. I know I shouldn't go, I know it's not within my powers to save the person it belongs to, I know it will only place myself in the line of fire, but I can't ignore the sound of pain. I have to go and see if my powers could possibly do anything to make this painful sound cease.

I go to the back of the nearest building and close my eyes, gathering everything my senses can find to help me get closer to the sound without being detected. I know the scream came from a young woman aged nineteen in human years and the auras of two dark forces of the highest rank are almost smothering what light she has left in this in between world.

I open my eyes and search the nearby area for any immediate danger. Once satisfied that I can move without being seen, I make my way behind building after building until I am almost upon the source of such distressful sounds. I flatten myself against a wall as I try in vain to make my body as silent as it can be so I can get close enough to let my eyes see what I may be up against.

My breathing is less than a whisper and my heart slows almost to the point of death, as my aura takes over and smothers whatever detectable sign of life I am emitting from my angelic form. Once I am but a mere walking ghost, I move in as close as I can, bending down low, placing my now cold hands on the filth below and crawl around the side of a barely standing shack. There are piles of wood standing up straight against this dwelling, giving me coverage to move in close to the source of distress. I slide my body against the half rotten wood of the wall and behind some of the standing timber, where I find a small gap. I lean my head in closer until my eyes finally reach the sight of horror which is almost within arm's reach of my body.

If I could gasp I would, for the sight before me is the most hideous thing my eyes have ever laid upon in all my existence.

A young, once beautiful woman is slouched over an old wine barrel. Her clothing hangs from her body in tatters, barely covering her flesh which is dripping with her red life force from the multiple wounds which have been so cruelly inflicted. Her breathing is laboured as she tries and whimpers for help from the two dark figures who are standing on either side of her withering form.

My brain screams at me to run away fast, as it becomes familiar with the sights before it. I have never sighted, even from afar, the figures before me, but my many lessons have made me very aware of who these tall, all black, menacing creatures are. Their name has been whispered for centuries amongst the villages who dwell in this waiting room of death. A name which holds almost as much fear as the one who is named Lucifer. The towering, wretched black figures my eyes are showing me are the Dolophonos.

If Lucifer were to leave his chamber in the darkest depths of Hell, and wander up towards the light to walk around this village of the condemned, there would still be some beings who would hold more fear for the Dolophonos than for the Devil himself, as it's these dark mythical creatures who act out the Devil's most horrendous of punishments. They carry out Satan's most painful of acts so he doesn't have to dirty his own hands.

As my brain still screams at me to run, I witness one of the dark ghosts move closer to the girl, bends down behind her, grabbing both her kicking feet in one of his black skeletal hands and brings them down to the filthy earth below, holding them in place while his companion moves over to a pile of large, long tree trunks and carefully selects the largest one he can find.

Ever so slowly, he moves to stand behind the girl, raises the long piece of heavy timber above his head before slamming it down with extreme force, dropping it across the back of the girl's heels, pinning her to the putrid earth beneath. She screams in absolute agony, arching herself up off the barrel she was placed over, I feel it course through me, pain and anguish welling within me as I feel her cries for help spear through my soul.

The Dolophonos move swiftly, gripping the girl's arms with their clawed fingers, blood running like streams down her skin as they bring her body back down to once more curve over the ancient barrel beneath her. One holds her down, wrapping his weathered fingers painfully around her neck, crushing them into her flesh, the other moves to the front where her head is limp, no longer able to make a sound as the pain she is suffering is robbing her of the ability to scream.

Watching through the cracked and broken sheet of wood, I see him grab her hands and stretch her arms out to their full extent as he lowers himself to his knees, pinning her hands. The other dark figure removes his hand from her neck and bends down to pick up two small boulders beside the barrel before making his way slowly towards her head. His larger than life form looms tall above her fractured body as he one by one drops the boulders onto her hands as his fellow comrade removes his own just before the boulders make contact with her fingers. Her flesh splits and spills out like a rotten tomato as the sound of bones cracking fill the air

The gargling sounds that emanate from her throat are sickening as both of the Dolophonos stand back and admire their handiwork, standing, silently watching as this poor defenceless shell of a human struggles to even draw breath.

They stand there staring at her, not moving, not acknowledging the whimpering, near silent pleas of the shattered and torn girl before them as she begs for forgiveness and pleads with them to just end her life.

I can't help but wonder at what crime she had committed in their eyes, for her to deserve such a barbaric punishment. They stand there for what seems like an eternity and just as I think they're about to turn away and leave this poor being in such a painful position, they move swiftly, flanking either side of her, each one of them raising a dark arm with an old fashioned whip in their grips and bringing them down at the exact same time with such a force I squeeze my eyes shut, not wanting to witness the possibility that they may have just cut her body in half.

I can't save her. I can't stop her torment. I can't rescue her soul before it endures another ounce of pain and that kills me inside. The powers I possess are nothing against the Devil's best creations.

My hiding place is so close to them I can't even risk moving to try and cause a distraction. I have never felt as helpless in my life as I do now, within arm's reach of someone in desperate need of my help, but without the power to save them from their pain.

I hear a strangled gargle come from the girl and force myself to open my eyes. Her body is still intact, but barely. Their whips have sliced off two large chunks of her flesh down the sides of her body beside her rib cage, which are now lying on the filthy earth beneath her knees. The gargling sound I heard is from the blood slowly dripping from her mouth, which has frozen open in a silent scream. Her breathing is heavy and I wonder how much of this torture she could possible endure before her soul is finally ripped from her shell.

The Dolophonos move, one behind her feet, the other to the front of her head, as they once more raise the whips above their head and bring them down with such force that the earth rattles for but a second. I flinch but refuse to close my eyes, as I still hold hope for a chance to save this suffering human. The lashes have landed on her back this time, one straight down her spine, the other across her middle on an angle, creating a cross that has now been permanently sliced into her flesh. She lifts her head in a silent screech, no energy left to make a noise, as I witness the flesh on her back start to peel back like it is lifting off one layer at a time.

They don't give her a reprieve as they raise their whips once more, this time landing them across the backs of her exposed thighs and the back of her neck, severing veins and tendons, making it impossible for her to lift her head in protest. It's as if the whole worlds have gone silent, all forced to watch this monstrosity, with the only noise the heavy rasping breath of the poor victim before my eyes.

Both creatures move to either side of her head and kneel down upon their knees, leaning slightly over her as one of them finally speaks with a very old and ancient accent. 'Tell us the story of what your eyes witnessed, and we may take pity on your atrocious form.'

The poor girl seems unable to reply even if she had the answers they seek. 'We hold no patience, so answer immediately or the *real* torture will commence,' the other one adds with a growl to his heavy tone.

She doesn't reply, and they don't waste any time following through with their threat. They both reach a hand out towards her face as I watch, astounded, as their pointed nails crackle and turn a deep glowing orange as if they were just removed from a raging fire. When they make contact with her face, I can hear her skin sear, the smell of burning flesh rushing through the air, assaulting my nostrils as they continue to viciously draw small x's all over her once white delicate cheeks.

The noise this poor girl is making doesn't even sound human. Her whimpers sound like that of a dying animal from the forest. She tries in vain to wriggle free from her restraints but these demonic savages have made sure she remains immobile, meeting her demise while slain over a wine barrel.

I am stuck here, unable to escape this heinous act I am being forced to witness. I am not oblivious to the long history of the Devil's many centuries of Satanic crimes, but I have never witnessed first hand the punishments he has ordered to be carried out. If this is what his most vile creatures are capable of, I would hate to be at the direct hand of the Devil himself.

While one of the Dolophonos continues his cutting patterns on her cheeks, the other raises both his hands, which have now returned to their normal black, clamps them together above his head, and begins a chant in an ancient language I can't decipher. A large deep purple ball of gas like substance starts to form in between his palms, a faint hissing sound vibrating through the air around us as it slowly grows louder with each passing second.

He steps in front of her, the mysterious wavering ball he holds beginning to swell as he continues to chant his sorcerer's words. I wait, anticipation twisting my heart tightly as to what this mysterious entity he holds contains, my brain still scrambling around for a way to end this viciousness.

As he looms over her, the hissing noise stops and the other Dolophonos stills. There is nothing but silence just before he whispers two words.

'Abeo Lam.'

My mind races, searching my memory, as I am sure I have heard those two words before. And just as my mind supplies me with their meaning *'die now,'* he squeezes the ball which releases a white fluid that rains down upon the girl's head as the smell of an acid like poison fills the air, stinging my eyes and burning my nostrils, as the victim releases a blood curdling scream of horror with the last of her life force.

The smell of her melting hair is like burning straw from a field as it fills the air surrounding us. I watch as her flesh starts to melt and drip to the ground below, her face now resembling a painting which has been left in the rain, colours running down, distorting and blending as one. He continues to guide the ball slowly down the rest of her body, flesh and veins dropping from bone like liquid wax. The scent of rotting flesh makes my stomach turn as my heart lurches in extreme pain at my helplessness to save this being before me. My powers alone are nothing compared to the Devil's minions. I hold myself as still as I can, despite my fight or flight reflex trying to kick in, telling me that flight is my only means of survival. I know how powerful these creatures are so it's only a matter of time before they will scent me here in my makeshift hiding place.

The poor girl is still whimpering and moving slightly by the time the acid rain reaches her legs, as she now resembles nothing more than a slab of meat that has been left to rot in the sun. She stops moving; she is now completely silent, but I can sense that her soul is still clinging to the last threads of its human shell.

Both Dolophonos move to the front of her head, standing, waiting, for what I do not know. Then one of these heinous creatures bends forward and places one long black finger at the top of her skull, pushing slightly into the exposed brain that's barely covered by what's left of her flesh. Time stands still. I hold my breath as I watch a line of large grey beetles, each with two sharp prickled claws, crawl from under his cloak, over his hand and down his finger and start to bury themselves into her brain.

I almost screech, throwing a hand over my mouth, as I hear the beetles clicking and clawing their way through her cerebral matter, shredding it like paper, consuming it, as I slowly feel her soul wither and disappear, now becoming the property of Lucifer. I feel like a part of me has died, knowing that the soul could have been saved one day if only I had reached her before this vile torture had even begun.

Three of the Devil's Hunters stumble upon the clearing, making the Dolophonos look their way, giving me what may be my only chance to quietly sneak away from this brothel of death. I move slightly but swiftly, knowing I may be in the gravest danger of my existence if they feel my presence moving in this world. I dare not look back, my complete concentration focused on every movement and step I have to take to rid myself of this malicious place.

As I leave the last of the village's buildings and enter the forgotten forest, I start to quicken my steps, desperate to leave these worlds behind, desperate to be rid the visions that are now flashing in my head, desperate to put as much distance between myself and all the hideous creatures the Devil has created.

Albion. Is he one of those creatures? No, he has too much good inside of him to be a creature of the Devil's hand, but that doesn't mean he wasn't created from evil. His parents were demons also, but how did they receive a child that is not consumed by darkness? How did he become the man he is hiding inside? Regardless of his true origin, he is and always has been a part of the dark world and all the vile depravity that comes with it. What acts of evil has he been a part of?

No! I don't want to know the answer to that. My head is still showing me visions of what I just witnessed, but instead of the Dolophonos, I am seeing Albion's face. I am not that naïve to not know that there is a possibility that Albion has taken part in such heinous acts, or even some that may have been worse. But I do have to ask my heart and soul how can I be so in love with someone capable of such sickening evil? Love, can I still tell Albion I love him after baring witness to such sickening acts, acts I know are a daily occurrence in the place he calls home?

Why, why has fate chosen this man for me to give my heart to when every fibre in my entire body is full of only good? The balance of life could never exist between us as a couple. We will never find a common ground to live upon. Every time I look into his soul, am I going to be reminded of all his past sins? I know there is a reason as to why my heart has opened up for him, but what if that reason turns out to be of Satan's design?

I know in my heart and soul that Albion's intentions towards me are true and honourable but what if he is being played himself, coerced by the Devil? Are we both being fooled into playing a life or death game of chess just for Lucifer's amusement?

My head has never been so confused in my life. I have always been a logical person but since laying eyes on my eternal saviour for the first time, I have felt like I haven't had one coherent thought. What in these worlds are wrong with me? Is this what love does to one's brain? I have read many a story about the foolish behaviour of mortals in love but never once thought I would play into that foolishness. So is this the result of a sorcerer's spell? Would my heart and soul be susceptible to such manipulation?

Whatever the reason for my recent revelations of love, I know now that saying those three little words aloud to Albion would only have given more power to whatever holds sway over me. I wasn't meant to say them. And I don't know if I ever will be.

20

Hidden Betrayal

ALBION

I reach the fall, the snapping auras of this group of would be killers nipping at my heels as I draw my blade. If I am to truly throw them from the scent of the woman who owns me completely then I know I have to make this convincing. Drawing my weapon from its sheath, I close my eyes, willing it to forgive me for what I am about to do. I feel its feral whimper in the back of my skull as I sink the blade deep into the meat of my side, leather, skin and flesh parting as I feel the razor honed edge skim across the plaster white face of my ribs.

I clench my teeth, screwing my eyes shut as I fall to my knees and yank my weapon free. I stare at the edge, the powdered white of my own bones coating it, as I watch my blood slip from the tip, pattering to the earth beneath me.

I force myself to stand as they arrive, chests heaving and eyes ablaze as I glare at them. None of them meet my gaze as I finally stagger to my full height. I watch one of them cower back, his movements furtive, submissive to a fault as I clutch at the self-inflicted wound in my side, their eyes dropping to it as I grimace slightly.

'You stupid children, this is your reward, to see me scarred and bleeding. Disobedience has a price and I just paid it for you. Disappear from my sight. I will deal with you when I return to the under croft. Be sure to make yourselves available upon my return. You do not want me to come seeking you out.'

I watch one of these self-proclaimed killers born of Lucifer raise his head, daring to meet my eye as I stride towards them. The sheen of fear that plays across his face makes a grin blossom behind the rictus of self-inflicted pain that is creeping over my features.

I glare at the ridiculous being as he opens his mouth to speak. I snap my hand forwards, fingers closing around his throat as I lift him from the floor.

'If you dare say a word, be it apology or otherwise, I will tear your tongue from your head and use it to polish my boots. Remove yourself from my sight.'

Without another word, they vanish as I move into the shaded awning of one of the tenements closest to the fall, the squat building little more than stacks of stone with a sheet metal roof lashed to it through wood lintel windows. The stink of their fear lace the air as I peel apart the split edges of my armour, the searing heat of my own opened flesh bathe my fingers as I watch my life's blood pulse from the wound.

'She's going to kill me for this if she ever finds out.'

My muttered self-admonishment flirts with my ears as I whisper a slow incantation, dragging my index finger along the weeping rent of flesh and sinew. I choke back a scream of utter agony as it begins to knit itself back together, twisting strands of muscle and skin, drawing my body whole as I collapse backwards, my form hitting the ramshackle wall with a hollow thunk before I slide to the floor panting like a dog in the sun.

I wait, sunlight bathing my face as it slowly drops through the sky. I cut too deep, I know I did, my wounds have never before taken this long to heal; then again I have never been sliced from buttock to navel with my own weapon before. I peel the leather of my shredded armour away, craning my neck to stare into the slowly sealing rent in my side. I catch site of my own rib, the pale grey shaft of bone glaring at me from the congealing viscous mass of flesh and blood.

I let my head slump back, my eyes dipping closed as I slip into a comatose slumber, my senses stretched wide, pinned to the world around me like a sheet of glass. The movement of anything larger than a mouse sends vibrations through my very soul, awakening me in an instant if I am healed or not.

The first notion I have of my not being alone is the darkening rays of the sun across my face. The loss of heat is palpable even in my near comatose state. Slowly my eyes stumble open, the sheer weight of my own lids drawing immensely on my meagre store of energy, the power my body has consumed in its need to heal my self-inflicted injury is far more than I would have ever thought. I will have to see Barbatos to find out just what he has crafted into the blade I wield.

Sluggishly, with all the speed of a paraplegic snail, I find the will to focus on whatever it is that is now staring back at me. A set of blazing orange orbs fills my vision as I struggle to comprehend who it is that is before me. The eyes are so eerily familiar but at the same time they're not ones I recognise.

I watch as they shift, the colours collapsing in on themselves as they turn a luminescent pink, I feel my stomach lurch as I watch them turn, the sight too much for my weakened state.

The voice that flows back at me drags my mind through fog and into the present as I feel hands grasp me under my arms, my eyes widening as I growl, willing myself not to cry out as I feel the wound in my side part slightly.

'Alp, please.'

My pitiful plea falls on deaf ears as I feel myself move upwards, Alp's limber frame hauling me upright as he tucks his shoulder into my armpit and begins the slow march back to my cell in the under croft.

'No, not there, take me where I tell you to. I need to heal away from prying eyes.'

I guide him to one of the small safe rooms I keep throughout the village, my steps growing weaker as the minutes trickle by. I know even in my dazed and weakened state that this is not my smartest of moves and yet, Alp is the one person in the entire damned kingdom that I can trust implicitly. I lean against the mud coated wall, bidding him to turn away as I trail my fingers over the sun baked surface until a subtle click resounds and my warded doorway opens up.

His steps falter as we enter the safe house, the sensory din that fills the outside world falling to nothing as he once more carries me forth, my bed meeting my falling form as Alp lets me slip from his grip.

The bear pelt sits soft against my skin as I sink into the wadded blankets and taut canvas below; the irony of such a demon needing a safe house so close to their own borders is not lost on me. Even as the infection slowly spreads through me, I cannot help but chuckle, my strained laugh drawing a concerned glance from my lifelong friend.

I force my body upright, gingerly dragging my armour off, letting the gore smeared lump of leather and mail fall to the floor at my feet. I watch through fog laden eyes as Alp moves towards me, his arms laden with gauze and bottles from my meagre store of medicinal aids.

'Why aren't you healing? A wound like this shouldn't have even slowed you down.'

I bite down on my teeth as Alp drags a pad of gauze through the gaping mouth in my side, the thick black tinged pool of coagulating blood that soaks it giving me pause as I watch Alp stare at it, his brow furrowed.

'Albion, what caused this? There are only a few weapons I know that would cause a wound like this, and all of them have been made by Barbatos.'

I turn my gaze away as he looks at me, his questioning gaze brushing aside his obvious curiosity as to where we are now sat.

'It was my own. I was momentarily disarmed in a confrontation with Gabriel's Sleepers and one of them turned my own weapon upon me.'

Alp returns to his ministrations, seemingly content with my recounting of one possible truth. It stings me in a way I have never before felt, to know that I am actively deceiving one of my oldest and truest friends. Even in the circles of Hell, Alp is one of a handful I truly trust and is one of a rapidly diminishing group that I would ever consider turning to for aid in my time of need.

I grind my teeth as I feel him peel my wound open further, the acidic pang of the cleansing lotion searing over the tender flesh as he begins to draw out whatever it is that is so afflicting me.

'Explains a lot. Barbatos' weapons are honed and cursed to pollute the user or ensure a lingering death should they end up being turned on the one they were made for, more than a little twisted, but Barbatos is an ...'

He pauses, searching out the right words as he continues to tease and pull at my flesh.

'Unusual individual. He is far older than many of those that dwell within our kingdom as you know, but was also the first to acquiesce to Lucifer's demands.'

I try not to scream as I feel him begin to stitch the wound closed, the bone shard needle slicing through my flesh the purest of agony. I struggle to fathom how something that small can create such inordinate pain.

Not even the wounds I have taken in battle can compare to this torture. I feel my flesh pull and move as he tugs each loop closed, my flesh slowly succumbing to the healing powers held within the tincture that has soaked through the threads and gauze.

The path winds down before me, twisting into the thick cloud of steam and heat that perpetually blankets the lower circles. I feel their grasping hands tug at my senses willing me to them, pale attempts at drawing me into their intoxicated dance of vice and salacious debauchery.

I slap aside their furtive touches and head deeper into these smoke stained corridors, my goal all too clear in my mind as I trudge onwards. Anger eats at me as I feel my stitches twist and stretch, blood weeping down my side as I grit my teeth. Barbatos will hear of this, I swear on it to all the souls of kin long dead, he will hear of it.

The doors ahead give me pause. The two hulking guards at the edges of the portal spare me a momentary glance as I stop, staring at the Sigel carved into the ebony face. I let my hand slip to my side, pressing at the wound that festers there, eating my resolve like maggots through rotting flesh.

I push the doors aside and stride through; the heat hits me with unbridled force. The air in my lungs sears them shut in a near instant as I feel the runes carved into my flesh glow, melting my human husk like sugar through water. The pale flesh of man slips like wet paper from me, pooling around my feet as I struggle to stay upright.

'You do not look in the halest of health, Albion. Shall I fetch the apothecary?'

I glare from behind hooded eyes as I watch Lucifer sip at the cup in his grip, my blood boiling in my veins as I finally regain control of my own flesh and step forwards.

'You saddled me with children. You tell me I will get sixteen of the best that form my ranks and yet I get sixteen pups barely off their mothers' teats.'

Lucifer holds my gaze as he sips slowly. With infuriating slowness and poise, he sets the cup back on a saucer and cradles his hands in his lap.

'Your point.'

I move slowly and with great care, stopping short of the small table in front of Lucifer.

'My point is, these children should not even be in armour let alone in the field. They're untrained, undisciplined, and ravenous. Not one even worthy of the armour of their fathers or their name and you saddled me with them, knowing what I was being sent after. You're either trying to get me killed or someone else is.'

With infinitesimal care, he plucks a small handkerchief from the table at his elbow and wipes away the last vestiges of whatever foul concoction is now fermenting in the pot on his table.

'Again, Albion, what pray tell is your point, and is there a logical end to this petulant tirade?'

I feel my heart slam against the inside of my chest, my anger boiling through me as he smirks at me, the taunting condescension bleeding from his eyes and quirked lips. The twirl of his hand as he motions for me to speak, dragging my ire to the fore, the shuddering force of its hammer blows against the gates of my own senses deafening as I struggle to keep it all in check.

'My point is, "Sire," that no matter what you think about sending these "children" to my side, they are in no way a substitute for the thousand strong cadre I have spent the last three hundred years training. It very nearly cost me my life having to watch their backs as well as my own. They are no more fit for combat than half of the boiled sots that fill your torture pits.'

I rein myself in before I let slip my true thoughts on this spiralling debacle. I take a step back as Lucifer rises to his feet, the billowing cloak around his shoulders casting a menacing blanket of shadow over his tautly honed frame.

'You may think me remiss in allying you with those "pups" as you have called them, but remember, Albion, everything has a reason. I had to be sure that you were up to the task of commanding even the most rough and unskilled of your cadre before I set you loose on anything with more skill. Would you pass command of the entire sixth legion on to someone like Alp for instance?

'The young fellow is excellent in his own field but he is far from command material. Yes, those children are nowhere near your calibre or skill, but I had to be sure you could work with even the most menial of provisions. To know how to do something with the most basic of tools sets you in grand stead for the larger tasks to come.'

He steps past me, a wave of his hand casting aside a lacquered ebony screen. Moving into his wake, I find myself moving out onto a small plateau, the crenelated stone railing ringing the balcony like shelf. I stare in amazement at the view before me, the glowing vista filled with the onyx black walls of our homeland, the weaving orange veins of fire and molten rock shimmering in the spectral pall of steam and vapour that hangs like a blanket over it all.

'Breath taking, isn't it? I often find myself caught by the majesty of it all, the single casting view that holds all of our kind in one sweeping expanse. From the pulsing thump of the under croft, the beating heart of this world, to the flowing rivers that ferry the damned to us on the back of Kharon. That poor soul was once like you and me; he spent so long trapped in those foul waters that he lost all semblance of what little of his human form remained. Then the vicious minions of Barbatos got their hooks and claws into him and now, if you cast your eye down, you will see for yourself what has become of him.'

I stare down, the heady drop to the waters below making my head spin as I spy the bloated hulk of the ferryman, his body warped and twisted, spine bent and split until it buckled, rails of iron and wood hammered into his tortured form. The rippling flesh of his back peeled away, hoisted aloft on the shards of his ribs to hang like wet leather, sodden sails of living flesh flapping in the heat soaked air, thick pulsing veins their rigging.

I tear my gaze away as I catch Lucifer staring at me, his eyes casting a knowing glare as I turn to face him once more.

'Is it any surprise your wounds haven't healed? Your weapon was created by a demon who commanded his minions to turn the bloated hulk of one of his own into a living boat! Is it that surprising that our own weaponry is toxic to not only our enemies, but ourselves as well? Barbatos may have little respect for me, but he has even less for you. Do not be taken in by his caring façade, Albion. You forget, it was his hand that helped end your father's life.'

I am rendered mute, unable to form even the weakest of responses. Is this some form of mental trap? Is he, in some churlish and spite filled way, trying to draw me out and trick me into spilling forth my deepest of thoughts by invoking the memory of my father? He is that cruel and vindictive, of that I have no doubt, but surely, even with all he has at his beck and call, there is no way he has an inkling of what has transpired between me and Arianwen.

I watch his face for any sign of malcontent and yet all I see is a passive acceptance of all that is before him. Could it be that he is truly warning me to be wary of a demon I thought was one of the few connections I had to my long dead lineage? As uncertain as this scenario is, I feel deep within myself that this is the only right answer to a situation that has left me doubting all I know.

'Albion, tread carefully from here on out. The forces you hold in your command are not just those of flesh and bone, but far deeper, deeper than even you, yourself, realise. Nothing in the world between Heaven and Hell, or even in those realms themselves, can prepare you for what lies inside your heart and soul.'

I stay rooted to the spot, his words ringing inside my mind as I struggle to fathom what I am hearing. I know my limits and surpassed them long ago, but this thinly veiled warning of my own abilities has left me with a sour taste on my tongue.

What could he know of me that I don't myself? I watch as Lucifer jerks his head in direction of the door, bidding me a cue to depart, one which I take gladly as I stride from his presence, my mind awash with conflicted thoughts and emotions. One thin veil of a thought bubbles to the surface, the unquenchable desire to forget.

I raise my eyes to the doors ahead of me, the under croft, the dwelling place of my kin and the one place I can truly lose myself and drop from the face of the universe for even the shortest of moments. I shove the doors aside, my head ducking low as I step deeper into the cavernous hall. The pounding music my kin so adore pours over me as I step to the bar. Slumping into a seat, I raise my hand, slamming my fist into the bar top and making those around me pause as the barman cautiously approaches my hunched form.

'Bruvow, now. Make it a triple.'

As I glare at the bubbling glass in front of me, its torrid green liquid smoking like the fires of redemption, I feel her eyes upon me. I raise my head as the bar man scurries away, her grinning scarlet eyes staring into my own. Even here that whore will not cease her hounding. I watch with a disenchanted and uncaring gaze as she saunters to my side, her hips swinging in an overtly sexual and all too obvious dance of lust and desire.

She wants me and has never made an attempt at keeping it anything but obvious. This slut, Jezebel of darkness, harlot of Hell is only interested in one thing from me: my title. She commands the lost maidens of the twelve circles and yet is still malcontent, so derisive of her own allotted station she wishes to latch herself to mine, and try as I might to shake her loose from my shadow, she still hounds my every waking moment.

'Albion, my sweet red knight, why so sour a gaze?'

I turn my eyes back to the glass in front me, snatching it up and sending the boiling concoction to the depths of my stomach, then let the glass crash back to the bar. I raise my hand with a smooth motion, drawing the barman's gaze and curtly point to the glass.

'Why so sour you ask? Well, partly because I am still healing, but mostly because you are so devoid of cognitive faculties to take the most monumental of hints, you slovenly whore.'

I feel her hand slide over my shoulder as she presses herself into my side. I fiercely repress my revulsion as she skates her hands down my back and chest, fingers dancing through the myriad of gaps and holes I have yet to repair.

'Now, now, why is my love so curt? A woman could be driven to thinking her man doesn't love her with words like those.'

She slips herself onto my lap as I glare into her eyes, the smouldering yellow of my own echoing back from her ruby red orbs. I raise my hand, encircling her throat and begin to squeeze as I bring my face a mere inch from hers.

'I will say this once and once only, you putrid harlot. I am not your man, I am not your love, you are lower in meaning and value to me than the dirt on which I walk. If you ever insinuate more than that again I will carve your head from your shoulders and feed it to the Dolophonos' wolves.'

I push her from my lap, rising to my feet as she lands with an indignant grunt on the flagstone floor beneath my feet. The glare of hatred in her eyes is palpable as I move towards my cell, my refilled glass clutched in my hand. I pass the barman, snatching the bottle from his hand as I do, the echoing vapours pouring from its neck as I drive my bottle filled fist into his face, silencing any feeble protest he was about to mount.

With a sigh laced in anger and confusion I kick my cell door closed before slumping to the floor, my back pressed against the rough-hewn timber of my chest of drawers and slowly begin to drink myself into oblivion.

I wake, aching and nauseated. Staggering to my feet, I feel the room spin as I reach out a hand, hoping to meet the cold stone of my cell walls and instead hit nothing but air. I lose my balance and crash back to the floor with a muffled growl of pain.

I feel warmth over my side as my stitches burst, a flood of puss and tainted blood spilling from the bottom of my leather tunic as I push myself upright. Dragging it off my shoulders, I toss it aside and yank my shaving mirror from the stand above me. Setting it on the floor, I stare into it, the rapidly closing wound on my side zipping itself shut as whatever foul taint that has so ailed me drips to the floor.

I roll to my knees, clutching at my chest of drawers as I stagger to my feet. The room tilts and spins as I slowly inch my way towards the shower and the shocking cold that awaits me.

My head cracks against the water stained stone as ice laced water crashes down on my shoulders. Images from the previous night dance through my mind as I stare at the split skin on my knuckles. I shake my head. Is this really what Arianwen wants, is this drunken sot anything close to the man she deserves in her life? I know with certainty I am teetering on the edge of her trust; if she knew of these past few hours, I know I would trip from that edge and be lost to her. That is something I will not do.

Lockdown

ARIANWEN

I feel it!

As soon as I step foot into Eden I feel it. Loss. A great loss of our kin. How could I have not felt it before? This spell of love has clouded my head to such an extent I didn't even scent who Albion and his league of brothers were fighting! As soon as I stepped into that forest his aura completely saturated all of my senses to a point where I couldn't feel the elimination of my fellow kin! How can that be? Standing here, after taking only one step over the threshold to our world, the grief of my kin suddenly hits me like a tidal wave.

Could I have done anything to help? If I was thinking clearly, could I have saved some of the sleepers? I know it must have been them who has perished because if it had been fellow Reclaimers, that would have been impossible not to have felt as we all have an unexplainable connection to each other's soul that nothing in these immortal worlds could ever mask.

As I get closer to our cottages, I see Anatiamoros coming my way. He steps right up in front of me and engulfs me in his arms.

'Thank the heavens you are okay, Arianwen. I could sense you entering the forest but then something seemed to take over your aura and I didn't know whether you were a part of the melee or not. Are you okay, child?' he asks as he stares at my cheek, my hand raising immediately to seek what he may be sighting. My fingers move over the graze on my cheek caused by Albion's lustful brutality.

'I'm fine, I just tripped trying to return here in a hurry,' I lie, hoping he doesn't look too closely.

'Gabriel has called a meeting to discuss the slaughter of half the sleepers that were sent out. It was foolish of him to send out such a large group. One or two at a time would have had a better chance of going unseen. Instead, we have lost the souls of our very own kin, young inexperienced kin at that. Too youthful to have met such a vicious end. They barely stood a chance. It's so sad. But who am I to question our leaders? Come child, we must go.'

He places a protective arm around my shoulder as we walk towards one of the meeting halls. A shiver runs through him as he pulls me in tighter, the worry he has experienced very evident in the tension bound up tightly in his shoulders. I am truly blessed to be cared for so deeply by my elderly mentor and my closest kin beyond my family. I would be lost without this great man's guidance.

We reach the opened ancient wooden door and walk through with two of Gabriel's close council and proceed to take a seat in one of the pews, facing a pacing Gabriel and a stone like unmoving Michael. I note it is only the leaders, all the council members and all of us Reclaimers in attendance. Once the door is locked and everyone is seated, Gabriel begins.

'Half our sleepers, half are dead! They were sent out to only gather information, most of them inexperienced in warfare. They were ambushed by a detachment of Lucifer's Hunters as if they were waiting for our kin to set foot into the forest, and slaughtered them to a man. It's almost as if they knew exactly where to find them. As well as this mysterious entity still looming over our heads, we now have to also concern ourselves with the possibility of a traitor amongst our ranks!'

I feel an instant sickness in my stomach as Michael, who was frozen only moments ago, turns and looks directly at me. I freeze my body language instantly, not wanting to give his assumptions any fuel to the fire that is starting in his head. Surely he can feel that I would never in a trillion lifetimes betray my kin in such a way. Just the thought of that makes my stomach heave as I force it to stay down and keep my eyes away from Michael's probing orbs.

'Until we discover why it was so easy for the Hunters to wipe out our kin, or we uncover the rat amongst us, as well as find this force that is screwing with the order of our immortal worlds, Eden is on lockdown! No one will leave this garden unless it is by direct order of Michael or myself. That includes no reclaiming. If a soul that resides in that wretched village is truly meant to be saved, then it will wait to seek its final demise. Am I clear?'

Murmurs erupt throughout the whole room as everyone starts to throw questions at Gabriel.

'Why were such youthful sleepers sent out in the first place? And why in such large numbers? Surely one or two at a time had a better chance of finding the information we seek and hiding if the need arose.'

I'm surprised that Anatiamoros is the first to fire off a question to Gabriel, but it is Michael who answers in a cold, calculating voice.

'Even though the reasoning behind our decisions is of no concern of yours, old man, I will grant you leniency for one of such advanced years, and we won't have to waste our time on such pitiful questions. This force that's appeared is more powerful than we first assumed, so we're saving our most experienced sleepers and our true army for when this entity decides to show its true purpose. Until then, you're all confined within these walls. Anyone caught outside without our direct permission will automatically be charged with treason and face the appropriate punishment.'

A shiver runs down my spine at the cold tone in Michael's voice as he yet again turns his eyes upon me, I feel Anatiamoros cast his gaze between Michael and I, silently asking why Michael is suspicious of me. One of the older Reclaimers speaks up. I turn my eyes towards him, his face showing true concern to the souls in need and asking how we are supposed to ignore a calling when it's emotionally and physically impossible to do so. The scorn that fills Michael's reply soaks the air around us, utterly destroying any form of objection or question that may have been brought to life.

Sometimes I believe that our fierce and great leaders are not as wise as they seem. If they're unable to realise that the gift of reclaiming, a gift from God, is just as much a part of us as the air that we breath and the blood that pumps through our veins, then how could they possibly be able to make the best decisions for our kin, including those who have yet to pass the gates of Heaven.

The rest of the meeting is the same arguments over and over again, the same talk of possible retaliation and the risk of war, something that they want to avoid thankfully, but still all-out war is a very real possibility, especially if this force shows its strength again. I know this is all the result of Albion and I meeting and sharing ourselves as one. A force, which I am still clueless as to its meaning, a force that seems to be unsettling both good and evil alike. A force I feel could one day cause more heartache than happiness.

The meeting finally ends, tensions running high between all with the arrangement of a clan meeting tomorrow to let our kin know of the lockdown and the announcement of the obligatory arrangements we are required to adhere to. I and my fellow Reclaimers seem to have the most difficult of hardships. We are not only confined to the walls of Eden, we are also supposed to endure the pain of hearing a calling and having to ignore the suffering of a soul in need because that is what our leaders have ruled. It is a sad day indeed when the gifts of God are to be silenced even for but a moment in time.

I have only just taken a mere few steps away from my fellow kin and around an old oak tree when I am confronted by Gabriel's false pouting face.

'Arianwen, my sweet angel, I know how much this lockdown will affect you. Believe me, if I had been able to find another solution I would have, just to avoid the suffering you may face,' he says as he slowly closes the distance between us. The false sympathy on his face raises my ire to boiling point by the time he is standing right in front of me.

'I'm not sure you even considered what a lockdown would do to me or my follow gifted ones, let alone the suffering souls who rely on us to reach the peace they have long awaited for,' I snarl at him, surprising even myself at the brave angry tone I am using to speak to one of my leaders. His face contorts from a sarcastic pout to an angry frown in but a second.

'It may be blatantly obvious the attraction I hold for you, but make no mistake, I am still your leader and that is not a tone I will accept from you. If I was already your husband I would gladly give you a spanking for speaking out of line to me, but ... I have a deep seated feeling that you may quite enjoy that. Am I right, *Arianwen?*'

He steps in closer to me as he says those last few words, caging me in against the old oak behind me, leaving me no room to avoid the contact he is about to make.

He slowly presses his body against mine, grabbing my hip with one hand as he reaches up with the other to tightly grip my chin. I start to panic as I realise his eyes are showing me his exact intentions at the same time I feel his length start to grow between our bodies.

'I can tell you like the thought of that, my sweet angel, by the subtle hitch in your breathing. You need to admit to yourself, Arianwen, we would make a beautiful and powerful partnership. The sooner you stop fighting it, the sooner we could be enjoying the fruits of our joining.'

I'm just about to put up a fight to stop the kiss I know is coming when I hear a large cough interrupt Gabriel's final advance. With a growl, he turns his head to the person who has interrupted us just in time.

'You have more important things to worry about than chasing a reluctant piece of arse!' Michael growls as Gabriel finally releases his grip on me and steps back, allowing me to take my first breath in what feels like forever.

'How dare you be so disrespectful in front of a lady. You were brought up to be more of a gentleman than that, Michael.'

I don't want to be here as it is, but if these two are going to start one of their famous quarrels, I do not want to be a part of it. When Michael doesn't offer the apology Gabriel has hinted at, he turns to me and grabs one of my hands.

'Accept my apology on his behalf, Arianwen. Until next time,' he says as he brings my hand up to his mouth and kisses the back of it. I try not to jump at the contact, just hoping this is my cue to leave. He drops my hand and nods. I take that opportunity to walk with haste away from them, but not before I hear Michael chastise Gabriel's actions.

'We could be at the brink of war and all you're thinking about is fucking that suspicious whore you have been lusting after for a century or more! When will you listen to me? She will be your ...' the breeze carries his last words away. I don't need to hear Michael's opinion of me. I know he has never liked me for some reason and frankly, I don't care. I am just thankful he's ending Gabriel's intentions before he could truly act on them.

I just hope when the day comes for him to choose a bride, I have turned him off so much that he will choose some other innocent girl to mould into his perfect trophy, one that is enamoured with him and willing to follow him around like a little puppy dog. That ... will never be me.

As painful as this lockdown will be, I think it is in my best interest to have some time apart from Albion. This man who owns my heart, who was leading a fight against and the cause of death of my own kin, only moments before he made me reach such a withering height of passion, is driving me to the point of craziness.

I know that fate has brought us together for a reason, a reason I know will be revealed to us when the time is right, but what would happen if I fight the hand of fate, what would happen if I fight the powerful love I feel for the man who has captured my heart and is holding it prisoner?

What could fate possibly do if I refuse to take the path it is so strongly trying to lay in front of me?

22

Screams of Silence

ALBION

I sit watching the world below me, my senses cast wide, a shivering net that encompasses everything within my sight, everything except the one person in this teeming world of inequity I wish to see.

This one solitary spot has been my home for the past three cycles and not once have I found challenge or battle. I curl my toes in my boots as my calf muscles flex, teasing out the night's cold, working loose the anarchic stillness that has seeped into the very fibres of my being.

I shift my vision, the world blurring in a dancing kaleidoscope of colour and light, yet still she cannot be found. The scurrying blue ghosts of the long since condemned flutter from one hovel to the next, prolonging their insignificant lives for a moment longer. I force myself to my feet, the groan in my joints rolling through my skull as I push my reach out further, hoping in vain to sense anything other than the chattering hairless apes below me.

I am greeted with silence, just as I have been for the last three days. Fear and worry have been my only companions, worry at the prospect that somehow I am the cause of this silence, that somehow I have brought down a calamity so great that she has been found wanting in the face of her lords. And fear, fear that if that is not what has come to pass and she may be in danger I am left wanting and powerless to protect her; for all my strength and skill, I am bound by my blood to be left naught but a mewling kitten in its mother's jaws when sent before those gates and the damned keepers that guard them.

I turn away from the edge of the plateau, slipping across it as silent as smoke on water and down the spider's crawl, this secluded hole leading me down into my private sanctum.

The mattress rises to catch me, folding around my body as I sink into its soft embrace. Her scent billows up around me, the soft spice of raw sunlight and apple blossom fills me, coiling through me with abandon as I sink into the turbulent memory of our first night together. I find a smile teasing my features as her eyes fill my mind, those glittering violet orbs sparkling with life, the soft crinkle of mirth at their corners as her musical laughter fills the room around me.

For the briefest of moments I snap free of my reverie, the hot press of skin flickering over my chest and arms. Flinging myself upright I stare around me, but nothing but silence, the irrepressible scream of that vacuous void. My heart sinks, a cold settling within me as I feel my sorrow rise. What could I have done to so drive her from me? I wish I knew what misstep I have taken to cause this chasm to widen between us so. If I knew what it was, if I knew the malady that so drove her to hide from my gaze then, maybe, with one chance at retribution I could undo my wrong and have her in my arms again.

But no, here I sit in this cold stone prison of my own design, locked away from the world in the cold and dark, the one place I know I belong. After all, what Angel could love a Demon? I am Hell spawn. Who was I to hope that one such as her could love a being like me?

Lying back, I slip into a fitful slumber. Torturous images of my ... no, she isn't mine, how could she be! Images of *her* dance past my mind's eye. Taunting, teasing, twisting my heart until I feel like I could burst from the pain that has so sealed my core.

I wake, the chill light of a new dawn licking the air, sending a bitter breeze into my home. I shake my head, her eyes still locked within sight as I step to the onyx bowl at the edge of my bathing pool. I smash the thick snow white layer of ice on its top with my fist, the pain making me smile slightly as her vision fades for the briefest of moments. I gasp, tasting the cold on my tongue. The crystal clear water hits my skin as I lean forwards, its frigid bite shocking me, stealing the air from my lungs as I plunge my head into its ice covered depths.

I stand there, iced lines of bitter cold trailing over my sleep heated form, rolling through the runes etched into my skin, those intricate lines of my lineage. The only thing my shell cannot erase. I turn, grabbing a towel from the shelf besides the pool. My mother swore by these, although I still cannot fathom why. Why waste time with frivolities such as these when your own body heat and day's labours dry you just as quickly.

My neck aches with tension. I know I need to relax, to wash away this pain that eats at my core. I know it's futile, she is the source of it all, and only she can cure it. But she is not here, nor, I fear, will she ever be again.

My eyes alight on the thin coils of rope hanging over my desk, the soft silk strands sitting like slumbering serpents on the oak pegs. I reach out, plucking one coil from where it lies, the smooth line slipping through my fingers as I let it play from one hand to the next. I slowly let myself slip on the edge of my bed, my feet carrying me backwards as I get lost in the simple action.

She invades my mind once more, her slim naked form standing there, soft and alluring as I find myself drawn towards her. The blood red silk rope in my hands slides through them as I fold it in two. I can feel her heat, the beat of her heart against my palm as I press the rope to her skin, ensnaring this glowing, lust soaked form of alabaster beauty; my eyes snap open. I stare at the line of knots and woven rope in my hands, a wanton, need driven smile flirting with my lips as the image of her coiled in my commanding embrace fills me with tumultuous desire. I will make her mine once more, no matter what has come between us.

✦ ✦ ✦

The fall stands before me, her scent caught on the spring winds as I tumble forwards, the spiced fragrance drawing forth her eyes once more as my wings snap free and I speed towards the one place I know I can never enter.

I coast lightly to the chirruping forest floor. The throbbing throng of life that envelopes me is deafening after the scream of silence I have been living in for the past three cycles. The faintest passage of mouse and insect alike makes me wince in sheer agony as I feel my wings slip past the sleeves of flesh that they call their home.

The crunch of twig and leaf gives me pause, my head snapping in all directions as I search for the source of the noise, until, with a wave of embarrassed self-derision washing over me, I realise there is no one to blame but myself. I lift my foot, the crushed remnants of the Drewen cast off filling the print of my foot.

There they stand, their heads pivoting towards me, the scarred corpse of the Drewen lying at their feet, the lump of dead timbre mocking me, chastising me, its presence an all too obvious reminder of how I had so cast it at these stone monoliths in my anger drowned state.

'Hear me. I beseech thee, guardians of Eden's path, let me pass. Throw open your doors and take pity on a man whose heart and soul lie beyond his reach. You yourselves know the ravages of heartache. I know of your lineage, of how you both once sat entwined in the gardens, guardians of humanity's sires. Please, I beg you ...'

I collapse to my knees, sorrow stealing my words as I bow my head before the keepers. I feel their eyes boring down on me, I hear them move, their forms slipping from the granite spires until they sit before me, towering monoliths of patient sentience.

Their voices roll over me, each rumbling note shaking the ground around me, sending the Drewen quivering into their shells.

'Sirrah, wot this, thy passage into these lands is something that we can nev'r deny. We can nay more deny thy entrance than we could Gabriel's birth. Ye are the soul of two worlds, slaved to the fate of another and born of eternity.'

I raise my head to the level of their eyes, my mind and soul struggling in disbelief at the knowledge pouring from these ancient stone guardians. I feel my soul tremble as the other begins to speak, the gravel filled growl making the hairs at my neck rise in fear as the stone dragon's lips move and my father's voice slips free.

'Child, ye are of both worlds and yet belong to neither. We recall that day well, the calm of night shatter'd by the cries of a newborn, your fate sealed at birth.'

I feel my throat tighten, my eyes widening as the other takes up this soul chilling yarn. I feel my heart freeze in my chest as I stare up into the maw of stone teeth and chiselled scales, my mother's silk tones filling the air as I crumble to the floor, my body crushed by the sheer weight of my sorrow.

'Nothing will erase this knowledge from us, nothing can take from us that 'ere lies the child of eternity, the soul of two worlds whose mirr'r lies beyond our gates. Rise, child, and know that thy soul is welcome hither nay matter who claims ownership.'

I cannot say exactly how long I lay there, even after the keepers slither back to their posts, once more ensconced in their place of watch. The words that tripped from their lips sear themselves into my mind as I rise, my mother and father, their voices, shattering all I thought I knew of myself. I'm a half breed, a creation of light and dark? I slump backwards, my back crashing into a Drewen, its aura quivering in tandem with the shaking of my soul.

One thought swims through my fog addled mind, one pervading note of knowledge. I am of both worlds, *both*. I rise to my feet, wiping away the haze of anguish from my heart and soul in a single move. My feet carry me forth, the gates parting like water through my fingers as I slowly step into a world no demon has ever been before. My armour shifts, moving over me like a second skin, its hue blossoming anew as I move into the realm of Angels and Demon killers, a world of certain death for an agent of the fallen, but, then, I am no ordinary demon.

23

Honesty

ARIANWEN

The pain is crippling. I want to scream, scream out loud; loud enough to startle the birds from their trees, enough to spook the innocent deer feeding in the nearby field, enough to seek help from the Lord himself for this affliction that has so consumed my body, heart and soul. This affliction which has me dreaming sweet dreams that are then slashed to pieces by horrifying nightmares.

My soul cries and my stomach twists as my heart convulses and stops beating for just a few seconds, frozen in time, leaving me to wonder if that was the last beat it will share before leaving me nothing but an empty shell. Once it starts again I take in a large gulp of air as if it may be my last, my last breath before my body finally crumbles under the weight of my breaking heart.

I have tried to push my love for Albion away, I have tried to fight it with every fibre I have within me, but with the pain increasing each day, I know what my body is telling me is the truth. That the love I have for Albion is real and will never leave me no matter how hard I tried to rid myself of it. It is a part of me, it is meant to be, and after three days of not seeing the man who holds my heart, I am feeling more ill than I have in my entire existence.

My heart is breaking because I have been denying it of what it craves, of what it needs to survive and flourish. But I needed to try, try and fight my emotions, try and find another way to exist without the love I feel so strongly for Albion. Because I know that a life with the demon who is a part of my soul, is a life full of fear, uncertainty and possible death. I don't see how we will ever find a middle ground to exist upon. Even though Anatiamoros has told me God is about to lift the lockdown for Reclaimers, I'm still not sure if it would be a good idea to see Albion or not.

After a reclaim, when I would walk through the forest and back to my own world, I would easily leave behind the wretched things my eyes sighted in the village and on my trek home through the forest; but now they follow me all the way into the sanctity of my world and if I choose the path that is now laid before me, the path I will walk hand in hand with the man I love, those horrid things will never leave me. Darkness will forever be a part of my life. Is that a life I am strong enough to live?

I gasp, startled by a sound amongst the tall vibrant trees beside my resting place. I look beyond the patch of grass and daisies I'm sitting on and into the towers of pine, searching for the entity that has disturbed my peace.

I see a faint silver glow behind one of the trees but before I have time to consider what it is, the glow moves and drifts into focus, I grip my chest with two hands as I realise who my eyes are trying to tell me it is.

It can't be possible! There is no way for a demon to enter Eden! Our walls cannot be penetrated by even the most powerful of sorcerers' spells, yet, if that magic is made by the Devil himself, could it overpower God's own?

Oh no! Is it true? Has all of this been a malicious trick? Has Albion been playing in Lucifer's game all along? As I look at the man who is holding my heart in his hands, a man who now looks more angelic than devilish, in a light grey version of the black leather suit that has always donned his Adonis like body, leather which has a luminous glow to it, almost making it unseen, a sickening feeling takes over my stomach.

My heartbreak and fear must show on my face as Albion rushes to me, speaking quickly as I take a few steps back as this demon before me steps further into the Garden of Eden.

'Arianwen, my angel, please let me explain, just listen! I beg you don't run from me, just listen, my love, just listen.'

I freeze, unable to move, unable to comprehend what is right in front of me. I step back further just as he reaches out to embrace me; pain etches on his face as he continues to speak quickly.

'I have been beset with fear and worry; it has been days since you last left Eden and I could wait no longer. I needed to see you, I had to see you. The darkness that took me, drew me to places I never knew I could fall, the fear that filled me at the thought of you meeting with foul play at the hands of that dark entity. I could still *feel* your aura but it was so distant, a pale shadow of the woman before me. I was beginning to doubt my own senses, you were so far from me that I couldn't even be sure if you were completely safe, even here. I had to see with my own eyes that the one I love is safe.

'I stood before the keepers that guard your world. I begged with them to see me pass through, even if it was only for a mo-ment. I still struggle with it all, Arianwen, the words they spoke, even as I fell to my knees, pleading with them, at what they told me. The words that still fill my mind with a cloud of astonished wonder. I finally know what has been hidden from me for so long. I finally comprehend what my mother had always tried to tell me. Things she told me in cryptic tongues, things only she knew I would need to know when it was time, when the time came where I would meet the woman that would take my heart in her hands and hold it for all eternity.

'She knew all along that I was a *half breed!* I am not of one world or the other, Arianwen. I am a child of eternity. My mother knew that one day I would need to use the hidden side of my true self to follow the woman I love into a world that has never belonged to me, this world. Arianwen, that woman is you. I was not born to this world but I have always had and always will have a right to be in it, to be with you. I know I can never reside here, but one day I hope I can walk hand in hand with the woman that owns me, for all this world to lay witness to. Don't you see, Arianwen ... this gives us a fighting chance.'

His animated face shows signs of excitement, but is also laced with uncertainty and fear as he takes a slow careful step towards me, not wanting me to retreat from him any further. He reaches one hand up slowly to cup my face, his thumb gently brushing over my soft skin, letting me feel that this is really him standing in front of me before he slowly brings his other hand up. I am cradled within his gentle strength. I am still trying to process every word that spilled from his mouth as my body starts to ignite at his first touch.

He leans in slowly, looking into my eyes, wanting from me belief at what he has just shared, belief that we will indeed have a fighting chance and find a way to co-exist between two worlds. His lips touch mine softly, as his eyes are still making certain that I do have faith in the love that we share, the love that has fated two immortal enemies to want an existence together. Two immortals that might not be so far apart in their worlds. What a revelation!

I lean into the kiss, opening my mouth to his probing tongue as he sighs, contented that I am still his. One of his hands travels slowly down my neck, his weathered rough skin creating a delicious friction as it continues to travel down my arm before grabbing me at my hip and pulling me in close to his body. A soft growl escapes his mouth as a low moan escapes mine, both our bodies rejoicing in their reunion. In a reunion that could become so much more.

The hand on my cheek slips into my hair and threads its way to the back of my head as he applies a slight pressure to bring me closer, his lips becoming more fervent as my body moulds into his, aligning perfectly as though it was created just for him. The hand on my hip slides around and splays over the cheek of my bottom as he pushes us closer, his shaft against my already wet centre sending sparks through my entire body. He anchors me to him, as if he still holds fear that I may run. But after his recent revelations, how could I ever run from this man again? He is not part of a game created by Lucifer, he is my love, sent to me by fate, a missing part of myself. A man who could possibly become a part of my life, here, in Eden.

My body hums in pleasure as our tongues dance a merry dance together in our mouths, consuming each other, feeding on the love that is pouring from every cell of our bodies. I need to tell him, he needs to know I love him. I may still hold uncertainty over our future and how we could possibly make it work, but being held so tightly by the man who owns my heart makes all of my fears seem insignificant compared to the love that is between us.

He bites my lip, but then soothes it by licking the wound he barely created. My tongue impatiently darts out to find his own, wanting to taste his arousal on the buds that coat it. Wanting to swallow down every essence his body has to offer, wanting to relish in the flavour of this rugged, solid bodied man. I run my hands up his back, feeling his rippled muscles contract under my touch as I move them over his leathered shoulders where I grab on hard, trying not to float away on this euphoric cloud we have created.

Just as I think he is going to take this further and pull me up so I can wrap myself like a vine around his form, he slows his kisses down, nibbling on the edges on my lips before resting his forehead on mine, looking deeply into my eyes.

'Are you still mine, Arianwen? Please tell me that you are, because I know now, more than ever, that you are the only one to love me for who I am, who I am inside.'

The sweet uncertain look on his face just melts my heart as I let my lips smile for the first time in days.

'Yes, Albion, I'm yours.'

His smile is blinding, as all the emotions he has been holding in rushes forth to show me exactly how much he cares, exactly how real this is, exactly how real *he* is. Yet he is looking at me with a painfully serious look, so much worry and fear still etched on his face, so I try and lighten the mood.

'So ... what is this new look that drapes your form?' I say with a cheeky grin.

I watch, fascinated that his cheeks redden slightly as a shy, almost boyish grin spreads from his lips. Who knew a demon could blush? It makes him look so young and innocent. It makes me believe that he could, one day, belong in this world of mine. Walking amongst the light ones. His beauty would be blinding within this world.

'When I finally found the strength to pass that threshold, I took one step over and everything shifted, my armour twisting to become this light grey. I move, but nothing is quite the same. I hear everything, feel everything, even now I can hear your sweet heart hum like the wings of a bird. I felt the change down to my very core, every part of my body singing in one serene moment.

'My wings tucked beneath my skin, I could always feel their solid ridges shifting as I move, even walking was a constant reminder of what lay just below my skin, but now, they seem to have softened, they feel as if they have all but vanished, replaced by something else altogether purer. The raging heat under my skin has cooled and my heart beats a calmer song, your song, Arianwen, and yet, I feel more powerful than I have in my entire existence. It all feels rather strange,' he says as he blushes slightly again.

This new vision of him is quite a sight, and yes, it does give my heart and soul hope, hope that one day we can find a way to be together in every sense of the word. That one day we could happily reside in the one world. I have an idea, an idea I hope he feels comfortable with. I grab one of his hands as I pull back from him slightly with a smile on my face. His curious grin is beautiful as he waits for me to speak.

'Albion, will you walk with me?'

His grin drops as he contemplates my request. 'That could be dangerous for you, Arianwen, I cannot take that chance.'

'We can stick to the far edges of Eden. I would like to share some of my world with you, some of the world you also belong to. Whether we understand why or not doesn't matter. Let's take this opportunity that has been given to us and wander around this beautiful garden.'

I wait, holding my breath, wanting so badly to share my home with this man, the man I love. He doesn't speak but nods with a slight grin on his face. The joy I feel inside is wonderful as I grip his hand harder and start to lead him with excitement in my steps from my patch of sunshine in the woods. I head to the far edges of Eden, showing him my favourite flowers on the way and many little hidden places that I have been visiting since a child.

He points out the places he remembers watching me as a child and then as I grew into a woman. I don't feel uncomfortable at all about being watched by him in secret for my entire existence; it feels comforting to know that this man who is so lovingly holding my hand while using his thumb to rub circles on my delicate skin had an unexplainable pull towards me before we had even meet face to face. It seems that we were always fated to be in each other's life.

I don't wish to break the silence, but there is a lot we need to talk about.

'Albion, how can we truly make this work? This world may never accept you regardless of the good you were created with, so where does that leave us? It would be too dangerous for me to live in your home; it may be safe inside, but I would have to come and go from your world to mine. That's where the danger may lie. What if I were intercepted by one of your brothers? I have laid witness to what they are capable of and ....' His face takes on a painful expression as I trail off, unable to complete my sentence.

Albion's brothers and fellow demons have all done what Albion has done himself. Regardless of the good he harbours inside, I would be a fool to believe he has lived his life as a saint.

'*Arianwen* ... I did what I had to do, to survive in my world. I'm loyal to my kin, I would lay my life down for some of them, but I have never truly felt one of them. I'm a Hunter, hunting your kind is what I do, it's what I was raised to do. I won't apologise for it. If you can't accept me for what I am, then at the very least find it in your heart to forgive me for what I have done. The demon you know, that's just a part of who I am. No matter how much I was or have been torn inside, I'm still bound by the law I was brought up to believe as the truth.

'When I was younger, I could feel something was wrong with me. I could feel that I never truly belonged. Even when I was ordered to commit a heinous act, I would be consumed by guilt afterwards, unlike my kin who stood rejoicing in our accomplishments. I didn't want to be different, I wanted to be normal, to be like those around me. I always felt my feelings were betraying my kin even as I hid them within myself.

'I soon learnt to control the torrent that constantly raged within me, hiding it beneath a veneer of calm viciousness and I never truly understood what it was, until now. Until you came into my life. My love for you has given me the strength to accept who I really am, who I have always been and who I want to become. My love for you has set me free.'

We have stopped walking as his honesty has me floored. To have always felt like that and never understood why must have been terrible to live with as a child and then to grow into an adult not knowing your true path must have been very difficult. I bring one hand up to cup his cheek and lay a sweet innocent kiss upon his lips. A kiss to say I am sorry you have been dealing with such internal conflict for your entire existence. I pray that from this day forth, he can find a way to live as the man he was always meant to be.

'Tell me about you, Arianwen. Tell me about your calling. When did you know that was your path in life?'

This is what we needed. This is how we are going to move forward. We both have to know what we are getting ourselves into, we should know each other well. And I am more than happy to tell him about my calling.

'I always knew I would be a Reclaimer, from my earliest memories I knew. It's not like that for all of my kind. Some find their path later in life, but me, I was born with my gift, with my calling. I remember being a toddler and seeing a butterfly fall down and die. I remember the devastation I held in my heart and this enormous need to save its soul so this beautiful creature could continue its exquisite life.

'I was too young to comprehend those feelings, but that wasn't the last time they visited me. I had them constantly throughout my childhood until one day I just knew what to do. I knew exactly how to save a soul. I started with a deer and other animals I would come across in Eden that had meet their natural length in life. Then when I was old enough, and wise enough, I heard my first human calling out directly to me, calling out for help and ... the rest is history.'

He looks at me with such pride and understanding that it brings water to my eyes and before I can control it, a human like tear starts to fall down my cheek. I used to believe humans' tears were a weakness, but now I know it's just another sign of emotion, emotions that swell to such an extent inside one's self that they just have to overflow. The fact that he understands, just by looking into my eyes, how much my calling is a part of me, makes my heart soar to new heights.

He kisses my tear away, cupping my face in his large strong hands and kisses my lips softly.

'My love, I want you to take a chance on me, a chance on us. I know by asking this, I'm asking you to give up a lot from your life. I know I am asking you to give up a traditional relationship, even marriage. I know that also means you'll be giving up the gift of motherhood. It breaks my heart to ask it of you, but please give us time to find a way to make this all work. I will find a way to leave my evil existence behind. I know it won't be easy and it may take some time, but we will find a way, Arianwen, I can feel it. Just please promise me you will give us a chance, please be patient, for me.'

How could I not take that leap of faith when he is laying his whole heart on the line for me? How could I deny the man I love? I do love him and I need to tell him. I need him to know that I will risk my life just to be in his arms.

'Albion, I *will* take a chance on us, a chance on you. Because I ... I ...'

I stumble as emotions start to boil over at the thought of the words I'm about to tell him and the impact they may have on both our lives. He brushes a thumb over my lips and looks at me adoringly as I take a deep breath in anticipation at laying my heart completely in his hands.

'Albion ... I love you.'

At first he looks shocked as my words take time to sink in, but as they begin to, his face starts to transform. His slight grin grows into a smile that takes over his entire face. His eyes light up brighter than a full moon as they begin to water, a sight I have never seen or heard of within a demon before, a lineage we now know is not the only part of him. He looks so young and free at this very second. This moment, right here, gives me more hope than I have ever had.

He wraps his arms around my waist and picks me up to spin me around in circles before stopping, with me still held high in his arms, looking down into his beautiful sensual eyes. He slowly slides me down his body until our eyes meet.

'I never thought I would ever hear those words said to me, me, a demon, a vicious worthless demon. I never knew I craved those words so desperately for an entire lifetime until right now, as they slipped past those luscious lips of yours. You've made me feel alive for the first time in my entire existence. You have made me feel like I am more. Thank you, my love. Thank you for believing in me, for believing in us. I will forever prove to you that I deserve those three little words. This, I promise you.'

Both our eyes are watering as he grips me tightly to his body and takes my lips in his, devouring me as if this is our first kiss, a first of many more to come. He kisses me as if I am the air he needs to breathe, as if I am the beat of his heart.

He kisses as if he has loved me for a lifetime.

Maybe he has.

24

Affirmation and Protection

ALBION

I stand, my lips locked to hers, her words still ringing in my mind as I feel my pain melt away, the anger of a generation falling from me in a tidal wave of exultation. She loves me, this angel in my arms; this woman who owns me heart and soul loves me. She sees through the vagaries of my beleaguered existence, the scars and tortured remnants of a pain filled past suffused by the knowledge of living within a realm and world that I never truly belonged to.

She looks past all of this to the man I really am, to the one true person hidden beneath the armour and layers of deceit and deception. Even now as we walk through the lush beds of spring flowers and fluttering birds that fill the canopy of greenery, her hand clasped in mine, I feel a rippling pool of serenity settle within me, its rolling waves drifting back and forth over the shores of my soul.

We drift quietly through the pathways, sculpted borders and swept paths lining our way. I reach out, my fingers dancing over the petals of flowers and the soft mint scented leaves of shrubs.

The turbulence within me melts with each step. Arianwen steps away from me for a moment, her face igniting like the sun as she turns and skips ahead. I stop, tasting the sun on my tongue as I slowly take in all that is around me, her scent caught on the floral spice that fills my lungs with each slow breath. I reach out, my fingers curling over the soft stems of the pastel coloured flowers, plucking them from where they lie, their beauty in that moment as bright as any sunrise. Footsteps to my left draw my attention as I rise once more to my feet, the bouquet in my hands snatching her gaze from mine.

'I ... I saw these and ... well ... the only thing in these realms that so echoes your beauty is what I now hold in my hands.'

She lifts the fragrant bundle from my grip, her eyes drifting closed as she inhales deeply, her cheeks glowing with a soft blush of happiness. She leans in, resting her head against my shoulder as I sigh, content in the moment as Arianwen curls in against my side, her hands snaring my arm in a gentle clutch as we near the soft waters of a pond.

Its surface slowly rocks, swathed in thick green pads, their expanse floating over the glass smooth waters, saffron pink blossoms opening as she nears. I stare in amazement as she settles at the water's edge, the pads of green moving, silent and serene as she steps forwards, her finger curling towards me, beckoning me to follow.

I move with the caution of a terrified cat, my footsteps tentative, wary of the sudden undulating surface beneath my feet. I feel the burn through my calves as I begin to inch my way towards my angel, her movements confident, almost arrogant as she moves away from me, her smooth cream coloured legs drawing my eye as she heads towards the small swatch of woodland in the middle of this lake.

The island's quiet form drinks her in as she vanishes with a sway of her hips, her body swallowed by the shadows and trees that fill this dot of land.

I follow on, mesmerised by my angel's movements, my mind lost to her sensual sway as I find myself all but gliding over the water, my early reticence gone, replaced by a calm confidence I never truly knew I possessed. Spending so many years living in the shadows of my parents and those around me, I became lost, disconnected from everything and everyone. Now as I watch her slip between the stands of oaks and maple, I cannot fathom the impact she has had on me and my life.

The sand laced shore sends me stumbling as I finally reach the edge of the copse of trees. I feel the cool kiss of the spring's breeze, the soft rustle of leaves grazing my ears as I spy my angel. Her sultry form draped over the small patch of lawn draws me in. I am caught like a moth to a flame. I move, my mind lost in a sea of emotions so virulent, so viscerally pure that for this one moment, amidst my unbridled happiness, I am terrified. Never have I felt more secure and yet so insignificant in a single moment than I do now.

Now I know my place in this world. It is with the maiden before me, the ethereal beauty who has so captured my heart and soul, but now, how can I stay, how can I keep her trapped in this limbo between worlds within which I find myself.

The keepers threw wide the door to my past, and here I am floundering and drowning in the outpouring, struggling to keep my head above the rising tide. Can I really drag her into it all, even now as she stares up at me, love and trust swimming in her gaze, can I really bring her into this storm that I can now call my existence?

Can I truly subject her to this, although I guess the true question is how can I not?

✦ ✦ ✦

I feel a tug at my fingers, my balance falling free as I tumble with a thump to the soft loamy turf besides this indomitable vixen. A girlish giggle coats the air as she turns, her legs sliding over my hips until she is lying astride me, her ankles curled over my knees, the bare dirt flecked soles of her feet peering over the edge of her shoulder as she stares into my eyes.

'I love you.'

The words drift from us both, blending in perfect unison as she giggles once more, her head resting over my heart as she traces her fingers over my palm. I breathe in deeply, her hair falling over my cheek as she nestles in tightly against my chest. I brush stray strands of burnished gold from her eyes as she gazes up at me, the innocence in her eyes bleeding forth as I slip my arms around her waist.

She squeals as I pull her upwards, her body moulding to mine as she settles against me once more. My lips graze her cheek and lips as her head finds the crook of my neck, her warmth bleeding into me as I wrap my arms around her, a heavy sigh beating its way free of my soul.

'Arianwen, do you trust me?'

I feel her move, her eyes finding mine as I turn my gaze towards her, her fingers rising, skating over my jaw as she stares up at me, brow furrowed in a worried puzzlement. 'Of course I do, why would you ask me that?'

I smile down at her, my eyes betraying me as I watch hers slowly dip, a deep brooding lust taking hold of her as she stares up from behind hooded lids.

A sly smile tugs at her as she slowly runs her hand along my inner thigh, fingers cupping me as she begins to grind her palm against my slowly hardening length.

'Not here, I have something else in mind.'

I sweep her up in my arms as my wings slip free, their velvet smooth form glistening in the dappled sunlight as I lift us both from this sculptured isle, the heavy throbbing beat of my wings echoing the drum of my own heart as Arianwen laughs, exultant in the sheer unadulterated abandon of the moment.

The touch of the rope against my palm makes me grin, her eyes tracing my every move as I slowly let its claret red length play through my fingers as I stand here in the cave that I call home. I watch as she bites her lip, drawing it into her mouth slightly, the nervous tick making my smile broaden as I watch her clench her thighs, her body sensing what's to come long before her mind makes the tentative connections to what her rapidly moistening core already knows.

'Remember when I asked if you trust me?'

She nods, her eyes wide with lust and caution as I continue my soft advance, the rope still sliding through my fingers.

'It's time for you to show me just how much.'

I am stood before her, the last few inches of plaited and coiled silk slipping from my grip in front of her eyes, as I let its end slide across her pale cheek, the splash of colour sending a fire to my loins as I get a glimpse of what's to come.

'Stand up.'

I step back, my angel rising, her shoulders slipping, head falling as her eyes drop to the floor. I stifle a gasp at her willingness, never before have I seen someone so willing, so eager to submit to the one they hold claim to.

'Step forwards and lose the dress.'

I stare at her as she moves once more, her hands sliding over the smooth cream of her shoulders, brushing the soft satin from her skin, letting it cascade down her arms, catching at her waist. She looks at me, waiting for some form of acknowledgement that she is doing right. I incline my head and watch as a soft smile teases the corners of her lips before her eyes fall once more and those slim delicate sources of my undoing tease the knot at her waist.

Soft firm breasts fill my vision as I step forwards, the silk rope once more travelling through my grip as I trail the end over her shoulder and collar bone, the strap of brassier making it skip and jump over her smooth, butter like skin. I stop, setting a small loop around her neck as I draw a slim blade from my hip, its point grazing up her spine before I slip it under the clasp of her under-garment and with a soft, near casual flick send it peeling away.

I flick my tongue over her earlobe, the coil of rope at her neck grazing over her skin as she tenses once more.

'Relax, Little Wing, the best is yet to come.'

Slowly, teasingly, I let the rope slip from her neck, its soft silk braid flowing over the contours of her firm and supple body, as I whisper into her ear.

'Remove the brassier, slowly.'

With almost reverent care she moves her arms, dancing fingers twirling as she guides the severed garment down her willowy length.

I move around her, her downcast gaze at odds with the soft almost pleased smile I see flirting with the corners of her lips. I watch as her skin begins to rise, the cold licking her form, nipples hardening as I play the rope across them. I grin as I track my gaze lower, the dark blossoming over her pouting lips telling me all I will ever need to know.

'Arms back.'

I watch as she brings her head up, brow furrowed as she stares at me, incomprehension dancing in her eyes. I smile softly, her gaze widening as she watches for it, waiting for it to reach my eyes, it never does.

I grab her wrist, pulling it back behind her as she whimpers at the sudden movement. I draw her other arm back along with it, my voice losing its warmth as I growl.

'Arms back, now keep them there.'

She doesn't move a muscle as I allow myself to smile again. I fold the rope in my hands before setting it just below her breasts. The soft milky white globes of succulent flesh tease my eyes as I watch them rise and fall with each breath she takes. I pin the rope to her, as I guide her around, her feet whispering over the small rug beneath them.

Slipping the lengths through the hoop between those smooth succulent mounds I give it a soft tug, making her jump as it sits flush to her skin. Leaning in, I set my lips scant millimetres from her ear, my warm breath tickling her pale skin.

'Now we shall see just how much you trust me, Little Wing.'

She stiffens under my touch, apprehension and pleasure running through her in equal measure as I slip the rope upwards, moving through the soft warmth of her breast. The valley of flesh moves against my hands as I flick my thumbs over the rigid nubs of her nipples, the soft pink pearls of flesh making her whimper and gasp in the chilled air around us both.

I drape the lengths of scarlet silk over her shoulders, as I grip her nipple between thumb and finger, a smile ghosting over my lips as she moans deep within her throat, the soft sound of her arousal running along her thighs filtering up to my ears as I pull, her body moving until her back is facing me, her movements guided by her succulent chest as I continue to tease and twist her overtly sensitive pearls.

She moans, the sound rising deep from within as I reach down between her legs, pressing my fingers into the soaked crotch of her panties, the gossamer material clinging to every fold of her silken maiden's cleft. The pouting lips draw my fingers in as I feel her quiver, the sodden cloth sinking between her swollen lips as her body tries in earnest to release her mounting pleasure.

I tap my fingers over her swollen button, the soft sensitive bundle making her shudder as my drenched fingers dance on its electric tip, the chill air rolling over her as I listen to the wet patter of my skin against hers.

Dragging my tongue over her neck I feel her shiver, her body shaking with desire, passion boiling up through her as I taste the sweet tang of her sweat on my tongue.

'You are mine, Little Wing, mine.'

I press my fingers deep into her, her warmth soaking through my invading digits as I curl them over the passion soaked cloth, teasing it free of her clutching core.

'Spread your legs, wide.'

I grin as she moves, obedient, silent, submissive to my command and presence. I stare at the polished sheen of her armour on my desk, her smile all too clear across her lips as I curl my hand around her panties and pull them down over her firm smooth thighs, the flesh pliant and warm under my hands as I watch her lift her feet, moving with me as she steps free of her sodden undergarment.

I smile, the twisting of my lips dark and lust soaked as I speak, my voice hoarse, soaked in my overflowing lust and need.

'Open your mouth.'

I see her brow rise, eyes widening as she obeys, my fingers curling her saturated panties into a ball of wet ecstasy. I lift her panties to her lips, the gargling noise bleeding from her throat, making my smile widen as I slip my free hand to her clitoris once more, my fingers twisting that bundle of pleasure, making her body tense with rippling desire as I push the arousal soaked ball past her lips, her juices running free down the sides of her mouth as I watch her swallow, tasting her pleasure.

I sink my fingers deep into her clutching core as my lips find her rock hard nipples, my teeth nipping at their tips as I feel her ripple and clutch at my thick fingers.

I pull them slowly from between her thighs, her wetness pooling in my palm as I lift my hand, cupping my palm, watching her juices flow over my skin as I raise it to my lips, letting her warmth slip across my lips and tongue, trickle down my throat as I taste the heavenly scent on my tongue. The exquisite pleasure that rolls through me makes my head swim as I rise, grasping the claret silk in my hands, sliding it between her shoulders and between thehoop that ensnares my angel.

My hands dance, twisting, turning, moving over her lustrous form, ensnaring her in my crimson embrace.

'Kneel.'

I watch her fall to her knees, her slow descent making my agates ache with need as I begin to pull apart the bindings of my trousers.

I step in front of her, my length springing free as I watch her eyes grow with wanton lust and shock at what I'm about to do. My leaking head rests against her lips as she slowly opens her mouth, letting the panties fall to the floor, as her lips instinctively slip over my swollen helmet as I begin to slowly disappear into her waiting throat.

I relish the feel of her warmth enveloping my throbbing manhood; her tongue slipping over my head makes me shiver as my fingers curl into her hair, the silk strands sliding through my slick fingers, her arousal clinging to her blonde hair as I force my length deeper into her.

Our lust fills the air, the thick sound of her mouth around my length exciting me beyond measure. I stare down at her, her eyes locking with my own as I drive my length between her wanton, throbbing lips. The plump pink cushions of my adoration slide along my rigid flesh, their smooth silk texture sending shivers of pleasure through my core as I feel my limit rise.

I close my fist, her gasp oozing free, little more than a liquid filled gargle as I drag her from my pinioning rod.

'Up, turn round and bend over.'

I grin, my spear twitching as I glide my hand over my spittle soaked length, her soft backside rising to my gaze as I stare at her swollen, plump lips, her juices sliding along her length as I rest my aching member between her cheeks, dragging it over her puckered hole and down, before I settle against her sex.

I listen to her impassioned gasping as she curls her fingers closed, her fists tightening as she bites down on the sheets of my bed, stifling her wanton moans as I begin to slip between her lips with agonising slowness.

Her near orgasmic moans filter through, coating my ears in a pleasure so fine I am all but driven to distraction. The firm warmth of her lustrous core draws me deeper as the sound of lust filled joining echoes around us.

I curl my fingers through the lattice work of scarlet rope locked around her arms, drawing this wanton angel up from my bed. I stare down, her back arching as she sinks deeper on to my invading member, my length disappearing between her flushed and swollen folds.

I feel her push back against me, willing me to drive deeper as I feel my seed boil, nearing the end as she growls. I send a ringing slap across her cheeks as I feel my thighs slap against hers, the rhythmic clap of skin on skin drowning out everything as I move faster, my ever increasing pace making her nubile form buck and sway in my grip as I reach forwards and grasp one soft pink bud in my fingers, twisting it, the feel of her flesh moving beneath my fingertips making me twitch; she groans, the sound echoing around us both as the feel of her flesh against mine makes me quiver and shake to my very soul

Her swollen nipple slips from my fingers as I smooth my hand over her soft cheeks, feeling the soft curves of her backside under my searching hand. I slowly slip down through her, the cleft of her backside feeling the aching heat seep into my fingers as she tenses beneath me, her head pivoting to meet my gaze as her eyes roll up; pleasure seeping from her every pore as I drive deeper into her.

Drool leaks from the corners of her mouth as I run my searching fingertip over her puckered ring. The feel of her fearful clenching draws me beyond my limits as I let slip a guttural moan, my length jerking within her as Arianwen goes limp, her body twitching as she clenches around me, milking my length of everything I have to offer. I fold over, driving as deep as I can, pouring my seed deep within her satin folds, gasping, our skin slick, soaked with the silk of our lovemaking.

I draw myself from her still clutching folds, a soft whimpering staccato moan slipping from Arianwen's mouth as she lies, chest heaving on the bed beneath me.

'On your knees.'

I curl my fingers through her hair as she sinks to her knees. I roll to the side, my sore and swollen length resting along my thigh as I feel my chest heave. Arianwen's golden tresses scrape over my sweat stained skin as I force her to move. The mattress beneath us rolls and dips as she shimmies onto her knees. Her soft plump breasts graze over my skin making my member twitch; I watch as she grins, her lascivious gaze speaking as she slowly inches her way towards me.

I grin as she pushes my knees apart with her shoulders as she edges further between my thighs. She leans forwards, my hand guiding her as she skates her tongue over my agates. I tip my head back as I groan, the wet warmth of her tongue over my tender eggs making me shiver as she runs it over the thin film of skin.

I listen to the soft lapping that emanates from between my thighs as she rolls her tongue over and over across my agates, my length swelling as I tug on her hair, her soft gasp making me shiver as cold air rushes over my spittle soaked sack. I reach forwards, lifting my hardening length up, her lips parting as I watch her eyes glaze with lust, her head falling forwards, eager to please as I feel her hair tug at my grip.

Her mouth envelopes me as I stare into her eyes, the sparkle within saying more than any words ever could. I watch as she begins to flush, her breathing coming ragged as she begins to take more of my ever swelling length down her throat. I feel my plump head nudge the back of her throat as she gags, her spittle slipping down her chin as I close my fist tighter into her hair, pulling her off my rigid flesh. I shuffle back against the wall, pulling her up onto the bed, her breasts swaying as she moves, her sodden sex drawing my gaze as she sits astride my legs, softly grinding against me as I stare into her eyes, those deep violet pools sealing my fate as I feel my heart fall, knowing now, that after this, there isn't any hope of someone else ever taking her place.

25

Trust and Devastation

ARIANWEN

The burn in my shoulders obliterates the minute his mouth wraps around my hardened raw nipple. The tug of the ropes intricately laced down my arms reminds me exactly how far I have been taken out of my own world and thrown into the world of ecstasy.

Pain bleeds into pleasure, pleasure bleeds into an ache, an ache only his touch can cure, an ache that has me floating on the cloud of euphoria, never wanting to fall back down to reality. My initial apprehension has completely deserted me, replaced with an excitement I can barely contain as I release another long drawn out moan when he replaces his mouth with his teeth on my over sensitive nipple.

He has positioned me straddling his thighs as he sits and leans his naked frame against the wall behind the bed, leaning forward to yet again feast on my exposed breasts as his fingers dig deep into the flesh of my hips, holding me in place, keeping me from what my body is craving, holding me on the edge of oblivion, not allowing the release I so insanely scream for.

My begging is ignored as he nips and sucks, enjoying my painful arousal and bringing me to the edge, only to move that final fall away from me yet again. I never knew my body could react in such a way, I've never known a craving to be as potent as the one he is building within every cell of my body.

I instinctively struggle, the slight burn of the ropes on my wrists sending a jolt of pain directly to the apex of my thighs, increasing the overwhelming feelings coursing through my veins. The thrill of the anticipation of another jolt of pain surprises my psyche, as I would never have imagined pain could be anything other than that, pain; but mixed with pleasure, it is a powerful aphrodisiac.

He swaps and bites my other nipple; my head flings back in a carnal scream as I feel like I can no longer endure this delicious torture 'Albion, please, I can't take it anymore, please, please Albion, no, no!'

I beg as he uses his teeth to tug my nipple hard before gripping my hips tighter, slowly bringing my body up higher, gliding me over his swollen thick shaft, my juices flowing over his skin, drowning him in my essence.

He releases his mouthful and leans back against the wall, gripping me tightly, rising me slightly above his shaft as it stands to attention, before he gently, agonisingly, lowers me down, spearing me with his manhood. I gasp at the first thrust, barely holding on to my sanity as my internal muscles start to clamp down around him before he has even had a chance to move, a deep growl emitting from his throat as he also is struggling to hold back another release.

I want to grab him, I want to anchor myself to his body, I want to slide over, touch and scratch his skin as a wildness takes over my form as I barely keep from falling over that high edge he has so deliciously built me up to stand upon. I desperately want to hold his face in my hands, but with his rope pattern binding my shoulders back, cinching my arms behind me, connecting them together all the way down to my wrists, I have no way to release the affection my fingers wish to thrust upon the lines of his handsome, sensual face.

He raises me once again in his powerful hold, but this time the gentleness has gone as his control snaps and he brings me down upon his shaft with an aching force, hitting that secret place inside, sending sparks shooting through my entire form as I *finally* fall, screaming *'Albion,'* as I clutch him with every piece of strength I have left, my internal muscles shuttering around him as a flood of arousal splashes from my centre.

My body feels as if electricity is shooting through my veins, setting my skin on fire as my vision blurs, making me feel faint as I struggle to catch a much needed breath. I am vaguely aware of his animalistic grunts as he continues to pump into me, holding on so tightly I can feel my skin begin to bruise. He calls my name over and over again like a prayer, like he is worshipping me and my body.

He suddenly sits up, grabbing my legs and wrapping them around his waist, before reaching around and sending two hands into my hair. He smashes my body hard against his chest, taking my lips in a rough, frantic kiss, a kiss that shows me how much this glorious man is affected by the love we share.

He thrusts hard twice more, growling loudly, then releasing the pressure he has held onto for so long, shooting his burning essence into my body, flooding my insides with what feels like a part of his very soul. His kisses start to slow as he continues to gently rock, bringing us back down from the greatest heights we have ever reached. Bringing us down to the raw honest love we share for each other.

'Arianwen.'

His voice is barely a whisper on his lips as he pulls back to look into my eyes, love shining brightly in his beautiful blue orbs; then he suddenly realises I am still bound up tightly.

'Oh, my sweet angel, let me untie you, my love,' he says as he gently raises me from his lap, his still semi hard shaft slipping from my centre as he places me in the centre of the bed.

He takes a moment to admire my form, tied and bound in the beautiful ancient art of Shibari, slowly running his hands over the rope lying above the tops of my breasts, following it over my shoulders and down the knots that flow all the way to my wrists.

He moves behind me and starts the delicate task of releasing all of the intricate knots and twists he had created not long after I first laid a finger on the rope, looking so pretty lying on his work bench.

When all of the rope is free of my body, my shoulders fall forward as my arms hang limp at my sides. He chuckles as he begins to rub my arms vigorously, bringing my circulation back to life. He tenderly guides me onto my stomach, stretching me out face down onto the soft mattress below, as he begins to massage my shoulders, then onto my arms and back, sensually rubbing to bring my body back to normal. I can't help the moan that escapes my lips as he once again lets a laugh slip from his lips.

'Don't let your body start heating up again, Arianwen, it needs to rest after what I just put it through. But don't worry, my sweet angel, we have a lifetime together to share our love in whatever way your heart desires.' He places a soft kiss to my cheek before lying down next to me, staring into my eyes and all the way into my soul.

I can't help but let those words slip from my lips again. 'I love you, Albion.'

He holds his breath, with such an intense stare into my eyes, before he releases it on a sigh, bringing his lips to mine, softly joining them together with a gentle touch as he whispers, 'I love you too, Arianwen, more than words could ever explain.'

The happiness I feel at this moment is something I never thought possible, not possible for such a simple existence us Angels live, but a happiness I know I will never let go of.

We lie like this, gently petting, looking adoringly into each other's eyes for what feels like forever before Albion breaks our silence. 'As much as I would like to lie here with you forever, we must return to our own worlds for now. I have a feeling that Lucifer has something planned and I need to be on full alert for whatever may become. I shall help you dress, my love.'

He grabs my clothes from a pile on the floor and begins to dress me, taking care of me so lovingly, returning me to the respectable angel I am.

Moments later, we cautiously leave his hidden home. As soon as we reach the edges of the forest, something feels wrong. Something deep in the pit of my stomach starts gnawing at my time honed sense of danger, filling my gut as I stop. I panic for a second, thinking maybe someone has witnessed me leave Albion's hidden place, when we both freeze at the sound of a piercing scream.

We carefully head closer to the source of the scream when the sounds of a conflict meets our ears. 'Arianwen, go, now.'

I think that maybe he has sensed that this could be Lucifer's doing and indeed it would be wise to hide in my world, but then I hear it, that familiar voice that has been such a comfort throughout my entire life.

'It's Anatiamoros!' I say as I start to run towards him, Albion fast on my heel; he grabs my arm before I can go any further.

'Arianwen, don't argue! Go now. I will do what I can for your kin.'

'No! You don't understand! Anatiamoros is not just a Reclaimer, he is family to me, Albion. I have to help him. I will not leave!'

He looks surprised at my outburst as I scream at him, fear gripping my sanity as the one true kin who understands me and means the world to me is involved in a fight with the Devil's minions. He is pained as to what to do, as his protective instincts are in full force over wanting to see me safe, no matter the costs.

'Trust me, Albion. Trust my gifts and abilities. I have fought my way out of battles before and with you by my side I know we can find a way out of this. Please trust me,' I say as I reach a hand up to cradle his cheek.

He lets out a low growl of frustration. 'Fine, stay *back* until I can find a way to distract them. Then, and only then, will you move in to get him out of there. Do not get involved, do you hear me?'

I nod yes, knowing no words of mine will set his heart at ease at what's about to happen. He grabs my cheeks within his large hands and kisses me fiercely, before giving me one last pained look. He lets me go before walking around to the other side of the conflict we are both about to enter.

As I get closer, I can scent the eight sleepers surrounding Anatiamoros' aura, as well as seven of the Devil's Hunters, all in close range of each other. I hear heated words and shots being fired as I reach close enough for my eyes to finally see the conflict in front of me. The sleepers, with weapons in hand, are scattered behind trees, with Anatiamoros furthest from the fight. His words rain free as he shouts for a cease fire, which goes unheard as the demon Hunters fire back with such weaponry never before seen by our world. The Devil's fancy toys are now being used by vile children.

I can sense Albion approaching his brothers and the moment they know he has stumbled upon them. A need to prove themselves in his presence washes like a tidal wave over them all. He growls a demand and all fire ceases for but a moment, giving me a chance to run to Anatiamoros and into the ring of war.

'You need to leave now, let the sleepers finish this off,' I say in a mad rush, wanting to get him away from this conflict.

'Arianwen, you go to safety, dear. I need to help these children before these Hunters obliterate them, before they even stand a chance. Go, I'll be fine.'

There is no way I am leaving him here, and if I am to be honest with myself, I could never walk away from any of my kin in need, regardless of their title.

I can hear an argument between Albion and one of his kin as I know they are getting ready to end this small cease fire. I brace myself for what I know is inevitable and the battle I'm about to fight, while the man I love will momentarily become my enemy.

Albion's voice roars, as one and then two more demons begins to fire again. Our sleepers move in closer to get a better shot, wanting to protect Anatiamoros and now me. I can't let this happen, I can't let this continue, the risk of the ones who are in my heart getting injured or killed is too high. I have to stop this!

I slip behind tree after tree, positioning myself closer with each slight movement. I've been created to go unseen when needed and this situation is no different. I slither right to the front line without anyone detecting me as I contemplate my next move. I need to create a diversion, I need to give my kin the opportunity to return to safety as the weapons the Hunters are using are unpredictable, and it is never good to fight with the unknown.

I have rarely had to do this before, but now, my unique reclaiming gift is truly needed. I direct all of my energy into one line of thought, to create what will become a simple smoke shield. It won't harm our enemy but may confuse them as to our whereabouts long enough for us to retreat to safety and to refrain Albion from taking any risks to keep me from harm.

I build the smoke from within my small frame as I get ready to blow it out of my mouth, with the guidance of my hands cupped up to my jaw. I use every piece of strength I have to release it and push it far enough out to give us a good coverage to retreat under. I step forward, pushing the smoke in the demons' direction, blinding their view of us. But what I don't expect is a large form running fast, straight for me.

As I let the last of the smoke go, I am left with just enough time to brace myself for impact as I grip the edges of my cloak, ready to use it as a shield, as I pull my left hand up to protect my face. I crouch low hoping this huge demon will fly over the top of me. As his massive bulk hits me, I push against the bottom of his legs and watch as he flies over the top of my small form.

I stand and spin quickly as he regains his footing and comes at me, an enormous blade flying in front of my face. He steps forward and once again, I bring my cloak up to block the blow of steel. He is shocked when the force of the connection of his weapon with my fabric armour sends the knife flying in the air, landing out of reach, yet closer to me.

I throw myself to the ground faster than he and reach the knife first, gripping the heavy metal in my hand, before I roll over and back up to my feet.

He just chuckles. He thinks it's amusing for a sweet innocent angel to be brandishing such a large weapon, as he reaches down to his boot and produces another blade for himself. He wastes no time in slashing in my direction, just missing my arm as I move swiftly to his side, taking the opportunity to fight back. I slice with all my strength and connect with his flesh, tearing a gash across the top of his arm, making him growl with anger as he comes back swinging at me again.

I jump back and send the knife carving through the air towards his shoulder, but I'm not fast enough. He grabs my wrist, trying to forcefully release the knife from my grip as he swings his other blade towards my stomach, narrowly missing my flesh, yet snagging on the edge of my cloak, ripping it. He brings his hand back, ready to strike again.

Just then I hear a vicious growl to our left, making both our heads whip in that direction. I see Albion come flying towards us, feet not touching the ground, as he collides with his fellow Hunter, knocking me down in the process as they crash to the floor a few feet away. Albion lands on top of the other Hunter as he reaches into his leather clad armour and pulls out two knives, brings them high above his head. Shock registers in his own kin's eyes, before he brings both hands down and rams his weapons in the demon's chest beneath him.

He killed for me. He killed one of his own to save me. But before I can even let that sink in, I hear Anatiamoros howl in pain, making me rise quickly to my feet and run in his direction, Albion's voice following in my wake.

'Arianwen, *no*!'

I reach a small clearing where my smoke has started to clear and see Anatiamoros clutching his side as he straightens, ready to fight his attacker again. The Hunter runs at him with a sword as he raises one hand with his cloak gripped tightly. But it's the demon's other hand he doesn't see, the Hunter keeping it low as he pulls the trigger on the gun clutched in his hand, sending a speeding bullet into the side Anatiamoros isn't protecting.

I scream at the same time as Anatiamoros' body falls to the ground, the killer turning his weapon my way, pulling the trigger. The all too familiar sound of a bullet speeding through the air, its whistling crack echoing through my ears as Albion grabs me around the waist, turning my body just in time to miss my would be assassin's shot. He lets me fall to the ground as he takes off after the demonic trigger man, not wanting him to alert his fellow brothers to Albion's protection of an Angel.

I run to my fallen mentor's side, raising his head to rest on my lap, feeling his life force draining swiftly as I know I am too late to save him from the fate he is about to meet. I have a gift, a gift to save human souls from the clutches of the Devil, but I am powerless to save this man in my hands, as the bullet that has entered his body was poisoned and cursed like all of the Devil's armoury.

I feel utterly helpless as he looks into my eyes with an undeniable peace I find hard to accept right now. 'Arianwen, you are the most gifted Reclaimer that has ever walked these worlds. Don't allow that power to fall into the wrong hands.'

He starts to choke on his words, but swallows down and continues. 'But remember that is not all you have to be. Follow the love that has made your cheeks glow and trust your heart. He will not let you down.'

Tears flow freely down my cheeks and onto the forest floor, as I feel Albion fall to his knees beside me, wrapping a caring arm around my shoulder. Anatiamoros turns his gaze from me and looks directly into Albion's eyes, not registering an ounce of shock at a demon embracing me with such affection.

'Take care of her and never forget her heart is a precious gift that you have been chosen to hold in your hands. Love and protect it always.'

I watch as Albion grasps Antiamoros' hand, clasping it tightly to his chest.

'You have my word, rest easy. I will die before harm comes to her.'

He smiles at me one more time before closing his eyes and leaving this immortal world for good, with that smile on his face for all eternity. Albion rises beside me as I hear the fighting continue around me. But I cannot move. I am frozen here in time not believing such a great man has left my world. How can this be? Anatiamoros was the longest serving Reclaimer for a reason. He had survived countless battles before this, so why was he taken now? Why was such a great man cut down in such a way? Why did God not intervene?

I am angry! How dare these heinous creatures take the life of one of Heaven's greatest gifts! I stand, rage boiling in my veins as I turn and take in the scene around me. Our sleepers are barely holding their ground as the Hunters continue to push forward, gaining on them, ready to finally take us heavenly creatures down.

I take two steps forwards, ready to make a stand with my fellow kin, when Albion grabs my hand and speaks with speed.

'Arianwen, take my hand, feel what we are capable of.'

I'm confused, my mind barely holding on as I know the shock loss of Anatiamoros will hit me soon.

'Ari, concentrate! Feel it, feel us, you know what we are and what we can do when we are together. Concentrate on that and we may just find a way for you and the rest of your kin to survive.'

He grabs my hand and I feel it! A colossal heat, an energy, a power that I hope will stop the slaughter that's about to take place.

26

Till the End of the Line

ALBION

Her hand burns in mine, the flesh of my palm searing as I let my eyes slip closed, visions of the skirmish around us dancing through my mind as I track every sound, every shuffle of shoe on dirt, every clang on blade against blade, every scream of pain.

My senses pour outwards as the tableau continues to play out in my mind's eyes. The copper taint of blood filters on the air, the pattering of life's glittering fluid flirting with my ears as I hear it drop into the dust at our feet, then, silence, all is engulfed in silence. Not a scream echoes, no rattle of mail, no clang of steel, no guttural howl of pain as blade meets flesh; just total and utter silence.

I open my eyes, Ari's hand still firmly clasped within my own. I can see the heat between us bleed out from between our fingers like the rays of the dawning sun. I cast my gaze around. The world is at a standstill, men, women, birds, even the air is frozen in time. Locked in place as if carved from stone, a world of statues dressed in the finery of war and death.

'Arianwen, my love, do not open your eyes, I beg you. Just follow me slowly and I will lead you from this, but I ask you not to look; this is something you do not want to see.'

I step away, Ari following in my wake, our hands still tightly locked together, whether from my own childish fear or from the sheer fact I cannot bare to let her go, I do not know.

I move towards one battling pair, a sleeper, his back bent double as a flamed hair huntress drives her blade deep into his throat. The glittering baubles of his life hang like rubies in the sky, arcing from her blade as she snarls, teeth bared, eyes blazing with feral fury. The terror and shock in his eyes is heart breaking. I can almost taste the finality of this moment; this snapshot of time is something that I know will be locked in my memory forever.

I glance around at the source of my life, my little angel. Not a word has issued from her and now I know why. She like the rest is locked in the moment, frozen like Medusa's garden of death.

I lead her to the edge of the clearing, past the carnage of war, her hand still grasped firmly within my own. I guide her to the floor, sheltering her within a pile of rocks that line the hollow of a tree.

Curling my fist over her palm, I draw from her whatever it is we have so conjured. The heat melts the flesh of my palm as I take it with my grasp. The pain is beyond anything I have ever felt as I smell my own flesh begin to roast.

I have to end this, and end it now; I draw my blade, moving towards that snarling harlot atop the Sleeper. I set my weapon against her throat, drawing it across her skin, watching as it slowly parts like dry parchment, the layers of her life peeling open showing me all that lies beyond.

I feel no remorse, no regret. They're not my kin, not my people. They never were. She is my only family and all that matters to me, in this life or any other, my silent angel.

Setting my weapon into the loop of my belt, I lift the sleeper's arm, turning his wrist, setting the edge of his blade to her throat and pushing deep, I feel the soft spring of her windpipe as it bends around the blade's edge.

'Sleep easy, soldier. One parting shot is no bad way to end.'

I turn, moving towards the static form of a female sleeper, her hand raised as the descending form of another of my former kinsmen bears down upon her. I draw her weapon from her hip, close her hand around its grip and set the point to his heart.

I take a fleeting moment and look upon the face of the demon I just condemned to death. I take a step back as the face jolts a memory loose, the tumbling collections of images falling free of my mind.

I knew him, I had trained him, dragged him by his boot straps from the ranks of raw recruits to the rank of captain in my legion. I shake my head as I stare at the bulge in his trousers, knowing all too well what he had in store for this slim waif. Any regret I had felt brewing drowns in a flood of ice and hatred. That is not what I had trained him to do. I had instilled honour, the value of life and of a clean death. Not battlefield rape. I tear the insignia from his chest, my scorn abating slightly as I move away. The filth will meet a just end at the hands of his former target, and to die without the honour I had so given him makes it all the more fitting.

I cast my sight around me. The other handful of Sleepers are holding their own, positions firm and locked in tight. I lift the side arm of one from its holster on his thigh and take aim at the knees of his closest assailant, sending the thick steel rounds through those tender joints. The crack of the weapon is deafening in the cloud of quiet that has blanketed this world. I set the weapon back and turn to Anatiamoros, his body only four feet away from this maelstrom. I spy his weapon, its gilded ornate form lying amidst the dust and debris at this man's feet. I pluck it from the ground, aiming into the brush to my left and fire three quick shots before setting the weapon into the fallen angel's hand.

'A parting gift, dear sir. I will hold true to my promise. No harm will ever come to her as long as I draw breath.'

I turn, slipping past them all and lift Arianwen from the floor, her body moulding to mine as I delve deeper into the undergrowth, before my hand opens. The charred remains of my glove and palm slip free as time falls in with vengeance and the sounds of war's orchestra once more fill the air.

Arianwen jerks in my grip as I stumble, both of us crashing to the floor. She stares at me with a dazed look of incomprehension in her eyes. I wave it away as I turn.

'Wait here. In three minutes follow after me and take the surviving Sleepers and go. I will guide my men away. Do not argue and do as I say.'

She nods as I slip through the brush, heading back towards the fight. Chaos reigns as I watch my men fumble, the screams of the one closest to me a soothing balm after all I have come to know.

I reach down, curling my hand through his collar as I fire three poorly placed shots at the trio of sleepers ahead of me, stone spraying over them as they fall for cover.

'Retreat, fall back to the under croft, move now!'

I watch as one races to snatch up the body of the feral whore I had sent to death's door, my growl staying the boy's hands as he turns and sprints past me, wings opening as I watch him take to the sky.

I leave them, dumping the now whimpering sack of blood and shattered bone at the door of the under croft as I turn towards the walkway.

'See to his wounds. I am going to finish the job you useless children failed to complete.'

Without another word, I leave. Their trembling adrenaline flushed forms glare at my back as I make my way free of this world of sulphur and smoke.

I crouch, low and hidden as I watch Arianwen and her team gather their fallen, the bodies of their kills lying in the hot noon day sun, skin already beginning to blacken as the pit from whence they came begins to reclaim them. I hold no pity; they met their ends at their own hands, paths already chosen. I just gave them a push.

I reach out, my aura caressing hers as I feel her sorrow leach into my heart. I know what that man meant to my angel, and the pain in my soul echoes her own. If I could return to the beginning and erase this all, maybe she would be happier. She wouldn't be here now, tears rolling over her anger flushed cheeks, mourning the death of a man so dear to her heart.

She turns her head in my direction as I shift forwards slightly, allowing her to see me for just a moment. I track the passage of her tears as they drift through the dust and grime that cakes her skin. The anger that blazes in her eyes makes me seize, my heart falling silent as I feel a cold pall settle in my stomach.

I pull away, drifting into the shadows and away from this scene of pain and anguish. I am of no use to anyone here. I cannot comfort the woman I love even in her hour of need for fear of the retribution of those around her, not only upon myself but also of her. What would they do if they knew she held the heart of a 'Demon,' if I can still own that title. I don't know what I am any more.

The doorway to my home looms before me as I slip inside, her scent hanging taut in the air, the glow of our impassioned coupling soaking through me as I head to my armoury and set aside the tools of my former life before slipping into the warmth of the bathing pool.

I need to clear my mind, make sense of all that has happened. Only then can I find a way to undo what has been done, and right the wrongs that have been cast at my angel's feet.

Can I really bear to ask her to give up on motherhood and all the normalcy of life with another angel? Can I offer anything close to that? I know I can't. I don't even truly know of my own origin, let alone what I can offer another living soul in return for their love and devotion.

I love my Little Wing, of that I have no doubt, but is my love enough to ensure she will be happy with me? That's if she chooses a life with me.

Grief

ARIANWEN

I watch every step my feet take. One after the other, heavy, dragging, barely able to take me to where I need to go, my body moving on its own. My heart feels like it has been filled with lead and has been dropped in the ocean, falling down to the bottom, unable to make its way to the top for a much needed breath to survive.

I don't see the grief stricken stares of my fellow kin as I follow behind the surviving sleepers who are now carrying Anatiamoros' shell, his soul long gone to stand with God behind the gates of Heaven, as we make our way to the great hall.

I can't lift my head as I know I am barely holding onto my composure, trying my hardest to not let the last strand of sanity break until I am behind the safe, closed doors of my home. I know questions need to be answered so all I have to do is keep myself together until I can finally let the grief out that is strangling me from the inside.

I barely have time to register what's happening when large fingers grip my arm painfully and drag me sideways, my feet sliding as I struggle to keep myself upright.

'What are you doing, Michael?' I hear Gabriel growl as he grabs my other arm, helping me to stand up straight as he continues to berate his brother. 'Have you no respect? She is in shock, can't you see that. Let her be!'

I can't even focus with my wet eyes, let alone understand why Michael is causing such pain in my arm. 'She needs to answer my questions now! Can't you see that this is suspicious, *brother*? The lockdown for Reclaimers was barely lifted before our sleepers were attacked. Why were two Reclaimers already in the forest? She *will* answer my questions now whether you like it or not!'

Michael continues to drag me forcefully, as his two personal guards stand to block Gabriel from following, fear now starting to come alive within me, telling me that what's about to unfold may not have a pleasant ending.

We reach a small door as Michael kicks it open before throwing me inside. I spread my hands out just in time to stop my face hitting the floor as my knees graze on the rough ground below. He slams the door closed behind him before I hear a jangle of keys and the tell tale sound of the lock clicking into place.

I lift my head and I'm met with complete malice from his burning stare, his silence more unsettling than his raging voice only moments before. He continues to glare, waiting for me to break, but regardless of the grief that is gripping my body and making me weak with sadness, I will not give in to his vicious antics. If he wants to know something, then he can damn well ask.

Silence. Both of us not wanting to be the first to give in to this battle of wills. He has always hated me for reasons unknown, but I do not deserve this treatment, as if I am the enemy, as if I am the Devil himself, thrown in an old filthy room ready to be broken, forced into a confession of something I have not committed.

'Why were you in the forest?' he lets out in a low frustrated voice, angry that he had to speak first.

'A soul was calling,' I struggle to get out as it is almost painful for an angel to lie.

'Why was Anatiamoros there also?'

'For the same reason. That is the only reason for us Reclaimers to enter the forgotten forest.'

I know he isn't convinced; the hatred seeping from his pores is like poison filling the cramped room. I move from my hands and knees and sit back on my heels, hands placed meekly on my lap, keeping my head high, not breaking our stare.

'Then tell me this, how did two Reclaimers, who were supposed to be focused on their calling, end up in the middle of a battle, a battle that our sleepers had barely begun? Why were you both in such close range of demon Hunters when part of your gifts are to sense such danger before it's near and stay well clear of it?' he yells, now standing directly in front of me, his large black shoes touching my knees as his towering bulk looms over me.

I choose my next words very carefully. 'Regardless of our title or the purpose we were created for, we would never walk away from our very own kin if we sensed they were in danger. I sensed the sleepers were in a battle so I went to assist and I would do it again if needed.'

He doesn't even let my words seep in before he is reaching down, wrapping his fingers around my throat and forcefully pulling me to my feet, then raising me up high until my toes leave the floor beneath me.

'*You're lying!*' he roars in my face as I struggle to breathe, hanging helpless in the air. '*Tell me the truth or I will treat you like the traitor I know you to be!*'

'It's the truth,' I squeeze out through the closing gap in my throat. He brings up his other hand. I go stiff with the sight of a small blade sticking out between his fingers, as he proceeds to point it at my right eye.

'Are you working with the enemy? Did you direct them to our sleepers' whereabouts? Were you the direct cause of death to your own *kin*?' he screams again, pushing the blade against the bottom of my eye, slightly piercing my skin.

The boiling rage so apparent in his eyes has me worried that I may not be able to talk my way out of this situation, and the possibility he may keep me locked up in this makeshift cell until he finds the answers he seeks terrifies me.

There is a large banging on the door followed by Gabriel's

angry voice.

'Michael, that's long enough! Release her now or let me in!'

I start to feel faint from the lack of air, my throat burning. He lets my feet touch the ground but keeps his fingers wrapped tightly around my throat, bringing my face close up to his so our noses almost touch.

'I will find out the truth, Arianwen. I have my ways,' he seethes as he uses a key to open the door before flinging it open and throwing me at Gabriel's feet.

He reaches for me, helping me to my feet, frowning deeply while reaching out to wipe the single drop of blood from under my eye. I pull out of his grip, take two steps back, then turn and retreat as fast as I can, out of the main doors and practically run from the two leaders who both want something from me I can never give.

My body aches as I uncurl myself from the ball I have been in for how long ... I don't know. I am in the middle of the lake on one of the large lily pads, calming my body after shattering completely at the loss of our greatest kin, the elder we all looked to for advice, and the man who loved me like the granddaughter he never had.

Who will I turn to now? Who will understand the fierce passion I have for my true calling? Who will help me from stumbling when life's obstacles get too large? My heart and soul give me the answer I am seeking in the form of a flutter in my heart as my thoughts turn to the man who holds my heart tightly in his grip. *Albion.*

If I didn't know before, the extent of his love for me ... I do now. He killed his own men to protect me, to protect my kin, to protect the world he may truly belong to. As heavy as my heart and soul is, I cannot sit here and grieve forever. I need answers. I need guidance. I need help.

I sit up with renewed determination to find the reason fate has thrown my life into turmoil and to find a way to take back control of my destiny. I stand tall, letting the last of the sunshine's rays warm my cold skin as I take a deep breath, bringing my form back to life, ready to fight for what I want. A life where Albion and I can co-exist.

✦ ✦ ✦

I reach the beautiful old world cottage, surrounded by flowers of every kind, the fragrance of which floods my senses, as I pause before I knock on the door, reminding myself of what I need to do. I need to seek answers, and this may be the only place I will find what I am looking for.

I knock softly and wait as I hear the occupant move towards the door. I take a deep breath just as the door opens and a sweet smile greets my nervous form. She looks the same as she did when I was a child, never changing, never ageing, always so willing to share her knowledge with anyone that seeks it. Her name is Claire, but everybody from within my world refers to her as 'The Bookkeeper.'

'Come child, I was just about to sit down for some tea, please join me,' she says in the kindest voice that has ever rung in my ears as she ushers me in and towards a little table in front of the window. The last rays of the sun shine through as we both take a seat and she begins to pour the boiling water into two cups. Two cups? Is she expecting somebody? Maybe I should go until another time.

'I was expecting you, Arianwen. I know you seek answers and I am here to help as much as I can.'

I am not shocked by her words as I suddenly remember the whispers I have heard for a lifetime about The Bookkeeper's gifts. Not only does her home house the oldest books in our histories, Claire herself has an uncanny ability to know exactly what book you are after and what page the information you seek lies upon.

We quietly sip our tea as I contemplate how to ask for the information I seek. She stands and breaks the silence. 'Shall we take a walk to the library, dear?'

I nod, rising also, and follow her retreating form. She comes to a heavy ancient carved door, with swirls of writing all over it in many different languages, some I recognise, some too old even for my earliest learnings.

She presses a large letter A in the centre of the door and it begins to open, old musty air floating past with a *swoosh.* The vision before me is amazing. There is an old stone staircase winding down, lit candles following the curved walls, but what is amazing is the shelves dug out of the old stone walls following the stairs, and they are overflowing with books.

I follow as she starts to descend the stairs, my eyes darting everywhere, taking in every little detail of these old ancient books sitting as if this has always been their home. I have heard of The Bookkeeper's Library, but have never had the privilege of stepping inside; she would always bring the books to us during the lessons throughout my life's education.

We continue to step deeper, shelves of books still lining the walls, but when she stops at the bottom of the stairs, I stand in silent awe. It is a large narrow room that seems to go on forever, as far as the eye can see. Tall bookshelves line either side of the room, small tables are scattered down the centre with a chair here and there. This is a reading room, the biggest one I have ever seen.

She doesn't waste time as she starts to walk along one side of the bookcases. She only walks a few metres before standing still. Standing, staring, and then turning to me with a smile. 'What information are you looking for, my dear?'

I am lost for words as I turn and look at the books she has stopped in front of. One title standing large and clear in front of my eyes. *Gabriel.*

Seeing my expression at the sight of that book, she grabs it from the shelf with a smile and makes her way to a small table with a chair on either side and indicates with her hand that I should sit. She looks at me, waiting for me to tell her what I seek.

'Why is Gabriel so interested in me? Are his intentions less than honourable?'

She doesn't seem surprised by my questions at all, as she still holds that small smile on her lips while opening the book and turning the pages. She stops, placing a finger on one and turns her attention back to me.

'Everybody seeks their perfect mate. It is nature's way of continuing a species and we immortals are no different. Gabriel was made to be a leader and protector of this world and his power has grown as he has proved his leadership through the centuries. He needs someone strong enough to support him in the good and the bad, someone to give him strength in his time of need and he sees that in you. You have an extraordinary gift, Arianwen, there is a reason you were created to be the most powerful Reclaimer of all time, and that reason will be revealed to you when the time is right.

'Gabriel knows the extent of your power, and that the two of you coming together in the union of marriage would create the most powerful duo our world has seen. How he would use that power is yet to be seen. I know the past, I know the present, but the future is not what I see.' As she finishes her words, the finger she had flying across the pages of the old worn paper while she was talking, also stops.

Her words make sense but don't put my mind at ease as to what Gabriel may use my power for. I know he and Michael are not only our leaders, but also our protectors. History has shown throughout all the worlds that not every act committed by a leader has been honourable. I just wish I knew his plans; it would make it much easier to plan a way out of them if I had even an inkling as to what was to come.

'Something else is bothering your beautiful mind, my sweet girl. I have many books. Is there anything else you wish to know?'

I blush slightly as my thoughts move to Albion and the uncertainty of our future, a future that has no guarantees.

'You are not the first one, you know.'

My eyes shoot up to hers, as I feel as if she can read my mind at this exact moment. 'Love has existed between Angels and Demons for all of existence. It's that forbidden thrill most of the time that causes such an attraction, but then true love has grown in some cases. None of them have lasted the test of time. It's near impossible to live between two worlds, but that doesn't mean your love won't be the first.'

I am saddened and thrilled at her words. I know in my heart that it is impossible, but I also feel as if fate will find us a way and that yes, we will be the first to make a life together for the rest of our existence.

'Will our fight to be together be worth the risk?' I ask with glassy eyes as the emotions of my love for Albion start to surface and boil over.

'All great love is worth it. But will it end well ... I cannot answer that, my dear. I am nothing more than the keeper of the past, I know the present, but the future has no meaning with me. To know what you seek, you need someone far older than I.'

She chuckles to herself as she closes the book in her hands. I sigh, still feeling lost and unsure of what step to take next.

'There is someone who may be able to shed light on your predicament, but it could be a great risk seeking her out.'

I think I know who she is referring to. In all my time as a Reclaimer and venturing into the village of the damned, I have heard many whispers of a lady who resides on the far edges of the forest who is called by many names. Fortune teller, sorcerer, witch, the one who sees all. Many villagers have met their death trying to get to her, so I am well aware of the risk.

'She will mean you no harm, but her words are known to be true. You have ventured many times into the forest so I'm sure you will be safe, but please, take extra care as the forest isn't always what it seems.' Her smile brightens as she continues. 'Go child, seek the answers you deserve; they may put your mind at ease.'

We stand and make our way back up the winding stairwell. I head to the door and turn to give her a thankful hug. 'I wish you all the best in your matters of the heart,' she says as she gives me another warm smile.

I walk away from her with optimism in my heart and the hope that I may eventually find the answers I am looking for.

As I walk through Eden, taking in all this beautiful garden has to offer, I think about what it would be like for Albion to make this his home. Would he ever be comfortable living here? Or would the constant stares and whispers of what he used to be prove to be too much for not only him, but for us to bear? Does he even have enough good in him to overrule the evil that has been bred into his very soul? All of this unknown is playing with my mind, making it hard to concentrate on anything at the moment.

As I pass under the stone gatekeepers and take my first step into the forest, the eternal dragons start to growl, letting the earth beneath my feet rumble. I look up to them as one begins to speak. 'Be careful with every step thou take, as evil is at play today.'

I stare back in confusion as evil has been in the forest every day I have step foot in it, so why is today any different? They don't offer any more, so I continue on my path to find a little shack at the far reaches of the forest.

I have never had a need to venture into this part of the forest, far from the village and the entrance to my home, even far from the edges of Hell itself. The absolute silence casts an eerie feel over my senses as I use them all to alert me to any danger that may be lurking. But all I can hear is my every step. Even though I am placing my feet with care and caution, the cracking sound of the dried rotten moss beneath my feet is the only sound echoing in my ears.

Something snags my right foot as I trip and only just manage to save myself with my other foot, looking back surprised to see a vine on my walkway that I hadn't noticed. I need to concentrate more as I cannot remain safe if I am tumbling all over the place. My eyes must still be sore from my earlier outpouring of emotions as I seem to not have my usual crystal clear vision.

Another vine snags a foot as I growl a sigh of frustration at myself for my carelessness. This has never happened before and this is not the place for it to start. I need to see this old lady as soon as I can and then leave this lurid place. I continue forth determined not to trip again, but as I concentrate on the placing of my feet, something flies past my head, just connecting with a few strands of my hair. I look up only to be met with the overhanging dead trees, their branches stretched out like skeletal fingers.

But it's while my vision has been raised towards the dark sky above that I feel movement over my feet. I try and jump back but I am stuck in place by the dried strands of moss over both feet that are now winding their way up my ankles. I try to shake it off but it only grips tighter. Something flies past my head again, this time grabbing a few strands of hair with it, pulling hard enough to rip it from my scalp and making me yelp.

I clasp a hand over my mouth, not wanting to draw attention to myself as I try and shake the moss from my feet which is now slowly making its way up my legs. I bend down to try and break it from my body as I notice the entire forest floor move and slither beneath me. As I am breaking pieces from my legs, something once again bumps into me, this time sending my whole body to the ground. I look up fast, only seeing a dark shadow hide in the highest trees.

Fear is starting to wind itself through my veins as I franticly claw at the moss that won't let go of my legs. That's when I hear it. *Arianwen,*' floats like a whisper through the stale air of this dead woodland. I don't want to come face to face with whatever entity is calling my name so I try with all my strength to break free.

As I free myself from the final piece of moss, I start to run but only get a mere few feet away before something wraps around both my bare arms. Vines hanging from the dead trees like snakes wind and coil their way around my flesh. Coated in small thorns, they cut into my skin as they slither around my form. I fight franticly, trying to release myself from their capture before they take complete control of me. I feel one arm start to rise as I realise they are trying to lift me in the air.

That can't happen, I will *not* let it happen. I will not be strung up high like an animal caught in a snare. I brace my feet on the ground and use all my strength to pull down, as again my name is whispered through the air. *'Arianwen.'* I fight, I pull, I rip at the vines on my arms as a swinging piece lands on the top of my head and starts to wind tightly in my hair.

'No!' I scream, uncaring now as to who could possible hear me as I grunt loudly, trying to escape this web I have been caught in. I tug down hard and get one arm free as I then use both hands to try and free my other. As I release the last of the vines from my arm, the vine in my hair pulls up, almost taking me from the ground below. I reach both hands up and wrap my fingers around the vine, thorns digging into the delicate flesh on my palm. Blood drips down my arms as I pull with all my might, my scalp aching with the pressure of my hair pulled tight.

I finally break the hold, but not without the vine taking a clump of my hair with it, my feet running as soon as they get a good grip on the ground. Black mist floats though the dead trees, hiding what direction I need to take to return to safety. *'Arianwen,'* the chilling voice sings again as I turn in circles, unsure as to what way to run. I have to move, regardless of what I may run into. Staying still is more of a risk.

The black mist starts to clog my throat, making it hard to take a breath as I begin to feel my vision swirl. I continue to turn in circles trying to get my bearings, trying to summon every gift I was created with to help me sense a way out of this cloud of malice. *'Arianwen.'* The whisper is closer this time, making my panic rise as I feel a branch of a tree swipe past my arm, causing a small gash. As I clamp my hand over it, trying to move forward, another branch scratches my neck. I wave my hands around wildly trying to stop their assault as my name continues to float on the air that surrounds me.

The mist starts to take form; hands reach out and brush past my hair as more grab my cloak from behind, trying to rip it from my body. I feel the black hands on my legs. One grabs my thigh, while another grabs at my waist. I twist and turn, trying to find a way out of this nightmare.

I feel something small, prickly, hairy, start to run over my feet and make its way up my legs. I look down to see that the mist has turned itself into a thousand spiders that have carpeted the ground and are now proceeding to crawl up my legs. I can't run, the misted hands are now holding me in place as the black spiders continue to crawl up my body, covering every inch of skin as I scream in terror while still hearing my name being called, *'Arianwen.'*

I struggle and fight, trying to shake these deathly creatures from my body as they crawl with rapid speed towards my head. Just as I'm about to let out a massive scream, it gets caught in my throat at the sight of a figure in front of me. A figure whispering my name, *'Arianwen.'* I know who it is. I have never laid eyes on this dark entity before, but my soul is screaming his name. Lucifer!

Just as he takes the final step to stand in front of me, the spiders crawl up my neck, rapidly covering my face. Before they cover my eyes, I see the Devil himself smirk at me before it all goes black.

I feel myself falling for forever before I finally land with a large thump on the ground. My eyes open immediately, fear gripping my heart at what I'm about to sight, but ... there is nothing! It's just the forest, as it was when I first stepped foot in it. The trees are still, the ground is solid and unmoving. There are no vines, no branches, no misted hands to grab at me, no spiders trying to crawl their way up my body. But most importantly, no Lucifer!

Did I imagine it all? Have I truly lost my mind? As I look around at this silent dead woodland, nothing moving, nothing breathing, no sound at all, I truly believe that maybe the recent events in my life have pushed me to the breaking point or beyond. My senses can't find another creature in this forest but me, so what just happened?

Was it the Devil's trickery at play or was it my mind, finally breaking to the point where I can no longer tell the difference between reality and fiction? Oh no, I feel like I am truly losing it.

I need him. I need home. I want to go home!

28

Passion and Hysteria

ALBION

The air sits fragrant and soft against my skin as the sunrise bathes me. The sour frown that teases my lips is one of sheer and utter self-loathing. If nothing else in my life was to come to pass, the love that will always grace me is something I know I can never relinquish. I know I never can, but does that stay the same for my angel?

My angel, my sweet, seductive, vivacious angel; the woman who came into my life as prey and stayed as the victor of my heart and soul. I have never known a love as pure as hers, as pure as what she lays upon my form, but after all that has happened can I still say that? Can I still say she, in anyway, still holds my heart in her hand?

I feel the Drewen move beneath me as I lie back against the trunk, the branch beneath my backside swaying with the wind as I close my eyes and let the world sit, quiet and still for a minute more.

The still air is shattered by the most soul crushing scream I have ever heard. I roll from the branch, my senses flying free as I ensnare the source of the echoing cry of fear and anguish. My heart bleeds cold as I feel the soft brush of the aura in distress.

'Arianwen.'

I hit the ground running, my movements a blur as I duck low, drawing my face guard tight to me and barrel headlong through everything in my path, my one thought, my only thought, is of reaching her before something foul truly befalls her.

Her pain, her fear, all rolls through me as I sprint towards the source of the shadowed outpouring of unadulterated grief and anguish. The one pervading thought fills me that despite it all, my woman, my angel, my love, is crying out for me. Nothing will keep me from her side. I draw my blade, its feral soul clawing at my mind as I roll to the left, the edge carving through the clutching strands of a Drewen, its whimpering core crying out as I duck low at its swinging strands of hate.

I see her glowing aura, the shimmering ball of energy filtering through the branches around me as they snag and clutch at my skin and armour, her wailing cries drawing fear and anger deep from my core.

Woe betide whatever has so afflicted my angel, for if I ever lay hand on it, nothing in this world, not God nor Devil will save it from my wrath.

✦ ✦ ✦

She lies there, quivering and tear streaked, her eyes wide, unseeing, their thousand yard stare sinking into my heart as she mumbles. Her words stilted, incoherent, little more than deranged baby babble; I ease her from the leaf strewn floor, her limp, fear weary form rolling into my grip as she curls against my chest, her fingers lacing around the straps of my armour as she buries her face into my chest.

'Dark ... so dark ... evil ... eyes watching, always watching.'

I brush my hand over her hair, the golden strands laced with blood, I cradle her tight to my body, a soft hushing whisper dusting her fevered, fear pricked ramblings as I let my wings unfurl.

'Hush, my darling ...'

I begin to speak, her fingers tightening their grip as she rolls her gaze to mine, her head smearing congealed hair and blood over my chest.

'Are we going home?'

Her words lance me, pinning me to the spot as I suddenly lose all control over my own words. I stutter and mumble as I stare down into the unfocused violet orbs that have so locked my mind away.

I smile, pasting it over my lips to hide the pain behind. I peel my eyes away from hers, the innocence and frailty almost too much to bear as I lift her against me, adjusting her weight as my wings unfurl further.

'Yes my love, we're going home.'

✦ ✦ ✦

The water swirls, soft blush pink as I squeeze the bunched rag in my fist, watching the glimmering liquid cascade over my knuckles, the twisting ribbons of my angel's lifeblood dancing through it as I brush her hair from her forehead. The stippled line of fevered sweat dapples her brow as I wipe the ice cooled cloth across her skin.

I brush the clinging strands from her cheek, my fingers brushing over her skin as I brush away the crusted line of blood beneath her eye, my mind sparking as I feel the malice and hate pour from beneath it, a sensation all too familiar. I stare down at her, questions dancing in my mind as she moves away from my tender touch.

Her child like whimpering moan makes my chest clench as she curls her fists into the pelt at her waist, her eyes screwing shut as she begins to toss in my bed.

She calls out my name, her voice soft, girlish, scared of every small noise that echoes over my home's walls. I let the cloth slip from my hand, sliding through the water to the bottom of the bowl. I run my hand over her shoulder, whispering gently into her ear as I hug her tightly to me, her soft willowy frame curling against mine as she begins to calm, her body softening, loosening to my touch. As I begin to rub my hand along her stomach, she issues a soft cooing moan as she drifts into a slow fitful slumber.

✦ ✦ ✦

I hear her move, the soft stirring of her lithe, sensual form giving me pause as I set my tools aside, the night's strain playing across me as I turn away from the delicate scroll work of Arianwen's armour and to the source of my inspiration.

The look of confusion in her eyes makes my heart dip as I watch her clutch the sheets to her breast, her naked form huddled amongst the bear skin and cotton sheets of my bed like a tree trapped in an ice flow, one lone spire of beauty amongst a crystalline sea of white.

'Albion ... how?'

I rise, the small stool sliding back beneath my work bench, its casters clattering over the chiselled stone floor. She watches my passage towards her as she curls her legs under her, a soft look of puzzlement listing in her eyes as I set myself down on the edge of the bed.

'I found you. You were calling out for me in the forest on the borders. Try not to move too quickly. You took a hit to the head; you were bleeding, confused and incoherent, terrified, babbling about monsters, darkness and evil trees.'

I run my hand up her neck as I lean in and plant a soft gentle kiss on her lips as I curl my fingers through hers.

'You asked me one thing that I still cannot shake from my head. Through all the fear and babbling, you asked me if "we" were going home, not to take you home, but if we were going home.'

I watch her as she shuffles across the bed, pulling me along with her, until I am sat, my back pressed to the stone wall and my angel tucked in at my hip, her head resting in the crook of my shoulder. I feel more than hear her sigh as she strokes her thumb along the back of my hand.

'Truly, Albion, my love, there is nowhere else I would ever call home. If you are not there it will never truly be my home, no matter what I am forced to call it.'

I cup the bottom of her chin, drawing her eyes to mine as I once more place a soft kiss upon her lips, the silk caress of her mouth on mine making my heart race as I feel the velvet brush of her tongue over my own.

'I love you, Arianwen, and have something for you, something that will ensure no harm will ever come to you again, not from Demon or Angel.'

I punctuate my words as I brush my thumb over the centimetre long scar below her right eye, the surprise and confusion in her eyes making me weak as I push off the bed, my angel shifting against the pillows behind us both.

'They interrogated me, Albion. When you left me, I went back with the others. I tried to explain what happened without revealing us, but Michael ...'

I raise my hand, patting the air as I lift her armour from the bench.

'I know all too well what that "Angel" is capable of. He is, after all, the one who cast out Lucifer. He isn't known as the Angel of Vengeance for being kind.'

I move to the side of my bed, the polished sheen of gold laced steel playing across her features as she stares at her own reflection. I set the armour on the bed in front of her. Her eyes widen as she takes in what I have just presented her: the intricate scroll work of birds in flight across the breast plate, the rolling filigree weaving over the contours of the sides accentuating every line and curve.

'Now I know that no matter what avails you, my love, you will carry my protection with you always.'

She traces her fingers over its glass smooth surface, a small tear welling in the corner of her eye as she looks up at me, adoration dancing in her eyes as she gently sets it at the side of the bed. Reaching out to me, she curls her hand into my waist band and pulls me towards her.

She shifts herself into my lap, her body shaking as I feel her bare skin beneath my hands. The scent of her hair fills my mind as she rests her head against me listening to the drum beat of my heart.

Her body quakes as she finally lets her walls down. The weight of loss and fear breaks over everything in its path as she begins to sob, her tears soaking my shirt, rolling down my skin as I gently rock her, my whispered words doing little to abate the weight of her grief.

After what feels like a life time of pent up anguish and fear finally slows to a tear stained trickle, she shifts, kissing my jaw as she leans her head into my neck, her words muffled as she curls her fingers through mine.

'Never have I thought that I could ever love you more; then you do this. I love you, Albion, with all my heart and soul.'

I softly draw her into a kiss, our lips meeting as the depth of my love for this winged beauty pours forth. I lift the sheets aside, drawing them back over us both as I feel her shiver. A soft giggle rolls up from my winged goddess as I nip at her collarbone, as she curls her arms around my neck.

Her body, soft and supple, moves against mine as she draws my shirt up and over my head, casting it aside. I draw my hands over her blemish free skin, the pale alabaster standing stark against the bronzed tone of my human shell. I lean in, trailing a line of butter-fly kisses down her neck and over her nubile chest, my lips flicker-ing over her rose tinted nipples.

Soft moans fill the air as I walk my way along her warm flesh to her lips, my tongue dancing with hers as we sink into each other, lost in our own bliss.

Her hands dance over my waist band as I feel the cord begin to unravel, the knot working free as her nimble fingers slip over my skin. I feel myself harden as her hands push my trousers down over my backside, her fingers digging into my firm flesh as she ravages my mouth.

I glide my hands up her sides, softly cupping her breasts as I feel her slim hand encircle my length, guiding it to her moist core; I feel her gasp against my lips as I slowly begin to slip between her sodden lips.

I feel her heat, the soft clutch of her as she draws me in. I groan in her mouth as she caresses my tongue with her own, the gentle velvet touch echoing her clenching core as I begin to draw myself from her.

Our joining is slow, unhurried, as she wraps her legs over my backside as I am once more enveloped in the woman that owns me completely.

29

Deception

ARIANWEN

One finger slowly trails down from the side of my breast, over my ribs, dipping at my waist, rising over my hips, travelling back until he splays his hand slowly over my behind, pushing with a gentle force until my wet centre once again meets his heated, hard flesh. I moan softly as he continues to nibble at the corner of my lips, displaying a gentleness beyond the façade of his rugged exterior.

His hand glides down my leg; he grips under my knee, bringing it up high until it is draped over his hip bone as he pushes his shaft against my dripping core. He slides me up slightly, friction causing a shiver of pleasure to roll through my body as he moves me back down, making that delicious ache build yet again in my body.

He moves back slightly to align his shaft with my wet core before pushing in, agonisingly slow. I feel his solid flesh sliding past my internal walls until he hits my resistance. He stills as my muscles clench tightly, enjoying this fullness that only he has given me. It starts to soothe my ache, an ache only he will give me.

He looks directly at me, his beautiful blue eyes shining with the love that is so evident in his every word, every movement. He starts to pull out gently before slowly rocking back in, as I can't help but close my eyes, overcome with the emotions flowing through my beating heart and the sweet song that is playing in my soul.

He keeps a slow steady pace as I feel his body start to tense, my centre gripping him harder with each slight thrust, a slow burn of ecstasy taking over both our bodies; it begins to bubble over, causing me to grip his shoulders tightly, my nails digging into his flesh as a shattering high hits me fast, unexpectedly, as I struggle to catch my breath at the waves of pleasure now simmering throughout me.

My wet centre strangles his manhood as I scream with pleasure. He grunts twice more before his body goes rigid as he reaches his release and pours his hot essence into my centre to meet with my overflowing juices.

His lips find mine in a sweet, gentle kiss that takes my breath away. I'm thankful he brought me here. To his home, to what feels like my home as well, to our bed, a bed we have shared the most intimate moments in, moments I thought only dreams were made of.

There is a lot happening in the worlds around us. To lie here for days is a luxury we cannot afford, so he rises and picks up my clothes, placing them on the bed beside me before again helping to dress me, a task he seems to relish in. I now know he loves taking care of me, even in the simplest of ways, and my heart melts every time he does something this sweet.

✦ ✦ ✦

He walks me to the safe entry of my world, underneath the stone dragon gatekeepers, ensuring I'm met with no harm. He leans in to kiss me goodbye, a shyness taking over him I have yet to experience. Is it the fact that the stone statues that surround us can see and hear what is going on beneath them?

My cheeks also blush at the thought as he deepens the kiss before pulling back to give me a serious look. 'Arianwen, don't leave your world alone. If you have a calling, I understand, but wait until you feel my presence before walking too far into the forest. If what you experienced in the far side of the forest was at the hand of Lucifer, it won't be the last you hear from him. I will go and listen to the gossips of my world for any clues. Please be careful. I need you safe, my love,' he whispers, giving me one last sweet kiss on my lips before turning and heading towards the pits of Hell.

I wander slowly through the garden, under the dark night skies, feeling the aftereffects of the love Albion and I both shared with our bodies and with our hearts. A feeling of contentment slowly settles in my heart for the first time since I discovered that Albion was indeed my eternal saviour. A demon, a man, who now owns my body, heart, and soul.

I reach my home and enter quietly; the rest of this house has retired long ago. I reach my room and suddenly... feel very alone. This has always been my safe haven, my place of peace and comfort, but as I undress the day's clothes and slip into a nightdress, I feel dread at having to crawl into my bed all alone.

The sheets are crisp and fresh, soft pure cotton, but they feel cold and the bed feels too big for just me. I roll to my side and reach a hand out, imagining that Albion grabs it and brings it up to his lips for a gentle kiss. My eyes start to water, a single tear slipping down my cheek and falling to the pillow below. I finally understand the need humans have to cry.

I am restless all night, the scene in the forest playing with my mind as I reach in my sleep for a man that is not there. The loss of Anatiamoros is still taking its toll on my heart, the grief I feel twisting tightly inside, embedding itself as a permanent scar, always a reminder of the cruel reality of our immortal worlds.

Eventually I sit up, looking outside my window and up to the moon sitting so high and pretty in the sky, imagining that there is nothing but silent peace up there. That's when I hear it. A calling. Torn at wanting to run to them straight away, and wanting to do as Albion had instructed and wait until I sense he is near, to deliver me to the soul in need safely and well protected.

I take a few deep breathes and try to ignore, just for a while; at least I'll try. I know Albion could be occupied as I can no longer feel his aura in the forest or the village. Pain is starting to run through my veins as I hear the calling again. Someone is in need, someone is in great pain and it is impossible for me to just sit here and do nothing.

I get up and get dressed, hoping that by the time I'm ready and entering the forest that Albion's aura will be close by. I make my way out quietly, just as the sky begins to change, ready to welcome the new day. I pass the gatekeepers, who are silent at the moment, and enter the forest, my senses searching for Albion as well as any danger that may be looming nearby.

I can't feel him, but what I do feel is the soul in need, almost frantic in their call for me. I know Albion is right, that Lucifer may be up to something, but it is impossible for me to ignore a soul who deserves a safe passage back to its Creator.

I have been Reclaiming for many years, so this is no different. I have been created with the abilities to slip in and out of the village without being detected; only sometimes will a Hunter catch my lingering scent as I enter the forest, but by then I am able to make my getaway without too much of a fight.

I take extra care as I reach the start of the rundown shacks and dwellings of the village, noting that it is near silent today. I can't hear the haggling at the makeshift market, or the fighting over the barely there necessities. I can't even hear the animals that are sometimes the source of food for the villagers.

An eerie feeling starts to flow through my veins as I become more cautious with each step. The silence is deafening as I begin to fear what might be at play behind the lack of sound.

I find the dwelling that houses my calling. It is quite large compared to most of the buildings that are just thrown together here. I imagine its use to be of some importance many centuries ago, but now it is like all the other shelters here, rundown and barely standing.

I grab the handle carefully, pulling down with ease, trying to avoid a click that would echo loudly in this quiet. I'm met with no noise, so I start to push the rough wooden door slowly, the bottom scratching slightly on the ancient floorboards beneath, the noise only a hush as all of my senses go into overdrive. I take in everything that is in this room, the only light coming from behind my form in the doorway and a small lit candle in the far corner of the large room.

As I pull the door closed behind me and make my way across the room, I am shocked at what my eyes are showing me. I first thought the soul in need was a young man, who is currently tightly curled into a ball on the floor in the corner, but all my senses start screaming at me that he is not alone. He is curled over a small young woman, protecting her, sheltering her, while both of their souls call out in need.

This is rare. I have read about this but never once experienced it for myself. All souls are individuals just like the human shells they resided in, and they all leave the earth at their own time. Even if they find companions in this waiting room of death, they still pass on their own when their time is right.

I make my way to stand in front of them, the girl mewing in pain and fear as the young man's body shakes around her, trying to hold on as tight as he can. Sending two souls to Heaven at once will take everything I have, but there is nothing to fear here as they will both be given the peace they have so earned.

As I kneel down onto the floor the girl starts to cry louder, barely able to contain her emotions as the man tries to shush her in a soothing tone. I move in closer and rest a gentle hand on her shoulder to try and give her comfort in her time of need. As the girl lifts her head and makes eye contact with me her crying stops instantly.

Before I have time to decipher the strange look that has suddenly taken over her face, she silently mouths the words 'I'm sorry' before the young man grabs her and pushes them both further into the corner.

It's then that I feel the rumble under my feet from the gate-keeper's roars and sense there is more than just this couple in the darkened room. I stand and swing around a split second too late as I feel a large blow hit the side of my head as my body flies across the room with the force.

My vision is blurred but I stand instantly, only just dodging a second blow by the demon who looks quite surprised that he missed. He raises his other hand and just before he swings, I see an ancient hammer ball with nails sticking out of its entire surface. As I raise my cloak to protect my face, the weapon makes contact with the side of my cloak, the cursed nails penetrating its protective forces and making contact with the crafted armour Albion gave to me only a matter of hours ago.

He moves fast, coming at me again, this time with more determination in his eyes. He swings his weapon. I try and move with haste but the weapon snags the end of my cloak and I am pulled down to the ground. I remove my cloak in an instant, shaking it from the nails which are captured in it. When it frees itself I swing the entire cloak at his head before he can avoid it; it crashes into the side of his skull, sending him crashing to the floor.

I know I may not survive this fight in the darkness of this room, against weapons that are cursed, so I turn, deciding that a fast retreat will work best. But when I turn, the blood in my veins instantly freezes.

Standing in the doorway, the light from outside silhouetting their forms, are two larger than life dark creatures looming over my angelic form.

It's the Dolophonos!

The last thought I have before a black cloud shoots out and grips my throat is ... this is death!

30

Day's of Future Past

ALBION

I watch as she vanishes beneath the dragon arch, my gaze tracking up into the still chiselled eyes, and have to turn my eyes away. The look of sardonic, smug confidence that leaches from them makes me burn with anger laced inferiority. How can it be that these ancient beings could know so much about my own past when all I have ever known is the dark depths of Hell and the fear and violence of growing up in a world of hedonism and vice?

She turns for a moment, stopping and gracing me with a small blown kiss and a smile that could melt the ice from around even the hardest heart. I find myself blushing slightly as I mouth the three little words that have come so easily for me. 'I love you.' Three words I will never be able to stop saying no matter what happens between us.

I move lightly, listening to the world around me slowly come to life. My eyes shift, the land around me glittering in a blanket of life. I wish Arianwen could see the world as I do, the sheer weight of life in this corner of the world an all too apparent reminder of what has been driven from mine.

My home calls my name as I scale the cliff face, the rocks and dirt grinding into my skin as I slowly surmount the border between my world and hers.

I'm bone weary, tired to my soul's soul, a depth of fatigue I have only felt once before in my life, the day of my training's end. A point where your body, after all has been said and done, finally gives in to the weight of exhaustion that has been hanging around your neck.

✦✦✦

I grasp the door to my home, dragging it aside, the weight almost too much to bear for my overtaxed and tired frame. With a grunt of exertion, it finally slides free and I stumble past before it slips closed behind me.

My bed calls my name as I stagger towards it, my armour slipping from me as I swat at the buckles and straps until it falls from my body.

I sink into my bed with a deep rolling sigh, my breath shallow and heavy as I almost immediately sink into a depthless slumber.

✦✦✦

The world is a storm of whispers, shadows so dark they blot out the sun. I stagger and stumble, my heart hammering in my chest as I cast my eyes around me blindly. The trees twist and move as I run. My legs shake, the fear inside me boiling up through me like steam through a chimney.

Voices draw me down pathways and through stands of these living oak shades, rank and file closing as I sprint for my life. I stumble, tumbling to the earth, tears springing to my eyes. I raise my hand and touch the warm saline that skates down my cheeks. I am crying, for the first time in my life I am crying.

A voice soothing and soft lifts my heart from this den of fear and loathing, the golden light of it filtering through the dark, guiding me towards a warmth so deep and loving that it can only be from one person.

I leave the grasp of the whispering shadows, stumbling into a clearing of white light. The thing that hits me first is not the heat of the sun or the fresh breeze that covers me in a cooling mist of relief, but the grass beneath my uncovered feet. I look down and can't help but frown; gone are the scarred runes and stressed toned skin of an adult. What greets my eyes is the soft putty like skin of a prepubescent boy.

I lift my hands to my eyes, disbelief availing me as I begin to tear open my shirt, the soft unblemished skin of youth sheathing my form as I hear the tinkling laughter that has been lost to my ears for over a hundred years.

'Mother?'

I watch as her eyes turn to me, the smile that blossoms on her smooth flawless alabaster features filling me with a sense of complete and utter safety. She pats at the grass, I move towards her, my head swimming as I try to fathom exactly what is happening. I reach her side, the smell of her perfume filling my mind as I sink to the ground. My voice high, the squeak of youth all too present as I cringe at the high pitched tones oozing from my mouth.

'Albion, my sweet boy, oh how I missed you.'

She sweeps me into her arms, her warmth overflowing, drowning my doubts and fears. I curl into her, her arms wrapping about me as she begins to hum. I find my eyes closing as the long lost lullaby drifts on the whispering breeze. I haven't felt such serenity and safety in many a long year.

'I wish I could stay here.'

I hear her smile, the soft cessation of her lilting song all too soon as she turns me to face her. Her hands smooth over my clothing as she drags her fingers through my hair.

'You never did comb your hair properly after bathing, no matter how many times I made you do it.'

She sighs as she looks at me, her head tilting to one side as she smiles.

'Albion, my boy, my shining sun, you know you can't stay here. There is another who needs you more than I.'

I stare at my mother's smiling face, her eyes glittering with love and pride as she strokes my cheek lovingly.

'Such a beautiful and strong man you've become, a heart of gold and light, to flourish as you have and keep the good that is locked within alive in such a place; I'm oh so proud of you my boy, my sweet Angel of Darkness.'

She slowly rises to her feet, the soft caress of her hand at my cheek drawing me with her as I am left staring into the eyes of a woman who nurtured and raised me to be the man that stands before her now.

I take her hand in mine as I pull her into a tight hug.

'Please, I beg you, don't leave me again. I fear that my soul will never heal this time.'

The look that passes over her face makes me pause; the vision of knowing love that stands before me settles in and she grasps my hand all the tighter.

'Albion, listen and listen well. The woman, the angel that holds your heart in her hand, has healed and brought your soul into the light. She is more to you than I can ever be. I will never truly be gone from your heart or your life, but she is the one who needs you now. She needs the man who brought her from the edge of possible destruction and gave her life true meaning. Within her lies the edge of your salvation and the meaning of true life; she needs you now more than ever as the darkness is closing in. Do not forsake her, Albion, now go, reclaim the woman you love and make her heart whole once more.'

I sit upright, motes of light dancing in my eyes as I try in vain to catch the embers of sleep that rise from my addled mind, my mother's touch and words sitting fresh on my heart as I swing my feet to the floor.

I gaze around me, the meaning of my mother's message all too clear as I begin to lace my armour to me, the heavy plates of leather and mail sitting tight to my body as I reach my armoury. I stare at the wall, my lineage of death played out over racks and rails. I lift my father's charge rod from its stand, the twin barrels laced with fine ruby inlays, the spiralled curls of red snaking their way from breach to muzzle. I flip it open as I slide two thick paper cartridges in and snap it closed. The holster on my thigh is heavy and familiar. I reach for my blade, the hunger within her calling to me as I slide her into the sheath in the small of my back.

My mind itches as my blade calls out, her frantic energy igniting my own as I slide two push blades into the sheaths on my hips.

I turn my eyes to my father's armour, the thick plates of ebony coloured steel drawing me in as I trace my hands over them. I lift his gauntlets from the mannequin as I slowly slip them on. Their living metal folds to my skin as I flex and clench my hands. Dare I risk taking these before it is time?

With a deep seated reluctance, I draw the gauntlet from my hand and set it back in place. I can hear the condescending scoff of my father as I turn and move towards my door; my sole focus lies in the woman who has reshaped my world and the perils that now ride at her heels.

Sweat rolls down my spine as I wait, crouched at the edge of a terraced roof, the street below me teeming with the unwashed as I stretch my senses outward, poring through all that reaches back, the fumbling ignorant grasps of the hairless apes below or the cautious, tentative touch of my former kin.

The air grows foul as I feel them approach me, the dark malevolence rolling out like fog from water, drenching everything it touches in pure unadulterated hate and malice. I turn my eyes, meeting the cold orbs of a Dolophonos.

'Malachai, I would say it's a pleasure, but then nothing that involves you could be even granted a meagre shred of positivity.'

A liquid chuckle boils up from behind the cloth wrap that folds around his rotted visage. I watch in disturbed interest as a centipede crawls over the edge of his wrap and drops to the floor, vanishing moments later as he shifts his foot, the poor insect vanishing into his form as the dark tendrils of his corporeal body lifts from the world like a sponge.

'His grace bids your attendance on an urgent matter; I won't state that refusal is not an option.'

I brush past the shadow demon, his body morphing around mine as I head to the far side of the roof.

'You just did.'

I stalk through the hallways, my body, aura, my merest glance sending the vapid shadows of my decrepit former kin scurrying for shelter. I spy Alp watching from a balcony above me, his eyes worried as he tracks the shifting changes in my Aura.

I don't even flinch as my meat suit begins to fall away, my armour morphing around me as the sodden lumps of steaming flesh fall to the floor, this routine standard every time I'm called to see the great one. Never before have I been as enraged as I am at this moment. I feel a familiar tug at my senses, the soft caress of a hand as familiar as time itself and yet all too weak and pale to place a finger upon. I close my eyes for a moment, trying in vain to lock it down and draw it in, but it is to no avail as I turn and move deeper into this toxic warren.

His presence hits me long before I reach his chambers, as it always does. I brush it aside as I march through the doorway. Malachai drops back, his sneering form vanishing like smoke through a window as I come to stand in front of Lucifer.

'You called.'

He sets the cup in hand on the table and nods at the door; it swings shut with an echoing thunk as I step closer to the table. He motions to a chair near my right leg as I watch it slide away from the table and closer to me. I take the cue and sit as Lucifer begins to pour a second cup.

'Why the theatrics? You've never bothered before.'

He stares at me from behind heavily lidded eyes as I watch his finger twitch and the cup slide over the polished table top, the onyx slab glowing as runes ignite, the cup beginning to steam as it finally settles seven inches from my right hand.

'Well I have never had a half breed and blood traitor before me before. None of the minions in the pit have been of as sallow a mind as to think they could continue courting the enemy without my noticing.'

I stay mute as he watches for a reaction, I feel sweat bead at my hair line, trailing droplets rolling down my neck as I swallow, the noise deafening in my ears as I watch his eyebrow quirk slightly.

'I thought as much, *half breed.*'

I feel my anger begin to rise as Lucifer stands, moving towards me as I let my hand slip surreptitiously to my hip.

'Do not bother, boy, it would be of little use to you. If a pig sticker like that with which you are contemplating use could offer me any form of threat, well, needless to say I wouldn't be standing here now.'

He motions to the cup at my hand and stares at me, eyes even and cold as ice.

'Drink, or are you going to refuse my hospitality as well as your fealty? Do you think it wise to be so blatantly offensive in the camp of your chosen enemy?'

I lift the cup to my lips and sip, the scalding brew searing my lips and throat as I feel it reach my stomach, a ball of glowing heat blossoming within me as I feel the threads of my mind dampen. I frown as the room dims momentarily before slipping back into focus.

My body feels wooden, hands like stumps as I force myself to drink once more before the cup slips from my grip and shatters over the floor.

'Now boy, as you have no doubt felt, there is a rather unique presence here. It's got a light and sweet edge to it, wouldn't you say?'

My head swims as I stare at the shards of the cup as I slump from the chair, my knees striking the floor painfully. I try to rise, my legs refusing to respond as I sink further into the embrace of whatever now flows through my veins.

'I can say with surety that you're fully aware of the effects that the Cudelare is having on your system. It's a potent little flower that grows on the fringes of Eden, a point of the three kingdoms where all borders intersect. Despite being heavily patrolled by my forces and those of my former kin, one can quite comfortably move through there without hindrance; but that has no bearing on this, does it?'

He curls his fingers around my chin, hate as pure and as black as night raining down from his eyes.

'You spurned all I offered, Albion. You could have ruled in my stead as King of Hell, as the ruler of an Army as vast as time itself, and you spurned me. For what, a simpering quimm and her doting eyes. I would have shown you the secrets of the universe, of points that even God has forgotten exist, but now, all I am going to offer you is the chance to have a seat at the floor of your own destruction as you sit and watch as I tear your world down around you, you and your little Reclaimer.'

I latch my hand around his ankle as I gasp through sodden lungs, my eyes swimming in darkness as I try in vain to drag my caster from its holster and make one last hole in history before my light is finally snuffed out.

His cackling laughter is punctuated by his booted foot meeting the side of my head as I'm sent skittering over the floor. My shoulders collide with the uncaring stone walls of his chambers, skulls and relics of lives long since dead, clattering around me in a spray of chipped bone and shattered pottery.

'So there is some fight still in you. Good, I would hate for you to miss my one final olive branch.'

He strides to me, lifting my head from the floor as I feel my scalp stretch, my neck near useless as I gurgle in response.

'Submit to me, Albion. Submit to my will, become my tool, my personal savant. Never before has there been one as pure in force and energy as you. You bend the world to your will, I have seen it, seen it when you cut down your own kin to save an angel. Bend to my orders and give yourself over to the darkness and I will let her go free, you have my word.'

He lets my head slip from his grip, my skull cracking off the chiselled rock beneath me.

I rasp, fighting for breath as I speak, black viscous ooze pouring from my lips as I stare through shadowed eyes.

'Yes.' Anything for my angel.

The word strikes my heart like a spear as I sink into the abyss, Malachai's laughter echoing as I feel him appear, before my mind finally goes dark and I sink into blessed oblivion.

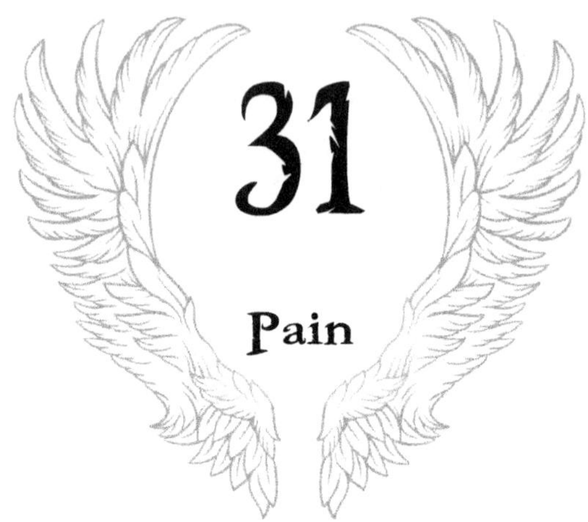

ARIANWEN

Drowning in the raging sea,
standing alone in the pouring rain.
Without you, not knowing how to be me,
desperately needing to feel your love again.

Lost, hurt, needing it to end,
lying broken, raw and bare.
Restrained by rules, wishing they could bend,
badly needing, wanting to follow you anywhere.

Into the heat, into the flame,
amongst the dark shadows of hell.
Not caring if anything at all remains.
Will my heart survive? Only time will tell.

Not different, not special, here I have no gifts,
complete devastation is what the devil sends.
If this is all that's left to live with,
what's the point? I would rather it all ends.

I feel my body being dragged, a rough surface scraping my back. I feel as heavy as lead, while my head is swimming in a fog. My senses are still alive but they are substantially dulled. It's dark, my vision is blurry, but I can make out the flickering of burning torches that slip by every now and then.

My breathing is slow and shallow; the stench of this place is suffocating me, clogging my throat with its vile air. Stale sweat and burnt flesh fills my airways, as the rotten sulphur scent burns me from my nostrils, down the back of my throat and all the way to my lungs.

My hearing is muffled, but that doesn't stop the agonising screams that are invading my head. The painful sickening shrills make my stomach turn with fear and threaten to stop my heart, which is in shock with the suffering it can sense. Pleading, begging, gasping, screaming, all creating a song of their own, a song of terrifying horror.

I can faintly feel the touch of fingers and the scraping of nails on my bare legs, as if they are reaching from the ground beneath me, desperately grabbing, trying to rip at my flesh as I am being dragged past them and their heavy, vicious, panting and primal screeches.

I am descending. Even though my head is raised slightly from the ground the rest of my body is sliding against, it feels lower than my feet, making me feel as though I'm about to fall, the feeling of vertigo giving me a sickening dizziness in my already swimming head. I am desperately trying to gain my bearings, willing all of my abilities to come back to life and save me from this horrendous nightmare.

I am taken down lower and lower, travelling forever, as I feel the flesh of my back split and bleed from the continual dragging on the uneven earth below me. The crippling heat begins to rise the lower we descend, my skin burning, feeling as though it's flaking away layers.

I feel like we are slowing down, but my captors' grips do not lessen on my wrists as they continue on their path. All of a sudden they stop. There is silence. All screaming and screeching are ceased. Then the sound of something very heavy being moved or dragged, as I am moved again. I vaguely notice that I am going under a large door frame and the sound must have been the two giant doors that stand tall on either side of this entrance.

They take a few more steps in, then stop. Still no sound except for my struggling heartbeat and my shallow breathing. Then suddenly, before I even realise what's happening, I'm being flipped over onto my stomach, dragged further, then my head and upper torso is plunged deep into water, while my hands are pinned to my back. All of my senses suddenly come to life and with the shock of that, I open my mouth to scream and water begins to fill my lungs.

I close my mouth but the damage is already done. As my senses bring my body back to life, I feel a crushing ache in my lungs, the torturous burning that steals my air, searing through me as I struggle to cope with the lack of oxygen. Fear and panic rushes through my veins as the ice cold water stings every piece of my submerged flesh.

I try in vain to struggle to freedom, but a solid pressure on my back keeps me deep in the water's grasp, black edging my vision as I begin to lose this fight, my throat closing as the tunnel begins to draw me in. There is no questioning, no explanation, nothing, just this. I have to be strong, I cannot lose faith, I will find a way out of this even if I die trying. I try and think, I try and wiggle, I also pray, I pray that God can hear me here, deep within what I suspect is the pit of Hell.

My body starts to weaken, the lack of air shutting down my system. The pressure on my chest is immense as I am pinned in this watery grave. I feel my last breath squeezing out between my tight lips, turning to bubbles, floating, dancing, twisting with what looks like droplets of blood that must be coming from the opened gash I feel on my neck, both swimming in my vision as if I'm wearing rose coloured glasses, as they race towards the faded light above the water's surface.

This is not my end. It can't be!

Just as I'm about to give my last fight, I am yanked up and out of the water and thrown to the ground. I lie coughing as I gasp continually, trying to return the air that was stolen from me and hopefully bring my body back to life.

Heaving, hacking, my head lolls to the left, rose tinged water pouring from my nose and mouth as I feel the cold burn of air through my lungs. Rasping, I draw in a long shuddering breath as I try to rise. Before I can regain any of my strength I am pulled up by my hair to a standing position. My legs shaking, unsteady as they barely hold me upright, my scalp aching as my hair is slowly ripped from its roots.

My captors, the Dolophonos, quickly each bend down and click shackles around my ankles, I'm still too weak to move or resist, before one steps back and yanks on a rope which pulls my feet from under me, sending my head flying backwards and slamming against the floor behind me before I am strung up like a piece of cattle, dangling in the air, blood running quickly to my head, as my vision swims from the blow to the floor.

I blink away the blurriness, not wanting my consciousness to slip away from me, even in the slightest, as my eyes take in the upside down room surrounding me. Both Dolophonos move to stand directly in front of me, in silence. There is not a sound but the rattles of the chains around my ankles and my body still gasping for much needed air.

My head is too heavy to remain looking up at them so I let it hang loose as the pounding in my ears increases with the blood flow building in my skull. I feel heat at my stomach, which is slightly exposed as my dress hangs in strips bedside my head, I have only just realised I am no longer wearing the armour Albion made for me.

Oh no! They will know, they will know that it was him, they will know he made it for me. Will they do the same to him, will they torture him for showing his love for the enemy? No! No!

I look to see what is causing the heat at the same time as it makes contact with my skin. I scream with all my might as my flesh burns, with a heat I have never felt before, from the hot sharp stone one of them is holding.

They move it over my skin as I feel my flesh start to blister and lift, peeling itself back like an orange peel as I scream and thrash, hanging in my restraints. The other one bends down and forcefully shoves a rolled up rag in my mouth to stifle my screeching as he then moves behind me, wrapping a large strap of leather around my throat and securing it with a metal pin to the floor, making my head immobile.

As I feel the heat increase on my stomach, now spreading out towards my hips, I realise my tongue has gone completely numb. I take a ragged breath in through my nose and scent that the cloth in my mouth is laced with a chemical. As my mind once again starts to go hazy, I try in vain to spit it out, to scream, scream in pain, scream for help. I begin to feel a new sensation beneath my burning flesh.

A sharp pinch makes my body flinch as I then feel the flesh at my hip start to peel back. I thrash wildly, despite my numerous restraints, as I feel a thin line of my flesh lift and peel all the way across my stomach and to my other hip, before the process starts again. Despite my lack of movement, I am hysterical inside, not wanting to die like a rabbit being skinned before it is thrown into a pot of boiling water.

My head becomes rapidly heavy as I feel one of the dark creatures move behind me and use a knife to slice the back of my dress before striking me with a hot whip on the soft flesh across my spine. It is then that I start to lose the fight to stay conscious.

✦ ✦ ✦

When I come to, I am on the move, pain shooting through me as I'm once again dragged down the dark corridors of Hell. The lower we go the more unbearable the heat is becoming as I feel the sweat drip down my face.

We stop and they lift me to my feet and turn me to face the largest set of doors I have ever seen in my life. I feel like an insect standing before these sky high ancient carved doors as they begin to slowly open. The Dolophonos each grab an arm and pull me forward fast, my feet scrambling to keep me upright as I desperately try and take in the sights of the room.

The room is round, very grand in size, and there are lit torches on the walls. I'm forcefully ushered across to the centre. A large pentagram is carved into the rough stone beneath my feet, which is surrounded by many throne like chairs filled with skeletal like creatures staring at me in silence as if waiting for an old theatre to raise the curtains for the show to begin.

Again I am surprised by the silence that surrounds us considering the deafening sounds of the dying when I was first brought down through the numerous levels of Hell. Which tells me exactly how deep we are buried.

I am placed between two tall pillars of wood, spread a metre apart as I am made to kneel before a large cloaked being with its back to me. Its robes are of different shades of black, the fabric looking older than Christ himself as its scent of charcoal invades the room.

The fabric rustles and the figure before me starts to move, slowly, turning, the front of its robes now facing me as I let my eyes rise up towards its head, which is covered in a black hood with ruby red crystals embedded around its edges. It stills and so does the entire room. Not a sound, not even my breath as I hold it in fear of what I know is about to be revealed to me.

The creature reaches up a cloaked hand and grabs the top of its hood, slowly pulling it back, as I gasp and automatically place my weakened hands over my mouth as my eyes confirm my mind's suspicion as to who it is that I'm kneeling before.

Lucifer!

'Welcome ... *Arianwen,*' he croons at me as I remain frozen on the spot, frozen in time, frozen in this room, kneeling in what must be Lucifer's court. I see his larger than life throne looming behind his layers of cloaks. Fear. Fear unlike anything I have ever felt in my life flushes through every cell of my being, as I know that to stand before the Devil himself is a death sentence.

My first thoughts are of Albion, and the guilt he will feel at me meeting my demise at the hands of the Devil himself. Then they wander to my parents and my two beautiful younger sisters and the grief I know will consume them when I fail to ever return to Eden.

Then my soul screams for all the souls in need that I will no longer be able to save, who will spend their existence living between worlds for all of eternity.

My eyes focus, yet again, on the dark lord standing in front of me. He nods his head to one of the Dolophonos and then to the other. He takes a step back as they move with extreme speed and wrap a chain around my waist that reaches out to be pinned at the posts either side of my being, then they move behind me and I feel a blade slice the remainder of my dress from my body and watch it fall to the floor as I kneel here in only my undergarments.

A Dolophonos moves to tie my two wrists together, while I feel the other one push a blade into the skin on the top of my back. I scream as I feel the blade slice down over the flesh that conceals my wings. I thrash about in panic, screaming at the top of my lungs as both of the Dolophonos slice open my back to reveal my wings in all their glory. I try and hold them in tight to my body, but the dark creatures holding them have the strength and power of the Devil behind them and almost too easily begin to force them out, unravelling them until they splay out to their full capacity.

Their celestial light is blinding to all that reside in this room as even the pits of Hell can't dull their beautiful glow. What happens next is the worst feeling in the world for an angel. They each grab hold of one of my wings and begin to stretch them, well beyond their capacity; the pain it causes is crippling as my heart begins to speed up and thump too hard against my chest, trying to jump out and away from such vicious treatment as I scream a high pitch shrill unlike anything that has ever left my lips.

They push my wings back against the wooden posts to my sides and what I see in their skeletal hands steals the air from my body and makes my heart stop beating. They are both holding sledge hammers in one hand and large, long nails in the other as they move in close, lifting a large boot sheathed foot and pinning my wings in place.

The heavy thunk as the first nails sink through my wings makes my stomach hurl its contents from my mouth and down the front of my chest as they ready themselves for more. The most sensitive part of an angel's body are their wings, so even though the nails are going through my feathers, nerves and webbing that hold them, my entire system is feeling every inch of the excruciating agony the sharp piercing pieces of metal are creating.

Tears run freely down my face as I screech loudly when the second lot of nails are slammed through my wings, making my body shudder violently. I feel my soul start to shatter.

I am vaguely aware of angry grunting and the sound of something heavy being dragged behind me, but my senses start to shut down when the third lot of nails are sliced through my feathers. My mouth opens in a silent scream as my head drops forward in defeat. I begin to lose faith and the slim possibility that I may somehow get out of here alive.

'Arianwen ... lift ... your ... head,' the Devil whispers just above my slumped form. I do as he bids, raising my head to his, as he slowly steps back, amused eyes fixed on mine as he takes a large step to my right.

I frown in confusion before my eyes leave his and look straight ahead as I'm met with a large figure down on its knees with a large black sack over its head. Two more Dolophonos stand either side of this figure and when they bend forward to each grab a side of the sack and start to raise it, my heart and soul begin to scream in utter devastation. Before the sack has even been completely removed, all of my senses howl in recognition as to who is beneath it.

'Albion!' I scream as my body comes back fighting, all my dulled senses fully alert and ready to fight for the battered and bleeding man who owns my heart. When the sack is finally off, and his eyes meet mine, I see ... disbelief. He seems to be in shock at what lies before him, his eyes widening, frozen at the sight of the woman he loves stretched and nailed to two wooden pillars in the deepest pits of Hell in the centre of Lucifer's court.

His eyes begin to water, causing mine to follow suit as our

worst nightmare has come true. The love we have created together will be the cause of our final demise. A love too grand and powerful to be contained in any one immortal world. Were we always doomed from the start? Lucifer throws something between us, the dull clang of metal echoing up as it hits the stone floor. I look down, my face reflected in the battered and scratched surface of my armour, the armour made by the hands of the man I love, hands that opened my mind to the possibility of being loved. Armour that is so clearly of this dark world, the armour which is now seen as a betrayal to his own people.

'Care to explain?'

Lucifer stares at Albion, his aura a shifting wall of black as I watch him raise his head in defiance, the question hanging between them. Albion's eyes have not left mine for a moment, locked in a stare of pure unadulterated love and devotion.

I see it in his eyes, the moment when he becomes determined to not let our love end this way. The moment he truly believes we can make it out alive. The moment he decides that our strength together will set us free.

He begins to thrash about violently in the restraints that are currently controlling his body, breaking two of them as he gets one arm free, trying to release the other before the Devil himself takes a step towards him, throwing his hand towards his face, a red snake like rope flying out and wrapping around Albion's neck, freezing his movements instantly.

'Agree to my terms, Albion, and we will unpin your *precious angel and set her free*,' Lucifer says in a sarcastic voice that practically sings those last few words.

Albion might not be able to move, but his eyes are fierce and the veins in his neck are throbbing and increasing in size. Lucifer nods to one of the Dolophonos who removes the metal face guard from him and the instant it releases Albion's mouth, he begins to roar!

'*What have you done?* Your quarrel is with me and only me. You gave me your word, Lucifer. *Let her go!*'

He screams so loud I feel the ground beneath my feet rumble.

His rage is overflowing which seems to make the Devil chuckle.

'Albion, Albion, Albion, you can see she is still alive, not much harm has come to her ... yet. Now as we are here, I want you to reaffirm in sound mind and body what you agreed to naught but an hour ago and I will set her free, as free as a bird.' He chuckles again, finding our pain highly entertaining.

'Agree to be my tool, Albion. Submit to my will, become my weapon. Bend to my orders and give yourself over to the darkness and I will let her go free ... all you have to do is say yes. You've said it before. All I ask is for you say it now, in front of all those you have wronged and jilted.'

'I know you too well, Lucifer. You have no intention of letting her go! Don't play me for a fool!' Albion roars at him.

The Devil, still not breaking his smile, turns to the Dolophonos flanking me and nods, causing my fear to choke me. I know what's to come will be made to sway Albion to agree to the terms Lucifer has demanded.

I hear them walk a few steps behind me before returning to stand at my back. I sense them raise something slowly above my head. As I raise my chin to look above, Albion screams wildly!

'No! No! No!'

I stare at the aged metal contraption they have in their hands and try to decipher what exactly it is, as Albion continues to yell and curse. The front of it looks like a mask of some sort but no eye holes, only a hole for a mouth to receive air. The top and back look something like a diver's helmet, as if it could cover the whole head and not let anything in ... or ... anything out!

Oh dear Lord, please save me.

The Devil speaks over Albion's abusive screams.

'I think it's time for a little education, I regret that these feathered buzzards are woefully under informed, so let's remedy that for our dear *Arianwen* and let her know exactly what it is that's hovering above her head, shall we? Yes ... I think *I* shall. This is one of my favourite toys so you should feel privileged to be about to wear it, sweet Angel of Albion's.

'It has been around since before my time, and despite all of the technology those weak earthlings have created over the centuries, this is still one of the most effective ... mmm ... tools, that has ever been created. It has been called many names over the sands of time but its most common epithet is "the mask of darkness," and I think it would look rather fetching on you, my dear, unless Albion has anything to tell us all?'

My body starts to shiver, all except my wings that have just about gone numb with pain. I look towards Albion, wanting to say many words, none of which make it out of my mouth. I stare directly into his eyes, trying to portray to him how much he means to me and how much his love has made me blossom under his tender guidance. The look of utter anguish that fills his face is the final blow to my heart as it begins to crumble, shattered by the loss it's about to endure.

I feel the Dolophonos move above me as I look up and see the evil piece of torture slowly lower towards my head.

Albion roars once again, making the entire room shake, dirt starting to trickle from the high roof above as his body starts to enlarge, rage transforming him into something I have yet to fully sight. I feel the mask touch the top of my head and slowly begin to slide down my hair; a deep burn in my temples increases and slowly slithers to the back of my head, stabbing into the top of my spine.

It feels like thousands of gossamer threads are slowly crawling to a destination deep within me, worming their way to my soul. I can feel it searching, prying out the good that dwells within me, drowning my God given gifts and abilities. I can feel it coursing through me, shooting through my paralysed form, fear making me scream as my soul tries in vain to fight this invasion of evil.

I stare straight at Albion, willing him to look me in the eyes, and when he does, I say the only thing that's important to me at this very moment.

'I love you.'

The last thing I see is Albion grow in size and his skin start to turn red, as he bursts through all of his restraints and lunges for me as the mask lowers, turning everything as black as the midnight sky. And just before I hear the click of the mask locking into place, I feel Albion's hand grip mine tightly as I feel the love he has for me surge through my veins and straight to my heart, just as all my senses die.

And all I am left with is pure black and my own thoughts that are starting to twist and swirl in a confused haze.

32

Unrepentant

ALBION

I watch as the helmet is lowered down upon her head, her screams filling my ears as I let slip my rage.

'Lucifer! You forget one thing.'

I push myself to my feet, my body straining at the shackles around my neck and arms as I slowly relinquish my form to all that I have kept locked away.

I feel my gums split, the opalescent white cubes of my teeth clattering to the floor as my true form begins to take hold, the sound of tearing silk filling my mind as my horns curl free, the sheaths of flawless bone scything through the air.

'I am the son of a Demon Knight, son of a Huntress of Hell, and the vengeance of a murdered clan. A vengeance you gave life, a vengeance that stands now before you as real as light and dark, a vengeance you left unshackled.'

My fingers distend as my claws snap free, my body shifting as I twist, my shackles and chains bursting like dandelions on a breeze. I thrust my hands out, encircling the heads of the two Dolophonos, and *squeeze.*

My skin aches as I feel my armour split and tear the age worn leather, finally giving way to the abuse it has suffered throughout my lifetime. I twist my arms as my coat peels away. Muffled, agonised, pleading cries of clemency fall on deaf ears as I feel their skulls collapse in my grip. Arianwen screams as I watch that helmet descend, the world around me slowing to a crawl as I launch myself forwards, an unbidden guttural roar finding its way free as I reach out to the pleading hand of my angel.

Malachai drifts to nothing as another of the Shadow race takes his place, their hands guiding home the cage around my woman. I feel his enveloping maliciousness fold over me as I send my hand arching backwards, spearing through his body and closing around his spine.

I stop the world around us, a pall of time drowned chaos as everything moves like insects caught in amber.

'You know, Malachai, I never had a quarrel with you, even when you murdered my mother and fed the eviscerated and flayed corpse of my father to Cerberus. I never held you responsible. One thing I do hold you to though, is predictability; even when we were children and you were put alongside us all, I could see through you. You have always been predictable. It's probably why now I have hold of your spine. To be honest, Malachai, I am surprised you have one, you always did have others do the deed. Goodbye, Malachai.'

I twist my hand, the feel of his spine sheering apart in my grip drawing a vicious grin from me as he crumbles to nothing around my invading hand. I let my fingers curl open, the shattered remnants of his bones crumbling on the air as I turn, once more closing my hand around Arianwen's.

The world bursts, light and dark collapsing, everything stopping in an instant as I stare at the woman before me, her face hidden behind the mask now sealed around her head.

I close my hand around the chains that bind her, ripping their mounts from the floor as I drive my chain wrapped fist through the faces of the Dolophonos around her, flesh and bone flowing around my hand as I send them reeling into oblivion one inch at a time.

I have changed many a time throughout my life, but never

before have I felt the power that flows through me, her touch infusing my core with an energy so raw, so primal that I fear I may bend to time's hand and cease to exist, and yet, as I pluck my fallen angel from where she lies, I have no fear, no fear of reprisal, no fear of failure. Even as the hounds of Hell snap at my heels, I know nothing they can lay in my path will deny my will as I cut my exit from their skin.

✦ ✦ ✦

She's like a cloud in my arms, her form fading as I race through the halls of my former home, the twisting corridors blurring past as I hear their footsteps at my heels. I stare down at the charred skin of my palm. If only she knew, knew what I had just done, all in the name of love for her. Would she be proud, would she still take me as hers and hold me safe within her heart, or would she turn from me and spurn me as I have the people I called kin for a lifetime?

The walkway spans my eye line, twisting as I race to its foot. I unfurl my wings, their beat drumming the air as I watch the hulking forms bear down upon me and my encapsulated angel, her eyes and lips lost from my gaze as we rise from the floor, my wings carrying us aloft as she groans in my grip.

The sun glares at us both, beating down upon us like a hammer on an anvil. I cradle her, holding her against me even as I feel her aura slowly slip away from me. My heart leaps in my chest; the mask, the steel hood of layered evil, I need to get it off of her! There is only one person I know I can trust with this and even then it is not a task I know I can make with a clear conscience.

✦ ✦ ✦

I stand there in the shadows of Garth's doorway, my heart breaking with every second that slips by as Arianwen's aura grows weaker.

'Hold on my love, please, just a few moments longer.'

I hammer my fist against the door, the echoing thumps rolling through the empty room beyond as I wait with growing anger and fear. She's cold to the touch as I push her hair from around her throat, the mask over her head hiding everything as I begin to feel the first vestige of tears prick my eyes. My mind is at odds with every new sensation and emotion that is welling up as I finally hear movement beyond this thin film of timber and iron.

'Damn it, Garth, open up! She's dying out here.'

The door swings open, the slowly widening crack showing the warm glow beyond. Without a moment's thought I smash it aside and sweep across the room. With a wave of one hand, I cast the crockery and flatware to the floor.

I listen to Garth's lacklustre sigh as he latches the door behind me and I set Arianwen's unconscious form down on the rough-hewn table.

'It's the mask.'

I watch Garth stop in his tracks, his face paling before he rapidly marches towards me, shoving me aside as I stand there, watching, unable to think of anything to help the woman I love who lies dying on a man's dining table.

'Help her, damn it.'

Garth's frantic movements draw my eyes as I watch him scramble through shelves and cupboards, their contents spilling forth in a frenzy of motion.

I watch as callipers, hammers, wrenches, all spiral away, clanging and clattering as jars of rivets and nails shatter across the floor. An exultant cry rattles my nerves as I watch Garth hop to his feet brandishing a roll of oiled leather and parchment.

'This, this is a mask of darkness, something I haven't seen in many a long year, but something I know intimately.'

Garth's hands trail over the mask, his fingers finding every dip, dent, and seam; his weathered, heat scarred hands draw on a lifetime of knowledge as he moves to the roll and lets it slide open.

I move, my feet carving a path through the debris to a chair as I sink into it, my head falling into my hands as I feel my tears threaten to break free.

Seconds burn minutes, minutes breed hours, all while I sit helpless, useless, powerless to even ease the suffering of the woman who owns me as she lies writhing in agony with every touch, every misplaced caress of the sheath of metal that encircles her head.

Her screams are daggers through my soul; I watch through pain reddened eyes as Garth begins to work.

'It has been so long, so long since I breathed life into these infernal instruments of pain and suffering. These are some of my greatest and worst creations, something that leaves me each and every night with that single thought.'

I mumble through my hands as I listen to another soul shattering scream issue forth from my angel.

'The thought of wanting to go back and undo the past, the thought that maybe, just maybe if you can go back and erase one action, then the ones who are hurting would never be there to begin with.'

My eyes fall on Arianwen, her fingers clawing at the table as Garth's eyes pore over the plans.

'Damn it, Garth, do something!'

I rise to my feet, Garth's eyes unmoving as he stares at the parchment, his fingers tracing over the lines and notations as Arianwen continues to scream from inside the sightless shell.

'Albion, she is not in pain, this mask is not a device of physical torture. It projects your worst fears and memories directly into your mind. It's as if she is living them out all at once, a swirling wall of primal anguish. It is not physical pain that you have to be worried over. It is what it will do to the mind, her mind, if she is not a strong willed woman ...'

He trails off; his unwillingness to finish is all the answer I need. I curl my hand into Arianwen's and, for the first time in my existence, feel the need to pray.

✦ ✦ ✦

I feel a hand on my shoulder, Garth's face grave as I rise from my knees, my muscles aching as I stare at Arianwen, our fingers still entwined.

'I need you to do something for me. It's to ease the transition between her masked mind and her present mind. Otherwise, when the mask comes off ... Well, she could shatter under the strain.'

He hands me a list, the spider scrawl that stains its face barely legible as I turn for the door.

'Garth.'

He looks up at me, pausing as he begins the slow process of reversing the demon snare that seals the mask around my Angel's visage.

'If she comes to harm, there will not be a place in any realm that you could hide, where I wouldn't find you.'

Garth nods as I move through the doorway. I head towards one of my safe rooms, the camouflaged door swinging open silently as I step inside and push it closed. The dark envelopes me as I reach out and drag my fingertip over the wick of a candle and let the soft glow light my path.

I carefully survey the room, my eyes taking in everything. I check the seals around the door, the wards and warnings that I carefully set into the frame. Nothing has been touched; the layer of dust that coats everything drills into my mind just how long it has been since I was last here.

I move to a small cabinet and pull it open, the hangers inside cluttered with various cloaks and dregs of old lives. I lift a set of lightweight sparring armour from one and move towards the dust laden table.

The air tastes fresh on my tongue as I move through the woodland surrounding Eden, Arianwen's scent still caught in the trees as I pass through woodsman's trails and animal runs, my senses stretched tighter than wire as I search in vain for a sign of this woman Garth has sent me in search of.

I shift my eyes, hoping that in some semblance of luck it leads me to finding this woman. I scan the world around me, the footsteps of the forest's denizens standing in stark glitter filled contrast to everything else around me.

The glowing crystal blue shadows of an ethereal's passage through the glade ahead of me gives me pause. I slip through the brush, falling to a knee as I tentatively taste the air around me, a soft fragrant aroma teasing me, guiding me to its source as I rise to my feet.

Its tantalising aroma all too familiar to my senses, and yet, as familiar as it is, I cannot fathom how I know it. I sink into my memories, desperate to find the source of this familiarity; but it's a lost cause. I shake my head, grinding the balls of my hands into my eyes as I growl.

I need to focus, I need to draw from my mind's eye the confusion and noise that has so polluted everything. Arianwen's life is sitting in the palm of my hand. She needs me now more than ever, and dallying here in the middle of the forest amongst the birds and insects is just one more nail in a coffin that is already being lowered into the ground.

I close my eyes, focusing in on the scent of this stranger, my mind sifting through the gloom and noise as I struggle to draw on what exactly it is that has so caught my mind.

It slithers in, the sudden realisation of what this scent means to me flooding through. Arianwen's nubile visage swims through me as I begin to move onwards. The soft curve of her features on the first day I ever saw her and the day I knew that she would forever be indelibly etched onto the tapestry of my life.

My memories draw me in as my feet lead me on, the way the sunlight plays off her skin, the cherubim lines to her teenage form. She was a striking sight even then, and as I sat watching from a rooftop, my back to the sun, I watch her turn her eyes glittering like an amethyst stone in white gold. I was forever changed at that one moment. Even as her eyes narrowed in a headstrong scowl of malice at being stalked by a green horned Hunter, my heart and soul knew that I would never find another who captivated me so.

Even now as she lies still and lifeless, trapped inside a cage so foul that my very soul cries out in anguish, I cannot help but see those same eyes, those same glowing orbs staring back at me, marking my soul as theirs for eternity.

I stop, the lingering scent shifting as my mind returns to the present. I cast my glance to my left and right, searching for a direction as a voice behind me makes me start, my body moving, rolling over my shoulder and coming up as my hand goes for a blade that is no longer there.

'Come now, Albion, no need to be so quick to aggression. Besides, your weapons are no good here. Why, they haven't been in your possession for the last twenty minutes. Your vaunted skills as a Hunter are leaving much to be desired. I am beginning to think Miss Arianwen was gravely mistaken when she extolled your virtues to me.'

I stare aghast at what she holds in her hands. I open my mind, my blade cooing softly in her grip as she sets my iron caster into the basket on her arm and strolls past me.

'Come on with you. We have a tincture to prepare, do we not? Or do you wish your soul mate's mind to be ground to dust when Garth is finished with his infernal machinations? I'm Cia, by the way, just in case you were wondering exactly what to call me.'

The room is dim, lit only by the guttering smoke blackened oil lamps in the far corners. A lone crow caws at us from its perch upon a beam as I duck my head to slip through the carved doorway. The raucous screech of the midnight bird grates at my ears as I cast a hateful glare in its direction, the woman's hand catching my ear a moment later as I feel the sting of her nails on my skin.

'She has been in this realm far longer than you. Now, fetch me a sprig from the basket atop the door. Cook loves hiding my specialised herbs up there.'

I reach up and do as I am asked. As she turns and quirks her brow, I drop the bundled herbs into her outstretched hand. She nods as I move towards a stool, the dour glare of that infernal crow following my every move as I watch this ancient woman go about her business.

'How, how do you know what I need?'

She stops, turning a soft motherly smile towards me before returning to her work.

'Albion, I am many things, but a gossip is not one of them. I am a seer, weaver of words, a healer; I am anything people need me to be when they are in their greatest hour of need. Arianwen came to me when she needed reassurance and guidance, although as I recall she was unavoidably detained.

'You've come to me when you need to heal the mind of the woman you love; the fact they are both the same person, well, that is an occurrence you can either chalk up to fate, or if you are so inclined, lay at the feet of destiny.'

She looks at me once more, the pot over the open fire glowing with an incandescent light. The soft hiss of steam curls up through her hands as she grinds the herbs, sprinkling them over the simmering concoction as I feel my heart gallop, urgent need and fear still battling within me.

'Personally, Albion, I would lean to the latter but then again, I am not one to meddle in the affairs of the short lived.'

Time crawls by as she continues to move about the room, leaves and stems, roots and bulbs, all slipping into the simmering water; finally, after an interminable wait she steps back, a satisfied smile on her face. I rise from the seat, my energy coursing as I watch her ladle it into an earthenware flask, the sound of the cork wedging into the neck deafening even over the crackle and snap of the still burning logs.

She turns to me, setting the bottle into the basket next to my caster and blade and holds it out; I take the proffered basket, my impatience burning a hole through my chest as I push through the door, a second crow skimming past my head and landing on the opposite side of the room to the other, a short sharp caw of acknowledgement seeing me from the room as I nod my thanks and move out into the winding woodland trails.

I move with anger in my stride as the world begins to blur. My weapons back where they belong and that woman's basket long gone, the bottle in my hand warm to the touch as I let my wings fold free, forcing my aura out like a beacon. I hear the dragon keepers roar.

The ground is cold, dead, as lifeless as a grave as I move with surety through alleys and back roads, never keeping to the thoroughfares, avoiding the main streets like a rat on the run from a cat.

They hunt me now. I can hear their panting breath, almost feel them at my neck. Their breath is hot and wet on my skin as I drop, spinning on the ball of my left foot, my knee digging into the hardened stone laced turf. My caster snaps free of my holster as I bring the sights to my eye and see nothing, nothing but empty air.

I grimace at my nervousness and rise once more, sprinting to the shadowed archway around Garth's doorway. I push inwards, the coarse timber catching my skin as I move through, Garth staring up expectantly as I enter.

'Come, come, quickly now boy, the seal is all but broken. I have kept the last turn of the screw waiting on its thread until you arrived. She cannot wait much longer.'

I watch as he lifts the lower plate free, her soft flushed lips coming into view, her chin quivering as I watch tears slip down the sides of her face, the soft crystal pearls rolling from under the beaten cowl of the infernal shell that still envelopes her head.

Her head lifts as Garth slowly begins to ease the rest of the helm free, her hair sodden, plastered to her scalp as I watch the few clinging strands flying free as her eyes stay sealed. Closed to the world, the violet pools my soul swims so freely through lost behind alabaster sheaths locked away from my sight.

'Why isn't she awake? What have you done!'

My hands wrap themselves through Garth's tunic as I wrench him free of gravity's embrace.

'Boy, there is naught we can do now but wait. Cia's potion is setting to work and if she is as strong as I think she is then she will be fine, but now we can do little more than wait. When I made these godforsaken pieces of tin, they were not designed to come off with the person alive.'

I stare into his face, my eyes searching, seeking for some hint of deception, but they find nothing, nothing but forthright honesty and a deep seated regret.

I nod as I set him down and turn away, turn back to the chair and my unflinching watch over the woman I love.

I watch her for what feels like an eternity, waiting, hoping for some sign of my angel coming back to me. She lies there, cold as ice and as still as stone. I feel my fears return, crushing me under their weight as I bury my head in my hands, stifling the need to weep. The sensation still confuses me even now as I watch the woman I love sit on the brink of oblivion.

Garth's hand ensnares my shoulder. I feel his fingers press into my flesh, the open tear in my armour widening under the press of his fire forged hands.

'Boy, she needs more care than we can provide. She needs her kin.'

I nod, my words failing me as I rise to my feet and move towards her, my hands shaking as I try in vain to hold back my fear and anguish.

'Thank you, Garth.'

I turn my head in his direction, the smith nodding as I lift my angel from the table, her body cold and limp as I rest her against my chest.

'Go boy, get her where she needs to be.'

I nod once more and move to the door.

'I won't forget this.'

With a beat of my wings, I am gone from his sight and the stifling warmth of his workshop; I glance down at the woman in my arms, her eyes twitching beneath her lids as she mewls and grimaces in my grasp.

'Hold on, my love, I will make this right.'

The ground rushes up to meet me as I crash through the thick green foliage that shields the entrance to Eden. I watch the gates swing inwards as I feel my body begin to shift, the silver glow enveloping us both as I step through those gates and into a realm I know I will never truly be welcome in.

I watch the door swing inwards, the tarnished glow of golden light flowing around the figure before me. I watch his eyes widen as I bow my head.

'It ... I did all I could.'

He says nothing as he lifts Arianwen from my arms, her absence sinking into my heart and soul like an ice coated spear. I watch as he turns, staring at me with the dispassionate gaze of a father. I stare into his eyes, the look within them sealing my pain within a vault of malice.

'If you truly love her, love her as I believe you do, stay away. You will bring her nothing but pain and agony, so if you love her let her go ... now.'

33

Lost Innocence

ARIANWEN

Visions, dreams, shadows all dance through my hazed mind, all melting and blurring into one. I am taking shallow breaths and I can feel my heart beating slowly in my chest so I know I am still alive, but when I blink my eyes, everything remains dark. My head feels different, larger, heavier, strange. I have a feeling of immense pressure surrounding my skull and sending pain through my ears as if they are about to pop.

I try and move, the weirdest sensation flowing through my limbs as I can feel them move, but at the same time, I can't. It is terribly confusing as I try and remember where I am, but don't come up with an answer. What was the last thing I remember doing? I think I was in the village, attending to a calling. I remember walking into a dwelling, seeing two souls in need and being surprised by that, but that's it. I can't remember anything after that. Did I hit my head? Not that I can recall. Why can't I remember anything?

Heat. I feel heat. My skin feels as if it is melting and the smell of coal is overpowering my senses. I have flashes behind my eyes of lit torches and deep water. The sensation of ripping flesh makes my form shiver, raising bumps on my skin. I feel my stomach start to turn as I hear the sounds of souls screaming in absolute agony as my memory brings up visions of faces frozen in a scream, reaching, clawing at my delicate flesh.

But my eyes remain blank, dark. I can feel myself blinking constantly, desperately trying to see where I am in this dreamlike state, but everything stays dark. Am I dreaming or more like having a nightmare? All of a sudden memories hit me! A dark forest trying to capture me; two souls in need which was a trick; large black creatures; Dolophonos! Being dragged, the flesh on my back ripping, water, cold, can't breathe, the world upside down, large doors, seeing the Devil standing before me, nails through my stretched out wings, the excruciating pain, the man I love battered and bleeding before me, him transforming into something found only in nightmares, a heaviness crushing my skull, the smell of hot iron and sweet herbs, my head floating on a cloud as light as a feather, cradled against Albion's chest, breathing in his unique smell, light kisses on my forehead, the worried hushed voices of my parents.

None of it makes sense. I feel as if something big has happened, but I'm unsure if it is real or just a state of dreaming. I fight the fogginess in my head but can't seem to grasp on to any type of reality as I feel myself slipping away.

I see Albion's eyes looking directly at me, pained beyond belief, then his skin is turning red as his body starts to enlarge, veins raising on his skin, muscles bulging from his form, breaking free of the restraints that bound him, trying to get to me as a veil of black is lowered over my head. NO! I wake up screaming, my vision blurred, but I can make out the shape of my bedroom and my father who is sitting on the edge of my bed, soothing me with a soft hand over my hair, telling me in his gentle voice that I'm home and I'm safe now. Just to rest and stay calm.

It all comes back to me. The visions I have been having were real! All of it was real! Oh no.

'Albion! Where is he?'

I raise my voice, which hurts my throat. My father tries to calm me down and keep me in my bed.

'He's gone, Arianwen, back to his world, where he belongs, and you don't. Please, sweetheart, lie back down and calm yourself.'

I try and sit up, wanting to go to Albion to make sure he is all right, that he escaped the clutches of the Devil too. I want to see with my own eyes that he is alive.

'Please, Arianwen, please lie back. Rest and we will talk.'

I calm slightly, lying back and taking a deep breathe to control the emotions that are threatening to boil over. I reach up to my head, touching, feeling, wanting to make sure that heavy mask is no longer there. Then I reach a hand down to my stomach, feeling where the flesh was peeled from me by the Devil's most evil, The Dolophonos, but I feel nothing but my smooth flesh under my probing fingertips.

My eyes start to water as I remember all of the horrendous treatment I received at the hands of those vile creatures.

'You only have a few red scratches and slight welts here and there, that's all that we can see, unless you healed before you were brought home to us,' my father tells me quietly.

But I have to know more. 'How did I get here? Who brought me home, Father?' He doesn't seem surprised by my question, but keeps a straight face when he answers me.

'The man whose heart you hold.'

I am shocked at my father's words and his calm composure when he tells me this and follows with more. 'I don't think I have ever seen a man more in love in all of my existence. But that doesn't mean that it's right. Whether he is man or demon, or from another immortal world entirely, he is not of *this* world that you call home and could never be a part of your life Arianwen. I hope you can see that now.'

No. I see the complete opposite. More than ever I know my

place is by Albion's side. That we were both saved from kneeling before the Devil and facing a death sentence for a reason and I fully intend to stay by his side regardless of what may come of it. He owns my heart and I own his. 'I need to see him. I need to know he is okay,' I tell my father and wait for his reply.

'Please, Arianwen, don't throw your life away and all you have worked so hard for just to satisfy childish matters of the heart. Yes, love can be important, but it's not *the* most important thing. It can cause more harm than good a lot of the time. Your loyalty towards your kin and our God is where your heart should lie, not wasted on some fantasy that can never be turned into reality. Please, for your own good, Arianwen, let him go.'

It breaks my heart that my father could see with his own eyes the love Albion has for me, yet can't believe that our love could survive living between worlds. I sit up and move past him to place my feet on the ground, blinking a few times to clear the final blurriness from my eyes. I reach for my sandals and proceed to put them on.

'Arianwen, you cannot leave. You need to rest. Whatever dark magic was cast over you could still be in your system, leaving you weak. You are staying here.' His voice is firm as he frowns at me. I reach for my cloak which is lying at the end of my bed. Did Albion find it and bring it here I wonder?

Before that thought can sink in, my mother enters the room, looks at the cloak in my hand and starts to panic. 'No, Arianwen, you are not going to him. No! He has put you in danger, you could have died. I will not let that type of danger reach you again. You will stay in this house, do you understand?'

I shake my head no and she looks at me in disbelief. 'It's impossible, it cannot work. Love between two worlds is destined to fail before it even has a chance to begin. Please trust me, Arianwen. It cannot be.'

Her always proper composure starts to slip as I see the panic rise in her eyes at my determined expression. 'You can't be serious, Arianwen. You would not only be risking *your* life but our lives and your sisters' lives by bringing evil that close to our family.'

'He is not evil, Mother, he is good. He is of both worlds; the gatekeepers told him he has the right to walk in *both* worlds. We don't understand it yet, but we will find out the truth. Together. I love him,' I plead with her as I watch her panicked expression turn to anger in a split second.

'Love can make the smartest people turn into fools, Arianwen, and I will not let you play the fool. You have more important things to think about than the flutters you get in your heart at the sight of the unattainable. You are not leaving this house!'

That's what she thinks. I continue to slip my cloak over my shoulders and stand from the bed, feeling slightly dizzy as I still to give my blood a chance to pump through my now standing legs as I take a deep breath.

'No, Arianwen, you can't!' She grabs my arm. 'Please be smart about this, please just stay and rest and give yourself time to think. You are not well, you are not thinking straight. Think about the consequences and what a life between worlds would truly be like. That is not a life for a gifted angel such as yourself. There will always be evil forces trying to strip you of your power. That is not a life you want to live.'

'Mother, the love I have for Albion is greater than any gift I was created with. We have been brought into each other's life for a reason. I feel it in my heart and in my soul. I need to have trust in what fate has in store for us. I need to go to him. Now.'

She remains silent for a minute as we both look into each other's eyes. She sees the unbreakable love I have for a demon, and I see a painful past she has been hiding for a lifetime, keeping it well hidden until now. I won't ask; I know she will tell me when the time is right. I can only hope whatever heartbreak she endured in her youth will give her some understanding as to my innate need to be with the man who holds my heart.

Both parents just look at me with pain and worry on their faces, knowing they can't stop me, as I continue to move past them, through the house, stop at the doorway and turn.

'If the love I have for Albion is half as strong as the love I feel for you both and my sisters, then our love with be strong enough to endure anything.'

I turn quickly, feeling my emotions start to twist my stomach as I slowly walk from my childhood home and to the home I wish to share with a demon, the man that I love.

As I make my way through the garden and come to the dragon gatekeepers, I can tell they have something to say, so I stand and wait beneath their tall, granite forms.

'Nice to see ye are well now, child. If thou follow thy heart, then hark out for our warnings. We will help thee keep safe between worlds.'

I smile at each of the twins, who understand my quest for love, before I continue cautiously through the forgotten forest, desperate to feel Albion's aura envelope mine once again. My nerves are more heightened after what happened in the pits of Hell and I hate how I feel as if I have lost my driving edge and confidence to walk this path I have been walking forever. Will I ever return to the same fearless and focused Angel I once was?

I walk slowly, jumping at every little noise and movement my senses find as I desperately search for Albion's whereabouts, worried that once he returned me to my family's home he may have not made it home safely.

I hear a branch crack behind me and spin quickly, grabbing the edges of my cloak, bringing it up ready to shield myself from an attack as my eyes meet those of a tiny old woman. She has an aged, light green cloak that has seen better days, but one that would have been very grand in its heyday. Her hair is a salt-n-pepper grey, pulled back into a low bun. She looks nothing like I thought she would as I instantly feel her magical aura and know exactly who she is. "*Cia,*" or better known as the teller of fortunes.

'I'm sorry you didn't get to seek me out the last time you entered the forest. So I took this opportunity to seek you out, the angel who has stolen the heart of a demon Hunter, the same one Lucifer wants to have standing beside him for all of eternity.'

I am shocked at how normal she sounds. My imagination was expecting the tones of the cranky old witch she is portrayed to be in children's fairy tales. But knowing what Lucifer has in store for Albion has my blood running cold in my veins.

I decide to get straight to the point, frustrated at the lack of clear understanding as to why Albion and I have been thrown together, desperate for some answer or at least some guidance.

'Will Albion and I be able to make a life together work?'

She looks up to the sky, pondering her answer before she brings her head back down to look me straight in the eye with a serious expression on her face. 'You are following the right path, but ... there may be destruction, war, death, but that is how it is supposed to be. The greatest love is only given to those who fight hard enough for it. For those who are strong enough to endure the lows that come with the highs. For those who will always put their love before anything else in these immortal worlds. For those who were created for each other.'

'Created for each other? How could that be? I am an Angel of God, born to my parents, and Albion is ... we are yet to discover how Albion's parents were capable of producing an offspring who has pure good inside his soul.' I go to ask more questions but she holds her hand up, halting me before I can open my mouth.

'One is not meant to know their entire future; the journey of your life will teach you slowly what you need to know. Now go and find the one who is holding your heart, waiting for reassurance that you are still his. Go and ease his worry, sweet angel. But one last word to the wise. Enemies can be found anywhere, even in one's own garden. Stay guarded.'

And with that she scuttles away quickly and soon blends in with the forgotten forest which looks the same as it always has, nothing moving, nothing reaching, nothing to scare me. The same place I have experienced incredible highs and devastating lows and discovered things that should only belong in nightmares.

But the most important thing is that I am indeed on the right path and, at that moment, my path is leading me straight into Albion's arms. I feel his aura, moving fast, running towards me, desperate to twist itself with mine, as it reaches for him in utter desperation.

I see him sprinting through the forest. I know he has scented me but that hasn't slowed him down. He comes flying towards me and doesn't stop until I am completely wrapped up in the glorious man that he is. He picks me up and spins me around, almost crushing my body to his as I feel the fear and crippling guilt flow from his every cell. He puts me down and stands back, holding onto my arms, making sure that what he is seeing is real.

'Albion,' I whisper. His name falling from my lips gives him the peace of mind he is looking for. His shoulders sag and he takes a step forward, but instead of holding me to him, he falls to his knees and wraps his arms around my waist, burying his head into my stomach.

Tears fall freely down my face as I am drenched in his heartbreak. I throw my arms around his head and hold him tightly, wanting to say so many words to make him feel better, to lessen the devastation at what had occurred in the Devil's court, to let him know that I am here for not only now, but for forever, but the words get stuck in my throat which has thickened with emotion.

I feel his body shudder with the overwhelming aftereffects of what we both endured at the hands of the Devil's minions. I still have no idea how Albion managed to get us both out of there, and right now I don't care. All I care about is being wrapped up in the man I love and to make him understand it wasn't his fault.

He raises his head and I am shocked to see wetness surrounding both eyes. Who knew a demon could cry.

'I am sorry I failed you, Arianwen. I am sorry you had to endure what you did at the hands of the Dolophonos. I will do everything in my power to never let that happen again. I will find a way to leave that world, I promise. Just please don't leave me, please have faith in me. I love you.'

My legs weaken with emotion as I fall to my knees to look into the eyes of the man who will be the only one to ever hold my heart. 'It wasn't your fault, my love. Lucifer is very smart and extremely powerful. You and I alone will never be a match for him, but if we stay hand in hand and give each other strength, we might just have a chance of avoiding his evil games for good. We will work it out Albion, I promise.'

He fists two handfuls of my hair and smashes his lips to mine, franticly wanting to believe the words I have spoken, wanting to feel that I am fine and I am his, always. He feasts on my moans as my body becomes a slave to his movements, desperately wanting to reconnect after the fear of almost losing him, almost losing my own life. He nibbles on my lips and then glides his tongue sensually over the seam before pushing his way through to dance with mine. The love that is coursing through my body right now would be enough to fill the entire earth with happiness and joy.

He pulls back and rests his forehead on mine, looking into my glassy eyes. 'I'm sorry,' he whispers as he looks at me, absolutely defeated that he couldn't keep me safe.

'It wasn't your fault. There was nothing you could have done. I knew the danger, yet I still ventured into the village. I could have tried harder to resist my calling, even long enough until I had found your guiding aura. As soon as I walked into the village I knew something was wrong, but I still proceeded forward. I should have turned and left, but ... my calling is my strongest sense. I couldn't turn my back on it. I still don't understand how the Devil could have possibly sent a false calling. And right now I don't care. All I care about is being in the arms of the one I love. Hold me tight, Albion, never let me go.'

With that he stands up, taking me with him and then throws me over his shoulder with a growl and I can't help but giggle as he slaps by bottom playfully before storming through the forest with determined steps towards his home. Our home.

If living in between worlds is what we have to do to be together, then that's what we will do.

Penance

ALBION

I feel her, soft and supple, the area around us aglow with our love as I cradle her in my arms, the soft bed beneath us little more than rags and pelts over a thin frame of canvas. I feel her fingers trail over the runes etched into my flesh, her soft violet orbs watching the path of her fingers through the valleys carved into my body.

'I love you.'

I glance down at the angel in my arms, her eyes still following her dancing fingers as her soft silky tones reach my ears again; I trail my fingers through her hair, the blonde strands of light sliding over my searching digits as she sighs in contentment.

'And I you, my Little Wing; from the very first moment I saw you playing as a young girl in Eden you've haunted my dreams and calmed my nightmares.'

I watch her smile, a soft kiss landing in the centre of the mark of Cain carved into the centre of my chest, the mark of all Hunters. I slide my hands along her sides, feeling her shiver and tense as they settle over her soft round buttocks; I lift her slightly, pulling her up, my lips meeting hers as I sit upright, her legs slipping past my thighs as she straddles me.

'Calmed your nightmares ...'

She loops her arms around my neck, crossing her wrists as she leans back slightly, her breasts rising, plump pink nipples flirting with my gaze as she smirks. The playful impish grin makes me twitch against her heated silk as she begins to softly gyrate against me.

'Here I was hoping I had caused a few vivid ones of my own creation.'

I draw her up from my lap, her wetness leaving me sodden as I feel my head slide over her pouting lips, a lust filled grin slipping free of my angel's features as she begins to slowly slip down my rapidly hardening flesh.

I hear the soft intake of breath as I latch my lips over her pink nibs; the pert taste of her ripe flesh on my tongue has me searing to new heights as I feel her push down on my invading length. The slow steady rhythm makes the makeshift cot squeak beneath us as I feel sunlight bathe my skin, the cool air washing over us both as I cast my glance to the left, Arianwen's movements slowing to nothing as her eyes follow mine.

'Sunlight.'

I hug her to me as she clenches tight, making me groan, her hips softly rocking as she nips at my lips before allowing me to speak any further.

'Darling, it's never in my life reached here. It's why I chose this spot.'

Her eyes lock with my own, the soft sensual rhythm echoed by the passing breeze that lifts her golden tresses into the newfound sun.

'Albion, right now I do not care whether you can see a man in the moon. You have me, I want you, so take me.'

I do as my angel commands. I lift her from the cot, letting her slowly slip from my length until we are just entwined within each other before her back hits the bed and I delve deep into her silk folds, relishing the gasping moan that echoes off the cliff face around us.

Her legs ensnare me, heels digging into my backside as I thrust deep. She bites her lip to keep from screaming as I feel my limit rise quickly. The need, the want, the lust filled agony of pure unadulterated passion fills us both as I feel her clench tightly around me as she claws at my back, the heady scent of my own blood tipping me past the point of no return as I join her in rapturous bliss.

I lift the heavy edge of one pelt around us as we sit at the edge of my watcher's nest, the sound of the wind in the trees and the lapping of waves filtering along the breeze.

'Albion, what do you think is past the edge of the water? No one ever speaks of it.'

I kiss her neck softly as she leans back against me, my hands curling into hers as I hug her close.

'Honestly, no one really knows. Many have guessed and none have been right. Your kin would know better than I, although I think the answer is plainly obvious, given the only beach port is in Eden.'

Arianwen pushes deeper into my embrace as I feel her naked form against me, the cool evening air making her shiver slightly as she turns in my grasp and plants a soft kiss on my lower jaw. I feel my stomach tighten as I think of the question that is burning through me, the one definitive statement of love and devotion that I have wanted to say from the moment we were first together.

'Ari, I ... I ... I have something to ask you.'

She turns her gaze on mine, a look of curious puzzlement burning through her eyes as she opens her mouth to speak. I feel a tingle at the edge of my senses, my mind screaming in an instant.

The world bursts into a frenzy of energy and movement, the ground beneath us shivering with a power so raw, so frantic that I feel the very plateau begin to shake under duress.

I'm yanked upwards, Arianwen screaming as I am dragged naked and kicking from her embrace. My throat tightens as I bellow with rage, my body burning with anger as I feel my claws shear through my skin, my horns tearing free of my scalp as I drag them against the rope that is slowly encircling my body.

My muscles tighten as my energy and rage bleed from within

me. I stare down as a grinning being I never thought I would ever see appears. His sneering visage makes my skin crawl as I watch him place a sack over Arianwen's head, her body sagging and going limp in moments as I roar like a man possessed.

'Michael, you vicious coward, I will rip your wings from your corpse! You mark my words, I will end you!'

The silver and red lines snake down from my shoulders as I feel the rope at my throat constrict, strangling my words as I feel my lungs shiver under the pressure. The energy within them drains me, my power waning; the taste of their power on my soul is all too familiar, the taint of Hell and the purity of Heaven coursing over me as I wheeze and gasp, clawing at my throat. Black hazes my vision, as I watch two of my former kin fall upon my prostrate soul mate, their hands roaming her body as I feel my wings snap free, the rope around me straining, groaning under my body's strength as Michael gloats, his voice staining the air.

'You flaunt your abilities, spit in the eye of your master, and still further tarnish the worth of one of our best and brightest stars. But here you are, a half breed cur, strung up and left to rot like the foul slab of dripping excrement you are. Come, half breed, show me this vaunted power that so destroyed Malachai and left Lucifer reeling.'

He cups his hand around his ear, leaning in as if straining to listen to something caught on the whispering wind.

'Ah, you can't, can you? I thought as much. You are nothing but a luck stained braggart, one that has thrust himself upon the virginity of a flourishing angel, tarnishing her name and sanctity for eternity. Why, if she could see you now ... although I know she can't.'

He turns, casting his eye on Arianwen's still naked form as the two Hunters lift her upright, their hands slipping over her skin as I watch one drag his putrescent fingers through her flushed lips, a lurid grin spreading over his face as he locks gazes with me, his hand rising, fingers slipping into his mouth.

I rail against my bonds viciously as Michael laughs, his throaty exhalation searing me as I watch him discard them all with a wave of his hand.

'Get that slut smeared piece of trash out of here. Her stink of lust filled betrayal is making me heave. Cover her over and take her to the gates. My men will take her from there.'

His eyes fall back upon me as I feel my skin split against the cliff face. I watch as Arianwen's unconscious form is slung over the shoulder of one Hunter as another sneers at me, spitting at my feet before launching himself into the sky.

My body skitters over stone and dirt as I feel the bonds around me release, my still trussed form crashing to the floor as two of Michael's guards appear at my side, the strutting peacock coming to kneel before my face as I roll to my side, my naked flesh battered and bruised as I come to a stop three feet from the plateau's edge.

'You have been weighed and measured and found wanting, in both my eyes and Lucifer's. After all, half breed, how do you hope to best me when I am the one who cast my own brother from the sight of God? Did you truly think your pitiful powers could best me? Hell, you never even had a chance to fully reveal yourself before you were trussed and hung like a turkey. Crawl back to the pit, Hell spawn. Lucifer, I know, will want a word with you. After all, he did help me find you.'

He pushes himself upright as he kicks dust into my eyes, the powdered grit searing my sockets as I feel it smear over the inside of my lids, scraping over the soft film of my eyeballs as I vainly try to quell the urge to blink.

'Honestly, the things you children think you can get away with; it's quite funny really, that whore colluding with the likes of you when she could have been the wife of the one of the most powerful generals in the holy legions. The things they do for the first swinging dick that shows interest. Stupid slut will now have to spend her days in a stupor because she is too headstrong and idiotic to be left unchecked. She'd probably come running back to you.'

He grabs my flaccid length, the rasp of his knife in its sheath making me freeze as I watch him bring it to bear.

'Maybe I should cut out the root of the problem now, save

everyone the trouble?'

He looks at me, a vicious glint in his eye as he sets the tip of his blade against my sack, the cold press of steel making my heart thunder in my chest.

'Michael, behave.'

The voice makes my soul fall as I feel his presence crash down upon me, his shadow falling across my dust coated form as I try not to shake, twisted in these two coloured vines. I feel Michael's blade flick over the wrinkled skin of my agates as he stands, its sharp bite drawing blood as it dips and skitters over my fear tensed flesh.

'Was that really necessary?'

Lucifer steps into my eye line as he moves to stand before Michael, the two of them staring into each other's eyes. To my overflowing amazement, they embrace, a joyful chuckle rising from both men as Lucifer holds his former kinsman at arm's length.

'You always were a twisted little shit, Michael, but it is good to see you, brother.'

Michael nods as he motions towards me, stepping to the edge of the cliff.

'As much as it pains me to say, Lucifer, this cannot be a lasting alliance. Father is already suspicious of us both for the noise that is falling at his door. We need to keep this quiet and away from his gaze, but you are right, it is damned good to see you, brother. I just wish next time it's under better terms. Try to keep them on a closer leash in future. I won't always be able to clean up your mess.'

Hands grab my bindings. My power is all but spent as I feel my meat suit fall from me, my demon form no longer able to hold the façade in place. Fingers curl through my hair, lifting my head as water douses my eyes. I cough, splutter, blink in pain as the ice cold liquid soaks through me, the fingers fall from my hair as I struggle to see, the blurred lines of my former king filling my vision as his voice drowns my mind.

'That should clear the grit from your gaze, Albion. My brother always was a petulant child. Even when we were children, he would be the one trapping butterflies and watching them wither and die. I once watched him set alight a small bird simply for singing near his window. Strange boy that one; but ours is not to reason why. Come, you have much to make amends for. I know Lilith has a few choice words for you. You hurt her feelings, you know.'

35

Whore

ARIANWEN

I open my eyes and I am in my room. I see my mother sitting on the edge of my bed, smiling at me, and I smile back. But something is not right. I know I am at home in my room but it feels like I'm not really here. She tells me that I'm still recovering but will be back to normal soon and that Gabriel has been so worried that he has been by every day to check on me. He brought special healing tea for me and treats for the rest of the family. My mother is talking to me about making a decision, a decision that will keep us all safe and that she needs my answer soon as the ceremony has been set for two days from now and that all of our kin are excited.

I frown and look down, trying to understand her words when she lifts my chin and says, 'I know you will make the *right* decision this time, Arianwen.'

Before I have a chance to ask a question, my two younger sisters come bursting in the room and tackle me in a big group hug. I'm happy to see them and I can feel myself smiling, but it somehow doesn't feel real. I almost feel as if I am floating on a cloud, feeling peaceful and happy, yet a niggling part of my psyche tells me there is something else I should be thinking about, there is something I am missing here.

All day I feel the same. I nap and when I wake, my mother or father is giving me tea or something light to eat. My sisters are talking in excited tones about the upcoming ceremony that the entire kin will be attending in the glass chapel and that they hope I agree so they can help me dress up and look like a pretty princess. I smile at them despite not understanding their words and having an internal war with my consciousness as to what is really going on.

There is a knock on the door and then Gabriel is standing in my doorway with a shy smile, apologising for the intrusion. My family all get up to leave us alone, which, despite my returning smile to his, I know is not a good idea. Something deep within me is trying to scream at me to run away, far from here, but all I can do is sit up against the pillows on my bed and smile politely at our leader. He grabs my hand in his and holds it gently, and even though I know I should pull it away, I don't. I just sit still quietly and listen to his words.

'Arianwen, I am so glad you are feeling better. You have more colour in your cheeks today,' he says while reaching up a hand and brushing a finger over my cheek. I let him, even though I know I don't like it, and his smile broadens as he keeps stroking my face and lets out a sigh.

'*Oh Arianwen*, you have no idea how much I have longed for you not to flinch at my touch. This is a joyous day indeed.' He continues to talk to me, smiling brightly as I just nod and smile politely, not really taking in any of the words that are flowing form his mouth.

'Your smile is so beautiful, my sweet angel. I wish I had seen it before now.'

The finger he was rubbing over my cheek slowly moves to my mouth. He glides it over my lips before moving in closer. Fear grips my heart at his intentions but my body will not move out of the way. But thank the heavens he only kisses the side of my mouth before pulling back.

'Please agree to the ceremony, Arianwen. I promise to make

you a very happy woman.'

He leans in to kiss the corner of my mouth again before rising and leaving the room with a large grin on his face. My brain is in overdrive, trying to put all the puzzle pieces together, but I just can't get it. I feel as if all of my senses are dulled, working much slower than their usual pace.

My sisters once again barge in my room, excited by my regal visitor, asking a million questions, saying how romantic it is and begging me to say yes. Yes to what? What is this ceremony they keep referring to? I feel tired again and settle down for a nap, hopeful that maybe after another rest I will feel more like myself.

The next day is much the same. I still don't feel right. But my mum can't keep the smile from her face and even my usually very composed father has been smiling a lot. Gabriel comes by again, bringing special tea just for me as he proceeds to pour a cup and offer it to me, this time in front of my family who are all crammed in my room chatting excitedly. He takes my hand in his and the room turns silent except for the pounding of my heart.

'Arianwen, I know you have been through a lot lately and that the ceremony is probably a lot sooner than you are comfortable with, but I think this is exactly what our community needs. Especially after the loss of Anatiamoros. I think a little bit of happiness and celebration would do you the world of good too. Please say yes, Arianwen.'

My heart is beating so fast I feel like it may jump out of my chest. I don't want to say yes to anything, especially something I don't understand. I feel wetness brim my eyes as I whisper, 'I don't understand,' not wanting to admit the weakness I am feeling at the moment.

Gabriel smiles at me softly. 'I think when it comes to you, Arianwen, I have always worn my heart on my sleeve, a heart you have so endearingly captured. And after the worry I have felt the past few days, my feelings for you have only intensified. I just wish we didn't have to go through the formalities of the ceremony so we could just celebrate here, surrounded by your family, the ones you love. But I have to stick with tradition.'

The room is still silent as he stares at me with a serious yet nervous expression. 'Will you take part, Arianwen, will you say yes?'

I feel trapped. I feel like my entire body is screaming on the inside for me to get up and run from this room, run from this house, run from the garden and run to ... run to ... arrrrr! I can't think straight. There is something there, something I am missing but I feel like I am being blocked from discovering the secrets of my mind, blocked from what I *need* to know.

Everyone is staring at me, waiting for me to respond, respond to a situation I don't have all the information about. If I say yes now, can I change my mind later when I regain full control of my thoughts? Surely there will be no harm if I say yes now only to buy myself some much needed time.

'Yes,' I whisper.

Gabriel instantly grabs my hand and brings it up to his mouth to kiss. My sisters squeal and jump up and down while my parents' smiles are blinding. I feel sick. I am barely holding onto the contents of my stomach as I feel the almost desperate need to scream at the top of my lungs. I am hoping they will all just leave me now so I can think, so I can fight this strange feeling in my brain, but my mother has other ideas.

She asks Gabriel to stay and have a meal with us and to everyone's surprise he says yes. Mother and the girls busy themselves in the kitchen while Gabriel, still seated on the edge of my bed, and my father, sitting on one of our kitchen chairs next to me, chat away happily about the coming and goings of Eden. The entire time Gabriel holds my hand in his, rubbing his thumb over my delicate skin. I stare at the movement; there's a memory tugging at my brain that I can't get a grasp on. It feels familiar but it's not. I have felt it before but not by his hand.

My body shudders violently as a memory almost reaches my thoughts only to disappear before I can see it. 'Are you okay sweetheart?' Gabriel asks with concern sketched across his face as my mother comes in announcing that dinner is ready.

'I think maybe Arianwen is not quite ready to sit up at the dining table, my dear. Maybe we could all bring our chairs in here and have an impromptu picnic of sorts,' my father says with a chuckle as they all agree. My plan to have some time alone shatters as they all start to pile in my small room.

Food is the last thing I want right now as my body feels as if it is so tightly wound it could snap. I still feel dull, slightly out of it as conversations continue around me, oblivious to the struggle I am experiencing. Gabriel tries to encourage me to eat but I keep refusing. My mother then pleads with me to try as Gabriel holds up a mouthful of food, hoping I will take it. The sooner I do what they say the sooner they may leave me alone. I nod and he brings it up to my mouth as I open and take the food he is offering.

His smile is so gentle and genuine, but it somehow doesn't sit well with him. Strange to me now, but true. He gives me two more mouthfuls, offering me encouraging smiles each time before I refuse any more. Then he helps me to wash it down with tea, the tea I am told is especially for me as it is a healing tea, specially made by our own healing specialist here at Eden. It is mostly sweet herbs I know well, but there is also a slight sour tang that I don't recognise.

My eyes start to feel heavy and the fog in my head feels like it is spreading to the rest of my body. I try and hide a yawn behind my hand but it's seen by all, as they rise and begin to clear dishes and chairs from the small room. Gabriel goes to take his dishes out when my mother stops him in the doorway and tells him that they will give him privacy to say his goodbyes.

He turns to me, and if I'm not mistaken, with a slight blush to his cheeks. He comes back to my bed and sits on the edge, grabbing my hand in his. He brings it up to his lips and kisses it softly before placing it back on my lap. He then brings his hands up to cradle my cheeks. Looking intently into my eyes, he says, 'You have made me a very happy man, Arianwen, happier than I ever thought I could be.'

He leans forward and places a light kiss to my lips. I flinch on the inside but outside remain still, which he takes as me being willing to his touch. He smiles as he repeats the kiss, still remaining gentle and slow. He sighs, whispering my name before he kisses me again, this time with a little more force as he slowly glides his lips over mine.

This is wrong. It feels wrong. It tastes wrong, he smells wrong, I feel wrong in his grip. I have to stop this, I *need* to stop this. My brain finally works how I want it to when I fake a jolt of pain, jumping in his grip which makes him release me instantly. 'Arianwen, I am so sorry, I just ... I just couldn't stop. It's the first time you have let me kiss you and now, after one small taste, I know I want to kiss those lips for the rest of my existence.'

He kisses me gently again before telling me to lie down so he can tuck me in. When the blankets are up tight around my chin, he kisses my forehead, says goodnight and leaves. I feel awful; my stomach starts to heave and I am lucky that my mother had placed a bucket under the edge of my bed in case this was to happen. I grab it just in time to catch the small amount of contents from my stomach as I heave until there is nothing left.

I grab the cup of tea on the table beside my bed and take a small sip to rinse out my mouth, but I have to spit it out in the bucket as well. Now that the tea has all but settled to the bottom of the cup, the sour taste I couldn't identify is much more prominent. It still has an herb like taste to it, but it is much more bitter than any other herb I have ever tasted before, certainly not something you would want to use in your tea. I bring the cup up to my nose, hoping the smell may indicate what it is, but as I take a big breath in, memories invade my thoughts instantly.

Dark cloaks; something familiar about one of them; looking up to a man's face that is blurred in my memory; a dark bag being placed over my head which contains a strong smell, the same smell as the herb in my tea. I gasp and drop the cup which falls to my floor with a loud smash. My mother comes in asking if I'm okay. The truth is I'm not. I'm not okay. Does this mean my tea has been laced? How many days have I been made to drink this damn tea? Is it the tea that has been keeping me in this zombie like state?

Anger starts to rise in my body.

'Arianwen, are you sure you're fine? Your cheeks look a little flushed. Maybe you're coming down with a fever.' She checks my head with her hand but is happy with the way it feels. 'Maybe it's all the excitement of today. I'll make you a fresh cup of tea before you sleep.'

I stop her, asking for a glass of water instead. When she returns and places it bedside my bed I ask her about the tea.

'Where is the tea from?' I'm hoping she has the answers.

'When Gabriel first came to see you, you were still unconscious, dear, so he immediately left to go see the healer, asking for anything that may help. When he returned, he brought the dried tea with him. It is freshly made each day, so he has been bringing a new bag with each of his visits. He says it is perfectly okay for all of us to have, but it is more important you get the healing you need. And the sooner the better, if you are going to be well enough to walk down the chapel's aisle tomorrow. Gabriel has assured us that if you are still too weak you will not be made to stand for too long. He will have a chair nearby if you feel unwell.'

This is all starting to make sense, just when my body is too exhausted to stay awake. I yawn, unable to keep my eyelids from dropping as I hear my mother say goodnight and leave my room as I fall into a fitful sleep.

✦ ✦ ✦

He is there. He is everywhere. All through my visions, flowing through my dreams, holding me, kissing me, loving me. Looking into my eyes with so much adoration that my heart skips a beat. He owns me and I own him and now that I have seen him in my dreams, nothing will block him from my mind when I wake. Albion will set me free.

My dreams finally unlock what the poison tea was keeping from me. All the realities, good and bad come flooding forth like a tidal wave over my senses. I remember lying in the arms of the man I love, basking in the sun's rays shining down on our entwined bodies, right before an ambush that shattered our small secluded peaceful world, an ambush neither of us sensed coming, an ambush that was so cleverly orchestrated and concealed that we didn't know what was upon us until the birds flew in fright from the trees above our heads and an army was surrounding us.

Regardless of the fact that Albion went instantly into protective mode and started transforming into his true demon self and grabbing my hand to combine our force, the power that was shot around his form was more than we could fight. It was more than the Devil's work; it was greater than any one immortal world could ever create. So the shock at seeing Michael standing before me just before he placed a bag over my head, a bag laced with the same herb I discovered in my tea, is no surprise now. Something as powerful as the spell that was cast over Albion and me could only have been created by the joining of two powerful leaders, two leaders from opposite sides of the worlds, from opposite sides of good and evil.

Michael's words resonate in my head, the words he whispered as he placed the bag over my head. *'To protect you both, you will do everything Gabriel asks of you and you will do it with an angelic smile on your face, you traitorous whore.'*

I wake and sit up in bed, startled at the viciousness of the words Michael spat at me and the realisation that one of our leaders, one of our greatest kin has been consorting with our immortal enemy, to the point that they combined their power. Is it for the good of our kind or for his own personal gain? Michael ... a Dark Angel? This means he is more dangerous than I ever thought possible. Does Gabriel know? Is he also working with the Devil? If he knows exactly what is in the tea he has been feeding me then maybe he and Michael are working towards a plan together.

I need to stay clear of Gabriel, of them both, as much as I can, at least until I can safely seek out Albion again. *Albion.* I can only just feel his aura. I need to go to him, I need to tell him what I now know. We need to leave here, we need to hide, we need to seek a world away from the ones who may want our power for themselves.

Just as I'm considering sneaking out my window so as not to involve my parents again, my door swings open and my sisters come bouncing in, followed by my mother carrying a large item in her arms. My sisters move out of the way as Mother lays it out on my bed and proceeds to unwrap the plain linen bag. I gasp at what I see and only now remember what today is. The day of the ceremony!

Michael's words once again ring in my ears and as I see my youngest sister munching on one of the biscuits Gabriel had brought for them; my idea of running starts to send fear through my entire being. Could they harm my sisters? Would they? If I refused to go through with this ceremony would they target the ones I love to get to me? To make me come out of hiding?

'Arianwen, we don't have much time. A crowd has already gathered in front of the chapel and people are waiting outside our house with bouquets of flowers ready to hand them to you,' my mother tells me excitedly as she takes the ancient gown and cloak from the bags lying on my bed.

'Ari, you are going to look like a princess!' my youngest sister Caronwen coos while smiling brightly at me.

I can still run, I can still hide, but if they want me bad enough, want Albion's and my power, then they will just continue to chase us, and the ones I have left behind will be the ones to suffer. Time is *not* on my side, but I am confident that I will find a way out of this situation. I will find a way to be free, free with the man who holds my heart.

Until then, I need to keep my loved ones close and my enemies closer. I have a plan. I turn to my sister, Briannel, the beautiful middle child of us girls. 'Will you help me do my hair?'

36

End of the Line

ALBION

The silence sits, squatting over me, waiting, watching, search-ing for the last shred of my sanity as I wait for my death to realise itself. Cold seeps into me as I sit chained to the floor, the collar around my neck chafing, biting through my flesh as it tries to heal over the invading iron ring.

I shift, chains rattling against the frigid stone, the sound of them echoing around my vacuous cell. The image of Arianwen's confused, fear laced eyes burn into my soul as I stare at the door only four feet away from me. The stench of urine and faeces fills the room as I listen to its slow trickle through the slatted drain beside me.

My legs stretch, the cold of the opposite wall filtering through the soles of my feet as I try in vain to abate the ache in my muscles, the searing, dull burn of fractured and cramped fragments of tissue. I wince sharply as the deep rent in my thigh opens once again, maggots tumbling from the wound as they eat away the rotten and torn flesh, their bloated bodies rolling from the blackened edges of my skin.

The buzz of flies mingles with the clink of my interminable bondage as I hear the sound of a key in my cell's lock. The door swings open, the sound of it striking the wall, shattering the invading silence that flows from the figure in the doorway. After standing there for what feels like forever, he finally speaks.

'Move, cur.'

I rise, my willingness to fight gone. Without her to fight for, what point is there to blind resistance? If at the end of the bloodshed and violence, you stand amidst the bodies of the dead with no light to reach for, then all it has become is senseless, wholesale murder, and where's the honour in that?

I force myself to rise on shaking muscles and weeping wounds, my legs nearly buckling as I lean backwards against the wall, my skin peeling off in pus soaked layers. The rampant burns across my shoulders and spine spill thick lines of infectious slime down my florid skin as it slips from my body. Thick slabs of my own dermis hang from the brickwork like blood soaked lichen.

My jailer steps forward, a jangling bunch of keys hanging from his belt as he moves to my side, his feet splashing through the river of liquid excrement that flows from the split and cracked bucket. The chains around my waist pin my arms to me as I listen to them rattle through the rings in the wall. I hear the pattering of footsteps, my second jailer appearing as I stand there, silent and still. They encircle me, the chains of my bondage and punishment clanking through the thick iron rings on their belts as they padlock them shut.

They march from my cell, dragging me in their wake as I stagger along behind them. My feet scrape over stone, the heat increasing with each step as I am led like a beast to slaughter, past the pits of the condemned, the souls of the long since departed, sitting writhing in agony for eternity in these pits of molten malice. The sounds of the torturers' playground filter through their screams as I see the doors to Lucifer's abode rise before me.

They push the doors aside, their armoured, muscled bulk filling the path with a wall of impassable anger as I stumble, my feet fighting to keep me aloft as I pitch forth, my body crashing to the floor at the Devil's feet.

'Ah, Albion, good of you to arrive. Punctual, as always.'

I am dragged upright, my body weak, near lifeless, hanging between these two demons like a wet rag.

'Set him in a chair. You two will not be needed from henceforth. You may take your leave. I do believe that Mr. Weiser will not be a problem, or am I wrong, Albion?'

He looks me over, appraising me. His eyes roam over my scarred and bloody form like a butcher searching for the choicest cuts from a carcass.

'No, I do not think this boy will be a problem.'

The chains drop from my waist as the two jailers depart, their footsteps fading to nothing as Lucifer sits, his eyes probing my face for any semblance of weakness. Let him find it, my fight departed the moment she was taken from me. All they can do now is destroy the physical form my soul used to inhabit.

'So, Albion, what are we to do with you?'

He sips at the cup in his hand, his brow rising as he hums, his question hanging in the air between us lost in a mist of my own fear and pain. The pain of my wounds is a pale replica of the gaping wound that strikes through the centre of my soul.

'Silence. Not unexpected, but a touch trite given your circumstances. I would, in your position, be grasping at any lifeline that floats by.'

He sets the cup down on the table at his elbow and folds his hands in his lap, a thoughtful expression slithering across his face as I stare through him, my eyes blank. Lucifer nods as he hunches forwards, elbows falling on knees as he rests his chin on his hands; a dark, all encompassing smile rolls across his lips as he reaches out, his pallid ice cold fingers encircling my chin as he lifts my head.

'Yes, this I can work with. You, Albion, are going to become all that I knew you could be from the first moment your father brought you to the under croft. Yes, I most certainly can work with this.'

He rises to his feet, a wave of his hand sending my shackles falling from me as my arms drop into my lap. He turns his back on me, a glimmer of my former self calling from the depths of my mind, calling to me, begging me to lift the chains from the floor, to loop them around his neck and pull, to squeeze the life from the man who has taken everything from me, one link at a time.

'I can tell what you're thinking. That's the small glimmer of fire that is still burning deep within your core, that spark that made you the Hunter you were and the traitor you became. Well, no, that's not a fair assessment; you're not a traitor. I know why you did it, Albion, and I applaud you for it. You sought out love in a world that is so filled with hate and anger that it has all but been wiped from existence; Hell, my own brother told you as much. The antiquated way with which they dole out women to the hierarchy is barbaric, even when set against the hedonism of this place.'

He turns back to me, a bottle in his right hand and two glasses in his left. He sets them down on the table, a rust coloured liquid slipping from the neck of the bottle, rolling into the glasses one after the other. He hands one to me, my wavering grip spilling the coarse grained liquid over my hands as I raise it to my lips.

'Now, Albion, after all is said and done, I still have to make an example out of you, to show the others that this is not tolerated, even from a legion commander. You did, after all, kill your own kin, one of my best Dolophonos, and subvert with an angel which brought the gaze of Heaven further to our door. The subversion of an angel I have no problem with, by the way, just the fact that you got my masochistic brother's attention as a result; a minor inconvenience but annoying none the less.'

He stares into the glass, watching the floating grains of barley and wheat that swirl through the dark alcoholic liquid. His gaze is almost thoughtful as I set the glass on the floor beside me. The pain that lances through me is blinding as I slump in the chair.

'Well, let's be on with it then. I think a public flogging and slow flaying will assure no one else follows in your ill advised footsteps, and I have no need to tell you that this will hurt worse than anything that has been imparted upon you up to this point.'

I find my voice as he moves away from me, the bottle clinking off others. He turns to me in surprise as my voice fills the room.

'Nothing you can do to me will ever equal the pain of what has already come to pass, Lucifer. Nothing. Not flogging, flaying, or being held spread eagled and eaten by the carrion crows could equal the anguish that so plagues my soul.'

Lucifer grins as he turns to me, my shackles snapping back around my wrists and throat with a flick of his wrist, his next words stoking the slowly glowing embers within me as I rise.

'Let's test that, shall we?'

✦✦✦

I scream, the sound a gargling, unintelligible mess of frantic pain and blood drenched misery. I feel the blade, I feel it as it peels away skin, cutting through the fat and sinew that binds it to my muscled frame. I long ago forgot the scent of my own blood, my mind so drenched in it that it has lost all meaning to me.

I watch as another sheet of my own rune etched flesh is sent falling to the floor, the mark of Cain already lying at my feet as I stare down at the slowly expanding pool of blood around the pole. My hands twitch as I feel the tip enter under my nail, its speared tip levering off the small sheet of bone as I feel my skin stretch.

'Hold, we need to make sure he doesn't truly expire. Bring in a Recounter.'

I hear its quivering footsteps, the shattered soul an unrepentant heathen, the body twisted, warped beyond the pale, its bloated bulk shuffling on stumps, its own fat greasing its path as it is planted at my feet.

I watch as the torturer's knife scythes through its throat, the blood cascading free, drenching me in a wave of gore. I retch, vomit boiling free of my mouth as my body begins to twist, my flesh growing like patches of hair on a mange riddled dog, sprouting from my muscles as the Recounter begins to bubble and hiss, its body melting into a viscous pool of putrescent muck.

Lucifer stands watching it all, his eyes impassive as he once more sends the dungeon keeper to work, and I once more begin to scream.

For days this lasts, each day a cycle of the last; my flesh is peeled from me, my blood soaks into the stone until it, in itself, becomes a part of me. My body warps each day as a Recounter is claimed and I am reborn for the next trial to begin. I lose count of how many times I watch as my innards boil free, landing like rope at my feet as my intestines coil forth in an undulating mass amidst the pile of rotting skin and fat.

The sweet scent of rancid meat filters up as I feel the blade hit home once more, but now it's ceased to matter, my cries little more than a whimper. I am done, my body is done, pain has ceased all meaning. Losing my angel, losing my very flesh in penance for my crime of simply loving another, I am done. Albion is dead; he lies here rotting into the floor.

What am I now, nothing more than a hacked and battered lump of sentient meat, capable of wielding a knife?

I am taken to my cell, my feet not even trying to support me as the door of my prison opens and I am sent tumbling in amidst the filth and decay.

Silence reigns over all as I lie there, her eyes still burning into my mind, the confusion, the fear, the pleading for me to save her. I quake as self-loathing and pain courses through me, my flesh stitching itself back in place as I push myself up onto the pile of straw in the corner, the thick strands of dried grain stalks spearing my exposed muscle as I sink into blackness. My mind shuts down as I try, in vain, to quell the thoughts that are slowly grinding away my sanity.

It feels like days I lie, unmoving, unfeeling, the sounds of my prison mates batting at my ears. Even the rats that so feasted on my decaying wounds have come to loath the sight of me, their scurrying forms fleeing at my merest whimper.

The door swings open, my jailers hoisting me up by my under-arms. The stench rising from me makes them heave as clotted faeces roll from what remains of my trousers, a streaked path leading from my cell as they drag me through the corridors.

Lucifer stands waiting as I find the strength to rise to my feet, my head bowed and heavy as I feel the chains of my bondage move, the guards shackling them to their belts, something they haven't done for many a moon.

'I think, Albion, it is time for a little trip, time for some air and a walk in the park. Come.'

I slip into step with my guards as Lucifer turns. I can feel their eyes upon me, the denizens of Hell lining the balconies and walkways as I am led, like a freak from a carnival, through the gamut of anger and hatred.

I can hear them, each spite filled remark, each hate laced curse; their voices ring true, speaking of my crimes against clan and kin. Vaunting me as an example of how far a Demon Knight can fall, and what awaits anyone who doesn't toe the line.

The crowds part as Lucifer leads me, guards flanking me, through the streets. A pack of Hunters skitter from roof to street, from door to alleyway, searching for anything that could harm their master, the masochistic Hell spawn that has vaunted mercy and handed agony in a single breath.

We march for hours, people gasping, the hairless apes around us falling in droves as they vanish at the sight of the King of Hell. I hear a scream, the rattle of gunfire and the thunk of dead flesh as a Reclaimer falls to the floor, body riddled with holes and throat lain open, her eyes wide and as flat as glass as she begins to fade, her form dissolving into light even as Lucifer reaches out and trails his fingers through the glittering mass of soul particles.

'A shame, really. I knew her mother. Lovely woman. I dare say there will be tears tonight when her companions send word of her demise, and of you.'

He turns his back to me as we slowly crest a hill, the sound of running water meeting my ears as I feel the air grow cold. Mud begins to grip at the torn soles of my feet as I slip and stumble, the annoyed grunts of my guards jolting my ears as they haul me to my feet, all but dragging me by chain up the hill as Lucifer vanishes from sight.

As I am finally thrown to the floor, the damp air soaking into what little remains of my clothing, I lie still, relishing the feel of water on my skin as the spray from the falls around us cascades like rain over my prostrate body.

'Albion, come, stand with me. I sincerely doubt you will want to miss this.'

I am pulled to his side as one of my guards unshackles me from his belt, handing the chain to Lucifer.

'Now tell me, what do you see?'

In a voice little more than a guttural whisper I reply, my throat parched and raw.

'Eden, I see Eden. I see the falls, I see the forest border.'

Lucifer smiles as he feeds the chain through his hands one link at a time, the motion drawing free a memory I franticly try to repress. The sight of her, the scarlet rope encircling her body as I lead her to the heights of pleasure and beyond, skewers me as I feel crimson tears slip free from my eyes. I bow my head, hoping to hide them from his gaze but it's to no avail, a derisive snort leaving him as he watches the first slip from my chin.

'Come now, boy, look harder and cease your crying. Tell me, what do you see?'

I look again, the throng of angels around the crystal cathedral drawing my eyes as I watch them file in slowly one by one.

'I see a ceremony; the cathedral is open, and people are going in.'

Lucifer chuckles as my words come through in a childish whisper.

'See anyone in particular?'

I let my eyes draw me closer, faces coming into view as I see Gabriel and Michael, their faces passive, arrogantly self assured as they stand at the foot of the alter, all the while the cathedral begins to fill.

The soft sound of a pipe organ fills the air as Lucifer grins at the sound.

'Ah good, it's starting. You certainly won't want to miss this part. Pay close attention to the doors at the far side of the aisle. You'll really want to see what happens next.'

I stare as they open, maidens in white stepping free as a figure, her face covered slightly by a shadow, sedately walks through the doors. Her pace is slow, measured, almost serene as she approaches Gabriel and stops. Time seems to stand still as I see her turn out of the shadow and her face comes into view.

My heart dies in that moment as I feel my body shake; ice floods my soul, drowning the final shreds of what remained of my former life in an instant. My knees buckle as I sink to the floor, tears flowing across my dirt smeared skin as I watch her look into the eyes of another man.

'How ... she was mine.'

I feel Lucifer's hand encircle my shoulder, his breath hot on my cheek as he leans in, his words sealing my coffin as I watch her lips move.

'I told you, you wouldn't want to miss this.'

He softly pats my shoulder as he lets the chain fall, a dull clink rising up as it hits the ground with a sodden thunk.

'Get him up and take him back. It's time to start on rebuilding this scrap of meat.'

37

Means to an End

ARIANWEN

My mother was right, there are, indeed, a few people waiting outside our home holding beautiful bunches of flowers, the colour of rainbows, the smell of eternal spring floating through my senses. My two sisters graciously take the bouquets for me as I concentrate on placing one foot in front of the other on the old cobblestone path before me.

My stride is determined, but I'm sure it is mistaken for excitement by my family and kin who surround my long walk through the Garden of Eden, to its far edges where the eternal chapel of glass sits secluded near a majestic waterfall, amongst the grand old pines that surround its glittering light.

The sooner I get this over with, the sooner the spotlight may be dropped from my every movement. Michael and Gabriel should see no need to shadow my every adventure after the commitment I make today. The minute I am released from the formalities, I will be gone. Gone to the man my heart is aching for, the man my heart is missing terribly. The man I know who will be standing by my side until I cease to exist.

But I cannot think about him now. To keep my emotions in check, I must push him to the back of my mind, for just a few hours at least. I need to keep my composure, not letting the outside world see the turmoil I have twirling around inside. I will not show my weakness. I will not give any more power to those who want to steal my own. I will get through this.

The longer I walk, the heavier my limbs feel, until the moment I see the first glimpses of the sun reflecting on the glass panes of the ancient chapel of my kin, and every step thereafter turns to lead. I have to do this. It is a means to an end, an end that will come in time. An end that may take a lot of work and struggles to get to, but an end that will ensure all I love will remain safe, including my Albion.

My nerves start to falter a little at the size of the crowd that is gathered in front of the entrance to the majestic towering chapel. All are smiling and happy to see me, happy to have something to celebrate after our recent losses. What would Anatiamoros think of my decision to go through with this? Would he understand? Yes, he would. He knows I would do anything for the ones I love.

My heart also starts to grow heavy as I make my way up the ancient carved steps and into the foyer. I am ushered into a room to my right and as the door begins to close, I see all of our kin start to usher in towards the main building. My sisters and mother help me out of the cloak that adorns my gown, a gown which is almost as old as life itself. The precious gems that have been embroidered into the ancient silk start to sparkle with the light that is shining through the small window of the room.

Gold thread is stitched in intricate patterns over my corset area and continues down the small sleeves on my arms. The layers of material hangs heavy on my frame, feeling like the weight of a million heavy shackles capturing my body in place, trapping me to a future I do not want to live. Attendants come in and out; all have a different purpose. One to tell my family what to do and where to sit, another to inspect that the ancient gown I am wearing is being worn the correct way. Another speaks to me about etiquette in front of such dignitaries of our world, another runs through the words of the ceremony and reminds me of the eloquent answers I need to say.

It is all too overwhelming, but I don't let it show. I nod when I'm supposed to and smile in the right places as everyone busies themselves around me, twirling like a tornado while I am frozen still, inside the eye of the storm. I control my mind, not letting it wander, as I know once I think of him I will not be able to control my boiling emotions. So I concentrate on my family and what I am doing for them, the sacrifice I am about to make in the hope it will keep them safe.

My father comes in quickly to kiss me on my cheek, telling me he will see me at the end of the aisle, then makes a hasty retreat away from all the girly chatter and tasks my sisters are seeing to. Mother checks my gown again; I notice her hands shake as she tucks a stray thread behind a gem. I grab one and give it a gentle squeeze as she raises glassy eyes to mine. The emotion I see swirling behind them is immense as she tries to blink it away. She squeezes my hand back and offers a small smile.

'Arianwen, I know. I know the struggles you have fought and the sacrifice you are making today. Please know that I am so very proud of your decision to go through with this. You *will* find your happiness one day and your heart will heal in time, I promise. Until then, know that your family is here for you, I am here for you. We will forever support you. I love you, my beautiful, strong daughter.'

Tears well in my eyes at my mother's words, but more so at the pain I see hidden in her soul. 'Will you tell me one day?' I quietly ask.

She looks shocked at my question, but quickly composes herself, offering me a small nod. She leans in and kisses my cheek before ushering my animated sisters out of the room, leaving me with only one attendant and thoughts of my mother's haunted past.

The attendant runs through the last of the details I need to know before telling me it may be a long wait until I am called and that someone one will come to collect me when it's time. Once I hear the door click in place, I let out the breath I had been holding forever. I am feeling nauseated and slightly faint, but I will not let my body lose strength now when I am this much closer to the end I am seeking.

I walk over to the small table in the corner of the room, pick up a glass of water and take a few sips to cleanse my body and soothe my dry throat. I then pick up a bunch of grapes and start picking them off and eating them one by one, thinking that the sugar in the sweet fruit is exactly what I need at this moment. But when they hit my stomach it starts to turn. I think I may still be suffering the effects of the tainted tea as my stomach has been upset since I woke a few days ago. I have only been able to eat small amounts before it protests. I take a few deep cleansing breaths with my hands held tightly over my stomach, when the most unbelievable event happens.

I feel a movement.

Beneath my fingertips I feel a distinct movement. I know it is not butterflies, as with them I feel a slight flutter in my entire stomach, but this, this is a definitive and precise movement. I am utterly shocked as I feel another, right under the palm of my hand, it is only slight but it is there. What ... I ... I don't understand. My mind is whirling at a hundred miles a second but the moment it lands on a vision of Albion's face, I feel a sharp strong push under my fingers!

Oh my lord! This can't be true! This is impossible! I have studied and read thousands of books and manuscripts as well as ancient scrolls and carved tablets and I know it is a well documented fact that an Angel and a Demon cannot conceive a child! But ... deep down inside, Albion is no demon. Despite witnessing with my own eyes Albion's transformation into a red monster of Hell, deep with his heart and soul, he is not a demon at all. As I listen to my heart and soul sing loud and clear I know that it is exactly what I am carrying in my fertile womb. A child. Mine and Albion's child!

My legs weaken and I fall to my knees with my hands still clutching my stomach tightly, protectively. A child. Mine and Albion's child. A child created out of the enormous love we share for each other. A child that feels like it was always meant to be a part of our lives. Is this the reason fate brought us together? To conceive a child of two worlds? To give us a gift that will enrich our lives through the struggles we will have, to find a life together? A child I envisage with his father's eyes and my lips. A child born of good, and not evil. A beautiful little cherub.

This changes everything, this changes our whole lives! If or when this gets out it will change our entire worlds! Nothing will be the same again and the danger for us and for that of my family will only intensify. And for our child! Oh no! Once the leaders of both worlds find out, they will want our child and not for good intentions.

I have to see Albion now! He will find a way to protect our child, to protect us until we can find a safe world to live in. I stand up on shaky legs and take deep breathes to steady the rising panic that is threatening to take over my body, a body that is threatening to send me into hysterics.

I steady myself for what I am about to do as I slowly walk towards the door, ready to flee from this mistake I was about to make. Just as I'm about to touch the handle, it starts to turn. I take a step back and as it opens, I am shocked to see Michael standing there with an angry scowl on his face.

'Arianwen ... it's time.'

The End

If you loved this book, please take the time to leave a review on Amazon and Goodreads

WE LOVE TO CHAT TO OUR READERS

If you want to get in touch with or stalk (in a healthy way)

either author, please use the links below.

You can email them both on:

cooperbooks100@gmail.com

Take an intimate look inside Heaven's Scent at our **Pinterest** board: www.pinterest.com/tmcoops/heavens-scent-series/

FIND RICKY ON HIS:

Facebook www.facebook.com/R.C.books

Twitter https://twitter.com/RJwC20

Instagram www.instagram.com/ricky_cooper_1/

Website www.ricky-cooper.co.uk/

FIND TANIA ON HER:

Facebook www.facebook.com/taniacooperbooks

Twitter https://twitter.com/TaniaTmcoops

Instagram www.instagram.com/taniacooper100/

Website www.taniacooperauthor.com.au/

PLAYLIST

Music is a huge part of both our lives and that includes our writing. If we were to list all the songs that each of us played while writing Heaven's Scent it might end up as long as the book, so here are the songs that made the most impact on the story and our writing:

Beast and the Harlot by Avenged Sevenfold
Pain by Rungran
Do I Wanna Know by Arctic Monkeys
Love Bites by Def Leppard
Nothing Else Matters by Metallica
Warrior by Beth Crowley
Once Upon a Dream by Lana Del Ray
Kettering by The Antlers
Starvation by Thomas Bergerson
Into Darkness by Thomas Bergerson
Take Me to Hell by Two steps from Hell
  (gave Tania nightmares)
Lost it All by Black Veil Brides
Bother [Explicit] by Stone Sour
Through The Glass by Stone Sour
From Can to Can't by Sound City
All of Me by John legend
Lost in Paradise by Evanesence
Running Up That Hill (Cover) by Placebo
Halo by Maluka
Reignite (Mass Effect Tribute) by Maluka
Carnival Of Rust by Poets Of The Fall
Locking Up The Sun by Poets Of The Fall
Before I Forget by Slipknot

My Demons by Starset
Falling Inside The Black by Skillet
Take Me Away by 7 Days Away
So Far Away by Staind
Vengeance by Zack Hemsey
Redemption by Zack Hemsey
Phenomenon by Thousand Foot Krutch

ACKNOWLEDGEMENTS

First and foremost we want to thank our readers. You ROCK! Without you, it is all just words on a page.

We would also like to thank our wonderful and patient beta readers: Terri Anne Browning, Nicole Layton, Sonia Ranger, Glenn Cooper, Leslie Whitaker, Shannon Sharpe, Sarah Beth, Mark Lewis, Lorraine Lilly Wickson, and Annmarie Amy Young. To all of you, a heartfelt thank you. Without your help and gentle tweaking we wouldn't have the polished work we do today, and our egos would have remained small.

Thank you to our assistant editor Sara Anne Jones, who not only instantly got our voices for the story, but also our sense of humour. There were many tears of laughter and we will forever have the word 'quimm' etched into our brain. A big thanks to our editor and words mistress Monique Lewis Happy of MHES. Your support goes above and beyond the call of duty. We are blessed to have both found you at the times we have needed you and love the support you have shown us as a collaborative writing team. And thank you to our cool and amazing cover artist Paul Chapman who gave us an awesome picture of the characters that live in our heads.

How you got in there is still a mystery.

Tania: I would like to thank my family and friends who have supported me during my long writing hours, especially Nicole Layton and Ann Gardner, who always believe in everything I do. And a big thanks to all the kinder and school mums who offer support and are always enquiring about where I'm up to in my writing adventures.

But my biggest thanks goes to my co-writer, best friend, and sometimes very stubborn pommy, Ricky. I am blessed to have you in my life. Your knowledge is endless and your support and belief in me has made me a better writer than I could ever have become alone. Thank you.

Ricky: There are too many people in my life I want to thank. My family: without them I literally wouldn't be here. The love and support they show me is beyond measure and something I am thankful for each and every day. I love you all more than words could ever say.

But above all, my biggest and greatest thank you goes to my best friend, confidante and co-writer, Tania. Your endless support, praise, and friendship has pushed me to reach for goals so far beyond my limits, not only as a writer but as a person, that I know

I would never have reached them on my own.

Thank you, Tania, for everything.

INDEX

NAMES & PHRASES

Abeo Lam – Latin for *die now*.

Abezethibou – (Abb-zayth-boo) Demon from the testament of Solomon, depicted with one red wing, formerly an angel named Amelouth, was trapped by Moses in a pillar of air in the Red Sea.

Acrestrian – (Ah-crest-rian) A fallen angel that lead a one man rebellion against Lucifer.

Agates – Old English for testicles.

Albion – Demon Hunter and General of the sixth legion.

Alp – Vampiric, shape shifting from German lore, associated with nightmares and demons such as the Succubus and Incubus.

Anatiamoros – (Anna-tia-moros) Leader of the Reclaimers

Arianwen – Reclaimer under Anatiamoros.

Barbatos – A fallen angel from before Lucifer and eighth of the seventy two spirits of Solomon. Formerly a member of the Angelic order of Virtue. A demon count who commands thirty legions, can talk in the tongues of any animal and is master of all sciences and knows of everything, past, present or future.

Bradawl – A leather worker and carpenter's tool, used for marking and piercing material.

Bruvow – Alcoholic drink brewed in the Undercroft.

Cia – (See-ah) Mystic and fortune teller, lives outside the borders of Eden, within the forest.

Drewen – Sentient trees that surround Eden

Estrastiel – (Es-tras-teal) Reclaimer under Anatiamoros.

Garth – Blacksmith in the Village of the Damned

Kharon – (Car-on) The boatman of the Underworld/Hell.

Malachai – (Mal-a-ky) Leader of the Dolophonos, a demon order dedicated to Lucifer who act as enforcers and assassins. Semi-corporeal beings, they can break down their own bodies at will, but in physical form manifest as a semi-necrotic corpse, swathed in black with their face hidden behind an Afghan Shemag.

Mark of Cain – Honorific scar carved into the chest of all Hunters, comes from the scar left upon Cain when he fought and killed Abel.

Moloch – Ammonite God demonized in Hebrew lore.

Reclaimer – A legion of Angels tasked with returning those souls held in limbo to Eden, they travel between the lands that border Heaven and Hell seeking them out regardless of the danger to themselves.

Recounter – A mutated and abused creature, created by Barbatos for use in long term torture; they are killed at the feet of those deserving long term punishment and restore the body of the victim to prolong the pain and agony that is inflicted.

Soul caster – Demon warriors who break off portions of their own soul to cast as spells and enchantments, created from the legion lead by the Demon Lord Udai.

Sigel – A mark or pictorial image denoting rank or clan in the demon world.

AVAILABLE NOW

Heaven's Scent series: Book 2

Between Worlds

'How can love survive when it's torn between two worlds?'